ALL WE'VE EVER DONE

A NOVEL

Brittany Sims

ISBN: 978-1-63821-519-6

Any references to historical events, real people, or real places are ued fictitiously. Names, characters, and places are products of the author's imagination.

Printed by Amazon in the United States

Author Picture by Maddi Rose Media

thenonbinarybarista.wordpress.com

CONTENTS

For all the people who have ever looked around and not
found what they were looking for, this novel is for you.
Sometimes, what we are looking for is hidden and it
is in the journey to find it that we also find ourselves.
Other times, we have to create what we want to find
elsewhere because others might not know they need it.

CHAPTER 1

Lucan wondered if he was making a mistake.

The pack his elf was caring knocked his daughter forward and she had said nothing. No word of protest, no snappy remark, and a scolding seemed beyond her capabilities. The man either had not seen her or ignored her, yet Rosalyn stood there straightening her dress then placing her hands behind her back. On occasion, she was strong-willed but it took some vexing to get it out of her.

"It was his mistake, Rosalyn." Lucan pointed at the man, but his voice was quiet enough that only she could hear his words. Her head jerked up at the attention from someone, and then paused a moment to recall what was said to her. He sighed, and then added, "You are allowed to voice your displeasure."

"I was not hurt," she said, raising her head. "I felt no need to say anything."

He sighed.

She looked like him, with her dark hair and hazel eyes, but inside she was her mother. The urge to finger the ring on the silver chain around his neck was like an itch he had to scratch, insatiable but he gritted his teeth and fought through it. He was not weak and he would make sure his daughter was not either.

"Rosalyn, you cannot be like this where we are going. You need to be strong and you need to pay attention." He looked into her eyes, wishing he could pass on strength to his daughter. She would have to dispel with the softness that was like an aura around her. "Can you do that?"

Rosalyn gave a half-hearted nod, barely a movement of her head. She reached up and grabbed her arms as if trying to hide her insecurities from view. Seventeen years in the kingdom of Helios was not enough education to give her the hardness and strength of the dark elves, which Lucan had hoped for. He glanced up at the castle she would inherit and the stone courtyard that seemed so big and expansive to him but swallowed her. The nod gave him little confidence that such hardness would ever present itself. If she were to fight the Vestans, she would need to make them fear her.

Though only the elves of the kingdom of Valandyl were called Vestan elves, he lumped in the light elves of Tadane in that name. What did it matter, they were all weak and not fit to exist in Lucan's mind. The war in the Three Kingdoms had been raging for centuries and, just as he had started it, he was intent on finishing victorious. What was the point of being king if the kingdom only went so far? The humans, the druids, and the rest of the creatures in the world could have their areas but he had his eyes on the whole of the elven kingdoms.

"Your Majesty, the King of Valandyl will be expecting you," ushered Lucan's steward.

"Yes," he grumbled. "Not that I care if I keep His Majesty up all night, but if I'm going to have a full day's ride ahead of me, I would prefer to ride during the light of day."

Though they had worked together for years, his steward, Jalen, always seemed to stand further away than social rules would dictate. Ever wary of a loud outburst from his King, he showered Lucan with niceties.

"But of course, Your Majesty. You wouldn't want to ride in the dark. Very wise of you, my King."

"Father?" Rosalyn interrupted.

"Yes, my daughter," Lucan mumbled.

'My daughter' was as close to a pet name that Lucan could muster. It was, however, more a statement of fact rather than complimenting her or expressing affection.

"Why are we going? Why would any of the Three Kingdoms come together for peace with the Elven War still going on."

"It is a duty we share," he began. Rosalyn's head cocked to one side in confusion, and so he felt compelled to go on. "Yes, I hate all those that are not in my kingdom, but I have a duty to prevent my people from dying in a war at the hands of those I hate. Those are the goals that I share with my fellow elves of the Three Kingdoms. The solutions are where we have different opinions, and that is why we convene."

"And what am I to learn?" She asked.

Lucan ushered with his head towards the horses and helped her onto the brown mare. As she was lifted onto the saddle, his eye caught sight of the mark on his left arm. The tattoo of a dragon with its narrow body and tail coiled around his wrist. It was a mark of pride, as he ensured that every dark elf had a dragon tattoo, or Corin, on their arm. Their journey made the mark seem more relevant somehow, and Lucan paused a moment.

"Hate," answered the King of the dark elves. "You are to learn a hatred of Vestan weakness."

He jumped onto his own horse and urged the animal forward with a malicious smile concerning his real goal for going to Valandyl.

CHAPTER 2

Rosalyn remembered the sun setting and guessed that it had been hours after that their convoy reached Valandyl, accompanied by her father's entourage of advisors and security. Lucan dismounted on his own, then took a few steps towards her horse to help her down. Her lungs gasped for air after her feet hit the ground. The dirty smell of the horse and dust that both animal and rider had picked up mixed with the sweat that ran down her forehead. Her muscles, unused to such a long ride without much stopping, felt like water pelted by rain, unsubstantial and quivering.

Doranen Balshon, the King of Valandyl, waited in the archway of the entrance to his palace until they had dismounted before coming forward to greet them. A small tapping echoed off the walls as he descended the stairs to the landing below. He was a slight elf, who carried himself with a contagious sense of calm and kindness. His demeanor gave one the impression that he was not to be taken seriously, and yet he had commanded armies that put up a fight against her father's forces since the war began. Something beneath his exterior was a match for those that challenged him, she thought.

"I hope the roads were clear," Doranen remarked.

She scanned his pale blue robes made of silk and found nothing alarming, and his hair was tied back without a fuss.

"Quite clear."

Her father's tone was civil, but both men were aware that no apology would follow the statement for arriving so late into the night. Lucan was unfazed by the journey, only his boots and the folds in his clothes gave any indication that he had been on horseback all day. For all his brusk, Rosalyn looked at Lucan and wished that she could be as unfazed by time and exertion as her father. It would require practice, another attribute to add to the never-ending list of attributes and qualities she had to master.

Lucan shook hands with Doranen as was their custom, though Lucan always made sure to initiate it by thrusting his tattooed hand as a not-so-subtle reminder that he was different from Doranen. When their hands released, her father looked back at her. She pulled the large bag over her shoulder as if she had the strength to carry it, but her father would have seen her catch hold of the saddle to keep her vertical. If her face showed as much exhaustion as she felt, any sign of weakness would embarrass him. She fidgeted with her saddlebag so that her face would not betray her. The bag felt more substantial than when she had packed it, and she feared what would happen should she have to let go of the horse.

"Our horses are tired," Lucan announced. "I'm afraid we rode without much delay."

Doranen nodded and gave the orders to his staff that the horses be taken to the stables to be watered and fed. Meanwhile, Lucan held his arm out to her, which she took with a nod of gratitude.

Lucan led her forward and indicated her presence with his hand. "I present the Princess of Helios, Rosalyn Lassehelin."

She gave what could only be defined broadly as a curtsy to the King of Valandyl, holding onto her father to keep from collapsing in the attempt. Her father jerked her upright. She forced her mouth into a smile as if she had straightened all on her own. Was it that the bow was too long or that she should not have bowed at all? She would have to ask her father later when they were alone.

"A true pleasure to finally meet you," Doranen said. His voice was sincere, and he accompanied his words with a respectful bow. "Come, your rooms are ready for you."

Rosalyn marveled at the palace walls as they were led

through the entry hall. The hall was accented with thin grey columns, decorated wooden beams, and light tapestries. Even the walls were highly decorated with murals of battles, heroes, and depictions of nature. The furniture she passed was all made of pale wood, and much of the terraces looked out onto the surrounding landscape. She did her best not to compare what she saw to the castle she came from, but the differences were stark and unavoidable.

"Your daughter will be sharing a room with my daughter," Doranen tossed over his shoulder in transit. He paused, then turned to look at his guests. "I thought it best for the sake of security, and our daughters are close in age. If you would like other accommodations, I can have a room made up for her, and it will only take a moment."

"I don't want any extra trouble," Rosalyn assured. "Your daughter's room will be fine."

Her father shot her a look, which Doranen either did not see or chose to ignore. She was accommodating Vestans, another thing her father would not be happy with. Perhaps it was best that she kept her mouth shut until bed, she thought, and possibly for the duration of their stay.

"I believe Emmelina is already in bed." Doranen motioned for the party to follow him further down the hall to his daughter's room. "She said that she would leave a candle or two lit in case you arrived tonight.

"Due to the meeting," Doranen continued, "I have increased security just in case, though I doubt we shall need it. More guards have been placed at the entrances and exits. Patrols have been increased."

Doranen elaborated on his security measures, unaware that neither of his guests were interested. Rosalyn knew her father would be analyzing each entrance and hallway for ways the King's preparations could be ruined or thwarted. Meanwhile, she tried her best to walk but felt more like she was hobbling along using her father as a crutch. She was glad that it was so late because it meant that she might avoid a lecture about her dreadful performance during her first meeting with Vestans.

"And here is your room, my dear."

The King of Valandyl stopped at a door halfway down one of the corridors and motioned for her to go in.

Lucan flashed a smile, though it was empty of any sincere emotion. "Do you mind giving me a moment with my daughter?"

"Of course," Doranen agreed with a half bow. "I will see to the preparations for the rest of your convoy."

Lucan's eyes followed Doranen until he was out of sight, then turned back to Rosalyn. "Don't be fooled by their niceties. They hide it but, in truth, they are just as cunning as we are."

"Father, please, I am far too tired for the lecture." Rosalyn turned to go inside the room. She reached for the doorknob, yet Lucan intercepted her hand. He made a sharp pull, causing Rosalyn to ricochet around with painful force.

"Listen to me," he ordered while giving her a hearty shake. "Remember that I brought you here to learn, not to make friends. You are a daughter of Helios, and therefore have no business with these people. Do you understand me?"

Rosalyn nodded. She had heard this lecture before and was not about to fight or argue. Lucan's eyes narrowed.

"I said, do you understand me?" Lucan yelled, grabbing his daughter and giving her another firm shake.

"Yes," Rosalyn cried.

She ripped herself from his grip and retreated into the room. She wanted to slam the door and, had she been in her room in Helios, she would have done so. Lucan did not fight her once she was inside for fear of causing a scene. She closed the door as quietly as she could and then sunk to the floor.

Despite the moonlight outside and the candles at the edge of the room, it took a moment for Rosalyn's eyes to adjust to the darkness. She could make out a figure asleep on the bed closest to her, and she hoped that the commotion with her father had not been overheard. Her arms began to weaken, and a deep soreness started where her father had grabbed her. Tears began to form in her eyes, but she focused on breathing them away. The figure, she assumed was Doranen's daughter, shifted. Fearing she had disturbed her new roommate, Rosalyn stood up and rushed towards her bed at the end of the room.

She dropped her bag by the foot of the bed, changed out of her clothes, and put on a simple sleeping gown. Her hair had started in a braid that morning, yet now it was a tangled and disheveled mess. She thought about redoing her braid, but instead removed the leather tie and straightened the runaway strands.

The bed seemed to be made for a large adult, and Rosalyn felt like it would swallow her up. Everything from the pillows and blankets to the mattress was comfortable, though ample for her size. Laying down eased away the tension from riding all day, and she let out a sigh of relief as she welcomed sleep.

"Excuse me."

Rosalyn's eyes opened, and her whole body tensed. She had hoped that the princess was asleep and that she had been quiet enough to go unnoticed.

"Are you still awake?" The girl asked.

"Yes," Rosalyn replied.

She sat up, unsure of what the girl would want from her. Had she heard the argument Rosalyn had had with her father? A wave of shame recoiled as if it would crash and flood her mind depending on how Doranen's daughter answered. She tried to force it away, as she was too tired to deal with those thoughts and feelings tonight.

"My name is Emmy."

Her voice was bright, despite her hushed tone.

"Rosalyn," she responded.

"You are probably tired, and I'll let you sleep, but I'm happy to have you here."

Rosalyn paused.

"Well, as I said, you are tired." Emmy rolled to the other side of her bed and tried to go to sleep. "Good night."

Rosalyn stared into the darkness of the room. As much as she did not want to believe it, she had grown up with the idea that everyone outside of Helios hated her and her kind. Yet, the Princess of Valandyl was happy to have her. It could be a trick, and maybe her first instinct was right. Emmy could have something diabolical planned. With the tension in the kingdom, Rosalyn would not be surprised.

Emmy, also, could be sincere.

Could be.

She had never had the opportunity to hope in the words "could be" before.

Rosalyn laid back down against the pillows, unsure if Emmy was still awake.

"Good night," she whispered into the darkness.

CHAPTER 3

Rosalyn did not want to wake up. The maid that had been assigned to her for the duration of her stay seemed to have other plans. Rather than call her name, the quiet woman decided that shaking her pillow was the best way to rouse her. As her head bobbled, Rosalyn rationalized that this particular method was more comfortable than if she had touched her and was better than shouting.

"Wake up, Lady Rosalyn," the maid called as if hearing her charge's thoughts. "Your father has asked to see you once you are dressed."

Rosalyn opened her eyes but had no intention of getting out of bed yet. After the journey from home to Valandyl the day before, she was grateful for the peace of a dreamless sleep. She stretched and recalled the enormity of her bed, her small body within it, and that she was sharing the room with the Princess of Valandyl. She heard movement and knew that every moment was only putting off the inevitable meeting of her roommate.

Rosalyn flung the comforter off her with regret. The day was already warm, and she wanted to linger in the feeling. Natural sunlight fell into the room in pale shades of pink and green from the stained glass balcony doors that replaced the far wall. Princess Emmelina was already up. Rosalyn stopped. Not Princess Emmelina, Emmy. That's what she had said her name was the night before. Rosalyn nodded to herself, then proceeded to get out of bed.

Contrary to the rest of the palace, Emmy's room was messy. Rosalyn had never thought of an elf with a messy room and looked around in doubt of what she saw. She had not dismissed the thought, but it was comical and strange to see the reality in one person. Emmy's wardrobe was open and clothes hung from the rack, yet enough clothes draped over her bed, on the dresser, and in clumps on the floor to fill the closet twice over. The owner of the bedroom was rushing to pick up pieces of fabric and shoving them into already full spaces.

"Do forgive all the stuff everywhere. I meant to have it cleaned up, but I've always been able to talk myself out of it." Emmy looked around, raised her eyebrows, and then shrugged. "Clearly."

If Rosalyn did not already feel small, Emmy reinforced it when Rosalyn got her first look at her. Emmy was tall, taller than the average elf and probably taller than Rosalyn's father. Her thin, dusty blonde hair was straight and fanned out around her shoulders. She smiled at her guest, in a way that made her eyes crinkle on the sides.

Rosalyn wanted to say something, but all words escaped her. Her father had made it clear that she was not to form bonds with the enemy, but he was not here and she did not want to make trouble for the rest of her stay. Of course, they were both royals, but she was a dark elf. How was she supposed to converse with her? After torturous minutes passed with no words said by either girl, Rosalyn decided to get dressed to avoid any further awkward silences.

At the end of her bed was a fitted purple dress, however, it was not one of the ones she had packed. She looked at it with a mix of longing and skepticism. The dress had to have been purchased by her father, as it looked expensive, and he only bought her new dresses or trinkets when he could use them to show off or prove a point. Her maid pointed to a few feet away from the bed, then set to work getting her ready for the day. Even away from home, she felt like a doll, lifeless and being instructed where to go and what to do. Yet, she reached out a timid hand and ran it across the soft fabric of her costume.

Rosalyn lifted her head to find that Emmy was watching

her. The maid took her sleeping gown and, with a small bow, left the room. She thought about requesting to wear it another night, but the woman was out the door before Rosalyn could stop her. The woman had been so quick that Rosalyn did not even have time to get a name.

"It's a beautiful dress," Emmy commented, walking closer.

Her voice was small, but Rosalyn forced out the words she wanted. "Thank you."

Emmy looked surprised when she spoke, but the look went away in an instant. If reading Emmy's reactions were anything like what her father had to deal with when he met with Doranen, she was beginning to understand why her father hated coming to Valandyl.

"Have you ever been to one of these meetings?" Rosalyn asked.

Emmy nodded, "Once, but I think I was only ten."

"I don't quite know what to expect."

"The last time it seemed quite boring," Emmy admitted with a laugh. "But that might have been because I was a child then. I remember your father though. He scared me, although I don't think that my age had anything to do with it. The way he would yell at my father and bang on the table."

Rosalyn opened her mouth to say something, but she could not think of a rebuttal. She was no longer a child, and she still found her father frightening. Often, that was a point of pride with him. She did not think Emmy was trying to be insulting, but the comment made her uncomfortable.

"Was that too much?" Emmy asked, taking a step back. "I didn't mean to offend you, and it feels like I did."

Rosalyn swallowed. She wanted to run outside and ignore the whole situation. Had she not been so tired last night, she would have had her own room and not had to make small talk with a girl she did not know about the last person she wanted to talk about. Her father would want her to be insulted, to cause a scene, but she shook her head. The almost comical way Emmy's body slumped and her attentive eyes pointed to her sincerity.

"It wasn't too much," she answered. "I don't think so. I have to go. My father's waiting for me."

The corner of Rosalyn's mouth tugged as if she were about to smile, but she turned towards the door before it was visible. In the short walk across the room, her stomach grew heavy. She did not need to turn around to see that her roommate still felt uneasy, and, even though her father would hate to hear it, she did as well. She grabbed onto the doorknob but used it to turn herself around.

"I'll see you at the meeting," she offered with a smile.

Emmy smiled back, indicating Rosalyn had made the right decision. Before anything else could be said, Rosalyn pulled on the door and left the room.

Her father's private secretary, Aldan, was standing down the hall. His hand was on the hilt of his sword, though she had never seen him use it and she often wondered if anyone had told him that private secretaries did not need weapons. Aldan had served her father since the King was a boy, and his entire deportment reflected his loyalty to his position while the grey in his hair pointed to his reliance in keeping the job. He acted as though a threat would be found around every corner, even though Lucan was intent on being the threat to everyone else. He watched her walk up to him, acknowledged her with a brief grunt, and then ushered her towards her father's room.

She lost track of where in the palace she was, but she knew her father's room before Aldan opened the heavy wooden door. The room was large enough to house a family. Doranen was trying to be impressive, she guessed, as they had passed other adequate rooms along the way. Aldan closed the door behind her without having to be told. Her training made her stop. The King would get to her when he saw fit.

The room had a large bed with sturdy posts, a table should the guest wish to eat in private that was covered with papers and her father's more decorative armor, and a shelf lined with books in the alcove. She tried to read the titles, but only the words "ethics" and "concordance" were visible from where she stood. The books were most likely placed there by some well-meaning staff member of the palace, hoping it would change her father but Rosalyn knew he would never touch them. Her eyes scanned the room for her father and found him in the far corner at the desk situated in the alcove.

Her father lounged like a giant cat at his desk, shuffling papers she could not make out and examining them with only passing attention. She wanted to fidget, as her body grew tense, but he would notice it. When he turned his attention to her, he gasped in a way that both inhabitants of the room knew was fake.

"My daughter, that dress is wonderful."

Her voice held no enthusiasm, "It was a lovely gift."

Rosalyn stepped to the side and sat down on Lucan's bed. She knew her father had slept, the wrinkles on the pillow told her so, but, aside from the observed marks, it looked as though the bed had not been used. Either he had had one of Doranen's staff make it or he had made it himself because Doranen's staff was too slow, but she could not be sure of which. The papers on his desk were all in neat piles. She thought back to her bedroom and how contrary it was to Emmy's room. Anything out of place was a personal offense to him, and she could not take the risk of angering him.

Lucan groaned, rubbing his cropped dark hair in irritation. "What is troubling you?"

"Nerves," she admitted. "I haven't been able to shake them since I walked out of Princess Emmelina's room."

"It's only a short walk from her room to mine," Lucan observed. "Your walk from your bedroom to my room at home is longer."

"I know."

Lucan stood up and walked over to her. His eyes and pace like that of a man half his age. Ever the strategist, he watched for flaws that could hurt his plan for the day. She caught sight of a slight tremor in her hands and shoved them underneath her. The meeting would happen just as Lucan wanted it to happen, and admitting to any of her feelings would only get in his way.

"Today is an important day," Lucan said, more to himself than to her. Rosalyn looked away, knowing that under the soldier exterior of her father was a rare giddiness that frightened her.

"How do you think your brother is getting on?" Her father asked without prompting. He turned towards the mirror near his desk and straightened his tunic.

"Probably has the run of the castle by now," she joked with a smirk.

Lucan turned back to her, "You should be more like him."

Rosalyn stood up wanting to protest. She glanced at the door. If anyone besides Aldan walked by, they would hear her yell. She clenched her fist and channeled all her anger into it. "I'm trying."

"Your brother doesn't need to try."

She looked at her father with an uncompromising glare. "I won't fail you."

After a cursory assessment, her father seemed unimpressed.

"Come," Lucan sighed. "It's time."

Lucan held out his hand, and, after she took it, held her hand high as he escorted his daughter to the main hall. Even in enemy territory, her father walked with the pride of his people in each step and she did her best to match.

Doranen's main hall had no doors. At first, Rosalyn thought it was a mistake and searched the archway for sockets or fixtures, but found none. Once inside, she realized that the whole room was open and bright. Small divots in the floor indicated that a large table was once in the middle of the room, but had been replaced with smaller rectangular tables set up for the leaders of all three kingdoms. In between every couple of tables was space designed for a speaker to come into the middle and deliver a call to action or explain their perspective. Rosalyn looked up at the stained glass ceiling and felt the voices of those in the room lift to the space above her. She was only pulled away when her father grabbed her by the shoulder and guided her to their table.

Lucan pulled out the high-backed wooden chair and motioned for her to sit down with a curt nod. She dropped her head and did as she was told. Rosalyn tried to make herself comfortable, her palms were sweaty and shaking. She had been daydreaming, and all she could focus on was that it would be another strike against her. The hair on the back of her neck prickled when she realized that Lucan's hand was still on the back of the chair, and she looked to her father for an explanation.

"I need to talk to Aldan," he explained. "I will be just over there. Stay here."

The bite in his last two words was enough to make her afraid to move. Like a wolf flashing his teeth, the words seemed to come from the front of his mouth. He tapped the top of the wood, then walked off to see to his business.

Rosalyn sat back in her chair, allowing herself to explore the room more. She noticed how the Vestans avoided her. When she did lock eyes with someone, they seemed to reach out to the nearest elf and pulled them in as a buffer or they would turn away entirely. Her father warned her about the prejudices of the two kingdoms towards her people, though this was the first time that she had seen it in action. She looked for a distraction, finding her eyes drawn across the room to the Princess of Valandyl. Emmy tossed a discrete wave, before walking over to Rosalyn with a male companion close on her heels.

"Is this the Princess that is staying with you?" the elf asked.

"You know she is," Emmy answered with a glance at her

companion before returning her eyes to her. "Rosalyn, this is my good friend, Azrael, the Prince of Tadane."

Rosalyn's eyes widened. If her father knew that she was talking to the Prince of the light elves, he would be furious. Her father hated those outside of Helios, but especially those from Tadane. Rosalyn glanced over at her father to see if he was watching, only to see he was distracted by what Aldan and his advisors were telling him. Out of the corner of her eye, she caught sight of Azrael's parents.

Queen Amrydalis and her husband, Aurelius, bore little resemblance to their son. While their son radiated with abundant energy, they seemed aged. They were the oldest of the elven rulers at over seven hundred years old, despite their son being in his twenties. Often believing that their age gave them ultimate authority, the King and Queen walked around with many attendants to match. Guards wearing the seal of Tadane were posted at every entrance, and the King and Queen were accompanied by eight that Rosalyn could see.

Rosalyn turned back to the Prince. His fair complexion highlighted the smile that appeared to be a permanent fixture of his face. He thrust his right hand out without hesitation. She took it, forcing herself to whisper her name in return.

"Emmy is right, you are a quiet one."

Azrael's voice was calm, though he looked at her with a strange examination. She averted her eyes, unable to look at what she could only assume was disdain for her. What else could it be, considering the reactions of the rest of the room?

"Stop being rude," Emmy scolded.

Rosalyn heard a small thud and looked up to see Emmy's hand coming away from her friend while he rubbed the newly sore spot on his arm.

Emmy chuckled, "I apologize for my friend's behavior."

"He's not wrong," Rosalyn said with a shrug.

Azrael's smile turned into a playful smirk.

"If I'm not wrong," he began. "Will you answer one question for me? I know quiet and I know contemplative. Which one are you?"

Emmy's mouth fell, and she made some incoherent noises before raising her hand to give him what Rosalyn assumed was another hard slap. As Azrael continued to study her, she noticed something in his voice was teasing her. There was nothing in his demeanor that challenged her, and, had he been her brother, she would have played along.

She raised her hand to silence Emmy's continued sputtering, then leaned in closer to him. "Oh, I'm afraid the answer to that is a *dark* secret."

Azrael's eyebrow shot up as if he had not expected her to respond. "People can't usually keep secrets around me."

"Well, when you figure it out, then you can en*light*en us all."

Prince Azrael smiled with all his teeth. Whatever test he had concocted for her, it seemed that she had passed.

"Oh, I like you," Emmy said abruptly. "You are more than a clever match for him."

Rosalyn tried not to smile, but the warmth of one pulled her mouth. She looked up at Emmy, the only Vestan elf to look at her without fear. Emmy said she liked her, but being surrounded by elves that kept casting side glances between her and her father made Emmy's affection feel fragile.

She tore her eyes away and looked for her father among the crowd. His mouth was still speaking to Aldan, yet his attention was on her. She wondered how long he had been staring at her, how much he had seen. His feet were urging back towards her, and his hand seemed to be ushering those around him forward.

"Emmy, if you could..."

Her voice trailed off. The shaking in her hands started again, and her breathing grew ragged.

At first, Emmy hesitated and reached out to help her. However, Rosalyn pulled away, knowing that her father would make a scene if Emmy laid a hand on her. A visible flash of understanding took over, and Emmy stepped back. Grabbing

Azrael by the arm, she pulled him along with her to the other side of the room.

"I will just talk to you after," Emmy tossed over her shoulder.

Rosalyn looked down at her hands to hide the smile from her father, who was walking towards her with greater speed. His eyes were dark and his fists were balled up tight, but no Vestan would have noticed the change in mood.

When he arrived at her side, he leaned in close to avoid prying ears. "What was all that?"

"Princess Emmelina was being civil," she shrugged. Her throat grew tight at the proximity of Lucan's arm as he coiled it along the edge of her chair, encircling her with his reach. In one swift motion, Lucan grabbed her under the chin with his other hand and forced her to look at him.

"I did not bring you here to make friends."

The anger in her burned hot, blazing past her fear. She leaned forward and grabbed the wrist of the hand that held her in place. Not enough to hurt and without any intention of ripping her father's hand off her, but enough to show her conviction.

"No," Rosalyn said through gritted teeth. "You brought me here to make a point."

The King's eyes narrowed. He had always scared her, but it was moments like these that she hoped scared him. Instead, he forced her closer and kissed the top of her head. His hand on her throat squeezed enough for her to gasp, but was over before she could pull away. No matter how fatherly the scene looked, her blood ran cold and she forced a cry for help down her throat.

"And what a point you shall make."

With two loud bangs on the table in front of him, Doranen called the meeting to order. The staff ushered those who were unsure of their place to their appointed seats. Doranen surveyed the scene, waiting until everyone was seated to begin.

"First, I would like to welcome you all here today. Before we get started, King Lucan of Helios has requested the floor."

Doranen held out his hand, beckoning him forward.

"Thank you," Lucan said with a bow of the head. "Before we discuss peace and our aims, I wanted to clear up an area of confusion that has plagued the Three Kingdoms."

Lucan inhaled, breathing in the attention of the room as he would air. He could feel their curiosity, as well as their fear of what he was going to say. She knew this was what he lived for when he was in complete control of those around him and he held the moment. Without warning, his face went soft and he relaxed his posture to a slump. It seemed unnatural to her, like a bow being pulled back before the eventual shot.

"The heir to the throne of Helios has long been in question. I have two children from two different women and they are close enough in age."

Lucan held out his hand, and, without further indication, Rosalyn stood up. Her anxiety was high, but she focused her energy on keeping her back straight and her breathing even. Once she had crossed the short distance between the table and where her father was standing, she took his hand with her left hand.

"I have chosen my firstborn, Rosalyn Eva Lassehelin, to be my heir."

Whispers erupted from all corners of the room.

"You are committed to this decision, King Lucan?" asked Queen Amrydalis, quieting some of the voices. Her eyes scanned the newly appointed heir with disapproval. "Your son would be the more logical choice."

"Rosalyn is my choice, and, consequently, she has remained unmarked." Her father raised her arm, allowing the loose sleeve to cascade down her bare wrist. A devious smile tore through the side of his face that sent a chill through her. "Unmarked until today."

Rosalyn felt like a puppet as her father guided her hand

down, the voice in her head told her to rip her hand from him. She wanted to believe that it was because of his grip on her arm that kept her in place, but she knew the reason why she let her father model her. As she took a breath, her lungs felt as though they were full of ice shards and her stomach hollow.

"Every dark elf has a corin," Lucan explained. "A tattoo on their left hand. It is a rite of passage, and it conveys their status among their people. While it is an honor to be marked, the process can be quite jarring."

Adjusting his grip like a shackle to him, Rosalyn could feel dark magic penetrate her skin. It cut its way through flesh, muscle, and bone like a sword but somehow going deeper even than that. She had seen the process done enough times to know the pain, but the scorching as deep as her soul was something no one had prepared her for. Her shoulder, as if separate from her, found the will to pull away but her father's magic was too strong.

All eyes in the room were drawn to her like something dying and they could not look away. The dark line writing itself onto her arm was like a cage, a physical representation of the distance between her and everyone in the room except for the man that stood smiling as she screamed. She fell to her knees clutching her arm. Taking on a life of its own, the mark formed a dragon that spread out until it had wrapped itself several times around her wrist. Her father towered over her, unconcerned. His heir was named, his power shown, and the attention of the room was under his command.

A scuffle of feet pulled his attention away, and he turned towards the Queen of Tadane. She was holding onto her son, begging him to be silent, and motioning for her husband to help her restrain her son.

"Is no one going to help her?" Azrael begged. His fidgeting was hard to ignore, though that is what the elves around him continued to do. "She's clearly in agony."

Rosalyn was shaking and still clutching her arm to her when she felt Azrael's hand on her shoulder. Azrael reached out for her hand.

"Princess Rosalyn, it's alright. Let me see."

"Azrael, don't," his mother called out, moving from her perch.

Like the pause just before a lightning strike, she felt a sudden halt. Azrael seemed frozen in place, gasping for breath. Rosalyn managed to look up to see the darkness of her mark infecting him. The veins in his arm black like a virus. She ripped her hand away from him, watching the color drain from his face and collapse beside her. She sputtered, but no words found their way out. She had not unleashed any magic on him or thought him any ill will, yet somehow her mark had hurt him with one touch.

"That's enough!" Doranen's voice echoed through the hall.

He was angry and, for the first time, Rosalyn feared someone more than her father. She staggered up and chose to run. No one bothered to stand in her way. Most of the elves seemed far too concerned with the Prince of Tadane lying unconscious in the middle of the room like some sort of pitiful sacrifice.

All she had wanted from today was to please her father, to earn his approval. He talked about how he imagined the scene of his daughter standing tall in the middle of the room with a bloody corin that would show the Vestans a glimpse of who she would be as queen. Her hand was indeed bleeding, and she tucked it into her stomach to salvage what she could. If Lucan had joy, it was not because of her. It was because Azrael had tried to help her and was hurt in front of everybody.

Because the meeting to discuss peace began with chaos that would distract the Vestans for hours.

She had fallen.

She had run.

Bitter tears soaked her cheeks.

As she looked back, she saw her father sitting in his appointed chair. Everyone was bustling about or standing around confused, except for the man who had caused the disturbance. He lounged in his seat like it was a throne, watching the madness with a terrible smile on his face.

CHAPTER 4

"Emmy," Doranen called. "Emmy, come here."

Emmy felt too stunned to move. The crowd of people swarmed the room, some focused on her friend while the others bickered and fought with any dark elf they could find. When her father realized she would not-- or rather could not-- move, he came over to her.

"Emmy," he said again.

She turned her body toward him. Her attention was still on catching any glimpse that would show her that Azrael would be alright.

"Did you hear me?"

Her mouth felt dry, so her voice seemed to scratch along her throat as she spoke. "Yes, I heard you."

"Go check on Princess Rosalyn."

She took a step toward the middle of the room. "Will Azrael be alright? I don't see him moving."

Her father lowered his head, took both her hands and cupped them in his.

"I know that none of this makes sense to you right now. Azrael is your friend, and, I assure you, that he will be fine. You are scared, as am I. But as scared as you are, I can only imagine how scared Rosalyn is."

With a tilt of her head, Emmy relived the last few minutes. Rosalyn's screams lingering in the air, and part of her thought that if she listened hard enough she could still hear them. Emmy had never heard screams like that, especially ones from someone so small. She shook the echoes of the prior scene away and nodded at her father's request.

"You'll make sure Azrael is taken care of, right?" She asked before leaving.

Her father rubbed her hands and smiled at her.

"Of course," he assured. "His mother has already sent for a healer. Now, go."

With a quick turn on her heal, she raced out of the room and charged down the hall in search of Rosalyn. She could not have gotten far, Emmy thought, since Rosalyn's familiarity with the castle only stretched as far as what she could have seen in a day. For a trained soldier, that could be enough to find a weakness or hiding spot.

However, Rosalyn was not a soldier.

Emmy reached her room only to find her door left open. As she neared the room enough to peer in, her heart seemed to push into her throat. The edge of the same dress she had admired earlier tempted her to look further as it laid in the doorway.

"Rosalyn?" she whispered.

She did not want to take any more steps toward the room, but her feet urged her closer with their own will.

Rosalyn Lassehelin resembled one of the mounds of clothes in other parts of her room; collapsed, limp, and out of place. Her breathing was ragged, her hair glued to her forehead from sweat, and blood dripped from her arm to the floor. Emmy rushed to her side, praying that she was not too late.

"He's going to be so angry with me," Rosalyn rasped. The fingers on her injured arm twitched, seemingly the only movement with her left arm that she was capable of. A sudden surge of pain shot through her making her bite her lip.

Emmy staggered up from the floor and called down the hall for anyone who was in earshot to come to help her. Bile rose up in her stomach as the smell of blood permeated the room. She whispered for Rosalyn to hold on, but, when help did not come right away, Emmy's pleas felt hollow.

She stood up, needing to clear her head. What she realized as she got a better look at the princess was how small

Rosalyn appeared. The girl had just been named the heir to the most powerful Kingdom of Elves and she looked like a child. How could someone like her turn into her father, Emmy wondered. Rosalyn's words repeated in Emmy's head as did many questions about Lucan's methods for training his daughter.

Movement out of the corner of her eye pulled her away and towards the man entering the room.

"Please, Absalom, hurry. I don't know what to do to help her," she beckoned.

Without any hesitancy, Absalom's trained eyes assessed Rosalyn before he picked her up and placed her on the bed. Rosalyn groaned as she failed to push herself out of his grasp. Had it not been for Absalom trying to keep her arm steady, Emmy guessed he could have picked Rosalyn up in only one arm due to her size and weight. Emmy followed, taking her place on the other side of the bed to give the physician space to do his work.

Absalom may have worked in her father's palace for years, yet she was still not used to the sight of him. His long withered hands worked with precision to check Rosalyn's heartbeat and his mismatched colored eyes inspected her arm. His thick dark hair was short enough that he did not need to tie it back, though he shook it out of his eyes from time to time. The bag around his shoulder clinked as bottles of healing draughts and other mysteries banged together. He pulled a bottle of a murky green liquid out of his bag and spread the contents over Rosalyn's arm. She winced and pulled away.

"Hold still, Princess Rosalyn," Absalom said without urgency.

"No." She pushed against Absalom's hand on her shoulder, though she was no match for his strength. "I need to get back. He'll be angry with me if I don't. Let me go."

"Stay in bed."

Emmy turned to see that Rosalyn's father had appeared in the doorway and walked towards her. He cleared his throat as a way of telling Emmy to move, but she did so more out of fear than obedience.

"Absalom, right?" Lucan asked.

Absalom nodded and pulled out a roll of bandages from the bag hanging across his torso.

Lucan glanced over at Rosalyn's injured arm. "Lift her arm, I want to see it."

Absalom obeyed, only raising her hand a few inches higher than before.

"I'm sorry," Rosalyn whimpered.

Lucan stiffened and looked straight ahead, "What have always said, Rosalyn?"

"Don't apologize."

Lucan nodded. "Give me your arm."

"Your majesty," Absalom interrupted. "Forgive me, but your daughter is weak. She should rest."

The change in Lucan's demeanor was sudden enough that it felt as though even the air around him stopped. He locked eyes with the man across from him, then held out his hand. Though he was speaking to his daughter, the challenge was given to Absalom.

"Give me your arm, Rosalyn," he commanded.

She winced, managing to drag her arm across to the other side with only a small whimper. The corner of Lucan's mouth tugged in a spiteful half smile. He grabbed Rosalyn by the wrist and twisted it around to look at her palm. Emmy covered her ears at the sound of the scream Rosalyn let out. Lucan's focus had switched from Absalom to his daughter's wrist and she wondered if resisting would only be another annoyance rather than a valid protest. He began mumbling to himself, half forgetting that other people were in the room.

"A fine mark. Good strong lines."

Emmy turned her attention back to Rosalyn. She did not know what she had expected from her new friend, but to see the looks of admiration on Rosalyn's tear-stained face was the last thing she had expected.

"I tried to fight through the pain," Rosalyn said. "Are you

angry with me?"

"I am," Lucan shrugged. "It will pass."

He released her hand, pulled out a handkerchief from his cloak, and wiped the residual concoction from her arm off his hand. Absalom lunged forward, catching her arm before it fell. He grabbed the bandages he had pulled out before and began applying them.

"You are named," Lucan continued. "That's all I care about."

The smile Emmy had seen in the main hall appeared and sank her stomach. "And besides, you took out the Prince of Tadane. Even better than I could have hoped for."

Emmy gasped. She half expected to see Lucan turn to the source of the noise, or Absalom to stop her. Neither man moved. Lucan seemed lost in his own world. The chuckle rattled his chest as though he were puffing himself up to appear more significant. While the laugh seemed odd, Emmy guessed that his intimidating size was a calculated move.

Rosalyn hesitated, "He's not..."

"Amry is fretting over him now." The glow was still present on his face even though the actual smile had faded. He laughed until he realized that his answer would not satisfy his daughter. With an added eye roll, Lucan emphasized, "He'll live. As will you."

"Would you like me to come back with you?" Rosalyn asked, trying to redeem herself.

Lucan scoffed. His face looked as though some foul smell had entered the room. "No, this doctor is correct. You need rest."

Had he been a typical father, he would have kissed her forehead or said something to alleviate the worry still on her face. Instead, Lucan left Rosalyn's side without another word. His last comment felt heavy in the air. It was a statement, not a sentiment, delivered like a command. Emmy half watched him leave the room until he turned and stopped in front of Absalom.

"A shade is an interesting choice for a healer," Lucan remarked in an uncharacteristically sweet tone. "Now, why would Doranen do that, I wonder."

Absalom's hands continued to work, showing none of the signs of shock that Emmy felt over Lucan's insensitive comment. He looked over the King's face, searching for any sign of a threat.

"I think he likes the poetry of it, Your Majesty."

Lucan ran the edge of his thumb across his mouth, "Poetry?"

Turning back to his patient, Absalom nodded and continued working. "Who better to care for the living than someone brought back from the dead."

Lucan's head tilted to the side, "I see."

He apparently did not, and Emmy knew enough about him to know he would not admit it. Lucan pivoted on his heels, then left the room. His daughter forced herself deeper into the bed and looked away from the rest of the occupants. She did not move when Emmy returned to the side of the bed and had no reaction aside from the occasional grown from Absalom's last few wraps of the bandages.

"Is that true?" Emmy asked when she was sure Lucan was down the hall. "Was hurting Azrael planned?"

Rosalyn's reaction was extreme. Her eyes widened, and she gripped the edge of the bed with her free hand. "No, I swear. I didn't know."

Absalom outstretched a hand to silence any further response from Emmy while the other stabilized his patient by the shoulder. Rosalyn looked at the hand on her shoulder, then to its owner as if she expected it to be someone else. She shrugged off Absalom's hand, returning her head to the other side of the pillow to avoid looking at them.

Tucking in the unfinished edge of the cloth bandage into the wrap, Absalom motioned for Emmy to follow him out of the room.

"Thank you," Rosalyn whispered as they walked away.

Emmy knew Absalom heard what Rosalyn had said, even though he said nothing. He fussed over the bag crossed over his shoulder, and she thought she saw a thin smile on his face.

"She will be alright," Absalom said in a hushed tone. "The pain will not ease for some time. I will send for someone to monitor her for the next few hours."

He turned to go, but she held out her hand to stop him. "That will not be necessary. I will watch over her."

Absalom looked taken aback by her offer, questioning her with his penetrating eyes. She squirmed under his gaze, though she could not blame him for his skepticism. He did not know about her father's instruction, and, while she did not think it would change Absalom's mind, it was still a reach for her to show any signs of caring for Rosalyn beyond the ordinary civility afforded to avoid aggravating the war.

"If that is what you wish, my lady," he said, with a bow of his head. "Do not hesitate to call for me if her condition changes."

As soon as the doctor left the room, Emmy made for Rosalyn's bedside. The color had yet to return to Rosalyn's face, that looked aged by pain. Her arm laid limp next to her, wrapped from her palm to just below her elbow. Her hair clung to her face, but she lacked the energy to brush it away.

"Thank you for staying with me," Rosalyn managed.

"Did you know that your father would do that? Any of that?"

"Of course I did," Rosalyn explained. "All elves of Helios are marked."

Emmy stammered, "All of them experience that?"

She could still hear Rosalyn's screams ringing in her head. Emmy found that she could not fathom the idea of her own father hurting her in such a way.

Rosalyn only nodded in response. Her face looked as though she could say more on the subject. Her instincts told her to ignore Emmy, and, after Lucan's behavior, Emmy could not blame her.

Yet, Rosalyn was grateful to her. She was under her father's thumb as evidenced by her obedience. The fact that aspects of Rosalyn's personality like kindness and gratitude kept showing themselves told Emmy that Rosalyn was different.

"Will Azrael recover?" Rosalyn asked, her voice wavering. Her eyes looked to Emmy with intense desperation and then changed to guilt. Horrified at the idea, she grabbed Emmy's sleeve and urged her to answer. "I mean he's not going to die, is he?"

"You do not have to worry about Azrael, my father says he will be fine."

Emmy smiled to reassure her, though she wondered about Azrael's condition as well. Rosalyn's face looked washed with relief, though some concern was still visible.

Rosalyn's ability to stay awake was lessening with each passing minute. She started apologizing, repeating her words and growing more agitated. "I did not mean to hurt him, I swear."

Emmy took Rosalyn's non-bandaged hand. As if her touch burned like fire, Rosalyn ripped her hand away.

"Let go of me," she screamed.

Emmy lifted her arms in surrender and took a step back.

Rosalyn covered her face with her free hand, wincing at her sudden outburst. Tears slipped through her fingers as she breathed herself through her own fear. It worked and she calmed down, though Emmy had never seen such control over emotions. Rosalyn crossed her free hand over her body and ran it across the upper part of her other arm, as though she were comforting herself.

"What if I hurt you too?" she observed.

"You are my friend," Emmy countered. "You won't hurt me."

"I've only known you a day, but I know that I don't want to hurt you. I didn't want to hurt Azrael. Please, leave me before I hurt you too."

Emmy reached out her hand to assure her friend nothing would happen but Rosalyn pushed herself further away.

"I said leave."

Emmy's eyes closed, and she breathed a sigh of regret.

"Go," Rosalyn pleaded.

Emmy backed up, despite her legs feeling like they were made of stone. It took all her strength to turn around, walk out of the room, and close the door. The instant she heard the sound of the door against the frame, she wished she could turn back. Less than two days, screams, and tears were all it took to turn a casual guest into a friend she was leaving in a room by herself. The air around her felt cold, but her ears burned. She leaned against the door and wished she could do more.

"What troubles you, my friend?"

Azrael, pale and coughing, walked towards her with his usual, albeit weakened, swagger.

"Should you be out of bed?" Emmy asked. "You look terrible."

He smiled and shrugged. "I look worse than I feel."

She tried to laugh, but the result was more like an exaggerated exhale than a chuckle. Even the fake smile she forced made her stomach lurch inside her. Her friend took a step towards her and examined her with soft eyes.

"You look worse than I do," he added.

Emmy opened her mouth to speak but found she had no words. The air she breathed felt insufficient somehow, and she had no idea if she was opening her mouth to protest or agree with Azrael's assessment of her. A sudden vision of the smear of blood on her floor came to the forefront of her mind.

Azrael cocked his head, "Has something happened?"

"I hardly know."

Her eyes were wide, despite staring at nothing in particular. She wiped her forehead with the edge of her sleeve.

"Come with me," Azrael suggested as he ushered her closer to him. "Everything will be made right."

Emmy agreed, letting Azrael take her by the elbow and lead her away. The room pulled at her to stay for Rosalyn's sake. She could not hear sounds from inside and hoped that meant Rosalyn was getting sleep as instructed. The door was thick, however, and could have been masking any sound. She shook her head loose of its thoughts and focused on what was in front of her.

Before being pulled away completely, she waved her hand at a maid walking by. "Tell Lord Absalom that I had to step out."

The girl curtsied and replied with a simple, "Yes, my lady."

Azrael and Emmy walked into the large yet enclosed kitchen. With only small windows towards the tops of the room to ventilate heat, the room felt humid. He directed her to a small table in the corner and she sat down on the nearest stool. The table was rarely used, as elves often ate in the large dining hall. Azrael pulled out a stool for himself but did not sit down. She watched him walk over to the cook and place an order. By the time she pulled her gaze away, the cook was pouring boiling water into a mug. The lines and patterns in the wood table seemed a better distraction as she processed all that had happened. Her focus was pulled back minutes later when Azrael set the drink down in front of her.

She waited for Azrael to say something, though she knew he would stay silent. The look on his face was one she had been privy to many times during the friendship. It was one she knew stemmed from love but she hated to be under its scrutiny. His eyes did not pry but his lips were formed in a tight line. Emmy found that she did not know where to start or how to speak her mind. She took a sip from the cup in front of her.

"I've never seen..."

"Did she hurt you?" Azrael asked after a few moments of silence.

"Of course not."

Azrael urged her further, "Then what is it?"

"If you could only see her, Azrael."

Her voice trailed off. She took a deep breath, then tried again.

"After she ran out of the room, my father asked me to look in on her. She was bleeding and her father only made her more afraid. And in spite of all that, all she could think about was our safety. She felt guilty for hurting you, and she pulled away from me."

"My mother said that you will not be affected," Azrael offered. His face now turned away in thought.

"Did she say why you were hurt?"

Emmy took a drink, this time tasting what Azrael had given her. The bitter tea took her by surprise more than the temperature.

"She said the mark on Rosalyn's hand is poisonous to my kin, but not yours." Azrael smiled and added, "It always comes down to magic. Light versus dark."

Emmy had grown up educated in the tension and prejudice surrounding the war. Even the mere mention of it made her scoff. It all seemed like such a mess that it would take a political miracle to satisfy all the pain that kept the different kingdoms from peace. She could recall her father mediating disputes between King Lucan and Azrael's parents countless times, most being petty arguments. Lucan reserved his more serious arguments for her father, but her father had managed to hide the bulk of those from her.

"But she did not want to hurt you. How can it come down to that?"

"Her dark magic against my light magic." Azrael was smiling, amused at something that Emmy failed to understand. "It would seem that even our bodies hate each other."

"You know I hate all this." She made a vague gesture to indicate all the fighting.

Her friend only nodded, "I know you do."

Emmy pushed her mug away and folded her hands in

front of her to indicate the seriousness of what she was about to say. "Be honest. Do you hate her? Rosalyn. Do you have some, even small, prejudice against her?"

Azrael sighed, scratching his head as he thought. He had a right to be wary of her after what happened with her marking. She was Lucan's daughter and heir, which gave her some amount of worrying attributes. Her people expected her to be fierce, bloodthirsty, and, above all, have an apparent disdain for Vestans. Yet, Emmy could not find any of those in the girl she was beginning to know.

"I should hate her," he started. "But, I don't. What happened was an accident, and I cannot hate her for an accident. An accident that wouldn't have happened if I had listened to my mother, who warned me to wear gloves this morning. And Rosalyn was just as surprised as I was when the mark affected me. I could see it in her eyes. If I assumed that she was like her father, I would be no better the likes of my parents."

Emmy nodded at her closest friend, knowing that their opinions were far from the opinions of the rulers fighting for peace in the main hall. While they gave her the benefit of the doubt, those in the other room did not have the luxury and had been hurt by her father enough times to warrant their mistrust.

She thought back to the look in Rosalyn's eyes when her father had been in her room, and it made Emmy pause. Rosalyn had been kind and thoughtful, but the desire to please her father had been just as apparent to Emmy since she met her. One had to be a rouse, and, if not, she wondered which feelings of Rosalyn's would win out. Eventually, Rosalyn would have to choose and Emmy's stomach sank as she knew that two days were not enough to defy years of loyalty.

CHAPTER 5

Rosalyn stared at the edge of the marble step and the adjoining grass that was the start of the garden of Valandyl. She had been staring at the edge for ten minutes, questioning the validity of her presence there. It had been two days since she was marked, and this was the first time that she had found the will to leave her bed in Princess Emmelina's room. The pain had kept her in bed the first day, and her legs were beginning to cramp from lack of movement. Spilling into the palace, the warmth of the day was perfect for a walk, and she had hoped that no one would be outside. The sun poking through the canopy of trees over the path seemed as foreign to her as the elves that flanked her. Back in Helios, the mountain terrain and high elevation kept the sun and warmth away.

A chill, like an echo, from her thoughts of home, pulled her back to the garden. She was in a beautiful place, and she would not let her thoughts of home tarnish her time here. The sun melted into her skin like a syrup and relaxed her down to the bone. She rolled her neck around, stretching the muscles, and rubbed the warmth on the surface of her sleeves into her arms.

Most of the garden was covered in shade, not because of the trees but because of the high walls that lined the edge.

Though there was a dozen of Doranen's elves in the garden, they made her feel like she was alone. The elves lowered their voices, made an obvious effort to keep their distance, and she caught them staring at her arm when they did bother to notice her. She forced herself to the least inhabited corner, shoving her head down and keeping her eyes focused on the ground in front of her. For all she knew, they had all seen her scream during her marking.

She looked at her wrapped hand that still felt scorched. All the stories she had heard about other Dark Elves getting their mark had done little to prepare her for the feeling of her father's white-hot hand pulling magic to the surface of her skin. Hidden under the wrap, she knew her tattoo waited for her. She would have to look at the corin mark once she had healed, and the thought only made the pain worse.

Though her head was down, she saw a bench at the top of her peripheral vision. She pushed aside her feelings about her arm and the elves around her and made her way to the bench perched in the corner. Low, hollow dings sounded above her from wind chimes in the trees, the birds conversed with each other, and the breeze made her pause to take it all in.

She rested her back against the tree, pulling her knees up close to her chest. The length of her dress covered her, and for once she was thankful that all of her dresses were too long for her. She stared out over her knees to the soft grass and decided to remove her short boots, placing them next to the bench with precision. The softness and intense color made her want to feel it for herself before she would go back to the stone and mud of Helios.

Rosalyn watched the people on the path with wavering curiosity. They frightened her with their relentless stares and judgments. Meanwhile, she loved to listen to their conversations and watch their behavior. They addressed each other with respect and talked in civil tones. She imagined that she was a flower or another blade of grass that these strange elves ignored as they continued on with their day and she could observe them from far off.

Until she caught eyes with the Prince of Tadane as he entered the garden.

He smiled, ended his conversation with one of his kin, and made his way over to her. The color had returned to his face, and, had she not been the one who had caused him pain, she would have thought him to be in pristine health. His clothes and hair caught the sunlight as he diverted from the shaded path. She wanted to look away from him or wave at him to leave her alone, but her body was frozen in place.

Azrael's smile seemed to grow with every step closer. The magic in him so strong that he radiated his own warmth and seemed to glow from some subtle light within him. This time, she did turn her face away and settled on her shoes as a distraction.

"Have you ever experienced a more lovely day?" he mused once he was in earshot.

"How are you feeling, Prince Azrael?" She asked, her voice just loud enough for him to hear. Her tone was overly civil, and she turned her head away in embarrassment. If he was angry with her, he did not show it on his face.

He sat down beside her and paused a moment to admire his surroundings before answering.

Her eyes strayed upward, but she still would not focus on the elf in front of her. The bench left little room for her to hide. Azrael had a broad chest that caused the fabric of his robes to brush against her arm. Her spine stiffened and she pulled her legs tighter into her chest to support her back.

"I am well." His voice was smooth and confident. "And you? Emmy told me about the pain you were in."

"Why would she...?" She started, her voice raised. Her instinct to lash out rippling under her skin. She closed her eyes and focused on breathing through her anger. Emmy's words were out of concern for her rather than malice. There was no need for an outburst, nor did she think that Azrael would understand why she would have one.

"I appreciate her concern, and yours." This time her voice was lower, and her temper was subdued. "My arm will heal in time, and the pain has lessened."

"That is good to hear. The other day, you were afraid. Trying to stay strong for whatever reason."

"For whatever reason?" she asked, trying not to sound like she was objecting.

The man paused, rethinking his words. "It seemed to me that you weren't being strong because of the pain, that's all I'm saying. I don't know you well enough to make a guess."

She opened her mouth to speak but thought better of it. Nothing she could say would explain her side and not embarrass her father. Like ringing in her ears, Rosalyn could imagine her father behind her telling her not to trust the light elf who pretended to care. He had looked at her before her marking like something intriguing, some foreign party trick to entertain him. Even now, she could not understand why he came over to her after what she had done to him.

"Do you ever speak your mind?" He asked without warning.

"I do not understand the question," She said, looking him straight in the eye for the first time. In actuality, she did understand his question though his bluntness took her by surprise.

"The two times that I've talked to you, you have barely said a word. You could have nothing to say, though I doubt it since you are Lucan's daughter. I can see in your eyes how you tailor your thoughts, and few of those thoughts make it out of your mouth."

He looked at her with the same examinatory look he had given her when they first met. Only this time, it was not a strange look but a curious one. The way he looked at her was piercing as though he could see through her blank expressions and banal answers. She wanted to back away from him or retreat against the wall to give her a semblance of strength. Rosalyn decided to put on her shoes and turned her face away so that Azrael could not see her expressions while she thought. Did he want her to speak her mind? The way he talked to her was inviting and playful, but no one dared speak to her that way in Helios. She could scream or speak her mind, as she wished, were she back home but the politics were so thick around them that it was stifling.

She heard him get up, and half expected him to walk away when she said nothing. Rather than watch him leave, she gathered her hair that hung loosely around her shoulders and started to braid it. She watched him out of the corner of her eye, only to find that his feet were planted a step away from her.

"Emmy and I were thinking of going for a walk today. Will you join us?" He smiled and held out his hand to help her up from the bench.

The muscles in her hand flexed yet she recoiled, afraid of hurting him again. Her breathing grew heavy and all the feelings from the marking ceremony came back to her. The defiance she felt towards her father, the estrangement from everyone in the room, and the warmth when Azrael reached out to help her. Though the pain made the moment drag on, she was able to feel the mark on her hand aching for the kill the instant his skin met hers. One touch was all it took for her to understand the differences between them and how their magic interacted. Worse still, there was a nagging in her brain to appease that ache days after.

"You will not hurt me if you use your other hand," he stated, nudging his own hand forward.

"How can you be sure?" she asked.

Rosalyn stood up and made her way towards the palace.

She could hear the sound of his clothes rustle and felt his presence follow her like a shadow. He only wanted her, followed her, because she was new. A curiosity that he could poke and prod until he figured out all he needed to for the story he would turn her into with his friends back home.

Just when she thought she could not hear him anymore, she felt his hand in her own. He did not grab or pull, but she ricocheted around anyway. It took a few seconds before Rosalyn realized that nothing was happening, and, when the realization occurred, she stared at their hands in shock.

"You could have been killed."

"And you could have been wrong," Azrael said, with a handsome smirk.

She pulled her hand away and placed it behind her back in case he decided to make for it again. All the warnings that her father had given were not enough to prepare her for a situation like this. What if he had been wrong? Azrael had reached out to her, not just physically but more than she thought someone from another kingdom would.

"Azrael," Emmy called from behind Rosalyn. Emmy turned to her and looked her over. "Are you alright? It looked like he was hurting you."

"I am fine," Rosalyn responded, still eyeing the Prince with suspicion. "He was just proving a point, that's all."

"Really, Emmy, what do you take me for?"

Emmy's eyes flashed between the two. Her voice dropped to a whisper, "I'm sorry. I misread the situation."

"All is well, my friend," he reassured. Azrael put his hand on Emmy's shoulder and she apologized again, though they all knew it was unnecessary.

"I should get back to my father." Rosalyn took a step away from them, biting her lip. "He may be wondering where I am."

"Wait," Azrael said. "Go, if you must, but we would still love it if you joined us for that walk."

She winced when hope made her stop. Rather than give in, she forced it down and crossed her arms. This elf had no idea what trouble he could get into by being friends with her or how her father's head would explode if he found out.

"Do you like getting hurt?" she snapped.

"Not particularly." He shrugged with a cocky smile. "Do you think I am a fool?"

She sputtered, "Why?"

"I know what is an accident and what is not. And I know that there is far more to you than most people see."

Emmy eased herself forward and put a hand on her arm. "We won't hurt you."

She unlaced her arms and ran a hand through her long hair. They wanted her, though Rosalyn could not figure out why. Azrael was a bit forward, which fostered concern, but Emmy's enthusiasm for her was genuine. If Emmy had any plans for using her in the future, she was the greatest liar that Rosalyn had ever encountered.

"Just a walk?"

"Just a walk," Azrael repeated.

"My father won't like it..."

He put his arm around Emmy, who nodded as though her life depended on it. Emmy's natural smile returned to her face. "He doesn't have to know."

Rosalyn's body grew tense, knowing that she should go to her father, yet a warmth found its way to her face, "Well, don't look at me to lead the way."

CHAPTER 6

As the rulers of the Three Kingdoms battled with each other in the name of peace down the hallway, Emmy found herself faced with a more sensitive undertaking. She managed to convince Rosalyn to sneak away from Emmy's room at times to take walks or have meals with Azrael and herself, but Rosalyn spent most of their time together with curious eyes and a closed mouth. She would answer questions that were asked of her, but she squirmed or gave an odd nervous chuckle with every response. Emmy had exchanged a few side glances with Azrael when Rosalyn's answers were shorter than expected. Though the progress was slow, they both knew how quickly she could shut down.

Emmy's hands fumbled around the top of her bed, though her focus was on the dark elf at the other end of her room. Rosalyn was sitting on her bed, with her bag already packed for the day. She was the shortest of the group and Emmy found it comical that Rosalyn's legs dangled off the side. Emmy turned back to her own pack of a change of clothes and a few snacks, then breathed a sigh of relief.

"Are you ready?" Emmy asked.

Rosalyn's head jerked up, "What?"

Emmy smiled at her friend's aloofness and repeated the question. "Are you ready to go to the waterfall?"

Rosalyn's eyes assessed her for any threat. When none was found, she nodded and added in a meek voice, "Yes."

Emmy slipped her hand under Rosalyn's and pulled her along with giddy excitement. She did her best to avoid any paths that might cause Rosalyn to worry about interacting with her father. Emmy counted four hallways between her room and the exit towards the stables where they planned to meet Azrael. She felt the jolt of hesitation from Rosalyn every time they passed someone she did not know or heard a voice other than Emmy beside her.

"Where do you go?" Emmy smiled, realizing how vague she sounded. "When you stare off, where does your mind wander off to?"

Rosalyn's eyes widened, then she jerked her head around to check the hallway for elves coming their way. "I live in my own mind, I guess. My father..."

"My father," she started again. "Prefers that I learn all I can from a situation so I'm often evaluating everything in my head."

Emmy's face puckered, "Evaluating?"

Her tone sounded rehearsed, even the phrasing did not fit with Rosalyn's normal speech. Emmy had seen her friend fidgeting and thought that she was nervous about being in Valandyl. Doing some evaluating of her own, Emmy tried to see more than Rosalyn had allowed her to see.

Emmy looked down, taking Rosalyn's hand. It was shaking, and Emmy gave it a squeeze. The shaking and nervousness all pointed to something, though Emmy knew she was missing the larger picture. She let the moment settle, and gestured for Rosalyn to continue to follow her down the hallway.

"I'm sorry that I get nervous." Rosalyn cleared her throat and breathed in again to summon up the courage to speak. When that was not enough, she forced an awkward shrug and a small laugh that seemed to ease her. "My father says that I overthink, and I think he's right."

"You don't need to apologize for anything."

Emmy gave a brief tug to start up their journey to the stables and wrapped Rosalyn's arm around her own. Once they were out of her father's palace, Emmy felt the stiffness fade from her friend as soon as the fresh air hit them. The elves that passed them made Rosalyn drop her head and veer away, but Emmy got the feeling that it was unconsciously done. The crowd had all but disappeared once they reached their destination.

Azrael greeted them with a wave as he pulled a horse alongside him. The grey mare was well groomed and already saddled. Another elf trailed behind him, casting a curious glance at Azrael then eyed the newcomers. Emmy smiled at him, and he returned the gesture. As his eyes moved on to Rosalyn, the man hesitated.

"I do apologize," he said, focusing his attention back on Emmy. "If Azrael knew his way around a horse, we would have been ready sooner."

Azrael wrapped the reins around the hitching rail then joined the three, staring at this companion with the afterglow of a joke that Emmy and Rosalyn had missed. Emmy had resigned herself to accepting that his glow was every bit as part of him as his hair or shape of his face. She could count on her hands all the times she had seen him without a smile or his face beaming.

"He likes to complain," Azrael said with a laugh.

Emmy put a hand on Rosalyn's shoulder, before gesturing over to the elf in front of them. "Rosalyn, meet Marcus."

They eyed each other, assessing the threat each posed. It could not have been more than a few seconds before Marcus put his hand out to shake Rosalyn's. She went to take it, but stopped and shoved her hand behind her back. Emmy caught sight of the bandage on Rosalyn's wrist, realizing why she had pulled her hand away.

"It's nice to meet you," Rosalyn whispered.

Emmy caught Azrael's eye and nudged her head towards Marcus. The awkwardness was obvious, and Rosalyn would insist on going back to hide in Emmy's room if they were not careful. Rosalyn let her head fall and shuffled her feet.

Azrael opened his mouth to say something, but Marcus shook his head. Though he looked hurt, his voice was calm. "I apologize, I forgot."

Rosalyn's head rose, "It's alright. After the incident the other day, I don't want to take any chances."

"Yes, I heard about that."

She shrugged and flashed a sarcastic smile, "I think you'd be hard pressed to find someone who hadn't."

Marcus' mouth dropped before Emmy had finished processing her friend's words. If Azrael had said it, his lightheartedness and familiarity would have made it into a joke. Coming from Rosalyn, the meaning exposed Lucan's actions and Rosalyn's place within them. It hit Emmy with full force for the first time the significance of Rosalyn as Lucan's heir and that the temporary peace that had brought Rosalyn to her would end.

But it did not have to end today.

"Well, let's change the subject, shall we?" She suggested, clearing her throat. "Marcus, how's your family?"

With a quick straightening of his already pristine shirt, Marcus' demeanor returned to his usual civility. "They are well. Unfortunately, work kept them from being here."

"What do they do?" Rosalyn asked.

"They are advisors to the King and Queen, but some have to stay behind when the royals are away."

The side of Rosalyn's mouth lifted, "You must be proud of them."

"I am. I hope one day to hold the same position."

Marcus looked towards Azrael as though he were putting his name in with him before he was crowned. Emmy knew as well as Azrael that Marcus thought of nothing else and that Azrael would hire him the moment he was able, but it never stopped Azrael from teasing him to the contrary. Azrael shrugged and faked hesitation, "That's if I think you are up to the job, old man."

A brief flash of worry passed over his friend's face but was gone as soon as Azrael's smile returned.

"He's messing with you," Emmy added. "We all know how hard you study."

Marcus nodded, "Thank you."

"I just have to prepare the other horse," Azrael interrupted, already turning towards the stables away from them. "And then we can leave."

Emmy watched him go. He knew that if he stayed, she would comment on the fact that he had promised he would be ready to go when she and Rosalyn arrived. The stables were an easy place for Rosalyn to be spotted, and the last thing they needed was for Lucan to hear from a stable boy some exaggerated tale. She had half a mind to run after him, but Marcus' sudden shuffling kept her there out of pure curiosity.

He crossed his arms and turned his attention to Rosalyn. "Do you mind if I ask you about something your father said? He mentioned your brother and I was wondering why he didn't come."

"Same as your parents, I guess."

"I've heard stories about him," Marcus replied. His eyes wide as though he were about to hear another one. "Are they true?"

Rosalyn took a step forward, "How could I possibly know what you've heard?"

"Well, I just thought you might shed some light on him."

Rosalyn's voice rose, "You talk about him like he's gossip, and I'm not going to add to it."

The change in Rosalyn's mood was as quick as a lightning strike. Her breathing came in gasps, her shoulders straightened, and her hands clenched tight. Emmy put her hand to her mouth. Rosalyn had been too introspective and timid to take on many of her father's more well-known attributes. Her temper, however, made Emmy wonder for the first time.

Like a storm moving past, the expression on Rosalyn's face cooled. She winced, unclenching her fists but looked down at them as though unsure what to do with them.

Emmy reached out to her, but Marcus grabbed Emmy's other wrist and pulled her back. She searched him for an explanation, but his attention was on Lucan's daughter. His other hand was at his hip, ready to pull the small knife concealed under his shirt.

"Excuse me," Rosalyn whispered. Emmy tried to follow after her, but Rosalyn waved her away. "I'm fine. I'm going to see if Azrael needs any help."

Emmy sighed, waiting until Rosalyn was out of earshot, before speaking. "You don't know that she would have hurt me."

"No," he answered as he let her go. "You're right. But you don't know for sure that she wouldn't have."

"You don't know her as I do."

"I shouldn't have to remind you that you've only known her for several days."

He was right, but Emmy refused to acknowledge that and give him the smug satisfaction. Marcus had not interacted with her like she had, as Azrael had.

"You're paranoid," she spat.

"I'd rather apologize to her for being wrong, than deal with the aftermath of my being right."

* * *

If she thought she would not be overheard, Rosalyn would have shouted out her frustration. She intertwined her fingers instead and wished she could just go back to Emmy's room to hide her embarrassment. She had let her anger out, or instead, she had set it loose. The fragile view of her was broken. She scoffed at how little it took for her to go from tentative friend to potential enemy, but also how quick Marcus reached for the knife that was so poorly concealed on his belt. He must have hoped that the coat he wore was enough to hide it, but Rosalyn had spotted the outline of the hilt the minute she saw him.

Once she reached the outside of the stables, she stopped

and took a breath. She had spent enough time in her father's to make her able to find a footing in the familiar setting. The knot in her stomach grew tighter when she saw Azrael, but being with a man that could make a joke about anything seemed more straightforward than going back to the others.

The brown horse that Azrael was working with pulled at the rope in his hand, which acted as a temporary bridle. Her inclination would have been to give the rope a firm tug in the direction she wanted the horse to go. She was surprised when instead Azrael kept his feet apart but still stood his ground. He clicked his tongue, ushering the horse to him, and ran his hand over the horse's long nose and down his neck.

"Good afternoon."

Azrael smiled at her, then returned his gaze to the horse. She wished that his eyes had stayed on her longer, but, if they had, he would have seen the light flush in her face. However quick, his attention filled her with a warmth like when she sat out in the sun.

He motioned for her to come closer, "Will you help me?"

"Of course. What can I do?"

"Hand me the bridle over there."

He pointed to a rack on the side of the corral near her. The horse eyed her as she moved away, but Azrael coaxed him back. She took the bridle off the rack, gave it to him, and he fixed it into place.

"There," Azrael said more to himself.

He took a couple tentative steps, and, when the horse followed, he gestured for her to come alongside him.

"You are good with him," she admired.

"Thank you," he said as he fell in line with her. "Sorry about that. He's a bit finicky. I got him saddled with no problem, but he hates being led around. I figured bringing the mare outside would give him some time to calm down before I put the bridle on."

She smirked, suddenly taking a liking to the horse.

"You know," he started. Even though he was taller than her, his head was bent and he looked at her through his thick eyelashes. "Marcus is a good man."

Rosalyn turned away from him.

"Why do you feel the need to say that?" she asked.

"You were scared of saying the wrong thing. I saw how hesitant you were."

He looked confident like he prided himself on discovering this nuance. She could not believe that he wore such a cocky smile when all around him smelled like hay and excrement, but the look was unmistakable on his face. Meanwhile, Rosalyn felt her insides turn. She had been scared that her every move or spoken word would be scrutinized when she came to Valandyl. Azrael's assessment only proved her assumption. Had he been watching her, waiting for some kind of slip up? His eyes on her seemed to change. Instead of seeing her, he was examining all her flaws and seeing all her pitiful tries in plain view. It was an intrusion, no less irritating or painful than that of her father.

Rosalyn's anger boiled, "You would be hesitant too if you could hurt someone with one touch. If everyone hated you because of an accident, or because you could just as easily do it again. I can't always tell with you Vestans and I'll not hurt anyone else."

She thought about apologizing. Her tone was harsh, though her words were accurate. The hesitancy she exhibited was all she could do to protect those around her, and she refused to apologize for being safe.

Azrael was the epitome of his race, with his light coloring and brown eyes. Even his face, with his high cheekbones that culminated in his square jaw and a bright smile that would make any attempt at disguise impossible. His friend, on the other hand, was different.

It was not until Marcus had mentioned his family and their positions that she had been sure of where he came from. His hair was darker than Emmy's and his face was soft. He would have to wait several more years for his brow ridge and cheekbones to catch up with his age. Valandyl was a reasonable guess, and one wrong one could result in trouble for her. Her accident with Azrael was forgivable, but another incident would be sure to be perceived as an attack.

She chewed on the inside of her cheek, "That was blunt."

"It was," he enunciated. "But thank you."

Her gaze softened, realizing her words had struck a chord with him. She breathed away her anger, wishing they could change the subject to anything else.

"So," she began. "How do you know about horses?"

"I used to travel between Valandyl and Tadane frequently, so the knowledge came with the territory. Or rather, the knowledge came from traveling between territories."

Azrael chuckled at his own attempt at a joke, which made Rosalyn smile. He opened his mouth to speak but stopped when he saw that their conversation would no longer be private. She wanted to make him stop, keep their conversation going. He had his jokes but even amongst all her recent actions, she never saw fear in his eyes. When the last of his attention was off her, she felt her frustration from earlier rising like an echo.

"It looks like you are finally ready," Azrael teased Marcus as they approached.

Marcus shrugged. He looked unfazed until Azrael was past him and he delivered a light slap to the back of Azrael's head. She knew the slap had not hurt, but Rosalyn could not help noting just how often the Prince of Tadane was slapped by his friends. It was all in jest, she understood that. What struck her was that no one, even a friend, would have the same freedom with her or her brother were they at home. Even the small thud from the slap and envisioning her father's reaction made her grab onto the saddle of the horse nearest her for support.

Emmy giggled, eyeing the two men as Azrael retaliated before making her way over to her. The way Emmy behaved around them and how Marcus had reached out to her suggested a friendship spanning years. She was only a few feet away, but Rosalyn felt as far as the castle in Helios like she was pulling Emmy away from those she really cared about.

"I'm afraid we can only take two horses today. Marcus just told me."

"What does that mean?"

"One horse can't take the weight of both Azrael and Marcus, and, since you just met Marcus, I was thinking you could ride with Azrael. Do you mind?"

Considering her recent outburst and her first interaction with the Prince, she minded. The idea of causing a scene or the trouble that would ensue of trying to find another horse was sure to cause Emmy stress and attract the attention of someone who would tell her father. She nodded in agreement and hoped her smile was convincing. At this point, she just wanted to leave whether she ran away to her temporary bed or went with them, the thought of staying out in the open any longer made her stomach turn.

Emmy called for the other two, and they came without protest. "So, we have the horses. Shall we get going?"

"How about you and Marcus go on?" Azrael suggested, running a hand through his blonde hair. "I need to grab one more thing, and I don't want to hold us up any further."

A laugh rumbled in her belly, and she would have let it escape from her mouth if it was not so tense from holding in a scream. The ease at which Emmy agreed and rode off with Marcus robbed her of breath. She had to make an excuse, any excuse, to get her out of this trip. One slip of her bandage or another outburst and even Emmy would not be able to forgive her.

"Why did you send them away?" Her voice hoarse and weak.

"Wait here."

"Why?"

"I'll only be a moment," he added over his shoulder.

As she watched him walk off, she grimaced at her own tone of voice. The weight of her new friends made her cover herself with her arms, looking for any kind of security. She looked around for something to ground her but even the architecture and the flora glared with a defiant difference. What had made her believe that she could be friends with these Vestans? Her father had warned her, and now everything felt like a complicated game that she was losing. So many rules, she thought, and so many ways for her to lose.

He rejoined her with a slight blush in his face from the physical exertion peeking out from under his pale skin. He paused, trying to figure out the right words to say. Even when he did speak, he stammered and rambled as though she were someone of a much higher social class and he did not know how to speak to her properly.

"I hope you do not think that I am saying what I am about to say out of fear or disgust. I want to do something kind, but I can see how it could be taken in way..."

His voice trailed off.

He looked at her with pleading eyes, only to realize that she had no idea what he was attempting to say. Somewhere between all his stammering, Rosalyn's stomach had leaped into her throat. She half expected him to ask her to stay behind, and that way she could avoid making excuses herself.

"This is not coming out how I wanted it to," he remarked when she said nothing.

He reached into the pocket of his robe and pulled out a small bundle of fabric.

Azrael chuckled nervously, "I thought you could wear it so that you would not have to worry about your mark."

He unfolded the fabric into its actual shape to reveal a single riding glove made of thick leather.

"Will it work?" Rosalyn asked, before allowing herself to get her hopes up.

"My father said that it is how my people interact with yours, so it should. The fabric is thick enough that your magic won't be able to penetrate it."

Rosalyn laced her fingers together and rested them against her mouth. She had not expected him to help her, and the kindness behind it made her want to retreat all the more. He was offering a chance for her to blend in, but she wondered why he could not see how unattainable that was. Covering her hand solved one problem, but she could still say the wrong thing or get angry again.

His eyes were soft. The glove in his hand shimmied as he inched it closer. The curiosity in his eyes had gone and had been replaced by something she had never seen before. Gentleness was there, but the other quality that made his gesture kinder was something more profound than she could name. She wanted to believe him, to take what he was offering, but the fear paralyzed her.

"You're nervous," he observed. Azrael pulled his hand back but took a step closer to her. "You don't have to be."

She took her eyes off him and forced herself to look at the palace that was so different from the one she was used to in Helios. It was her reminder, a totem of sorts to keep her from getting too involved. No matter how close she got to Emmy and Azrael, she would return to a life in Helios where her father's eyes would be on her. The training that Princess Emmelina would never receive and the discipline that Prince Azrael did not need made the outing seem like a foolhardy distraction.

"I feel so different like I don't belong with you or Emmy." She looked at the glove again, then crossed her arms in front of her to close herself off from him. "I appreciate the gesture."

"Don't go."

Rosalyn froze. She had not even turned to leave or made any excuses yet, but he already was trying to get her to stay. Though her thoughts raced, had her intentions been that obvious. Her voice was weak, "I didn't say..."

"But you were going to, weren't you?"

She nodded.

Rosalyn squirmed under his gaze, "Why do you want me to stay?"

"Because you are original," he replied without much thought.

Rosalyn scoffed and started walking away. If being there for their own amusement was all she was, she would be better off alone. The anger fueled her forward, yet was all but extinguished when Azrael reached out to stop her. He turned her around with gentle touch that made her want to cry. She pressed her lips together and shook his hand off her.

"Because I'm a novelty, you mean," she corrected.

Azrael shook his head, "You feel things I've never felt before."

He paused when her eyebrows knit together and looked around for a better answer. A small smile returned to his face, and, by some magic, she did not understand, made her relax her arms.

"Because you are sad, I think, and Emmy and I want to make you happy." His smile grew and bent his head down to her. "And because I like being with you."

"Even though, I..." her words dropped off.

"Yes," he said, not waiting for her to finish. "Even though, everything."

Azrael outstretched his hand once again and offered her the glove. He could have had ulterior motives and his words were just niceties to lure her in, but she forced those thoughts away.

"Thank you."

Her words felt breathless and inadequate. He beamed, as she took the glove from his hand and pulled it on over her bandaged left hand.

"We better catch up with the others." He grabbed her now gloved hand without fear and led her to the horse. "They'll think we decided to go off on our own."

Azrael hiked up onto the horse first, then reached down

to help her get on behind him.

"Would they really think that?" she said into the back of his robes.

He shrugged, "Well, I wouldn't put it past ourselves."

She pulled her head back and rested her hands on the edge of the saddle behind her.

"It was a joke," he laughed.

"Well, it wasn't amusing, and I'm not sure what it means."

Azrael adjusted the reins, then turned his face towards her as best he could. "It means that I would just as soon as run off and spend the day with you, as I would spend the day with friends I've known my entire life."

She felt the word in her throat and knew it would stay in there like a bug trying to crawl its way out if she did not say it. "Why?"

He chuckled, "You ask so many questions."

Even though the crane of his neck gave him only a partial view of her, she knew she had his full attention. At home, it was rare for her to get the same focus from her father or even her brother since he was always running off on some errand to please Lucan.

"Why would you spend your time with me?" she asked. Her voice was not much more than a whisper.

"I already said, because I like being with you."

He had said it already, but this time was different. The sudden tenderness in his voice made her stop. She did not know that she had been holding her breath until the smile that crept onto her face made her release it. A sigh of relief came from him when he saw her smile, then he straightened his posture.

"Hold on tight, Rosalyn. We don't have far to go, but we'll be riding fast."

With a click of his tongue and small kick to the horse's side, they were off. The wind whipped at her face and she clung to Azrael. At first, the force of the horse's hooves against the forest floor made her teeth rattle but she soon drowned it out. She closed her eyes and replayed Azrael saying her name in her head until they arrived.

CHAPTER 7

Azrael was told countless times by his father that he would grow tired with horseback riding as he continued traveling between kingdoms. Yet, all the trips across the border and two trips to the Elestren had not taken away the rush he felt every time the wind hit his face or dulled the beauty of the trees as they spun past him. Having Rosalyn's arms around his waist made him wish he was going on a longer trip. It had to have been only twenty minutes by the time he saw Emmy near the shoreline taking off her boots and Marcus rummaging through his saddle. The dust swarmed around their horse when Azrael instructed it to stop. Marcus coughed as the breeze blew the dust into his face.

The pressure of Rosalyn's arms eased around his middle, he swung his leg over the horse, and slipped down before helping Rosalyn. Out of the corner of his eye, he saw Marcus flinch when he steadied Rosalyn with his hand on her gloved one.

Despite Emmy's kind words about Rosalyn, Marcus' first instinct was skepticism. He saw the incident in the main hall as his parents did, an attack at worst or a sign of future relations between Tadane and Helios at best. Azrael had been quiet with Marcus since he had no concrete reasons for his affection for her. His experience with dark elves had told him to take all the necessary precautions, which he had assured Marcus and his parents that he was doing more times than he could remember.

"Rosalyn," Emmy called from the water. "Come join me, you will love it."

His companion thanked him, and she sauntered over to

her friend. He watched her leave, before turning to tie up his horse. She approached the water timidly, as though she had never seen it before. While Emmy was already knee deep, Rosalyn stopped at the water's edge and skimmed the top of the pool with the tips of her fingers. Emmy and Rosalyn started talking, but the distance blocked Azrael from hearing what was said.

"You didn't join Emmy?" Azrael asked Marcus as he got closer.

"I wanted to wait for you, and Emmy was burning up. So we came up with the current arrangement. Besides, Emmy left her bag here and the horses needed to be secured."

Marcus smirked, knowing that they had been suckled into doing the legwork. Azrael let out an exaggerated sigh but set to work with no real complaint. As he got to work, however, he found Marcus' eyes on him. Marcus would look away when their eyes caught each other, but Azrael could not shake the feeling once he was aware of it.

"Go on," Azrael urged. "Say what you want to say."

"Azrael..."

The anxiety and hesitancy caused Marcus to straighten his spine, and Azrael did the same as the feelings seeped into him. Marcus put down Emmy's bag and walked over as though to hide their conversation from the other two.

"I trust your instincts, Azrael," Marcus stated. "But, allow me to ask, are you sure about Rosalyn?"

Azrael stopped what he was doing, and let his hands fall to his side. He should have known that his friendship would bring about questions, though he found he had no desire to answer them.

"Emmy likes her well enough, and what I have experienced has shown her to be unlike her father."

He wanted to add that he could feel it in his gut, but he knew Marcus would not give that reason much credence.

"Emmy does not have the experience that we do with her kind." Marcus paused, knowing that Azrael would object.

"I do not wish to dig up the past."

The memories hit him square in the chest like an unexpected punch. He wiped the beads of sweat that lined the back of his neck and tried to breathe through the influx. If he could just get through the moment, he knew from experience that the anxiety and fear would fade.

"Leave it alone," Azrael countered through the pain starting in his head.

"All I wanted to say was be cautious of her."

"I am."

He had not realized how close he had gotten to Marcus or that his hands were in tight fists until he was already recovering from raising his voice. He turned towards Emmy and Rosalyn and was glad when he saw them laughing about something they had not heard. He dreaded to think what Rosalyn's reaction would have been or the questions that may have been asked if his past with dark elves came to light. He wiped his face and dropped his voice to a whisper.

"Do not bring up what happened in front of them. Rosalyn is just starting to open up and, if she hears about that, she may not talk to us again. Besides, I," Azrael stopped, feeling uneasy. "I never told Emmelina about what happened."

"How could you not tell her?" Marcus exclaimed.

"Just leave it alone."

They finished with the horses in silence, then made their way over to the waterfall and the women who had migrated to the beach. Emmy was trying to contain her laughter at a story, and Rosalyn had her hand up to block the broad smile that lit up her face.

Marcus tapped Emmy on the shoulder as he sat down. "What are we laughing at?"

"Azrael," Emmy confessed, suppressing another laugh. "I was telling her about your first dance experience."

Azrael paused, taking an extra minute before joining them on the sand as he recalled the event. His cheeks flushed.

"Of all the stories to tell, you tell her that one. It isn't my fault that my mother made me dance in front of the court after only one lesson."

"I remember that," Marcus insisted, unable to suppress a smirk. "The Queen's feet were sore for a few days."

"And you did not get punished at all for that?" Rosalyn asked sheepishly.

"No, but I was in dance lessons for a few months. So, I felt like I was being punished for something."

Rosalyn laughed but said nothing further.

"Well," Azrael began, looking at Rosalyn with a playful grin. "It's only fair that you share an embarrassing dance story. What was your first grand ball like?"

At that moment, everyone noticed the change. There was a sharp intake of breath and Rosalyn's eyes darted to the ground. Her nervousness made Azrael's stomach turn, and he had the sudden urge to mimic Rosalyn's fussing with her glove despite not wearing one.

Emmy placed a gentle hand on Rosalyn's back, "It cannot be that bad."

"No, it's not like that," Rosalyn stammered. She looked toward Emmy, feeling that the Princess of Valandyl would be the least judgemental. "The last ball was before I was born. My father is not one for dancing."

"That is not something to get worked up over," Emmy replied.

"So you've never danced before?"

The shock in Azrael's voice was evident, though the condescension appeared like an unintentional afterthought. He wished that he could somehow grab it and pull it back, as though a physical object that he could hide from view. However, the effect of the question was immediate. Rosalyn pulled her knees up to her chest, her wet feet pulling sand in their wake.

"Not really," she muttered.

He stood up, dusted off the sand on his clothes, and held out his hand.

"I'll teach you."

Rosalyn's posture relaxed and she stared at his hand. Her face was blank and, for the first time, Azrael could not decipher what she was feeling. He looked towards Emmy, hoping for support, but she was grinning like a child with a secret. He hoped to remedy the situation and give Rosalyn a positive experience, yet Emmy's face made him wonder if he was not putting her on display. Before Rosalyn could form the words in her head, Emmy nudged her forward.

"You wouldn't want all those dance lessons to go to waste, would you?" she added.

Rosalyn sputtered but placed a timid hand in his and he whisked her up from the beach. He did not let go of the hand he used to hoist her up and wrapped his free hand around her waist.

"One, two, three, four... One, two, three, four..."

He started dancing a simple square, using slow steps so that Rosalyn could follow. She was light on her feet, moving with him when he expected resistance. Her eyes met his. Their rhythm faltered and she looked back towards Emmy. As soon as her focus shifted, Azrael felt her feet pause altogether but the momentum kept her moving. Rosalyn stumbled, her face flushed, and she pulled away from him entirely.

Azrael stopped and waited for her to regain her footing.

"Maybe I'm not made for dancing."

Rosalyn took a few steps back, feeling like she had embarrassed Azrael as much as herself. She looked down at her hands, that she had smashed together when she pulled away and further intertwined her fingers to avoid Azrael from taking her hand to try again.

Azrael's head tilted to one side, and he stepped forward to bridge the gap that Rosalyn had made. His voice low and gentle. "Rosalyn, look at me. You were doing well until you looked away. Forget about Emmy and Marcus, and try to imagine that it is just the two of us here. Can you do that?"

"I don't want to mess up," she confessed.

He held out his hand once more, "Let me guide you."

She returned her hands to where they were on his body, this time with a small amount of confidence brought on by his willingness to go on. Her eyes watched her feet as they moved at first, but migrated up to Azrael's face when repetition took the mystery out of her movements.

As their feet glided over the hard shoreline, Azrael felt a hyper-awareness of the situation he was in. Though his dancing did not falter, his counting dropped off. The Prince of Tadane was dancing with the Princess of Helios on a beach outside Valandyl. The political ramifications were endless. Part of him knew that Marcus would worry enough for everyone, even if he did not concern himself with what the world would think. The physical sensations took over. Her hand in his, and the natural smile on her face that seemed foreign but filled him with a mysterious sense of accomplishment.

"Are you brave enough to try a turn?" Azrael asked, his tone pleasant and light-hearted.

"Do you think I'm ready?"

"We shall see, won't we?"

With a gentle pull, Azrael lifted Rosalyn's hand above her head in a smooth and easy to follow movement. She spun faster than she expected and lost her balance, though Azrael was prepared to catch her. Rosalyn clutched his shoulder for support.

"I guess I wasn't ready for that."

Her anxiety spiked again, as her eyes moved from her hands to the two others on the beach. Rosalyn let go of his shoulders with one quick release, while Azrael let his arms hang down loosely.

"The first turn is always difficult. But now, you have had your first dance."

She beamed.

Azrael bowed with a flourish, and Rosalyn returned with a small bow of her own.

"It was a pleasure," Azrael added.

Emmy clapped, "Well done. Rosalyn, are you sure you haven't done that before?"

"Quite sure."

"How come you never teach me, Azrael?" Emmy faked earnestness but laughed by the end of her question.

"Because you've been a natural dancer since you were six."

Marcus cleared his throat, "Emmy, you taught me."

"True."

Azrael looked beyond his friends, to the top of the stone formation that made up the base of the waterfall. After his brief dance, his muscles were electrified and brimming with energy. The heat of the day was descending on them, which made him giddy. He stretched his arms, flexed his muscles, and released the tensions in his shoulder blades.

"I'm feeling adventurous today."

Emmy groaned, "Oh no, please don't."

"You don't even know what I want to do."

He knew she did, and he did his best not to laugh when her eyes rolled.

"It's what you always want to do."

Marcus stood up, placing his hands on his hips at the ready. "I'm in."

He smiled, then turned back towards Emmy. "See, Marcus is in and he's the rational one."

Emmy sneered and crossed her arms.

Azrael shrugged it off, then turned to his dance partner. "What do you say, Rosalyn? We're going to jump from the top of the waterfall. You in?"

"You just saw a healer a week ago," Emmy inserted before Rosalyn could answer. "It shouldn't become a habit."

Rosalyn shifted her weight away from them, not enough to make a difference but enough to be noticed.

"What do you say?" Azrael asked again.

"No."

"It's not that high. Are you scared?"

Rosalyn smirked, and her face lifted at the sudden influx of confidence. "No, but you should be."

"Oh, and why is that?"

"Think about it. If I go up there, and I land on the water wrong or hit a rock, any damage to me and my father..."

Her voice trailed off.

"King Lucan's head would explode," Marcus finished behind him.

Her eyes stayed on him. At first, he thought that she was watching for signs of a threat, something he had noticed her do, but this time was different. There was a challenge sparking in her strong amber eyes, as she anticipated him to keep petitioning her. Until now, he had only seen her as timid or reacting out of fear. The fire in her stayed with him and the desire to see it again seemed unquenchable.

"Exactly," she said with a small laugh and turned her attention on Emmy. "Best not chance it."

"Suit yourself."

He noticed Emmy's confused glare before he heard his voice come back to him in a tone more disappointed than he had intended. He wiped his face, then motioned for Marcus that they should get going. Marcus was at his heel, and they turned towards the path they had followed several times.

"We'll watch you test your mother's patience from down here."

He turned around but kept walking with the confidence that Marcus would stop him from backing himself into a tree. "Emmy, you know I'm not just testing her's, but yours as well."

While Emmy's smile was dripping with sarcasm, his last image before he turned was Rosalyn stifling another laugh and that gave him confidence. He had made the dive several times, but the adrenaline and fear hit him every time he climbed the ridge. That numbness that made his legs feel like water and the unnerving crunch of the small rocks grating underneath him as he neared the edge.

Marcus jumped first.

Azrael's stomach dropped as the water engulfed him, and, for a split second, he reconsidered what he was about to do. He took a step back.

The preparation was the worst part of the whole stunt. He told himself that he would be fine, he worked through the doubts, thought about the fact that Rosalyn would be watching, and circled back to his doubts until he knew what he had to do. His eyes focused on the horizon.

He ran, letting his body takeover.

His feet propelled him off.

The freefall.

It was the moment he lived for, that moment when his body felt weightless. The earth pulled him down and the water swallowed him. His body felt the smack of impact and the chill, but he succumbed to it. The blues and bubbles wrapped around him as he blearily searched to orient himself. Surfacing, his body began feeling what the adrenaline had pushed off and he did his best to get to shore. His arms made terrible plopping sounds next to his ears as he swam forward.

Emmy began a slow and sardonic clap once he was close enough to hear it, but waited to speak until only his knees remained in the water. "Well, you did it. Have you got that out of your system?"

He took a huge breath, "For today."

"Well," Emmy began as she got up from her spot. "I'm burning up."

Azrael turned around and gestured to the entirety of the pool away from the waterfall. "Why didn't you get in then?"

"You could have splashed me."

"Or landed on you," Rosalyn added.

Emmy nodded and tried to look as though she agreed with Rosalyn's point, but laughed under her breath.

"Well, nothing is stopping you now."

Though it was not reflected in his voice, Azrael had a sudden desire for Emmy to leave. He had just had time with Rosalyn all to himself, but still, he wanted more. His own people would suggest some kind of dark elf spell as the reason, and, while he knew that no such spell had been cast, the real reason seemed just as foreign. Had she said something that had caught him by the ear or done something to keep him interested? He wondered how her normal behavior had struck such a chord with him.

Emmy shrugged. "Are you coming, Rosalyn?"

"No, I'm fine."

Emmy's feet made sharp ripples in the water as she turned around, her posture rigid. She seemed annoyed, though Azrael had a suspicion that was residual and directed more towards his jump. She was nervous, concerned. Her vulnerability made his hands shake, and breath catch in his throat.

"Go," Rosalyn said, waving them away. "I don't really want to get all wet, but I know you want to."

Azrael straightened. He hoped that his excitement was not as obvious as he thought, and pulled his shoulders in to hide it from view. Emmy cast a look towards him, and he realized that rather than being successful in avoiding attention, his awkward straight but somehow still hunched posture was painfully noticeable.

He coughed, clearing his throat. "I'll keep her company."

"You landed wrong, didn't you?"

Azrael laughed and decided to use Emmy's sarcasm as a cover. "You can't ruin that jump for me."

With a roll of her eyes, Emmy walked away and into the water. He felt a wave of nostalgia and remembered all the times that Emmy, Marcus, and himself had come to this beach as they grew up. He turned to his companion, marveling at their new addition. She caught him staring at her, and he rushed for something to excuse him.

He waved towards the waterfall, "Do you have places like this at home?"

"We do, but it is often so cold that they aren't popular places to spend a day."

As she spoke, her body relaxed as though her words gave

herself permission to soak up the warmth that she was not used to in Helios. She watched Emmy and the crashing of the waterfall with new eyes. Was it doubt she felt, Azrael wondered. He sat down next to her. Her anxiety elevated enough for his heart rate to speed up, but the spike settled as quickly as it had come on.

"So what do you do to spend a day in Helios?"

Rosalyn's eyes narrowed, her defenses going up. The movement was tiny, but he saw her shoulders inch away from him. Lucan was careful with what information about his kingdom got out, no doubt Rosalyn had inherited his fear of the wrong piece of knowledge being used against them. He wanted to reach out, to comfort her in the only way he knew how. A nagging voice in his head caused him to hesitate, recalling the way her mark had made his skin crawl. His eyes drifted back to his friends in the water and noticed that Marcus was watching him. Whether it was his parents or Marcus, the cycle of fear that he was apart of seemed like a fog around him.

"You don't have to be afraid of me. Emmy and I aren't trying to trap you or find some detail about you that we can take to our parents. When Emmy and I are together, we are just ourselves without titles. You don't have to be the Princess of Helios when you are with us. Just Rosalyn will be fine."

A stray piece of hair fell into her face and she pulled it back, avoiding eye contact.

"I don't know who that is," she admitted.

"Who are you when you are at home? Like when you are with your friends or your brother. When you are in your room?"

Rosalyn kicked her legs forward and wrapped her arms around her. "I don't make the distinction and neither should you because I won't be here long enough for it to matter."

"Rosalyn..."

He reached out again, this time without hesitation, but she jerked further away.

"Don't," she demanded. "How long will it take after I

leave for you and Emmy to treat me like some interesting story you can tell? How long until whatever I do here will be drowned out by something my father does? You and Emmy should face the reality that we will be enemies one day. We shouldn't try to kid ourselves otherwise."

He backed away, but his mind stopped at her last sentence. She stopped too. There was so much advance and retreat with her, he noticed, and how quickly she moved from one state to another. She was the youngest of their group, yet so much more aware of how their actions impacted the future. If his parents could look beyond their prejudice, they would have appreciated that about her. Marcus had his rules and his parents had their tradition, but Rosalyn had fire. Every feeling she felt burned with an intensity that he had never experienced before.

"You don't have to stay with me," she excused. Her breathing returned to normal, and her face blanked. "You should be enjoying yourself with Emmy and Marcus."

Azrael reached down and dug his hands in the sand. He grabbed at it in clumps, channeling all his frustrations into pushing the tiny rocks as close together as he could get them. The heat made his clothes stick to his skin, but a soft summer breeze broke up the humidity. Her movements appearing as lithe as her father when he got his way. Even as she tried to relax, he could see the weight of the world in her eyes but then something else.

He paused.

Her height had masked it, or maybe he was not looking for it, to begin with. Her arms stretched tight enough to reveal a surprising amount of muscle. She came from a long line of warriors, so he should have expected some training under her belt. The Prince of Helios was rumored to be an expert archer with accuracy up to 300 paces. Something about her strength and the hard set of her jaw pointed to a defiance in her that gave him hope.

"Maybe that is the inevitable fate for us, but it doesn't

mean the inevitable has to be now."

"What would be the point?" she asked.

"Because I like your mouth."

The words were out before he could stop them.

Rosalyn's eyes widened, "What?"

"That came out wrong."

"Clearly," she said, holding back a smile.

He took a breath and gathered his thoughts with more care. The blush in his cheeks radiated heat. His pale skin would give away his embarrassment, so he tried to laugh his way through it.

"I just meant that I like it when you are mouthy. When you forget about your father, you tease me and I enjoy it. I didn't expect to like you as much as I do."

His flush deepened, but he did not regret any of what he had said. When she relaxed, he felt better and comfortable enough to release the tension that had built up.

"I like you and Emmy too," she confessed in a hushed tone. "I don't really have friends at home. When you have a father like mine, even in Helios, it scares people away."

"Well, then allow me to be your second friend."

"Second?"

Azrael let a toothy grin escape, "I think Emmy would push me off that ledge if I claimed to be your first."

"So, tell me something, new friend," she began, attempting to speak through her laughter. "Did you land wrong?"

Azrael looked away, rubbing the flat of his back. He had been able to fake it in the distance between the water and where he had sat down, but the impact still made his back smart with a burning numbness.

"Yes," he admitted. "I still can't really feel my back. It practically slapped the water."

Her laugh grew.

"Don't laugh, it hurt."

She covered her mouth, but it only served to encourage her further and inspire laughter in himself.

"You didn't tell Emmy because you knew she'd laugh at you."

He shrugged, "Or scold me."

"True."

Azrael leaned in closer to her, "Our secret?"

"Only if I get to keep laughing at your expense."

"Deal."

He leaned a hand over himself to her, and they shook in a mock ceremony.

"I don't take back what I said earlier. I do like your mouth, and by that, I mean that I like your smile."

Though the last of giggling finished its run, her smile did not fade and he was fixed to it. It took extra work but getting her to smile made his insides leap. All kinds of wistful thoughts swirled in his head. The endless smirks that Emmy did not hide told him that it was not just his imagination. He wanted to believe in them, no matter how impossible.

CHAPTER 8

Later that night, Emmy unpacked. Rosalyn had come in with her but decided that she would make her way to the kitchen for a drink. Meanwhile, Emmy wanted to change her clothes and get rid of her heavy bag. Her skin felt raw from the sand and water, as well as her hair was clumping together. She ran a thick bristled brush through her hair, but it still felt tacky and limp to the touch. With an audible sigh to no one in particular, she dropped the brush on the top of her bed and left the room to join Rosalyn.

The entire day had been spent talking and laughing, but her mind kept flashing to a single moment. She had known Azrael since they were children, yet she had never seen him look as happy as he had when he danced with Rosalyn. For a brief moment, Emmy had watched her oldest friend and her newest one dance in unison as if there was music that only they could hear. Rosalyn's timidity melted away, and their dance became one fluid motion. The trust that Rosalyn had in Azrael to lead her and the confidence that Azrael had in his steps made the simple dance seem choreographed and beautiful.

A unity of any kind between the two would be extraordinary, Emmy thought to herself. If they could reconcile their differences, the union could make for a better world. However, she knew that voicing such a thought to anyone outside her own group would be dangerous. Lucan would sooner kill his daughter before allowing her to be involved with a light elf, and the Queen of Tadane would dismiss the entire relationship as dark elf magic. Even their magic fought against each other because of Rosalyn's mark, making the interaction between them a constant struggle. To Emmy's knowledge, no light and dark elf pairing had ever been attempted; though she knew no one would report such an occurrence.

She pushed her thoughts on the subject aside and decided to join Rosalyn. The walk to the kitchen was far from her room so she hummed to pass the time. It was a habit she did often, consequently receiving the occasional stare from the elves she passed.

"Emmelina," she heard from behind. "You should be in bed. It's late."

Emmy winced, recognizing her father's voice. "Father, it isn't even midnight yet? I am meeting Princess Rosalyn in the kitchen, but I promise that I will retire soon."

Her father looked tired, mitigating between Lucan and Amrydalis for hours had taken a definite toll. The lines on the side of his eyes seemed deeper under the strain of it all. How her father managed the two rulers with such grace was beyond what she could fathom.

"How are the two of you getting along? No trouble?"

"We are getting along quite well. Why would you think there would be trouble?" She knew why, even her father could not escape the prejudice that plagued the elven kingdoms.

"The environment that she has grown up in is not the best environment for raising children. It can be hard forming relationships with people." His hesitancy was obvious, and his words came out slower than usual. He took a moment, rolled his shoulders, and allowed himself to slink back into his professionalism. "However, I am glad to hear that she is able to rise above it."

"What about her environment made it so bad?" she asked.

Her father looked at her as if she were a small child. A look familiar to her father's face and she had grown to detest it.

"I never said the word bad," Doranen corrected. "Dark elves are a brutal race, and Rosalyn is not exempt from that because she is a Princess."

"I don't understand," Emmy said. Her father looked like he was going to say more, but voices down the corridor made him pause. If King Lucan or any of his elves heard Doranen's comments, it would only lead to a fight and political strife.

"The point is that you two are growing closer and that is a good thing. Perhaps there is hope for your generation and the future of the Three Kingdoms. Goodnight, my dear." Doranen pulled his daughter close, kissed her forehead, and turned to retire to his own room. She knew better than to ask for more information. Her father was discreet, a character trait that he prided himself on.

Emmy continued on to the kitchen, her mind distracted by her father's comments. Overall, the dark elves and their culture were widely rumored but facts were scarce. The wall of secrecy and soldiers unlike elsewhere in the Three Kingdoms stood as a terrible model of where the world was falling away, where force trumped trust. Rosalyn's father had tight control over his kingdom, and every facet was a well-regulated secret. The idea that Rosalyn had grown up in such an environment left Emmy speechless.

As she entered the kitchen, the familiar smells of flour and warm butter greeted her. The cooks were baking the pastries for the next day, saving themselves from rushing in the morning. Emmy greeted the cook on duty, then made her way to the table where Rosalyn was sitting. The glove Rosalyn had been wearing all day was laying limp near her glass of water.

For the first time, Emmy had a good look at the mark on her friend's hand. The wounds and redness had decreased, though the dark pigment stood out against her pale skin. Starting at her palm, the dragon mark matched her father's though the lines were more delicate. The tail of the dragon wrapped around her wrist, but Rosalyn's other hand obscured some of the rings. Her mark took over her entire arm, ending just below her elbow. Over the past few days, Emmy had noticed Rosalyn make a great effort to hide her mark as best she could.

"How is your arm?" Emmy asked. Rosalyn's head popped up at the sound of her voice and the attention of her friend. Her eyes flickered between Emmy and her hand, growing self-conscious.

"Oh, it's fine," Rosalyn stammered. "Sorry, it was warm in here, so I took the glove off. I can put it back on if it bothers you."

"I don't mind," she excused as she sat down across from her. "Did you enjoy today? I know Marcus can be rather critical at times, but he is a good friend when you get down to it."

"I had a wonderful time," Rosalyn responded. "Today was one of the best days I have had in years."

"Really?" Emmy beamed, allowing herself to enjoy the pride of planning a good day. A smirk followed as her pride grew into something else. "If you don't mind me saying, you seemed to be having a wonderful time dancing with Azrael."

A subtle blush and large smile appeared on Rosalyn's face that she tried to hide by lowering her head.

"He's a good teacher, and I was..."

"A willing student?" Emmy filled in, her tone and smile mischievous.

"Don't talk like that, please. People might think the unthinkable." She looked around and hoped that Emmy would say nothing more.

"You wouldn't have to worry. Azrael and I are not involved so you wouldn't be intruding on anything."

"That is far from the point. If anyone ever thought," she started. Rosalyn shut her mouth and chewed over her next words. "You two are my friends, and that is all I want. Our friendship is dangerous enough without rumors of deeper involvement."

With a reluctant sigh, Emmy forced her smirk away. "I understand."

Rosalyn was scared, small, but, with sudden clarity, Emmy saw what had gone unnoticed. The girl in front of her had inherited Lucan's intellect and cunning that so often was masked by his power and anger. Rosalyn was sizing her up, weighing out information and opinion with what she gained with each interaction. It was not so much a malicious assessment, but Emmy had a distinct suspicion that it was a developed survival instinct. When Rosalyn's face softened, Emmy realized that she had passed another round of Rosalyn's internal screening process.

"He was critical, but I was scared so..."

Emmy stopped, "Sorry, start over."

"Marcus," she clarified. "He was critical, sure, but I believe you about his being a good friend. He and Azrael seem close."

"You could tell that? They seemed off today."

"True, but only good friends behave like that. My brother and I are the same way."

Rosalyn's size and fear returned. Emmy wondered if she was aware she had slipped into her father's nature for a moment. As the last of Rosalyn's words registered, Emmy realized that it was not a slip, but rather a part of her that never stopped. She had been watching all of them, assessing, and that she did the same in Helios.

"It's good that you are close with him," Emmy added when she remembered she had not said anything. "I always thought I'd be close with my siblings if I had any."

"To be honest, my brother is my only friend back in Helios, so it has been nice spending time with new people." Rosalyn had mentioned her brother on occasion and was the only dark elf who she spoke of fondly.

"You don't speak well of Helios," Emmy pushed.

Rosalyn looked away and pulled her arms in close. "You wouldn't either."

"Why a dragon?" Emmy asked, desperate to keep the conversation on Rosalyn without being overly forceful. She pointed at Rosalyn's mark to clarify her question.

"There is a myth that our race was created by the blending of elven blood with dragon blood. My people believed that this union would give us the strength and ferocity of dragons. I do not personally believe in the story, but the image of the dragon has always been a symbol. Every mark is slightly different though because it is based on the dark elf's personality. It's a common party trick for dark elves to be able to read each other as a palm reader would."

"I had no idea."

"My father would be cross with me if he knew I told you that." Rosalyn shifted, but her eyes were fixed on her friend. She laughed to cover her nervousness. There was something pleasing about Rosalyn's laugh and voice, a lower register than her own that was breathy and light. "You two have a way of making me say more than I should. Although, I have found that Azrael seems to know everything I say before I say it."

There were times when Emmy felt that Rosalyn had been her friend for years, yet this was a moment where she realized how little Rosalyn knew about the two of them. "Azrael tends to do that, it's the empath part of him."

"I don't understand what that means."

"Most light elves are magical empaths, it means they can read how others are feeling like an aura around them. Azrael is a powerful one, so he tends to guess what people are thinking based on the emotions that he can sense. It can be irritating, I'll admit."

"Why would he do that?"

Rosalyn's gaze grew strong, though Emmy quickly tried to defuse the anger she could see starting in her friend. "It is an ability that he cannot turn off."

Rosalyn rested her hand on the back of her neck, but she did not say anything right away. She sipped at her drink, and, when she was done, rotated the glass while she thought.

"I feel like I should have known that," she commented.

"Azrael is not exactly forthcoming about it, so there is no way you could have known."

"I am increasingly aware that you and Azrael know

more about me then I could have imagined, yet I feel that I know little about the two of you. And, I don't know what that says about me." Rosalyn paused and stared fixated on her glass. "Maybe I'm overthinking this."

"Maybe you just need something stronger than water," Emmy offered, trying to brighten up the moment, though it was unsuccessful.

The sounds of the kitchen that went somehow ignored during their conversation roared back into her ears. The pots in the sink that clinked together as they were washed. How the baker ran his calloused hand over the wooden surface to spread the flour around. She also became aware of Rosalyn's suspicious glances and worried looks at those around them and what they might overhear. They both drew so much attention that Emmy had learned to ignore, and Rosalyn had learned to fear.

Emmy pushed her cup away from her with the tip of her finger and covered her thoughts with a smile. "I think I will head to bed early tonight."

Rosalyn grabbed her glove and glass as if to get up, though Emmy stopped her.

"Stay and get something else to drink. Don't let this conversation spoil the day for you. Everything will be better tomorrow, I promise."

"Alright," Rosalyn said, setting her two items back on the table.

"Goodnight."

Emmy left. The doors were opened and closed by smiling attendants, and she nodded in gratitude at their service. They were not men that she had seen before, but shrugged to herself at the new hires. She had not been walking long, however, when she heard the sound of glass shattering. Rosalyn must have dropped her glass, and Emmy paused in case her friend called for help.

Instead, she heard the sound of wood scraping the stone floor, the scuffle of feet, the sound of the glass being stepped on and broken, and a chair fell over. She pushed the doors open, only to see Rosalyn knocked out and being dragged out the back door.

Emmy froze, unsure whether to go after the men who had Rosalyn or fetch her father's guards. Before she could make a decision, two hands grabbed her from behind and shoved her into the table. The table slid out from under her, and she fell on top of the glass that had been knocked to the floor, presumably during Rosalyn's struggle. The man who had come from behind stood over her but watched his accomplice exit the building.

She noticed his dark hair and pale skin, sure, but it was hands that stuck with her. There was something about how still they were, hanging above her that made them threatening. She could feel them around her arms, or worse, her neck. Before he even opened his mouth, she found all will to resist stolen from her.

"This is none of your concern," he stated with an even tone, before leaving the room.

The glass shards had managed to only make surface cuts in part of Emmy's arm, though she found it difficult to get up. Her whole body seemed unsteady, but she ran to her father's room with as much haste as she could muster. The rest of the night progressed in a haze as she recounted her experience numerous times while the elves moved around her in a frenzy. The details seemed irrelevant, but what she knew was the princess of Helios had been kidnapped and no one had answers as to why.

CHAPTER 9

Azrael laced up his leather gauntlets with precision, and with the surety of an action he had done many times. The leather was good quality, but the edges had been worn by time and the elements. He grabbed his belt that held his sword within arms reach, affixing them to his waist, and turned to the other occupant in the room. The gloves made him feel overdressed, but he was optimistic that they would be needed on his expedition.

After Emmy had been interviewed, he had felt it best not to leave her alone. Lucan let his temper make his interview with her more frightening than it should have been, and Doranen's protests at Lucan's temper dragged the whole affair out. He had taken her to his room, though Emmy sat on his bed without a word. He had heard pieces of the interview, trying to listen while having to go back and forth to convey the night's happenings to his parents.

"Can I get you anything? A hot drink maybe?" Azrael offered.

Emmelina was afraid, wringing the corner of a blanket with all-too-diligent focus. The lingering effects of King Lucan's intimidating interrogation, the concern for Rosalyn, and the fear that Rosalyn could be dead came in waves. Her posture was rigid, sitting on the edge of the bed, at the ready should someone come in to announce that she had been found. Azrael doubted such an occurrence would happen, but he had no intention of vocalizing that thought to her. Emmy did not stay sitting for long and began to pace from one side of the room to the other.

"A drink is not going to help, or bring her back any faster." Her fear was quickly turning into agitation, and nothing but Rosalyn's return would calm her. He walked into the direct path of her pacing, forcing her to stop and look at him.

"We will find her," Azrael assured.

His stomach tightened, and Emmy's worry soon seeped into his own mind. He knew that the group charged with finding her, of which he was apart of, would find Rosalyn, yet her doubt was infectious to him. A pain at the front of his head started, a common trend when he was around strong emotions.

"I know that we will find her. I am more concerned with the condition that she is in when we do." She turned away, not out of defiance but restlessness. "They hit her over the head. She was knocked out. What if they hurt her more? Who knows what they could be doing while we are standing here doing nothing."

"Then I need to go. Lucan's men will be going on another survey of the area. They plan on going all the way to the border. There are some caves in the mountains near there, and they need to be searched."

"Please be careful, Azrael." Emmelina's tone was hopeful, though her body language and face looked as though she had already given up.

* * *

The tension was well-masked, Azrael thought as he scoured the area with eighteen soldiers of the Three Kingdoms. No one spoke outside of their own group, yet all were concerned with finding the Princess of Helios. He felt with equal weight the disdainful stares of the dark elves on him and the anxiousness of Doranen's men at having a royal in their company. Marcus did not meet the eyes of any of the dark elves but kept a steady hand on the hilt of his sword in case one of them grew feisty and tried to please King Lucan by attacking the Prince of Tadane.

They approached the entrance to the cave, with Lucan's man, Aldan, at the front. For a group of soldiers, they moved with a surprising lightness of foot. The tunnels began to fracture into multiple trails, slowly separating the group into factions. Azrael had never been in a cave before because Helios was the only kingdom of the three that backed up against a series of mountains, and half expected to find piles of skeletons around every corner like in the stories he grew up hearing. The tunnels and alcoves showed signs of transient inhabitants, yet that seemed to be all the group could find.

"Azrael," Marcus called from a distant alcove. "I found a passageway that leads downward."

Azrael hastened over to Marcus, seeing the doorway built into the stone. The darkly speckled rock had rough etchings along the sides of various spells and warnings.

"The engravings are all meant to keep outsiders from seeing this entrance," Marcus explained, answering the question Azrael had not yet asked.

"How did you find it?" he mumbled as he inspected the spellbound border. There was an odd feeling when he looked directly at it. His eyes felt compelled to look away as if the door was so terrifying that no one should ever see it.

"I was inspecting the alcove and patting down the walls. The spells written into the stone kept me from seeing it right away, but, once I found it, I walked through it." Marcus paused, pinching the bridge of his nose as he thought. “You need to walk in the door because I think I might have found her."

The dread in Marcus's voice made Azrael uneasy. His friend was not the type to be at a loss for words. Before he could ask for clarification, the feeling hit him as soon as he stepped past the entrance. While no one was in the staircase from what he could see, he could feel powerful emotion emanating from the bottom of the passageway as clear as he could feel the stone beneath his boots. Excruciating pain, confusion, and fear hit him all at once. He stepped away from the passage, and back towards Marcus.

"I can't say who, but it is clear that someone is suffering down there," Marcus said somberly.

Azrael forced his subjectivity away; if he let his feelings cloud his judgment then Rosalyn would wind up dead. "Go find the dark elves and tell them what you found."

"Are you going down there?" Marcus asked.

"If Rosalyn is down there, she may not have much time." Azrael turned towards the passage, but Marcus pulled him back.

"Whoever kidnapped her is going after royals. You would be putting your life at risk going down there."

Azrael sighed, "I'll be cautious. Now, go."

His friend left with haste and reluctance. Azrael turned back towards the stairs, this time unencumbered. As he passed through the archway, the mixture of emotions returned to him. The stairs, if they could be called that, were giant slabs misshapenly stacked on top of one another down a long, vertical shaft. He guessed he was half a mile down when the staircase ended and he entered a tunnel with dying torches ensconced on the walls. Every flicker of the burning embers bounced off the cracks in the stone making Azrael nervous that the movement was someone lurking in the tunnels.

With every step, the emotions and feelings became more intense. Usually, when his empathic abilities picked up on someone's emotions, he could feel them as he could feel the wind. What he sensed now was harsh and violent pulls on his mind to recognize the agony coming from someone inside.

The light from one of the larger alcoves shown out into the tunnel, drawing him forward like a beacon. Azrael heard a groan from one of the occupants in the room, the sound of a forceful slap, and then the sound of someone pacing.

"One more noise out of you and I won't wait to give you another beating. That will shut you up, won't it?" said a man.

Azrael waited until the pacing was further away, and

glanced around the corner. There was the elf who had talked before, as well as a female elf strung up by her hands. The rope holding her was tied to a rock jutting out from the rest of the wall and made it so that her feet could not touch the floor. Her hair covered her face, though he could see that she had been severely beaten and her muscles were straining in their current position.

Hearing footsteps behind him, Azrael backed against the wall and as deep into a shadowed corner as he could. He hoped that it was one elf that could be taken down with little noise, though his chances were negligible. A feeling of relief swept through him when he saw that it was Marcus approaching, and he crept towards him still wary of alerting the occupants of the next room.

"Did you find them? Aldan and the others?" Azrael whispered.

"Yes," replied Marcus. "They met a group of their own kind on the other side, and told us to come in from this entrance."

"There is only one elf inside, and then another tied up."

Marcus nodded.

Azrael crossed to the other side of the doorway, waited for Marcus, and they both went in with their swords drawn. The elf walking about the room was startled at the two light elves storming in, but as well as the mix of elves entering in from the other passageway that Azrael had not yet seen. Aldan and the rest of the company had cornered the elves that opposed them, leaving the elf on guard alone to defend their prisoner. The lone guard did not have time to draw his weapon before Marcus had his sword at his throat from behind.

"Stand down," Marcus ordered, then called over his shoulder. "I have him, Azrael."

The elf reached towards his belt, still hoping to defend himself. His face begged for pity, though his eyes wavered between Marcus's blade and the other entrance where he hoped reinforcements would appear. He soon realized that this company of elves had managed to subdue his entire group and that no one would be coming to his aid.

As Aldan and his men began rounding up the elves from outside the room and within, Azrael withdrew to attend to the female elf that was still restrained. He held on to her with one arm, then pulled out a knife and cut the rope. Azrael was prepared for her dead weight and lowered her into his arms as he knelt down on to the ground. He found it impossible to hide his relief when he recognized that it was Rosalyn. Despite her condition, Azrael took a moment to be thankful that she was alive and found.

"Rosalyn, it's alright." He tried to get her to look at him, yet she struggled in his arms. She put her arms in front of her face like a shield, shut her eyes, and recoiled away from him. He did not let her go, but he loosened his grip. "It's me, Azrael."

"Azrael?" she echoed. She thrashed around, so he placed her on the floor in front of him. "Please don't hurt me. Please."

"I'm not going to hurt you, I swear." Rosalyn's whole body paused, as she processed his words. "I'm here to save you. I'm going to make sure that those elves never hurt you again."

"I've never been saved before," she said, more to herself than in response to Azrael. Her right hand ventured up towards him, which he took hold of with both of his hands. Rosalyn with weak strength pulled him towards her.

"Save me," she whispered. Her desperate plea was matched by the outflow of tears that began. Azrael picked her up again, feeling her sudden change in emotion as she clung to him. He could feel her mind screaming for help, this time loud enough to cause him physical distress. A throbbing pain in his head that made it hard for him to focus on the present. Marcus must have felt it too, as he came over to him with a pained expression on his face.

"Give her to Aldan," Marcus said loud enough for only Azrael to hear. "He will want to take her anyway, and they won't understand if you try to walk her out of here."

Azrael looked at his friend, then returned his gaze to the

girl in his arms. It was confusing enough why the Prince of Tadane had asked to accompany the mission, but requesting to bring her back would cause trouble for both him and Rosalyn. He looked down at her once more, wishing the politics did not matter.

"Get Aldan, and tell him she needs immediate attention." Azrael watched Marcus walk off towards the elves that were subduing Rosalyn's abductors.

"Don't let me go," Rosalyn pleaded.

He smoothed out her hair and held her tighter, "You're safe now. Aldan will get you back to your father."

Aldan rushed over, cast a quick glare laced with confusion at Azrael's tenderness, then took her from him. Rosalyn began to fight them both, pushing away with her right hand and cradling the other.

"Wait," Azrael called.

He was not sure if he had said it to Aldan or Rosalyn, but both seemed to stop what they were doing. Thankful that he had worn gloves, Azrael pulled down Rosalyn's left sleeve. Her arm had been smashed and the dark bruising made most of her tattoo disappear. The sight of it made Aldan's jaw drop.

"Give her to me," Aldan commanded, even though Azrael's light grip on her arm was not enough to restrain her in any way.

When Aldan pulled the girl into his arms and stood up, he struggled. A man of Aldan's role in Lucan's court would have to be in fit shape. It was not until Aldan glanced around, looking for something that Azrael could not name, that he realized that Aldan's strain was more in his head than his body. Rosalyn's emotions drowned everyone out with their intensity but Aldan's tight jaw and the way his eyes glazed over told Azrael all he needed to know.

Once Rosalyn was settled in his arms, Aldan barked out orders. The scene was cleared, the dark elves secured their newest prisoners, and they all made their way back up to the surface.

CHAPTER 10

Lucan's voice boomed through the halls of Doranen's palace, "Where is she? Where is my daughter?"

A wobbly elf of Doranen's, who kept looking back at him, led the way towards Doranen's infirmary. The man assured him that it was "just this way" so many times that Lucan wanted to throttle him and start kicking down doors. It would probably be faster. To his immediate relief, they arrived but, before the elf could open the door, Lucan blazed past him and barged in.

Doranen, who was already in the room, hurried over to calm the distressed father. It was belittling, his attitude now and when his sniveling daughter reported the incident. He was not some insignificant father whose daughter was a victim of a senseless crime and Doranen did not care as much as he claimed. He was only trying to cover for his mistakes.

"Your daughter is in quite a state, but the important thing is that she is alive. My best physician, Absalom, is attending to her now."

"Your best physician?" Lucan flesh burned with rage, and he wanted to tear Doranen in half. "You claimed that you had your best security on duty while we were here, and yet rogue elves kidnapped my daughter. Why should I trust your doctors?"

"Lucan, I assure you..."

"You can assure me of nothing."

His voice was like acid. Lucan felt like he could not breath, the rage simultaneously suffocated him and forced his thoughts into an avalanche of words.

"At best, this was an attack by my men that your guards let slip past them because of your incompetence. At worst, this was an attack by you when we agreed on peace and you are trying to cover up your own crimes. She is a young girl, barely out of the womb."

As though hearing that she was the subject of conversation, an unfettered scream from his daughter pulled Lucan away. The sound resonated in his ears, grating on his skin and echoing in the hollows of his head.

He leaned in close to Doranen, "If the latter proves true, your kingdom will fall. I will make sure of it."

Lucan looked past the King of Valandyl to see that Rosalyn was being held down on a bed by Absalom and a few attendants. She was frightened, resisting those around her, and pleading with them to let her go. Lucan pushed past Doranen and went to his daughter's side. She was using all the energy she had to fight those restraining her. Absalom was examining the source of the blood trail in her hair, keeping a steady grip on her arm so as not to injure her further as she thrashed about. Lucan ushered for the attendant on her right to move and took his place.

"No, let me go," Rosalyn yelled with her eyes shut. She dared not open them for fear of what she might see, yet her fear turned to bargaining. "Please. I'll be good, I swear. Stop hurting me, please."

"Rosalyn, you are safe," Absalom coddled. "But you have to stop fighting us. I need to examine you. You have to lay still."

Rosalyn could barely speak as she gasped for breath, "I'm not fighting. I'll be good."

Lucan took his daughter's face in his hands, "Rosalyn, it's your father. Look at your father, child."

Rosalyn stopped and opened her eyes, "Papa?"

Lucan paused; his daughter had not called him that since she was a little girl, since before her mother left. She looked around the room at the unfamiliar faces that stared at her then returned to her father, as though in disbelief that he knew her either.

Rosalyn allowed herself to relax, and Lucan felt her entire body go limp. Honest tears streamed from her eyes and into her hair, though she tried to wipe them away with her right hand. She took a moment, breathing and assessing the room before acknowledging her father again.

"I need you to tell me who did this to you." Lucan's voice was low and gentle.

He became aware that he was showing this level of gentleness in front of others, though he pushed the feelings of vulnerability away. Regardless of his daughter's condition, he would not let them see. He cast a quick glance up to find Doranen, though he only saw Absalom who was taking advantage of Rosalyn's calm to examine her other wounds.

Lucan returned to his daughter and repeated himself, "Tell me who did this."

"They hurt me," Rosalyn sobbed. "Papa, they just kept hitting me, and they wouldn't stop. I tried to be strong. I tried to fight them."

Rosalyn held her right hand up in defense, reliving the memory of the beatings in her head. Her hand showed damage to her nails, fresh cuts to her palms and fingertips, and bruising on a couple of fingers. One of them even looked broken, so he reached over to grab Absalom's attention.

Rosalyn noticed Lucan's focus on her hand and she began to explain amongst her sobs, "I didn't want to go, I swear. When they were taking me to the caves, I grabbed onto a tree and held on. I fought, but they ripped me away. They ended up hitting my head to get me to stop."

Rosalyn instinctively reached to the back of her head, only to pull her hand away with blood from her hair. She looked at her hand as though she had no idea why there was blood and started panicking like she was being hit all over again.

"I woke up and I didn't know where I was."

She shut her eyes and started pushing away from Absalom and Lucan again. Absalom tried to restrain her, but Lucan motioned for him to stop. Her hair was sticking to her forehead, and she was feigning consciousness.

Absalom had moved from her hand to try to examine Rosalyn's head wound. "Your majesty, she needs to sleep."

Lucan grasped his daughter by the shoulders to force her focus back on him and her eyes opened wide in shock. "Rosalyn, I will punish those we found and I will find anyone connected to them. But I need you to tell me who they are."

"Dark elves," she blurted out.

"Are you sure?" Lucan asked. "Marks can be faked."

"They were dark elves," she repeated. "I swear."

Lucan let go of his daughter. He would not be able to get more from her until she calmed down.

"Rest now."

"Papa..." she whispered. She reached out for his hand, which he let her take. "They kept saying, 'we don't want you.' They would hit me again and again, saying 'we don't want you.' Why did they keep hurting me if they didn't want me?"

She paused, smiling like she had done something she was proud of and wanted to share with her father. "Then I figured it out. I've only been your heir for a couple of weeks, but they didn't want me. They wanted me dead. The people don't want me.

"It hurts, my whole body hurts." Rosalyn began crying again, and her grip on her father's wrist tightened. "I tried to be strong, Papa. They would take my arm, and tell me that I didn't deserve my mark. They grabbed a rock, and I begged them not to hurt me. I'm sorry, Papa, but I begged and pleaded with them.

"Stop hitting me, please," she screamed. Rosalyn's anxiety was building, reliving the torture of her imprisonment again more vividly. "I'll do anything, just please stop hurting me. Father, make it stop."

Lucan stared at what was left of his daughter, feeling

pity towards her and a renewed anger towards her captors. He clenched his teeth in an attempt to force his anger away. An unfamiliar pull in his chest increased as Rosalyn begged for his help. When her outburst became hysterical, he turned towards Absalom.

“Is there anything you can give her?” Lucan asked, sounding vulnerable for the first time.

Absalom nodded and placed his long, pale hand behind her head. Rosalyn's eyes widened at his touch, then fluttered as Absalom’s magic coursed through her body like poison in her veins.

“Don’t fight it,” Absalom remarked in a mild tone of voice.

"Rest, my girl," Lucan added. His voice, though gentle, was more reminiscent of a low growl then sweet words. His hand lifted of its own accord before he could stop it, though he felt no regret when the back of his fingers grazed Rosalyn’s cheek. While Absalom and Doranen might think his demeanor coarse, Rosalyn was aware of the break from character in her father. She stopped resisting and was asleep in seconds.

Lucan sighed, letting his head fall down almost to his chest. He had expected backlash on his decision to make Rosalyn his heir, but abducting Rosalyn to kill her was not something he had considered. Lucan lifted his head up when he heard Doranen's voice.

"What is your assessment, Absalom?"

The physician sighed, giving Rosalyn a once over before answering. “The damage is extensive. For one thing, her left arm has been shattered. If it wasn’t for the magic in her corin tattoo, I would think the hand would never regain full function. It would seem, King Lucan, the elves who took your daughter were trying to prove a point. The rest of her body shows signs of severe beatings, sleep deprivation, and it doesn’t look like they fed her much.”

Doranen tapped on Absalom’s shoulder, as though to remind the Doctor he was still there. “What do you mean about her arm?"

"The tattoo protects itself," Lucan answered as he shook his head. Was this really the time for useless questions? The Vestan king could have waited to ask for a history lesson on dark elves, but the man seemed not to feel any awkwardness.

Absalom, on the other hand, hesitated between Lucan's anger and his loyalty to his king. His affection for Doranen won out, as Lucan knew it would, and Absalom turned to face Doranen as he explained.

"The magic that acts as ink also protects the area around it. If Rosalyn's testimony is accurate, then her attackers would have known that they could hurt her arm as much as they wanted without risking her life."

"You suspect something," Doranen observed.

"It's just a theory, Your Majesties."

Lucan clenched his fist, wanting to punch the nearest hard surface. "Out with it."

"I don't think her kidnappers wanted to kill her."

"Your evidence?" Lucan asked.

"All of the damage done to her, aside from her arm, was meant to restrain her. Most of the other damage is on her wrists where she was bound, or on her arms near her shoulders where they grabbed her. On her head to subdue her when she resisted them."

Doranen took a step forward so he could see the young girl clearly. "Then why did they take her?"

Lucan sighed, refusing to let the small feeling in the pit of his stomach have any power over him. "They wanted me to change my mind."

"That is my theory, Your Majesties."

"Will she heal?" Lucan growled.

"She will need time and patience, but yes, she will heal."

Lucan did not want to believe Absalom's report on his daughter, as though accepting her condition would make the situation his fault. He had done all he could, though his mistake was trusting Doranen's word about the security measures taken in Valandyl.

"I'll take her home, where she can rest in her own bed. In Helios, I can keep her safe from any future attacks. At least I can say with certainty that she will be safe there."

"You are, of course, welcome to do that, Your Majesty," said Absalom hesitantly. "However, I would not recommend that course of action."

Lucan raised his eyebrow, "Why?"

"In my own opinion," Absalom prefaced. "If she was captured by dark elves, then taking her to a place filled with dark elves would only terrify her further."

"And your solution would be what? I leave her in Valandyl for the rest of her life, frightened of her own people. Frightened of the elves that she will one day lead."

Lucan's anger extended to every part of his body and he wondered if he had ever felt anything else. These Vestans did not understand his life or the true meaning behind this attack. Why should they? This was not their world, and Rosalyn was his responsibility. He cast a death glare in Absalom's direction before turning to exit the room.

"King Lucan, that is not what I meant at all," Absalom called out after him. "All I meant is that she may need time to heal and to process what has happened. But please, you know her better than I do."

"Yes, I do," Lucan asserted.

He cast a glance at his daughter and then relented. For now, he would look for any elves involved and give her the time she needed to heal. No harm could come to her by staying in Valandyl for a couple more days as she recovered so long as his men were there to protect her. "She may stay here until I have finished my business with King Doranen and the rulers of Tadane. My guards will stand outside."

Absalom nodded, "Of course."

CHAPTER 11

Azrael pressed the door to the infirmary open, aware of every sound he made amongst the quiet. The door creaked as it scraped across the floor, and he had half a mind to shush it. He peered into the vast and warm room. Candles and sticks of incense billowed up to the ceiling, filling the room with musk. Patients occupied two of the eight beds lining the round walls. The first patient, a kitchen girl by the look of her, who had come down with an illness, was fast asleep. The other patient stared blindly out the window nearest her bed, watching the rain fall down the colored glass panes.

After the initial night, Rosalyn had refused to see anyone apart from Absalom. He had made a comment that she had not warmed to him either but put up with him only because her father wished it. According to Emmy, who had been pestering Absalom since her return, Rosalyn had not been sleeping well the past few nights and spoke only to her father or to Absalom when needed. Her body language was one of restless defeat; she squirmed as if she was confined to an undesirable bed, tucking the blanket around her legs that created long moments of stiff inactivity. Azrael took his time crossing the room, not wanting to alarm her with the sound of his feet on the hard floor.

"Isn't it a little early for you, Absalom?" she asked without looking over her shoulder.

"It is, and I'd imagine that is why Absalom is still asleep."

Rosalyn swiveled around towards his voice but remained fixed to her bed. Her breathing quickened, and her body tightened like a stone. She stared at him in disbelief that he was in the room, "Why are you here?"

He returned her stares with stares of his own, his being well aware of Rosalyn's existence. She avoided his gaze and focused her attention back on the fragments of light slipping through the glass of the window and the rain trickling down. The only difference from when he came in was that she pulled her knees up to her chest and refused to look at him.

"I couldn't sleep and I'm told that you haven't been able to sleep much either."

He smiled, hoping she would look up and see it.

She did not.

"I said I didn't want any visitors."

"We were concerned."

"We?" she asked, casting a glance over his shoulder.

"Emmy and I," he responded. "She's been so worried that I swear she will dig a rut in the floor if she keeps pacing they way she has been."

Rosalyn's face softened at the thought of Emmy, yet she began to fidget. She took hold of her pillow and held it close to her chest. Azrael shifted his weight, startling Rosalyn and causing her breathing to quicken. She clutched the pillow as if it were a shield.

"I'm sorry," she whispered.

Azrael realized that he had thought that the few days between Rosalyn being brought back would have calmed her mind. Only now did he see that the incident was as fresh as when he had cut her hands free in the caves. He was scared of making her anxiousness worse, but he was also afraid of her pulling away.

She took a few deep breaths, then sat up and looked him straight in the eye. For the first time, Azrael saw the resemblance between King Lucan and his daughter. The look in her eyes dared the room to look away and captured the attention of the ones brave enough to stare. It was shocking, coming from a girl so young and looking so frail covered in bedsheets.

"I appreciate the concern from both of you, but it is no longer necessary. As soon as I am healed, my father and I will go back to Helios.

"I imagine we won't see each other again for some time," she added with faint regret. She turned her head, breaking the spell. Rosalyn leaned back against the bed frame and folded her bent legs to the side. Her anxiety began to spike again, and she held her arms. "I would appreciate it if you would leave now."

Azrael surveyed her, unsure if he wanted to acquiesce or try to get her to talk about what had happened. He paused, realizing that to get her to talk would mean that he would have to open up about his past as well. Azrael eased his way forward, cautious of her eyes on him until he sat down at the edge of the bed.

"It's easier to pull away," he started.

"Don't lecture me," she snapped. In a split second, her anxiety switched to anger before he could process the change. "You cannot judge me based on what you think I'm feeling or how you think I'm processing what happened to me."

"I wish I could turn it off," he tried.

"Well, you can't." She looked away, yet her tone stayed the same. "So stop pretending like you know anything about me. And stop believing that you know what I'm thinking."

"You're right, I don't," he admitted. "It was unfair of me to judge."

"What could you possibly..." Rosalyn started again, then she stopped. Her look softened, and Azrael felt uncomfortable as she studied him. After a brief moment of recognition, her face went blank and she laid back.

"Now, it's my turn to read you. Something happened to you."

Her words were matter-of-fact, she was not guessing that something had happened but intuitively knew.

Azrael sighed, uncomfortable with the idea of lying. "I was attacked in Tadane."

Her face darkened, “Attacked by dark elves, you mean.”

Azrael nodded. He took a deep breath, fully aware that this was the first time recounting the incident to anyone.

“I was in my room talking with Marcus when they broke in. They said Marcus was in the way, so they stabbed him and left him there. After that, they took me to my parents’ throne room and I was held at knifepoint for what felt like hours. I don’t really know how long it was.”

"And Marcus?" She interrupted. "I mean, obviously he survived."

"Thankfully, he was found soon after and rushed to the infirmary."

Azrael remembered many trips to his friend’s bedside. They joked about the pain they were both in, and Marcus complained about the bed frame. Occasionally, they would pause to gather up their courage so they could talk about the incident but then they would reconsider. Even now, the first time the incident had been brought up by either of them was when Marcus was warning Azrael by the waterfall.

“After the incident, I couldn’t stay in Tadane so I moved to Valandyl. I haven’t stayed in Tadane any longer than six months since it happened.”

He paused when he saw the impact of his words on her face. Azrael straightened his back and adjusted his position on the bed.

“Rosalyn,” he said, as he reconsidered elaborating more but thought better of it. “You’re right, I don’t know what you’re thinking. I do know that it can be easier to push people away. That life becomes boiled down to vulnerability, and all you see are security flaws and the ways people can hurt you. No one can live when they are constantly afraid, and, if you are afraid, it only allows the captors their satisfaction. The satisfaction of them winning, of them taking everything from you.”

Rosalyn rubbed the back of her neck and weighed her words before speaking. “They didn’t want me. Those dark elves took me because they didn't want me as their queen. Can I be that bad of an heir already?"

He took a deep breath, "If you live in fear and aim to please elves like that, you will be."

"You are wiser than you appear," Rosalyn commented after processing the meaning of his words.

Azrael smirked, "Sometimes."

The corners of her mouth lifted, not quite a smile but enough. While her face was brighter because of the smile, Azrael noticed for the first time how tired she looked. She rubbed her eyes and grabbed onto her pillow again for comfort.

"It looks like lack of sleep is catching up with you," Azrael remarked. She stopped rubbing her eyes, straightened her posture, then sighed knowing his assessment was correct.

"I'm sorry," she said out of habit. "I do enjoy talking to you, and, if we're being honest, I'd rather talk to you than sleep. I've been afraid to close my eyes because of the nightmares."

"They will go away, but you should sleep. I'll come visit you later if you'd like?" Azrael felt the feeling of companionship, though he could not tell whether it came from Rosalyn or himself.

"I'd like that," she said with a rare smile. Despite her lethargy, this smile was radiant and he found it hard to focus on anything else. His eyes turned away, but only because his body carried him off the bed and his head followed.

"Good," he replied. Rosalyn laughed at his stammering, which only made the lightness worse. "Great. I mean, I'd like that too. To see you. Not now, later. After you have gotten some sleep."

He left the room more reluctantly than he cared to admit. The warmth he felt from Rosalyn drained from him as he walked out the door. Without much warning, he felt something new. Something darker, that turned his stomach at its sudden onset though he could not place the source.

"Prince Azrael?"

As soon as he heard King Lucan Lassehelin's voice, what he felt made sense.

"Good morning, your majesty," Azrael said with all due civility.

Lucan was not as civil, cutting straight through the usual niceties. "Why were you in there?"

Azrael realized just how odd it was for the Prince of Tadane to be coming out of the infirmary early in the morning and searched for an excuse that would please Lucan. He straightened his posture and tried his best to be as obliging as possible, hoping he could convince Rosalyn's father that nothing inappropriate had occurred.

"I was concerned about Princess Rosalyn's condition. I couldn't sleep, so I decided to check in on her. She was awake, but verging on sleep so I let her be."

Lucan looked pleased enough with his answer, and his displeasure subsided. He waved his comment away. "You were the one that found her, correct?"

"A friend and I found her," Azrael corrected modestly. "Along with Aldan and the rest of the convoy, of course."

"Why did you help?" Lucan asked without warning. He paused to wait for an answer but felt the need to clarify. "Help look for her, I mean."

Azrael knew the lengths that Emmy had gone to for Rosalyn to avoid catching the attention of her father. He had found it odd at first, yet soon realized why such measures were necessary as he listened to Lucan's rhetoric in the meetings with the other Elven rulers. Azrael thought for a moment before answering, doing his best to downplay the connection between them.

"She has been staying with Princess Emmelina, who is a dear friend of mine, and your daughter was in trouble."

Lucan glared at him in obvious disbelief, "Is that all?"

"Are those reasons insufficient?" Azrael did his best to make his tone as docile as he could manage. If Lucan perceived any threat, he would lash out and take action.

Lucan's facial expression relaxed, taking a small step back to assess the young Prince in front of him. His eyes were just as striking as Rosalyn's, yet they made Azrael feel exposed. It was as if Lucan could see through every lie and perception to reveal the flaws in his character. Azrael did his best refrain from fidgeting, though his body ached to do so.

When Lucan finally spoke, it startled Azrael with his calmness. "You are admirable, Prince Azrael. You give me hope for your people. Good Morning."

Lucan passed him, and Azrael let out the breath he had been holding. Azrael found he had a whole new level of respect for Rosalyn, considering she had to endure Lucan's gaze regularly.

CHAPTER 12

Rosalyn lifted her still sensitive right hand to knock on the door. After her three habitual raps on the wood, she pulled her hand back realizing the pain in some of her fingers from the force exerted. Her other hand was still bandaged up to her elbow, leaving only her fingertips exposed.

"Come in," called the voice inside.

Rosalyn pushed the door open and was welcomed by the sight of Emmy near her dresser. She did not look up at first, focusing on the top of her chest of drawers.

"Emmy," Rosalyn nudged.

Emmy looked up at her friend, and Rosalyn saw her face transform. The flash of recognition then excitement and relief. Emmy ran across the room and embraced Rosalyn as if they had been away from each other for years. Rosalyn groaned in pain at Emmy's force but did not let go of her. The Princess of Valandyl pulled back, alarmed at the expression of pain and searched for the source.

"I'm still sore from what happened," Rosalyn explained. She took a deep breath until her sore muscles relaxed.

"Of course, I understand. I'm just glad that you're safe now." Emmy ushered Rosalyn further into the room. "Have a seat."

Rosalyn thanked Emmy as she lowered down onto the bed closest to the door. Emmy grabbed the clothes off her bed and scattered them about the room as if each one belonged there. When she finally sat back down, Rosalyn's mind flashed back.

In the caves, she would look for any distraction from

her captors' torment. Her only solace was thinking about the time she had spent in Valandyl, reliving the moments in her head throughout the day. Emmy's fussing over the placement of objects in her room and her meandering from one side of the room to the other was a source of continual relief.

"Would it be alright if I stayed with you tonight?" Rosalyn asked, pulling herself away from the past.

"Of course," Emmy said a little too quickly. She took a moment to calm herself, then spoke again. "I would love to have you."

"Thank you."

Rosalyn was grateful to Emmy but more grateful that she would no longer be sleeping in a room where she was on display. The formation of the beds in Doranen's infirmary left no room for privacy, and Absalom's constant checking, while endearing, was driving her mad.

Emmy paused, her body inward, and Rosalyn knew the question before Emmy even spoke. "How are you?"

It was the question that she had received so often, that she half wondered if she would get any other topic of conversation for the rest of her life. Sure, she was a victim, but was she doomed to be treated like one forever?

"Sometimes, I feel as though it was nothing. Like, it was just something that happened, but it's over." She wanted to shove the more serious feelings down into her stomach, but it had the habit of forcing its way up until it was out. "Other times, I'm still there. In the cave, and they're hitting me."

Her body shuddered.

"You are safe," Emmy said.

"Am I?"

Her friend's eyes widened. The concern and pity were clear on Emmy's face, but it made her want to run. Instead, she looked away.

"I get like this," Rosalyn excused. "I panic and... it's nothing."

"Rosalyn."

She turned back.

Emmy was older than she was. Not just because, when they stood next to each other, Emmy towered over her, but the way her soft face had grown into itself. When her friend spoke, it was that even pitch that one gains when they have to be in the company of adults rather than children. Her uneven dimples on the side of her smile that clung to childhood. Rosalyn winced, tears pooling on her eyelids.

"I kept picturing you, Azrael, my brother. Your face, your hair, your eyes. I mapped out every room and hallway here in my head. Anything to keep my focus not where I was. Is that wrong?"

Emmy took her hand, "Of course not. You did what you needed to do."

Nerves sent shockwaves through her body. It was just a hand on her own, but she froze. She took a deep breath, wanting more than anything to focus on Emmy's thin, warm fingers that held her. Her heartbeat pulsed in the pads of her fingers. When the anxiety began to fade, she pulled her shoulders back and forced a smile.

"I heard you missed me," she mused.

Emmy stood up again. Rosalyn presumed it was to keep cleaning but was surprised when Emmy started pacing just as Azrael had described in great length. Emmy would pause, look at Rosalyn, and then start to pace again.

"Rosalyn, there's something that I keep coming back to. A thought that I don't want to think about."

"And what thought is that?"

Emmy wiped her hands on her dress, then clapped them in front of her to get them to stay in one spot. It took her a while to form the words that eventually found their way out of her mouth. "I froze. When they were taking you, I froze. And I keep thinking that if I had done something..."

"Emmy," Rosalyn interjected. "This wasn't your fault."

Rosalyn had not considered the idea that Emmy could have done something, even in the moment. While the torture was fresh in her mind, the moment of abduction felt like a distant memory.

"But I just stood there."

Emmy crossed the distance between where she was standing and her bed. She sat down reluctantly, seeming more at peace when she was pacing.

"I kept thinking that I could go get my father, but then I would be leaving you alone with them. I wanted to stay there and fight, but I've never had any training. I knew I couldn't take them." She looked at Rosalyn, then let her gaze fall to her lap. "I feel like I let you down."

Rosalyn took hold of Emmy's shoulder and waited until Emmy looked her in the eyes before speaking. "I don't blame you, for any of it. You did what you could, and that's all I can expect from you."

"You've been so brave throughout this entire ordeal," Emmy commented.

Rosalyn rolled her eyes, "I don't know why people keep calling me brave."

"Because you survived," Emmy answered simply. "You stayed alive."

Rosalyn scoffed, but her demeanor was one of resignation. "But that's just it. I mean, I've always believed that bravery is something you choose and I don't feel like I chose any of it. I didn't choose to stay alive, my body did that and the people who had me chose not to kill me. Tell me I'm strong. Tell me I'm lucky. But I don't feel brave, and I feel like a liar when I have to smile and thank people for such comments."

"You are strong. Stronger than the men who took you. I hope you don't take anything they said to heart. They don't matter."

"Azrael said the same thing."

Emmy's eyebrow raised of its own accord. "When did you talk to Azrael?"

"He visited me yesterday morning, and we talked about the incident." Rosalyn's voice was calm though she felt a smile tug at the sides of her mouth. He was the one that suggested she move back in with Emmy to help her feel safer at night.

"I thought I heard you didn't want visitors. I would have come to see you if I had known." Emmy looked hurt.

"I didn't," Rosalyn said quickly. Emmy's expression softened, and Rosalyn continued explaining. "Azrael came in the early morning to check on me, and I hadn't been sleeping. He asked how I was feeling, which became the start of a conversation that was longer than I anticipated. He came to see me later on after we had both gotten some sleep."

"Azrael visited you twice?" Emmy managed to get out her words, despite the shock clearly displayed on her face.

Rosalyn fidgeted on the bed for a moment and straightened the blanket near her. She did not look up, but replied, "Yes."

"Didn't he find you?" Emmy asked. The shock was subsiding, changing into a smile. A smile that Rosalyn found dangerous because of its implications.

"Yes," Rosalyn replied again. "Why is that relevant?"

Emmy's smile grew wider, making Rosalyn more nervous. "I have never seen him go out of his way like this, that's all."

"I'm sure he would do it for you, had you been kidnapped." Rosalyn stood up to avoid the mischievous look on Emmy's face and walked over near the bed that she had stayed in. She ran her fingers across the top of the bedside table absentmindedly, wishing she was back in her own room in Helios.

Emmy migrated to the other side of the room, and lowered her voice, "But that's just it. I haven't been taken. He's done all this for you."

Rosalyn opened her mouth to respond but found she had no words. As she thought about Azrael's actions over the past few weeks, Rosalyn felt a warmth grow from an unknown place in her body. He encouraged her to open up, yet made her feel like the outside world did not exist.

A confident knock on Emmy's door was all that Rosalyn needed to remember that the world was real. Both girls instinctively looked towards the sound, and one of Doranen's attendants entered.

"I'm sure he's just being kind," Rosalyn tossed over her shoulder, as she turned away to let Emmy deal with her father's man. Emmy turned reluctantly towards him and ushered him to speak.

"Your father wanted me to let you know that he is waiting for you in the dining room, Your Highness."

"Thank you," Emmy said. Her voice, while exasperated, still held onto her usual kindness. "I'll be there in a minute."

The man smiled and gave a polite bow, "Of course."

Even though her right hand was covered, the man paused and stared at her. She knew he knew who she was without having to see her mark. Her hair and eyes darker than Emmy's, her resemblance to her father, the way her ears and jaw were a stronger curve than the elves around her. Whatever it was, she wanted to change. To file down the sharp points of her until she was soft.

He left, and Emmy turned back towards Rosalyn unaware. She had laid down on her bed with her legs dangling off one side. At first, Emmy did not say a word. She crawled onto the opposite half of the bed. Rosalyn's face showed nothing of the thoughts in her head, only a false focus on the blanket underneath her. Emmy fixated for the first time on the conglomeration of bruises reaching around her shoulder stemming from her back.

"I'm sorry," Emmy whispered.

Rosalyn shifted her focus to her friend, "Why are you sorry?"

"I have to go," she admitted. "My father schedules time with me. We both know that he's busy, so we try to have lunch whenever we can."

Rosalyn sat up like she were the one that was claiming to leave. Instead, she crossed her legs and straightened out the bed behind her.

“If he’s waiting, then you should go. I will be fine here.”

“Are you sure? I hate to leave you alone.”

Rosalyn turned her head back towards Emmy and flashed a smile that she hoped looked reassuring. She stood, extending a hand to Emmy to help her up. "I think I’ll just walk down to your father’s library. At home, I love to read and haven’t had much chance to while I've been here."

Emmy and Rosalyn left the room together but parted ways midway through the palace. At first, Rosalyn walked through the halls in a state of peace. The hallway was washed with light from the windows overhead and the tapestries glowed bright with the color of thousands of strings. Elves greeted her as they passed one another, and the palace felt familiar.

As the sunlight moved, however, her mood shifted. She remembered the feeling of foreign arms grabbing her from behind. She stood only a few feet from the doors of the library, yet she felt like running back to Emmy's room.

"Princess Rosalyn."

She looked up to see Aldan walking towards her. "Are you well? You look distressed."

"Am I well?" She repeated, the word choice sounding strange coming from her mouth. It took her a moment to comprehend him, as she forced away the memories. "Yes, I am well. Thank you."

"You should be resting," he muttered.

"I am, or will be." Aldan looked less than pleased. "I came to get a book."

He pursed his lips, turning back towards the way he came. "I'm keeping your father waiting, but do get back to resting. The sooner you are healed and your father is done with his business, we can leave this infernal place. They are all politicians, the lot of them if you ask me."

"Yes, sir." Her tone was demure, knowing the risks if she were to argue. He gave an obligatory bow in her direction, then departed down the hallway like a loyal dog.

She watched him walk off, waiting until Aldan was out of sight before grabbing the brass knob of the library door. Rosalyn hurried inside, yet paused when she saw the room in front of her. Her father's library was hollow, filled with ignored books. While the room was considerably smaller than her father's library, the shelves lined the walls and left the middle of the room open for the readers making it appear large. The wood floors were covered with large rugs, adding to the closeness of the room. She fell back against the door with a contented sigh.

Rosalyn walked over to the nearest bookshelf, took out one of the more decorative books on the shelf, and fingered it like a precious gem. She put it back and turned to take another look around the room. She noticed that she was not alone, and walked over to the elf she recognized.

"May I sit with you?" She asked.

Azrael looked up from his spot at the thick wooden table, and his lips formed a quick smile. He picked up the books he had in the chair next to him and shoved them to the middle of the table. He stared up at her for a moment, then realized he had not responded to her question. He laughed at himself, "Of course, do sit down. What brings you here?"

"Emmy is meeting with her father, and I thought I would read while she's gone." She reached for the top book on the stack in front of Azrael and started thumbing through it.

"Ah, yes, Emmy and Doranen's father and daughter time," Azrael said to himself, rather than to her. His eyes glazed over for a moment in thought, then he shook his head out of it. His smile returned, though his eyes went back to the book in his hand.

"Don't worry," he taunted. "I'm just as envious as you are."

"I'm not..." Rosalyn started. She had been fighting the feelings of jealousy from the moment Emmy explained where she was expected to be. "I should know better than to lie to you at this point."

"You should." He flashed a smile with mock arrogance, but the smile changed to playfulness. She smiled back but hid it while scanning the book in her hands. It was a history book, a genre she rarely read.

"I just had a thought," Azrael remarked. He put his book on the table and looked her straight in the eyes. "If you're willing to give up books for a short time, that is."

"A single thought? How exciting," she commented. The boldness in her tone surprised her, yet she felt at ease when Azrael chuckled.

"You're becoming more comfortable around me," he observed.

She knew he was right, though that fact brought with it dangerous implications. Rosalyn knew if she had any sense she should casually leave, but the unrelenting smile on her face inclined her to stay.

"Is that the thought?" She asked, ignoring his previous comment.

"No, just an observation. My thought was since our parents are not the sort to spend quality time with their children, we could go to the street fair that's happening in the city square."

"I don't know." Talking with Azrael in the library was one thing, going out in public was another. "I don't want my father to come looking for me, and I'm nowhere to be found. He's been on edge ever since what happened."

"We could stay for only an hour," he offered. "If it would put your mind at ease. I just think that it would be a crime to stay inside on such a beautiful day."

Her mind filled with the many reasons why she should say no and the punishments her father would deal out to her were she to be caught. Yet, she could feel the urge within her telling her to go. The euphoria she experienced was reminiscent of a muscle moving for the first time. She was slow to accept it at first, and now it had become the thing she wanted most.

"I would love to go," Rosalyn admitted.

Azrael stood up and held a hand out for her. She took it, realizing as he pulled her from her the library and through the hallway outside that he held her tattooed hand. The bandages were what stood in the way of hurting him, yet he held it without fear.

CHAPTER 13

The walk to the city square was brief, and Azrael was disappointed that they arrived so quickly. His disappointment was short lived, as soon as he saw Rosalyn's face light up at the booths and elves in attendance. She cast a short glance at him to validate the reality of everything around her, then walked on unencumbered. The air smelt of fresh food and wildflowers, all mingling together in the excitement.

“Have you ever been to something like this?” he asked. The borders between Helios and the rest of the elven kingdoms had been closed for centuries, leaving much of daily life up to speculation. “I confess that I don’t even know if they have street fairs in Helios. I would assume they do."

"They do, but not like this," she narrated. Despite the wonder on her face and confident stride, Rosalyn did not stray far from his side. "There are outdoor markets for people to get food, and things like that, but I can’t say that I have had much experience with them. I spend most of my time in the castle."

Azrael had heard stories of the castle in Helios and had dreamed when he was younger of being the first outside elf to see it. However, he had met many advisors and scouts that had been inside since then so the appeal died out. They had described it as not just a tall building, but an imposing one. It stood out from all the buildings around it with spires and sweeping architectural lines. The elves had claimed that the sheer size of the building not only dwarfed all who entered but had the terrifying effect of being swallowed.

He had never before thought about what it would be like to live in such a monstrosity. While the castle fit what Azrael knew of Lucan, he could not imagine Rosalyn growing up in such a place. He was also surprised that Rosalyn found the castle more comforting than the outside city.

"That sounds painfully isolated," Azrael said after much thought.

Rosalyn paused, turning around as if he had brought up an idea she had never heard before.

"I guess, but I'm not so isolated now. Am I?" She flashed a winsome smile, then turned to keep walking through the crowd.

"No, you are not," He replied, charmed by her boldness. "Can I ask you about something?"

"Of course." Her eyes were distracted by a cart of fresh vegetables as she spoke, but soon her attention was back on him once they passed.

"I don't want to bring up bad memories," Azrael cautioned. "About your abduction, I mean."

She waved her hand as if she were swatting away a fly, "It's fine."

"When I found you, you said that you had never been saved before. Do you remember that?"

Her mood darkened, and he regretted bringing up the subject.

"I remember," she stated without elaboration.

"It's an odd statement to make." He carried on, only because ending the conversation now would seem out of place. "What did you mean?"

He felt his insides grow tight in embarrassment and shame, though he realized that it was not his embarrassment that he was feeling. Rosalyn reached up to the tip of her bandage on her left arm and picked at the ends.

"My father gets angry. The whole incident made me think of those times when his anger just... erupts. And it's easy to think that his anger is just a normal part of life. That all fathers treat their children that way."

She smiled humorlessly, "You've ruined me."

Her last words caught him by surprise, “How have I done that?”

“I think,” she started slowly. “I'm always going to wish you were there. To save me, I mean. I never did say thank you. You didn't have to help look for me but you did."

"I wanted to help a friend."

He was unsure of what to make of Rosalyn's admission of her father's temper and it was still baffling to him that Rosalyn grew up among the more terrifying aspects of Helios. However, he was sure of his intentions when he joined the convoy that he wanted to help bring Rosalyn to safety.

Rosalyn turned away from him and walked onward. She meandered from booth to booth, admiring the different wares of each merchant. Her eyes seemed to scan every cart and table within seconds, though she made no contact with anyone. Azrael could feel a quiet anxiousness under all her curiosity and wonder.

A table off to the side caught her eye, and she was drawn toward it like a bee to honey. The table was covered in a royal blue tablecloth of velvet with handmade candles sitting in neat rows overtop. The colors were vibrant, and each candle's flame was dazzling and bright. The young elf was placing more candles behind the rows she had already formed when Rosalyn walked over. The woman tossed a brief greeting before grabbing a couple more candles from the crate behind her.

"These are beautiful," Rosalyn admired.

"Thank you, miss." The elf put the last candle in a row and then smiled at her two potential customers. "I make them all myself. It's a decent hobby to pass the time."

"A hobby?" Rosalyn picked up a lavender scented candle, and examined it from all angles, looking pleased. "These are good enough to be used in a royal court. Even a ball, were there to be one."

"I do appreciate the compliment, miss, but I'm sure I could never make candles good enough for such a fanciful occasion. If you like the lavender, you might like the honeysuckle as well. Let me get you one."

Rosalyn set the candle back down, while the woman dug behind her table. Azrael took hold of her arm and pulled her close enough to whisper, "Ana travels to Tadane as well. A true artisan, but a truly humble one."

Rosalyn smiled at Azrael but was then drawn back by the merchant. "I'm afraid I didn't bring any, I'm sorry."

"It's fine, we were merely browsing. Thank you for your time." Both women smiled cordially at each other, and then Rosalyn continued walking.

Azrael followed, allowing Rosalyn the freedom to explore at her leisure. He mused at how she ambled to each side of the path to gaze at each cart and stand. Like a shy child, she swayed and stood on the tips of her toes to see but did not allow herself to go any closer.

"Prince Azrael," a voice called from amongst the crowd.

He looked around until a jovial elf with a patch of flour on the front of his robe waved him down. "I'm glad you could join us today."

Azrael gestured Rosalyn over, and she agreed happily. The warm smell of bread wafted from this area of the market, adding a feeling of summer to the spring day.

"Simon, it was a beautiful day and I couldn't resist. How are you?"

"Doing well," he commented in a husky voice. "I just brought out something new you might like."

Simon ushered both of them to the opposite end of the table and uncovered two loaves of sweet bread. As Azrael and Rosalyn moved toward the plate, Azrael turned his head towards his companion.

"More to the point, I think you will like this."

"You know all their names? I'm surprised."

Azrael chuckled, "I wish I could say I know all their names, but I only know the ones that travel between Tadane and Valandyl."

"Here we are." Simon waved his hand over the tray as if

it were an award he was presenting. "Tried it and had huge success with the wife. Brought it here, and the reviews I've had are amazing."

"Do tell us more," Azrael urged.

Simon breathed in confidence, puffing up his already thick torso. Azrael's skin felt warm and tingled in response to Simon's excitement. "Olive oil bread with orange zest and a grapefruit glaze. Try a piece."

Azrael took a piece and offered it to Rosalyn first. "I bet you don't get much citrus up in the mountains. Try this and tell me what you think?"

Rosalyn broke off a small piece and popped it into her mouth. Her reaction was immediate and honest. Her head fell back, her eyes closed, and a brightness filled her cheeks. "It's delicious. Thank you. Really, I've never had something taste so good."

"You're quite welcome, my dear. Prince Azrael, who's your friend?"

Azrael and Rosalyn shared a glance, and he could feel her nervousness rise up. The wars had cost lives, and the hatred ran deep on both sides. If Azrael said her name to the wrong person or a volatile person overheard who she was, Rosalyn's safety would be threatened.

"Just a friend of Princess Emmelina's that I've had the pleasure of getting to know while she is in town." Simon's eyes narrowed, in suspicion, but did not press the issue further.

"Well, I hope you enjoy your stay." He extended a hand towards her for a handshake, to ease away the tension of not knowing her name.

Rosalyn pulled her left hand behind her back and stepped away from the two men. Simon's brows furrowed, he glanced over her entire body and then had a moment of realization. His mouth opened wide, though his words barely made their way out. "What is your name?"

Simon's anger made Azrael's limbs numb and his heart pound in his chest. The anger he felt worried him, and he wondered if Simon would lash out towards Rosalyn. He put his hands up as a form of surrender, but it also blocked Simon's access to her. "Simon, it's alright."

"If that's who I think it is, I want nothing to do with her," Simon said through gritted teeth.

"It's nothing to worry about," Azrael said again.

Simon reached under his table for a leather bag. Azrael saw the shape of a knife, but Simon paused to reconsider. The tension did not leave his shoulders, but he slid the bag away with a sobering breath. "Her people killed my brother and countless others. I'm not a violent man, so I'm asking you to leave."

Azrael stepped closer to explain the situation. Before any words reached his throat, he felt a hand grab his arm from behind him.

"I'm sorry, sir," Rosalyn apologized. She looked back towards Azrael and then bowed her head towards Simon. "I understand, and won't trouble you further. Good day to you."

Her calm and resignation faded from within him as she dismissed herself, though Azrael's frustration did not subside. They both watched her go, and Azrael turned to follow her. However, Simon reached out and grabbed his arm. "I don't know why you are with her, but nothing good can come from her or her kind. Stay here if you need to."

"Thank you for your time and your opinions, Simon." Azrael gave a quick bow with only his head, slipped out of his grasp, and left before he could be stopped a second time. He looked around for Rosalyn, only to find her sitting on a bench at the end of the row.

She did not want to be seen; if her body language did not convey it clearly enough, her mind screamed it. Her back was straight, and her face was turned towards a round stage just past her. He felt her embarrassment and fear, but she felt shame above all else.

"I'm sorry about Simon," Azrael said as he sat down next to her. His words felt inadequate as he sputtered on. "I didn't know... I didn't think that he would act like that."

"It's understandable."

"I should go back and say something."

He stood up, unsure of what he would say but convicted that he would say something.

She grabbed his hand, "No. It won't change anything."

Rosalyn watched and waited until he sat down before speaking. "I have no illusions about what the outside world thinks of my people, and what they must think of me."

Azrael stared ahead of him. Only a week before Rosalyn arrived, he and Marcus were joking about what to do if Lucan started killing should he not get his way and trying to guess how much the mysterious Princess of Helios would be like Lucan. Emmy had given Rosalyn the benefit of the doubt, hoping that she would be kind. She had promised him, however, that she would alert her father should Rosalyn do anything to make her nervous or uncomfortable. They had assumed the worst, just as Simon had. Azrael rubbed his hands together feeling the onset of a grime he knew was more emotional than physical.

He was pulled back by a small thud. A group of musicians were setting up their instruments at the stage that was situated between them and the fair's end when the third chair dropped the bow to his violin. He turned towards her, wishing that he had not already proven her words true.

"But we could say something. Make it right."

Azrael felt that he was only echoing his earlier statement. This time, however, he was saying it more to convince himself that if he protested that it would make up for his comments with Marcus.

"I admire that about you and Emmy. Both of you believe that people's minds can be changed so readily."

"You've changed mine," he admitted. He felt her shame leave and a warmth replace it.

"Then that is good enough for me." The bright smile she had shown him in the infirmary returned. She stood up, and Azrael realized that his hour was approaching its end. He looked around for any excuse to keep her longer. The musicians had finished warming up and were preparing to play. The sounds of the strings being plucked and tuned weakened his resolve as though a reminder that bravado was easier than consistency.

"Rosalyn, wait." She turned around and he held out his hand, "Dance with me."

Rosalyn looked at his hand as if taking it would release her from bondage. It was a dance, but they both knew that it was something more. That they had been circling around each other, growing closer but watching each move. The connotations and implications were unavoidable, yet their connection was like a growing voice in their heads that drowned out everyone else.

She placed her hand in his, and he pulled her on the stage. Two of the violins started a quick back and forth base, and was then joined by the third chair with the low melody floating above them.

Azrael noted that they were rigid at first, moving slow and awkward. He focused on keeping his back straight, while Rosalyn was watching her feet. Once she familiarized herself with the steps and looked up at him, the nervousness melted away. He relaxed his arm around her waist, and let his fingers hold her other hand as opposed to holding it up like a prop.

He felt her doubt begin when elves walked over and started to listen to the trio. She did not let go, but she started panicking. "People are coming. What if they..."

Azrael turned her away so that her back was facing the crowd. "Rosalyn, they don't matter."

She breathed heavily, feeling their eyes bore into her. "They don't want me. They will figure out who I am and then they won't want me here."

"They don't matter," he repeated. "I want you here."

Azrael knew that his words were true, though he realized the desperation in his voice. Every part of him wanted to shield her from all that scared her, from all that scared himself. The eyes of the crowd, the knife in Simon's bag, and all the dangers he could not foresee. As he felt her hands begin to retract, he knew he wanted to follow.

They both realized that they had stopped dancing when the music picked up. Rosalyn looked at him for a long time, before gesturing to continue dancing. As he moved alongside her, she relied on him as he led her around the stage. The elves that watched them faded away, even the musicians seem to disappear from their perceptions so that the music felt like a phantom around them.

Rosalyn leaned in closer and let her head rest on his chest. He had not expected it, but he wrapped his arms around her when she did. If she got scared and ran off, he knew a part of him would not recover. In this moment, everything felt right. Azrael stroked her hair, holding her securely with the other hand.

The violin's melody rose, and the song itself started to crescendo. In a move reminiscent of more experienced dancers, Azrael and Rosalyn assumed their former dancing position. He gave her a small push and spun her around. She was caught off guard but her reliance on his lead allowed the move to be carried out with ease. He took the spin to return her home slower.

As they fell back into rhythm, a unique feeling of happiness descended. He noticed his own happiness as the song reached its apex, yet the warmth and elation from Rosalyn mix with his own. Her smile was the biggest he had ever seen, and he was enthralled. He felt as if his feelings would bubble over as if the building melody lifted his feelings so close to the surface that he could not contain them any longer.

Azrael kissed her. He did not remember bending down or how one of his hands had moved upward to pull her closer to him. His stomach dropped and his body felt like water, but he enjoyed both feelings because he knew they were symptoms of something deeper. Her lips moved with his, and she held onto his shoulders with a firm grip.

Though it lasted only a moment, the moment was still. There was a security that each emotion felt was raw and natural. As their lips parted, their thoughts and feelings settled.

Azrael sensed Rosalyn's calm dissipate, and a storm of emotions replace it. Her eyes widened, and her mouth dropped of its own accord. The dominating emotion she felt was fear, causing Azrael's own breathing to quicken.

"What have I done?" she managed to say out loud. She looked around at the musicians and spectators that looked puzzled at her sudden change in character. Rosalyn ripped herself out of his arms and took off towards the palace. He cast a glance around him at the confused stares from the other elves before chasing after her.

He followed her to the gates of the palace's garden, where she began pacing back and forth. She was startled when he approached her.

"That," she started, pointing back towards the stage. "That should have never happened."

"But it did happen," Azrael said plainly.

Her breathing came out in wheezes, "Do you have any idea what my father would do to me if he found out?"

Her phrasing felt awkward, though her conviction made him worry. If his parents found out, they would scold him and send him back to Tadane for some time to contemplate what he had done. Yet, Rosalyn's fear pointed to something worse.

"No, you have no idea. Do you?" She patronized. She looked at him as if he were a child and, although he was older and taller, her gaze leveled him.

"I'm sorry," she said vaguely.

"For what?"

"For snapping," she explained. Rosalyn paused, her embarrassment peaking. She straightened her shoulders and continued with forced civility. "And for what happened. It would be better for both of us if we kept our distance."

Azrael wanted to protest, but she had turned and

started walking away before he could say anything. The opinions of others did not matter compared to the feelings he experienced when he was with her. He looked to see how far she had walked, only to see her walking back toward him.

"I realized something," she stated. Her emotions were usually recognizable, but he could not pinpoint a dominant emotion this time.

"And what did you realize?" He asked.

Rosalyn spoke with conviction, yet she crossed and rubbed her arms. "I realized that I'm not sorry about what happened. I should be. Every inch of me is telling me that I should be sorry for what happened, but I'm not."

"I'm not either. Rosalyn, I know that you're terrified, but I know that I would take the risk if it meant that we could spend more time together."

"Would it be worth it?" Her doubt surfacing, though she sounded more hopeful than she had before. "I don't know how much longer I will be in Valandyl."

"Whether I have two days or two hundred years, I would gladly spend my time with you."

Rosalyn stared at him for a moment. Her body fixed to its place, and he knew she was searching for any hint of threat or deceit. He wished in this moment that he could project his emotions, rather than receive emotions from others.

With a release of her hands, her fear dissipated and a hard strength appeared. She walked up closer to him, and they kissed again. She may not have been brave before, but, this time, she was taking what she wanted. He wrapped his arms around her and forced his mind to be quiet. He was here with her and wanted to stay in this moment for however long it lasted.

CHAPTER 14

Rosalyn took tentative steps in front of her to combat the darkness. The moon was high above her head, she knew that from earlier, but Azrael had his hands over her eyes that blocked her from seeing the sky or anything else.

“Just a bit further," Azrael whispered.

They had agreed to meet late that night to avoid anyone discovering the relationship between them. The hallways of the palace were lit only by candles on the tables and stands, but it made Rosalyn nervous that someone could be lurking there and spot them. Azrael assured her that no one suspected anything to warrant suspicion, but she still searched for partially open doors and deep shadows. Rosalyn followed Azrael into the trees away from Doranen's palace, though she became less sure with every step.

She stopped and twisted around before Azrael could stop her. The trees shivered around her from the breeze, and the darkness made her doubt all the good intentions of the man in front of her. “How do I know this isn't a trick?"

“You don't," Azrael answered with a coy smile. "But I promise it's not."

She contemplated his answer, but she was not convinced. Her head slouched to one side, and she crossed her arms.

“If it is a trick, tell your father that I lied to you and I'll be surprised if he doesn't personally run me through." He smiled at the thought, then his excitement grew as a new thought came to him. "No, I can do better. If it is a trick, your father can hold his sword out in front of him and I will charge at it."

She could not help but imagine the scene that Azrael was painting, and it all made her laugh because of the absurdity. "I will hold you to that."

Azrael smiled, "By all means, please do. Now, turn around. We are almost there."

She turned, and Azrael's hands returned to their former position of covering her eyes. He waited until she started walking again to guide her in the direction he desired, navigating her around trees and other foliage.

"Where are we going anyway?"

"There is a clearing up ahead."

Rosalyn could hear the smile in his voice. He stopped her, though he did not remove his hands right away. "Now, close your eyes. I need to do something first."

She shut them as she was told, though she focused on the sounds around her. If she heard Azrael stray too far, she would open her eyes. His footsteps did move away from her, but they stayed within a reasonable distance. She also listened for the sounds of any other bodies in the area, in case he had brought her out to humiliate her in front of elves he knew.

The night was quiet. Crickets were out, but the birds seemed to be asleep by now. She heard the sounds of a chert striking a firesteel, which gave her the indication that a fire was being lit and that meant Azrael planned on staying in this section of the forest for a while unless the trick took time, few people would bother with a long setup or so she convinced herself.

"Now, open your eyes."

When she saw the scene in front of her, she gasped. The fire she had suspected was growing bright and warm rapidly, casting light on the edge of the small clearing of trees. Azrael eased himself around her and went to a large satchel that she assumed he had brought out earlier. He pulled out a few candles, a taper to light them, and a lush maroon blanket before turning to explain.

“I thought we could just…” his voice dropped as a light nervousness appeared. She smiled and waved for him to continue. “Just, I mean, I thought I could live up to what I said and spend my few days with you.”

“With a fire under the stars,” she added.

“And,” he turned, grabbed the candles, and began lighting them. “With these candles from Anna. She did bring honeysuckle after all.”

“You did all this?” She took in the scene and opportunity they had again before she turned her attention back to Azrael.

He smiled, then motioned for her to sit down. “Well, I figured that I may only have the chance to spoil you for a short time.”

The flames danced as they burnt their wicks, and she breathed in the warm, floral scents. Azrael grabbed another blanket and offered it to her, which she took with a nod of thanks. She thought about the time he would have set aside to make this possible. He had no desire to trick her or leave her alone in the forest. She said it in her head like a mantra, forcing her doubt into her hands and squeezing the blanket to release it all.

“No one has ever done anything like this for me before," she thought out loud.

“Nonsense, I bet you have a hundred suitors back in Helios who would give you anything you wanted."

“No," she replied with a chuckle. "No such suitors exist.”

“Really?”

“After my mother left," she began. Rosalyn wondered if Azrael would be interested, but looked up at the stars so she could not gauge his interest. If he was going to stay, he would have to face her past eventually. "My father wasn’t the biggest proponent of marriage. I asked him about it once, and he said that there would be plenty of time for that later. But, I'm grateful. It's one thing that I don't have to worry about."

Azrael looked puzzled, "I never thought I would say this,

but your father is a rare exception."

"Your mother?"

"Oh, she tries and I can tell she has grand plans for me later. But, for now, I'm happy to make my own decisions."

Rosalyn smiled, then turned her attention back to the stars above her. The trees opened up in a ragged circle, allowing both of them an unencumbered window to the sky above.

"You know all the merchants' names. But do you know any of their names?" She motioned with her head towards the opening, and Azrael's eyes followed.

"No, do you?"

"A few," Rosalyn admitted modestly. She had read half of the books her father owned on astronomy and skimmed the other half.

Azrael opened his hand for her to take, and, after she took it, said, "Tell me."

"That cluster there," she opened, pointing towards the sky. "Those are called the eight mountains. The astronomers of old thought that they resembled a mountain range in the realm. That mountain range is now home to the Elestren. And that one there."

"The red one?" he clarified.

"Yes, that one. That one is called Arianna's heart. Legend says that there was a girl."

"A girl named Arianna, I assume." His interruption caught her off guard, but his attempt to fill in the story amused her.

"Correct," she smiled and gave his hand a light squeeze. "She was held captive by her parents with no hope of seeing the outside world, so she threw her heart in the sky so that she could travel without leaving her room. And that one."

She paused, realizing that she was telling more than she had planned. She exhaled and smiled at Azrael. "I'm sorry."

Azrael had been leaning up against the tree with a look that Rosalyn could only describe as admiration. The smile on his face was small, yet resided deep in his cheeks.

"I take it you know more than a few," he said.

"I spend most of my time in my father's library. My favorite books are on magic, and they often relate to astronomy."

Azrael donned a puzzled expression once again, "Why would you read books on magic?"

Rosalyn bit her lip and removed her hand from his. She looked at the candles around her and willed them to move. The muscles in her left arm flexed, and she felt rather than saw the candles rise from their places in the ground.

Azrael leaned forward, watching them move with only fragile acceptance that what he saw was happening. He cast a quick glance back at her, before standing up to get an even closer look. Azrael reached up to touch them, the tips of his fingers pricking with curiosity. Rosalyn stood up to get a better look at his face, the candles trembling as she got to her feet.

"This kind of magic is unheard of in elves," Azrael thought out loud. "Can all dark elves do this?"

"No," Rosalyn shrugged. "Just me."

Azrael turned around, and Rosalyn placed the candles back in their place. "Elves can't do this kind of magic, but druids can. My mother was a druid."

Rosalyn waited for Azrael to say something, yet he stood there without a word. She would have thought he was scared, but he was calm and smiling. He bridged the gap between the two of them, took hold of her face, and kissed her full in the mouth.

She wrapped her arms around his neck, "What was that for?"

"You are unparalleled." His expression had not changed, yet his voice held a desperation that Rosalyn had not heard and she doubted that anyone else had heard it from him either.

CHAPTER 15

Emmelina closed the book she had been reading with a dramatic flourish and tapped on the cover. She resigned herself to get off of her bed and paced the length of the room. She walked to her window and looked out to the forest as if she could see her two friends together. The sun glossed over her face and seemed to search the exposed parts of her body. She flashed a spiteful smirk and walked back over to her bed to put the book on her dresser.

Emmelina was startled by a knock at her door, but she was even more shocked to see Rosalyn's father walk in after the knocking. His pace was quick like everything was a trifle and he could not be bothered with trifles.

"Princess Emmelina," his tone was grinding but formal. "Have you seen my daughter, recently?"

Emmy's heart rate spiked. "Your daughter? No, I haven't seen her all day."

"Was she here when you awoke this morning?" The bite in his voice ate at her.

Emmy sputtered, "Yes, she was."

Lucan tilted his head, his agitation growing. "When did she leave? Do you know where she went?"

Flashbacks of her interrogation with Lucan when Rosalyn had been kidnapped surfaced, only this time Emmy did not have her father telling Lucan to be kinder to her. She tried to think of an excuse or a plausible place for Rosalyn to be, but her mind drew a blank. Her voice grew quiet and her body retreated.

"I don't know."

Lucan took a dominant step forward. "These are simple questions. How can you not know? What aren't you telling me?"

Despite the fact that Lucan had stayed near the door, Emmy felt caged. Lucan turned from her and yelled for Aldan. When his man came, he cast a quick glance back at her then returned to him. "Fetch Doranen, now."

She wanted to Lucan to leave, though she did not realize how much until Aldan left the room without him. The way he watched her from the doorway made her scared to move and ache to run away at the same time. His body like stone except for the way he breathed, inflating his chest and torso like a wolf.

Torturous minutes passed until Doranen entered Emmy's room with an alarmed expression and Aldan close on his heels. "King Lucan, can I help you with something?"

Lucan had perched himself against the wall of nearest the exit, causing Doranen to have to walk in the room then turn around, in between Lucan and his daughter, to face the King of Helios.

"I'm looking for my daughter," Lucan stated. "Princess Emmelina knows something, yet she remains silent or stupid."

When her father turned and walked over to her, she felt comforted but in trouble. His eyes narrowed, though his voice remained even. "Emmy, is that true?"

Emmy looked back and forth between the two men of power, wishing that she could say nothing. She let her head sink and shifted her weight between her feet. She heard Lucan remove himself from the wall, and tell Aldan to have his security start searching the castle. Meanwhile, her father put his hand on her shoulder.

"This is a serious matter," he said as he lifted her face to look at him. "You must tell the King if you know."

Lucan scoffed, "She does know."

"I know that," yelled Doranen. Lucan's face flinched,

having never seen Doranen react in such a way. Doranen turned back to Emmy, his face already back to its normal calm. "Emmy, where is she?"

"Rosalyn is in the forest." She sighed, feeling guilt working its way through her body. "In a clearing just south of the gardens."

"She doesn't know this area," Lucan said more to himself than to the room. "Why would she be there?"

Emmy took a deep breath, knowing that what she was about to say would anger Rosalyn's father. She exhaled, "She isn't alone."

In an instant, every elf in the room saw Lucan's body change. His eyes turned black, his knuckles turned white, and his whole body shook. He breathed out through his nose, reminiscent of a dragon fuming.

"Aldan, with me," Lucan commanded. He stomped out of the room, Aldan struggling to keep up.

Doranen watched them leave, then turned back in alarm. "Who is she with?"

"Azrael," Emmy whispered.

With as much haste as Lucan had mustered, both father and daughter bolted out of the room towards the gardens. Emmy led them, with Doranen and a few guards that he had motioned to follow him along the way. Lucan and Aldan were just approaching because they had been meandering through the forest while Emmy knew where her friends had gone.

Emmy could see through the trees the outline of Azrael and Rosalyn. Azrael had both of his arms wrapped around her, and Rosalyn placed a kiss on his cheek. They looked happy, which made Emmy feel sick knowing that soon their moment would be interrupted. Lucan's temper had only grown in the distance from her room to the clearing.

"Rosalyn," roared Lucan.

Rosalyn gasped and ripped herself from Azrael's arms, "Father?"

Lucan grabbed Azrael by his shirt and pulled him bodily

from Rosalyn's vicinity. "Get away from my daughter."

"Prince Azrael, you need to come inside with me." Doranen stepped in between Lucan and the prince to protect Azrael from any more assaults.

Lucan grabbed Rosalyn by the arm, though his attention was on Doranen. "You are just going to take him inside? He was inappropriate with my daughter."

"I will handle it," Doranen insisted.

Emmy held out her hand for Azrael to take, but he looked frozen in place. When he did not move, Emmy reached out and grabbed his hand. Azrael tried to pull away, and Lucan was drawn to the motion. Rosalyn struggled against the stone hard grip of her father and mouthed for Azrael to go. Emmy did not know why Azrael gave up, but, after a few moments, he retreated back to her.

Doranen's eyes caught Azrael's movement and sighed in relief. "Good, come with us."

Azrael turned around to get one last glance at Rosalyn, though it was Lucan who registered the gesture first. He pulled Rosalyn behind him, and then pushed her to the ground.

“Do as you are told, Prince Azrael. I need to deal with my daughter’s indecency.” Lucan’s last word was spoken with such malice, Emmy would have thought he was talking about a greater crime.

Doranen ushered Azrael away, but it was only when Emmy pulled at Azrael’s shoulders did he move. His body was dead weight that moved only because of the pressure Emmy had put on him, making it look like he was progressively falling with instinct catching his weight with his feet. Lucan’s yelling started as soon as they left the area. It was then that Doranen put his hand on Azrael’s other shoulder and began to push, knowing that Azrael would react.

CHAPTER 16

Rosalyn had one goal when she woke up and that was to remain still, a goal she now intended to break. Just as her body had started to heal from her kidnapping, it felt as though her father had reopened her wounds. While her left arm remained intact, her torso had taken the brunt of it. She had not yet looked, but she could imagine the bruises forming under her skin that would soon appear. Breathing seemed unbearable, moving at all seemed like it would kill her.

Her father had refused to let her out of sight since he caught her, and she had been forced to sleep on the floor in front of the hearth of his room. She could not tell if her back hurt because of the floor or her injuries, though she suspected that it was both. The fire had helped to soothe her strained muscles the night before. However, she awoke to marble that was cold under her fingers and the sun had not been up for long enough to absorb the warmth.

Lucan was snoring, an otherwise comical sound save for Lucan's particular sound was reminiscent of a bear attack. Despite the snoring, Rosalyn cast a quick glance towards her father to make sure he was asleep before attempting to get up. She felt the familiar dichotomy of her body feeling able to do the action, but her muscles refused to move without protest. She suppressed the urge to scream and did her best to breathe through the pain. She took a long final breath, then walked out of his room.

"Get back inside."

Rosalyn turned to see Aldan in his usual place outside his king's door, mimicking the anger in her father that she had hoped to avoid.

"I was going to grab my belongings while everyone was asleep."

Aldan scoffed and grabbed her arm, shoving her towards the door. "You really think I believe that? You are going to run to your Vestan friends the second you can."

"The castle is still asleep, and I will only be a minute."

Aldan's eyes narrowed, his head falling to the side as if it were attached to a weight. He let go of her, and then ushered her in the direction that his head fell. "We will go get your things."

She made her way towards Emmy's room with Aldan following her like a vulture. As much as she hoped that she could run to Azrael and Emmy like Aldan had said, her father's punishment made her hope that Emmy would be asleep as she packed. Her stomach felt hollow, but dwelling on her feelings for them would only make the pain she felt worse.

Aldan stopped at the door, "I don't want to start any rumors, so I'll wait here. Be quick. I don't care what people say, I will come to get you if you aren't outside in five minutes."

She opened and closed the door with enough quickness that would make Aldan nervous of a side plot, but she had none. Her friends were asleep and she could slip away unnoticed. Her bag was folded against the bed undisturbed. As she picked up the last of her things, she heard a voice from under the blankets of the bed on the other side of the room. "Rosalyn?"

"I thought you were asleep," she whispered, motioning for Emmy to answer quiet enough so Aldan would not hear.

"I've been trying to all night." Rosalyn looked at the door, paranoid that even the sound of Emmy getting out of bed would be enough to have Aldan barge in and drag her back to her father. "But without much success. Rosalyn, I am sorry. I tried lying, but your father."

"Believe me," Rosalyn interrupted. "I know what my father can be like. You have nothing to apologize for. I can't stay long, or Aldan will suspect something."

The hollowness of her stomach and the pain of her injuries were incomparable to the feelings she felt being with Emmy knowing that she was leaving in a matter of hours. Emmy wanted her to be happy and had shown that in her actions and kind words. For years, her father and those closest to her in Helios had expressed verbal sentiments though they were ephemeral.

She embraced Emmy, "Thank you for everything."

"I'll miss you." Rosalyn heard Emmy say into her shoulder.

She parroted Emmy's comment, then turned to leave. Rosalyn wanted to stay and entertained the idea of running away. She knew her father all too well, and he would send out the army to find her if he deemed it necessary. She did not know the area, she did not know where she would go, and, with her mark, she was too recognizable to hide anywhere that she could end up. Her body felt disjointed, moving despite the emotional weight within her.

Rosalyn appeared to be held by the room as if she was stuck to the floor and cursed to watch the future before her. Everything around her aged, and elves came and gone. Emmy would make new friends, and the Rosalyn that Emmy knew would be drowned out by the reports of a more violent Rosalyn. She would be reduced to a conversation between Emmy and Azrael, a simple "remember when" that would take on a mythic quality. She shut her eyes tight, and let out a slow breath.

"Rosalyn."

Emmy's voice was just loud enough to stop her from leaving, but not loud enough to hear from outside the room. Rosalyn stopped near the door, barely turning her body. "Is there anything you want me to say to Azrael for you?"

She felt choked by all that she wanted to say to Azrael, though everything she thought of seemed wrong. Despite how open she had been with Emmy, Rosalyn felt as if she were talking to a stranger. She could not pinpoint how she felt about Azrael, and, whatever she did feel, she would have to banish them from her mind by the time she returned to Helios. A spasm of pain shook her as if her own body was reminded of the consequences for feeling anything but hatred for the Prince of Tadane.

"How could I possibly say all that I'm thinking in a message conveyed through a friend?" she speculated. "No, best not say anything. Goodbye, Princess Emmelina."

Rosalyn exited the room, with her bag held down by her side. Aldan grabbed her by the arm and proceeded to scold her for how long she took. His words blurred amongst the pain she felt from the force of his hand and the desperate desire to go back to Emmy's room that harrowed her mind. Lucan's yelling came into the storm of internal and external voices, it was then that she shut down. She understood that she had fallen to the floor, by feeling the stone with her hands rather than experience her body drop. All she knew was that by tomorrow night, she would be in Helios and Valandyl would be a fading dream.

CHAPTER 17

Dorian Lassehelin proceeded down the level stairway, taking each step with care but noticeable haste. The bottom of his cloak and his boots were still wet with fresh mud from his latest patrol. Dark elves bowed to him as he passed, and he nodded back to those who caught his eye.

"She is claimed by her father, and then she goes and does this. Hardly appropriate behavior for the future queen."

Dorian heard the words before seeing the voice that spoke them. He turned the corner to see his father's steward talking to one of Lucan's generals. The steward, Casimir, was a well-built man, with black hair that grazed the top of his shoulders. He saw Dorian out of the corner of his eye, then he ushered the general away. Dorian chuckled then continued to the cells. He had heard his sister was back from Valandyl, and, while he was anxious to see her, he had not expected to visit her in his father's dungeon.

"Get in there." Aldan had his hand gripped around his sister's arm, and was shoving her inside the bare room. The cell door scraped against the stone foundations as Aldan closed the door. After he slid the bolt home, he glared at the Princess and said, "Your father will deal with you when he returns."

Dorian watched him leave, waiting to make sure Aldan had ascended the stairs before going over to the prisoner inside. His sister had pulled herself up and was leaning against the wall. He stopped at the door, "What happened? Aldan is furious, and why isn't father with you?"

"He didn't trust me to stay on." Rosalyn rubbed the back of her neck, recognizing her brother's voice without having to look up. "And he's right."

Dorian's eyes narrowed.

"What did you do?" he asked, his voice elevated.

Had she different parentage, she would have stuttered yet Rosalyn's voice was even. "I was inappropriate with the Prince of Tadane."

"You were what?" The impact of her words hit him like an icy wind, freezing his whole body in place.

She only nodded. It did not answer his question, but an acknowledgment of her actions. She dragged herself over to the cell door and gripped the bars. The top of her head was at eye-level to him, a fact that under lighter circumstances he would have pointed out to tease her.

"You were inappropriate?" Dorian asked again.

“I...” she turned away, searching for words. “I got caught up.”

“In a Vestan? How? Why?”

“I don’t know. The usual way, and the usual reasons.” She forced her jaw into a tight line, refusing to let her emotions spill out. “I’ve never done anything like this before.”

Dorian wiped his face, then stopped as his eyes traveled down. “Rosalyn, the glove.”

She tucked her dark hair behind her ear and reached for her brother's hand. He took her hand with his left and then held out his right.

"I want to see it."

Rosalyn sighed, pushing away from the barrier. With a wave of her hand, the bolt on the cell door slid over and the door creaked open.

"I don't know why they keep putting you in here. It's not much of prison when the prisoner can walk out when she wishes."

Rosalyn took off the glove she was wearing and held out her hand. When he took hold of her wrist to examine the mark, she shivered. The mark was outlined in faint red, that would not go away for a couple of weeks yet. Out of the corner of his eye, Dorian saw his sister's attempts to avoid looking at it.

She always seemed fiercer when he saw her profile. All her power and ferocity, that was so often dwarfed by her size, rested in her face. It was a trait he wished that he had inherited from their father. Some said he had, but being in the company of his father and his sister always made him doubt he was capable of inspiring such fear. He let go of her arm, and she smoothed the sleeve of her dress over it as if it were to somehow escape from its covering.

"You can't even look at it," Dorian observed.

"Oh, I'm sorry. The whole experience was delightful and I'd happily do it again."

"It's important."

"You think I should grateful?"

"I think you should feel honored. Humbled even."

Rosalyn shrugged his comment away, "You should be careful when father gets back."

"Why?" Dorian asked, wary of what else could have happened on this trip.

"There was an attempt on my life," Rosalyn admitted casually. "He will probably ask you if you were involved."

Dorian leaned against the wall, more to steady his thoughts than his body. His mind was swimming with questions, though only one made its way out of his mouth. "Why would he think I was involved?"

"They wanted you to be father's heir instead of me."

She walked over to him and used the wall to slide down to the floor. He followed her down, exhaling his breath, and taking in all that he had heard.

"My head is spinning."

"I don't think father believes you are involved, but I wouldn't give him any reason to suspect."

"I wasn't involved. I wouldn't even think to..."

"I know."

He gave her another once over. Only months older than

him, they felt more like twins than half-siblings. He let his legs straighten out, and hers followed but landed a foot short. The lines at the corner of her eyes and in her cheeks. The mud and dust on her shoes and the bottom of her skirt. Her hair fell limp on her shoulder. She was made to walk all or most of the way home. Her posture was rigid, and a wince when she tried to relax told him what she would not.

"Are you alright?" He asked, knowing the answer.

"No," she sighed, leaning her head on his shoulder. "Not yet anyway."

Dorian shifted her forward so he could put his arm around her. He rested his cheek on her head, feeling her hair tickle his lips. "I'm glad your back."

CHAPTER 18

Five Years Later

Lucan groaned as he felt the mud sink into his shoes. The cemetery was always muddy, and that was one of the many reasons he stayed away from it. He saw the figure he was looking for sitting on a stone bench, and, after wiping his boot on a patch of grass, made his way towards her.

"Rosalyn?" He took a quick glance around. "You shouldn't be out here. It's too exposed."

Rosalyn seemed unconcerned.

"The ones that tried to hurt you, they wanted the war to end."

He scoffed, "They were shortsighted elves that could not see the future."

"And you?"

No one had asked him that. It was not the first assassination attempt during his reign and he knew that it would not be the last. So far, no one had ever gotten close enough to seriously hurt him. The one poisoning he had survived only left him out for the night it happened, but he crafted a story that it had been a bigger ordeal. He hated looking weak but sometimes it proved useful. The battle he led a few weeks later was won with such fervor because his soldiers sought revenge.

He turned back to his daughter, "I'm fine, of course. There are few out there that can match your brother in skill with a bow, and he's one of the few that I would worry about if I had reason."

"I knew you were fine," she snickered. "Dorian informed me just after it happened. I meant you can see the future?"

"My vision is good."

His daughter looked straight ahead, though her body language gave her father no quarter. She had her legs crossed, and it looked as if she were lounging amongst the dead. On closer inspection, her knuckles were white from holding the stone bench that she was sitting on so hard and her spine was uncomfortably straight.

"Why do you come here? It's depressing."

"A king who doesn't visit his own people. Now, that is depressing." Her voice held a defiant tone that had become more common in his interactions with his daughter. Even though she was sitting, the strength and power in her eyes would have leveled even the most experienced soldier.

His jaw clenched, "Rosalyn, don't start that. It's a graveyard. A relic."

"Are they not your people too?"

"They are dead."

"Because of a war you started."

"That they agreed to," he retorted. "Don't assume that because they are dead, that they died with hatred for me in their hearts."

"But they are dead nonetheless." Rosalyn's voice dropped to a whisper. "And their families grieve their absence."

"They are not my concern."

She tightened her fists, "Not your concern?"

"No," he roared.

His voice echoed off the stone markers and his temper's effect in a place reserved for silence hung around him. He gritted his teeth and planted his feet in the mud.

"Do not be taken by every sad face, because, no matter what you do as queen, sad and angry faces will always exist around you."

"It is your job to help them," she whimpered.

"Those families are not warriors. Those families did not swear allegiance to me in the same way."

"You are a king. You should..."

"Should what?" he interrupted. "You're right. I am the King.

"Rosalyn, you have magic through heritage. I have it by rite. All the ceremony and image you hate only reinforce my power. My power to send these elves to their deaths. I don't wish for them to be alive because they died with honor and Helios is where it is now because of their sacrifice."

"That's not what our people would want."

Lucan scoffed, "What would you know of our people?"

"More than you think," she snapped. Rosalyn turned her attention back to the graves in front of her. She gathered her long hair and pulled it all to one side.

After a bout of silence, she stood up and faced her father. "I've been sitting out here, just wondering. All this is worth it to you? All the lives lost to further your war?"

Lucan shifted, knowing that this conversation could have taken place inside. The graveyard was massive, despite the current trend of a funeral pyre. He wished he could say that the graves were from before his time, though he would not do the elves entombed here the disservice.

Lucan breathed in strength, "As long as I win, it is worth it."

"This is about winning?" Rosalyn objected.

"This is about dominance," he corrected.

If Rosalyn's tone did not show her displeasure with his response, her body language conveyed it clearly enough. "And what is the point in dominating Vestans?"

"The only thing that matters is the domination of Vestans," Lucan roared. "We attack them so that they do not attack us."

"That is ridiculous," Rosalyn insisted. "Yet you have made it impossible for anyone to tell you so. You are killing our people because of your own prejudice and hate. And furthermore."

With his anger carrying his swing, he slapped her mid-sentence. Lucan would not tolerate the way his daughter talked to him, his anger rising. She had not yet recovered from the slap before he grabbed her and pulled her in close.

"I'm killing our people to fight Vestan weakness, is that what you want to hear?" he said through gritted teeth.

Rosalyn wrestled herself free from his grip, her tone changing from defiance to strength. "You are using force to keep anyone from protesting. The lives of our people matter more than the existence of Vestans and their weaknesses."

Lucan assessed his daughter, scanning her from head to toe. She was young, and the attitude she had with him would cool with time. Rosalyn was not the first to protest, and, like the others, she would see reason with enough persuasion.

"In time," Lucan warned. "I hope you see their true nature. I just hope that you come to realize it soon."

CHAPTER 19

Twenty Years Later

Lucan advanced into his daughter's room, past her bed, and separated the curtains. The previously dark room was flooded with blinding light, causing Rosalyn to wake up startled. He glanced out her window, the sun just over the horizon.

"What's the emergency?" Rosalyn asked, straightening her hair.

"Doranen's elves are set to arrive in a week and you are far from ready."

Rosalyn's face soured, "No one reasonable is ready to wake up at dawn."

With the quickness of a hunter, Lucan rushed to the bedside and grabbed his daughter under her chin. Her breathing quickened and her eyes widened, fearing what he would do next.

"Don't be smart with me," he growled. "I expect you to behave, and you will do so sooner rather than later."

He let her go and turned his attention towards the door and called out, "Freya."

The lady's maid walked in and bowed to her King. Freya had only two ways that she was capable of looking at people. The first was how she could look at someone she had known for years, only to look at them as if they had never met and were meeting under tense circumstances. Her brow would be furrowed, she would stay at arm's length, and she would watch every gesture with the hyper-awareness of a squirrel.

The second look was one of not entitlement, but a slow infecting disdain for all around her. Lucan could not decipher which glance she wore much of the time.

"I want her to look presentable," he told Freya. "And I want her hair washed."

"She'll be fixed up until she is to your liking, Your Majesty" Freya replied, tossing her hair behind her ear. "I'll fetch some hot water."

As she did so, Lucan made his way to the dark wood wardrobe that rested on the wall opposite of the window. He did not have an interest in what his daughter wore, just so long as it conveyed confidence and wealth. A maroon dress with sleeves that needed to be wrapped by hand and a matching section around her waist was the favorable option. The dress required a certain air of superiority, which, with the right posture, Rosalyn could fake until she grew the confidence organically.

Freya returned with a few servants trailing behind, all carrying items to help her wash Rosalyn's hair. They set up a station, and then all but Freya left. Lucan pulled Rosalyn out of bed to the sound of her moaning over the force he used on her. He ignored his daughter, grabbed a chair on the way over, and sat her down in it when they reached the area Freya had set up.

Rosalyn sat through Freya's pulling and clawing at her hair during the wash and after. Every strand was brushed free of her natural curl and pulled into a tight bun. Freya gathered small sections into braids and other decorative flourishes.

"Is this alright?" Freya asked as if nothing Lucan said would make her add or subtract from any part.

Lucan pointed to the dress, "Her hair is fine. Get her dressed, please." The last word was said more to encourage haste, rather than out of politeness.

The way in which Freya stripped and clothed Rosalyn was clinical in nature. Lucan averted his eyes for the most part, though he saw Rosalyn attempt to cover herself and whimpered when Freya smacked her hands away. Rosalyn took on the characteristics of a doll, being moved and dressed without any concern for her body.

"Could you loosen...?" Rosalyn started. She would have finished her question, except she was interrupted by a sharp pull on the lacing up the back of the dress by her maid.

"You won't notice it after a while," Freya replied.

Lucan rapped his knuckles on the wall in impatience, "Rosalyn, stop pestering her. I want to get this meeting underway."

Rosalyn straightened her posture and directed her gaze towards her father. "What meeting?"

"A princess shouldn't ask questions," Lucan heard Freya say under her breath.

"If you must know," Lucan groaned. "I've convened the council to talk about the ball next week. Some details need to be smoothed out."

"Stay still," Freya commanded. She had lifted Rosalyn's arms and began wrapping the sleeves. The fabric seemed uncooperative, and Freya's frustration was growing with every coil. Rosalyn grimaced but stayed stiff in an attempt to please the room.

"Why do you want me in attendance this morning?" Rosalyn asked.

Lucan rolled his eyes, "Because one day you will be queen, and meetings such as this will become commonplace."

He was getting impatient because he knew that were he the only royal going to this meeting, he would be there twenty minutes early. "Are you ready yet, Rosalyn?"

"If she would stop fidgeting," Freya uttered as she stepped back. "She's good enough."

"I'd say so," Lucan replied as if it were tiresome to do so. "We need to get going."

He grabbed Rosalyn's wrist and pulled her out of the room with as much haste as he could muster. Rosalyn tried with minimal success to keep up behind him, her shoes making a distracting clapping sound against the marble floor. The length of her dress cascading and flowing as she walked, and Lucan liked the way she caught the eye of the few people that were awake and in the hallway.

Lucan paused before the doors to the dining hall and waited until they were opened for him. He cast one last glance at his daughter before going in. Her posture was tentatively straight, yet her head sagged down. He pulled her head up so that it was level with the floor. "Let your head fall and you will have lost the respect of the room."

She exhaled, "Yes, father."

Lucan caught a trace of sardonicism in her voice and was surprised that it had taken this long for it to rear its head. Rosalyn's rebellion must have been impeded by the early morning start, and she yawned as if to confirm Lucan's theory. He heard the rushing footsteps of those inside the large room and knew the doors would be open soon.

"Make no mistake, my daughter. When you go in there, you carry not just your reputation on your shoulders but mine as well. Queen or Princess, you must keep the attention of that room. Lose it and you lose your power."

"How do I do that?" Rosalyn asked.

Lucan smirked, "Well, fear and violence have always worked for me."

"And what if I don't want to use those methods?"

"Then you will not be the Queen that I want," Lucan muttered.

Rosalyn's head cocked to the side and Lucan thought he saw the echoes of a smirk not unlike the one he just wore. "That would be your problem, not mine."

The large wooden doors opened, cutting off any response from Lucan unless he wanted it heard by others. He faced forward. He would not allow his body to shift or his face to show the vexation caused by his daughter. Lucan brimmed with annoyance, causing a heatwave through his body and an odd sickness in his belly.

Lucan pulled Rosalyn through the room and nodded at the advisors standing around the table, Casimir, Cyrus, and Jalen. They greeted their King and Princess with versions of "Good morning," which Lucan drowned out. When he reached the head of the table, he released Rosalyn's hand. She could manage to seat herself, and, after that quip, he was not in the mood to perform the usual pleasantries of seating her. He sat down in the ornate wooden chair, and everyone in the room followed suit with their own seats.

"I know you are all quite hungry," Lucan began. "I will try to keep this meeting short as I'm sure we all could smell the product of our cook's labors on our way here."

There were a few hearty grunts from some of the more burly elves at the table, which made Lucan grin.

"The matter at hand is the ball in one week's time. This will be the first time in over a hundred years since any Vestans were on our land."

"Why do they have to come at all?" Casimir asked. "It's a security risk."

Lucan rolled his eyes, "They are coming because I said so." He pursed his lips, realizing how childish he must have sounded. Wiping his face with his hand, he thought of how he could recover.

"Perhaps," asserted Rosalyn. "You could explain your reasoning. You, most of all, wouldn't invite them without a reason."

Lucan inhaled, mentally preparing his speech. He surveyed those sitting at the table and used their curiosity to inspire him further. After he thanked Rosalyn for the cover with a small nod, he gripped the edge of the table and began to explain himself.

"Every action or surrender is boiled down to who has the power. We are letting them in, yes, but it is to show them who has control. What I want to discuss this morning is how we can best show them our power at the ball. It must be a clear message to Doranen Balshon and the pompous King and Queen of Tadane exactly who will win this war."

Casimir and Jalen nodded in approval, while Cyrus stroked his beard in thought.

"What are you thinking?" asked Cyrus. His question was monotone, giving Lucan the impression that any questions he posed were nonthreatening.

"Well, all eyes will be on us, " Lucan replied. "We need a display of some kind that will unnerve our guests."

Casimir tapped on his armrest, "We could always get the Vestans drunk. Catch them off guard."

For a second, Lucan entertained the idea. Lucan imagined Doranen's robes misshapen and the way he would slur words that Doranen never would say were he sober. Queen Amrydalis and her husband were so rigid in their behavior that he wondered if alcohol would even work on them and he doubted that they would put themselves in such a position. The plan was illogical, and Lucan did not have to think about it too long to realize all the reasons the idea was a foolish one. He dismissed Casimir with a look and hoped that someone would have another suggestion.

Jalen cleared his throat, "There is a different kind of embarrassment. A night of revelry perhaps."

Lucan nodded, more in acknowledgment than in agreement. "Elaborate."

"The Vestans believe us to be an uncivilized group." Getting up, Jalen began to pace as was common when he presented ideas. "Why don't we use that to our advantage. Play along. Our entertainment for the evening could be a play or presentation of a sexual nature. Have courtesans, whether real or pretend, just so long as it offends their sensibilities."

Lucan smirked, "There could be something to that."

"There is always the blood route," Cyrus interjected. "Slaughter a deer or a boar for the evening meal in front of them."

Lucan sat back in his chair, and let the ideas roll around in his head. They were all decent suggestions, though he favored Jalen's plan. Doranen was easy as far as finding something to make him uncomfortable. The debauchery was sure to make the Tadanians squirm in their seats. Lucan chuckled at the thought, and he imagined the real incident would be hilarious.

Lucan suppressed a laugh, "Rosalyn, thoughts?"

"They are all good suggestions," she said reluctantly.

Lucan groaned and tapped his fingers against his temple. Rosalyn opened her mouth to say something. He could not listen because he found her stammering disappointing.

"Well, if those are all the ideas we have," Lucan paused.

"A spy," Rosalyn interrupted.

"What?"

Rosalyn straightened her shoulders, and she changed her expression to one Lucan recognized as one he wore often. "Revelry and blood won't work."

"Why?" Lucan growled.

She turned and lowered her voice, "Fear and violence, remember?"

More out of curiosity than anything, Lucan motioned for Rosalyn to proceed. She turned to the other advisors and projected a confidence that took the room by surprise.

"Revelry may embarrass them, but it will only reinforce their idea of our lack of civility and prove our own."

Cyrus raised his hand to get Rosalyn's attention, "What's wrong with blood?"

"A deer or a boar?" she scoffed. "Do you really think that they have never had a feast of their own or that they have never been hunting? It won't work."

"Then what will?" Lucan interjected. "You mentioned a spy."

Rosalyn turned her body towards him. Her jaw was rigid, yet her eyes and interest begged for her father's attention.

"At the ball, make a grand statement that you found their spy and rage at the dishonor and broken trust after opening your doors to them."

"Have we found a spy?" Cyrus asked, looking as if someone would hand him such a report. "I don't recall hearing that."

"That's just it," Rosalyn was answering Cyrus's question, yet her focus remained on her father. "You have men that would die for you. Use one."

Lucan ran his hand across his mouth, "Whose spy would he be?"

"We don't have to say. Admit you don't know where the spy is from."

"And what if they know we are lying?"

"We know they have spies here, and we use them on occasion. If they can prove the spy doesn't belong to them, they would have to admit to the ones they have in place. And by the time they get home and realize that no spy has been found, they will know they have been played."

As Lucan thought through Rosalyn's plan, he was aware of the smile forming on his face. His daughter's idea showed force and cunning. He was proud of her, and the feeling was hard to hide.

"Does anyone object?" Lucan asked.

Jalen, who was standing behind his own chair, tapped on the corner and grunted in approval. Lucan saw Casimir's face contort, and he opened his mouth to protest. With one glare, Lucan silenced him. His daughter sat at the edge of her seat, searching the room for opinions. Cyrus, catching the exchange between Lucan and Casimir and seeing Jalen's compliance, nodded.

Cyrus interlocked his fingers, "We shall start making all the necessary arrangements."

"Meeting adjourned," Lucan concluded.

He made his pleasantries with his advisors but shuffled them out. Rosalyn stayed in her chair, only nodding when she was addressed. She wanted her father's approval, and, for the first time in a while, he was willing to give it.

Lucan closed the door behind his men, "I'm rather impressed with how you handled that."

She turned her head toward him, though she kept her eyes looking ahead of her. "Is it really such a shock? You've been training me for decades."

"Don't act so surprised," Lucan quipped.

"I'm invisible to you," Rosalyn urged. She stood up with such force that her chair fell back. "No matter what I do."

"Then do what you did just now and make me see you."

Lucan found he was on the verge of letting his temper rule him when he realized his opening. Training Rosalyn had been an arduous task for many years, with little of the results that Lucan had hoped for. For all her strength and will, there was a persistent softness that he attributed to her mother. He had done his best to get her to behave like she should and punished her when she disobeyed, yet her nature continued to get in Lucan's way.

"It was your idea," he said with confidence. "You kill the spy."

Rosalyn looked up at him, alarmed. "You want me to do what?"

"You want me to see you? Stop acting like a child and prove yourself."

Rosalyn turned away from him and wrapped her arms around herself. He could hear her breathing grow heavy amongst her sniffling, and she rubbed her arms. "I've killed for you already."

"There isn't a quota," Lucan snapped.

"I don't want to kill," she whined.

Lucan shook his head, "This is why you are so disappointing."

The weight of his statement made her head fall. Her reaction was pathetic, allowing herself to be dejected over a death. In Lucan's beginning days as King, he had come to realize that killing those in his way was a means to an end. He would admit he was skittish at the idea when he was young, but he had grown accustomed. By the time he was Rosalyn's age, he had not only accepted his job as a soldier prince but enjoyed it.

"Your head should be up," he said and lifted it to its proper place. Rosalyn's sad eyes turned to anger, a transformation that Lucan enjoyed. It was her anger that would change her into the queen she should be, not her gentility. "You are a foolish girl, having a problem with killing. It's what we do."

"It's what you do."

Rosalyn's eyes turned black and the fire inside her burned through her skin.

Lucan cocked his head, "I know what this is all about. It's those Vestan friends of yours."

Rosalyn chuckled humorlessly, "You can't let that go, can you?"

"You don't want to kill in front of your good friends, lest they think you actually behave like the rest of your people."

"That isn't it," Rosalyn insisted. She exhaled, turned her head down, and tried to calm herself.

Lucan reached out and grabbed her chin, using force more to show his control than out of necessity. "What did I say?"

Rosalyn raised her hand, and it was then that Lucan felt his control over his body vanish. He was flung against the wall, and, when he looked up from the floor, he saw his daughter smiling above him. It was a smile Lucan recognized, a smile that came from tasting control.

"I hadn't thought about it," she commented in a gloating tone. With a flick of her arm, Rosalyn lifted him off the floor and kept him pinned to the wall. The guards moved in to protect their King, yet Rosalyn held them in place as well. "Maybe I will go to my Vestan friends. If I'm such a disappointment to you, why not rub it in. I'll tell them everything."

"They won't accept you," he wheezed. "They won't look past your arm."

"And my people can't look past a mistake from 20 years

ago." Rosalyn released him, his body making a terrible thud as he hit the ground. "And you can't look past the simple fact that I came from the woman that left you humiliated."

"Enough," Lucan boomed, silencing his daughter. Rosalyn had her magic, but Lucan had a magic that was no match for his daughter. He could feel the ink in her arm and pulled, his own mark feeling the sensation of use.

Rosalyn screamed, collapsing under the weight of the pain. He alone had control of the corin marks of the dark elves, a magic rite that he had come to possess once he was made King. The pain he caused in Rosalyn, and had caused in others, was a mystery to him. Some had compared it to a fire being lit inside their skin, while others only said that they would rather have their arm removed than feel the pain that came from his power. Truth be told, Lucan did not care what those who angered him felt. If they understood why he was hurting them, he was satisfied.

"Hurting me only proves that I'm right," Rosalyn said through gritted teeth. "And that one day, I'll leave you just like she did."

Lucan's vision went red, no one dared mention Rosalyn's mother. He grabbed Rosalyn's arm and lifted her as high as he could, intensifying his magic towards her. He was not sure when he had started hitting her, only that by the time he realized his actions, he knew it was not his first punch thrown.

"You will do as I say, or be punished until you do." He heard himself say the words, rather than his thoughts willing the words out or the sensation of his mouth moving to form the words he had said. His ears felt clogged, and all sense of time and sound fell away. If it was not for the movement of his body and the sweat seeping into his clothes, he would have forgotten himself entirely.

A pounding in his head grew louder until the sound focused into what he realized was the voice of someone in the room. "King Lucan, please stop."

He was pulled back to his body by Rosalyn's guard,

Kieran, who held back the arm that had been punishing his daughter. He had positioned himself in the way of his fist. There were beads of sweat seen amongst the tiny bristles of hair on Kieran's shaved head.

"Surely," he began. "Your daughter has gotten your message by now."

Lucan looked down at the body in his hand. Rosalyn's eyes fluttered, but that was the only movement her body was capable of. He let her go, without realizing that she was unable to catch herself. Kieran bent down to her level and felt her neck for a pulse. She groaned, as her guard picked her up when the pulse was not found immediately.

"Take her back to her room." Lucan rubbed his head and walked towards the table. His head felt heavy, a tension headache starting.

"May I call for a doctor?" Kieran asked.

"Very well, if you must."

CHAPTER 20

As Kieran held the door open for him, Lucan saw his daughter avoid his gaze. She gave her brother behind him some attention before lowering her head. For once, it was not rebellion he saw but fear. She was trembling, though she tried to cover for it by holding onto the armrests of the chair she was sitting in. He moved casually towards her, motioning for her brother to stay at the back of the room.

"I need you to come down, and be there to greet Doranen and his company." His tone was matter-of-fact, and he looked straight at the wall above her rather than make eye contact. The room was cool and he second-guessed if she was shaking because of him. "The duty falls on both of you to be there when dignitaries arrive."

Rosalyn's posture was rigid and her face blank, only moving her head to look at her father. "You made it quite clear the nature of my interaction with foreign dignitaries."

"Don't get smart with me," he scolded.

Rosalyn's entire demeanor changed. Her body jerked away and reached for his hand as if it could save her life. Her face held the most drastic change, going from emotionless to fear and desperation with nothing in between.

"I'll go," she pleaded. "I'll do what you want, just please don't hurt me again."

Dorian took a step forward, "When did you hurt her?"

"Wait downstairs."

His son sputtered, but one glare sent him off.

"The bruises?" Lucan asked without clarification. When Rosalyn did not respond right away, he bent down and lifted her head up just enough for her to look him in the eye.

"When I stand, the pain is so intense that it robs me of breath."

He thought back to that morning when he saw for the first time that her whole right side was splashed with purple and green bruises that spread around her torso. Any extension of the muscles in her back sent painful tremors through the core of her body. She had resigned herself to her room since the incident, for fear of agitating her body or angering her father further.

Lucan stood up, examining the state his daughter was in. He had always admired and, if he was being honest, feared the strength of his daughter's will, yet he saw none in this moment. Her eyes were pleading for mercy, and she watched his every move, fearing that he would lash out. She shivered from the cold of the winter morning, though she dared not get up to close her window or start a fire. A small part of him wanted to use this weakness to his advantage, yet he found he could only be her father.

"I was too hard on you. I see that now. I apologize, my daughter."

He hoped that she would say something, yet Rosalyn remained silent and distant. Lucan stood up and proceeded to close the window. The click of the lock sliding into home caught her attention. She pushed herself up from her chair with great difficulty and made her way over to her father.

Lucan took hold of Rosalyn's shoulders and looked her square in the eye, "Rosalyn, I need you by my side. Without you, I am nothing."

He could see her rolling his words around in her head like clockwork. The people needed an heir to believe in as much as their King, a support that could be relied on should the worst happen. More so, it was hard for him to acknowledge how much he wanted his daughter to follow him. That kind of desire could be his downfall, were someone to take advantage of it, but he could not ignore it. Like an itch in his brain, the desire left him always coming back to Rosalyn despite the feelings of others.

She nodded more to herself than to him, and, with conviction, stated, "I am at your side."

"Then we must go," he said and motioned towards the door. Rosalyn walked with caution, avoiding movements that would stretch her bruised skin. Lucan saw her grimace and held the door open for his daughter. His fingers could not grip the door as a moment of excitement built up in him at Rosalyn's answer.

The soft heels of their boots made little noise as they walked down the hallways, though their status cleared a path among the crowd. The black marble pillars appeared to stunt all those who passed through, yet Lucan and Rosalyn were experienced in the fortitude it took to walk down the hallway with heads held high.

Lucan coiled his arm around his daughter and pulled her close so that his words would not be overheard. "She is going to try to talk to you, isn't she? Doranen's daughter."

"It is possible," she acknowledged.

Lucan deliberated, making nods of his head and small grunts as he thought.

"I'll give you leniency with her," he bargained. "But, you are not to speak with the Prince of Tadane. Understand?"

"Yes, father."

They descended the final stairway that led to the courtyard in front of the castle. Rosalyn's aubergine dress was a swirl of fabric starting at her neck and tapered down around her body, making her look regal yet highlighting her young figure. Her arms were exposed that served to distinguish her from the rest of the crowd, while the folds and bare skin drew the eye to her corin, the ink on her hand matched the color of her dress. Lucan had talked to his daughter's lady's maid earlier and asked that even her hair be pulled to one side in order to focus all eyes towards her mark.

Dorian was leaning against the castle wall when they

arrived. More specifically, he was leaning against Lucan's great grandfather that had been carved into the side of the door along with many other past kings and queens. When Dorian saw them, he hastened up and met them at the bottom stair.

He motioned for Dorian to walk near Rosalyn, "And take her hand."

King Doranen and his company rode up on pale horses in a cloud of dust. Despite the journey, their horses seemed rowdy and ready to go further. Doranen's bodyguard disembarked from his horse first, walked over to his master, and took control of the reigns so his master could get off safely. Once Doranen's feet were planted on the ground, the guard hastened to the Princess' horse to perform the same service.

"King Doranen," Lucan flashed a charming smile. "A pleasure."

"It is indeed." Doranen's voice was hollow, a clear sign that he was tired from the rough ride to Helios. He glanced over his shoulder at his daughter, who was being helped down from her saddle. Lucan motioned to Rosalyn immediately, hoping to avoid interaction between the two princesses.

"You remember my daughter," Lucan noted.

"I do," Doranen said, with a weak paternal smile. "You look well, Princess Rosalyn."

Emmelina appeared behind him and stopped on his side closest to Rosalyn. She intertwined her arm around his, yet her focus was on Rosalyn. Lucan frowned at her enthusiasm and concentration on his daughter, hating the politics that forbade him from reprimanding her. Doranen gestured towards his daughter, "And my daughter."

"Your Majesty." Emmelina bowed her head low, looking once towards him before returning her gaze back to her original target. Despite the pain that made her cling to her brother for physical support, Rosalyn was squirming at the attention being placed on her. "It is good to see you again, Rosalyn."

At the sound of her name, Rosalyn's squirming stopped

and her whole body turned stiff as a metal bar. She turned to her father who gave a small nod, then looked at Emmelina without hesitation. "And you, Princess Emmelina."

Rosalyn gave a small curtsy, though Lucan noticed the slight movement from Dorian as he stabled her descent and helped her back up. To anyone that did not know of Rosalyn's injuries, they would think that Dorian was putting a protective arm around his sister. Rosalyn's eyes hinted of her gratitude, then she turned back to the Princess of Valandyl and motioned towards him. "This is my brother, Prince Dorian Lassehelin."

Emmelina smiled, parroting her father's civility, "Nice to meet you."

Before an awkward silence dawned, and Lucan could feel one approaching, he took a step forward that separated his guests from his children. He waved Aldan over, "My private secretary will show you to your rooms."

CHAPTER 21

Emmy's mind kept flashing back to the one word her father had used to describe where Rosalyn had grown up, and that word was brutal. Everywhere she turned, there were men at arms with hard faces and dark intentions. There were no murals or tapestries on the walls, such as could be found in Valandyl, only bare stone with cold glass cut into sharp corners that lined the corridors. The harlequin design of the windows made the walls look sinister, like rows of teeth consuming all those inside. Intricate molding wove itself on the walls and ceiling, and it would have been something to marvel at in better light. However, the designs only highlighted the number of shadows and crevices in which one could hide.

Rosalyn had been quiet the day before when Emmy and her father had arrived, though she had not expected Rosalyn to be welcoming with King Lucan standing next to her. Nor had she had expected Rosalyn to be so reliant on her family. Rosalyn was reigned in by her brother, who kept a hand on her at all times, and she looked to her father as though to get permission to speak. It had taken time for Rosalyn to get comfortable when she was in Valandyl, but Emmy had viewed Rosalyn as a strong and independent elf. Her conduct yesterday was a complete reversal, and Emmy was struck at that moment by just how much time had elapsed since she last saw Rosalyn of Helios.

Emmy put her architectural anxiety aside and moved through the crowded hallway while scanning the room for a specific person. Prince Dorian took after his father, which explained the resemblance between him and his sister. He was the type of man experienced in weaving through a crowd unseen if he wished. He was narrow in build, but with muscle definition that his layers of clothing could not hide. Many years around her father's garrison and guards told her what the Prince would not, that he played an active role in the war. It had been speculated across the Three Kingdoms what his role was, but Dorian was an elf born for the shadows.

She walked up behind him and tapped on his back. "Prince Dorian?"

He turned around, then breathed out in frustration. Crossing his arms in front of him, Dorian took on an air that he was late for something. He sized her up before speaking, "You can drop the title. Just Dorian will be fine."

"Right," she hesitated. He shrugged off the title, then, with a motion she almost missed, motioned for her to walk with him. He walked at a brisk pace, and Emmy had to make a distinct effort to keep up with him. "I was hoping that you could help me find your sister."

"My sister is quite busy," he said over his shoulder. His pitch was low, much like Rosalyn's voice. "I don't know how good of an idea that would be."

Emmy tried her best to match his pace until she gave up, ran ahead, and stopped in front of him. She took a moment to compose herself, knowing she had to force herself to be heard.

"I only want to speak with her for a few minutes. Please." She grimaced at the want that filled her last word.

The opposition in his face faded and was replaced by a vulnerability that she had seen on Rosalyn's face years earlier. He nudged his head to the side towards the end of the hallway, "Right this way."

A few minutes later, Dorian knocked on a door. "Rosalyn, you have someone asking for you."

He opened the door, and Emmy peaked her head around him. Rosalyn was sitting at a desk on the adjacent wall, the train of her dress cascading around her chair. She looked confused until she saw Emmy behind her brother's shoulder. Rosalyn stood up and ushered them inside.

"May I speak to you for a minute?" Emmy asked.

She walked in, but Dorian stayed perched near the entrance. While one hand rested on the doorknob, Dorian tapped his pointer finger on his thigh in impatience. Rosalyn peered her head around Emmy and waved away her brother. "It's alright, Dorian."

"Father will not be happy with this," he grumbled.

"It's fine," she assured. "Thank you."

"I'll be outside," Dorian announced and bowed his head. He left the room but purposely left the door ajar. Contrary to her own room, Emmy noted that Rosalyn's bedroom was immaculate. Dark wood furniture such as her bed, a desk, and a wardrobe were its main occupants aside from the owner. Rosalyn's bedroom was also bare. There was little on the desk, and the only reason that there were so many blankets around the room was to combat the weather. Everything was functional, and nothing was unnecessary.

Emmy had been too flustered from the journey the day before to get a good look at Rosalyn, but she took a moment to observe her in her element. Though she was still a foot shorter than Emmy, Rosalyn showcased all the signs of etiquette training which gave her a more significant presence. Her spine was erect, her shoulders pulled back, and her head stayed level with the floor as she walked.

"Would you care for a chair?" Rosalyn asked. Her words were enunciated and clear, pointing toward speech training. Doranen had asked Emmy to attend classes or be tutored in public speaking, but she had stalled the need for such training for now. Emmy refused the chair, even though Rosalyn returned to her own.

Rosalyn sat as social customs dictated, knees together with her feet stationed near one of the chair legs, and held herself like a queen. Her eyes were calm, but her eyebrows were raised as if she were hearing a proposition. Rosalyn moved slowly, lounging in her seat and her fingers lingering across all that they touched.

"I'm sorry to intrude," Emmy murmured, feeling self-conscious under the weight of Rosalyn's gaze. She inhaled, forcing confidence from somewhere unknown in her body. "I just wanted the chance to speak with you, since so much time has gone by. How are you?"

Rosalyn's left eyebrow arched higher. "I am well. And you?"

"I am well too," Emmy answered. Her palms felt sweaty, and she shifted her weight between her two feet. She attempted to make small talk, feeling embarrassed at the fact that her skills at conversation seemed to have disappeared. "I never realized how much like your father you look until I saw you and your brother together. You and Dorian could pass for twins."

Rosalyn smiled, "We're close, he and I. It helps that we are close in age as well."

"You grew up together."

"He was my first friend, before you."

Emmy relaxed at the warmth Rosalyn exhibited towards her brother. Her face was bright, and it was the only time since she had arrived that she had seen Rosalyn with authentic emotion on her face. Rosalyn shifted and looked towards the open door. Emmy turned to see the disgruntled stares from the passersby before they continued on and whispered to their companions.

Rosalyn tapped the side of her chair and hesitated. "Emmy, this isn't a good time for me,"

"Dorian said you were busy."

She had understood when Rosalyn was under the eyes of her father in Valandyl, that they should be careful. In Helios, Emmy did not have the same protection and Rosalyn could get in more trouble if unwanted observers decided to twist the facts when they reported to King Lucan.

"I know you weren't in Valandyl for that long but I've missed you."

Rosalyn's even expression faltered, and she stood up and tucked her chair in to cover the change. She cleared her throat, "I've missed you too."

Rosalyn cast another glance at the door, then faced Emmy. Her posture like that of a dignitary much older, "You're staying in the guest rooms in the south hallway, correct?"

"I believe so," Emmy replied. "I've gotten turned around a dozen times already."

"The hallways are designed to do that," Rosalyn commented with a half-hearted laugh. "May I call on you tomorrow morning? There is too much foot traffic right now."

"Of course." Emmy held back a grimace at how positive and accommodating she sounded. She backed out of the room, with as much of a casual air as she could muster. "I'll see you tomorrow then."

"Goodnight, Princess Emmelina."

Emmy hoped Rosalyn's smile was genuine, turning towards the door and leaving the room.

It took her by surprise that Rosalyn had used her full name. Emmy had dismissed it when they greeted each other in front of King Lucan because he would have found the informality of it appalling. This time, they were by themselves with no one to judge anything Rosalyn had said and she chose to stick with formality. It felt like a slap. It was another reminder of the gap of time between when Rosalyn hugged Emmy before leaving Valandyl and now.

She was barely out of the room before Dorian slipped behind her and shut the door. Emmy heard Dorian's voice through the wood, "If father catches you, you know what he'll do."

Emmy had not intended to listen in, but Dorian's voice held a concern that worried her. The door was unlatched, and, after checking to see no one noticed her, she leaned in close to hear Rosalyn's response.

"He said it's fine," Rosalyn assured. "He gave me a short leash with Emmelina. I'm allowed to talk to her."

Dorian sighed, “Fine, but please tread warily. I don’t want you hurt again.”

“I know.”

Emmy backed away, hearing a shuffling of feet coming towards the door.

CHAPTER 22

Emmy awoke to knocking at her door, and her bodyguard easing the door open.

"Your Highness?" The hesitation in his voice was unmistakable. "I'm sorry to wake you, but there is someone who wishes to see you. She said that she is expected."

She ignored her guard's stammering, got out of bed, and put on a robe before walking over to see her guest. When she saw Rosalyn, her sleepiness vanished.

"Yes," she began, turning towards her guard. "She is expected. Thank you."

"If you should need anything..."

"I'll be sure to call." She flashed a smile, and her guard left with a reluctant sigh. Emmy opened her door wide and allowed Rosalyn to enter.

Despite it being early, Rosalyn looked put together and held a tray of breakfast food. Her long hair was tied up on the top of her head, allowing her face to be presented without distraction. High collared and long-sleeved, her black dress was sleek and well fitted to the curves of her body. She placed the tray casually on the small table at the edge of Emmy's bed with the grace of a lady's maid.

"Good morning," Rosalyn greeted. Her voice was clear and bright, indicating she had been awake for some time. "I brought you breakfast. I didn't know what you liked so I asked our cook to make whatever is the most popular."

"Well, it smells wonderful. Thank you."

Emmy walked towards the smells of bacon and sweet corn cakes, followed up by the humid warmth from the tea, eggs, and potatoes. She took a piece of bacon and nibbled on it to inspire an appetite. Rosalyn stood with a casual but stiff posture, and, while she looked comfortable, her silence created an awkwardness that Emmy could not ignore.

"You are different," Emmy observed.

She did not think that Rosalyn's posture and formality could get any worse until she saw her facade falter. There was hope in Rosalyn's eyes, that changed to sadness. She avoided looking at Emmy's face and rubbed her hands together as if she were trying to get something off of them.

"How so?" Rosalyn asked, taking a seat on Emmy's bed.

Emmy ripped a piece of the corn cake and eased herself to the same side of the bed. Rosalyn shifted when the bed dipped down, but she did not move away. Emmy popped the piece of corn cake in her mouth, before speaking.

"You look older."

Rosalyn chuckled, "It's been over two decades since we last spoke. I am older."

Emmy shrugged, consenting to Rosalyn's point. "You're more confident when you speak as well."

"Dark elves value honesty, at least with each other. We would rather have someone yell out their thoughts rather than keeping it bottled up. When a dark elf is silent, that usually means a plot is underway. But in Valandyl, I was so afraid that I would offend someone or say the wrong thing that I chose to say the least amount of words."

An authentic smile appeared on Rosalyn's face, without warning. She paused, her back relaxing enough to make her posture seem natural.

"You haven't changed at all."

"Well," Emmy started, turning her body towards Rosalyn. "I'm not exactly the same. I've taken up swordsmanship."

Rosalyn's eyebrows shot up, "That is new."

"My father hasn't been happy about it." Emmy had a sudden flashback of the time she told her father that she was thinking about sword lessons. She had to fight for weeks to pick up a sword, let alone get an instructor willing to teach her. “I think he worries that I'll enlist in the military one day, only to be placed on the front line.”

“It's natural to worry,” Rosalyn commented. Her facial expression changed after she thought through Emmy’s revelation. "You are careful, right?"

"Of course," Emmy assured.

"That's good," she said with a nod. Rosalyn breathed out and tugged at a fold in her hair. After some thought, she pursed her lips and her shoulders made a gradual slump inward. "Emmy, please be cautious while you are here. There is no shortage of elves that are eager to please my father. They could hurt you if given the opportunity."

Emmy nodded and stood up to grab more of what was on the tray that Rosalyn had brought in. "I will,” she added after she saw Rosalyn waiting for an answer.

“I mean it,” Rosalyn stressed. “Don't go anywhere alone and please don't underestimate anyone.”

Emmy paused, “You sound scared.”

“Concerned,” she corrected.

“Everyone is concerned it seems.” Emmy rolled her eyes, believing that Rosalyn would react just like her father. “When I trained with Azrael, he was so worried that...”

Emmy clamped her mouth shut, feeling her eyes widen. If Emmy had not been so concerned at Rosalyn’s reaction, she would have smirked at Rosalyn’s head snapping up like she used to do when someone would call her name in Valandyl.

Rosalyn could not hide the visceral signs of her interest. Her eyes widened too, yet she inhaled out of excitement. She shifted forward and rubbed her thumb across her wrist. When Rosalyn realized her own reaction, she stood up and pulled her arms behind her back. She relaxed her face, smiled, and ambled her way around the room. “It's fine.”

“I'm sorry.” Emmy tried to catch Rosalyn’s eye, though she kept her gaze high on where the wall met the ceiling. “I didn't think.”

"I don't mean to overstep," Rosalyn started. She ran her top teeth against her bottom lip and attempted to speak. It took some stammering before she finished the sentence she had started. "But, um, how is he?"

"He's doing well, as far as I know."

Rosalyn's head cocked to one side, "As far you know?"

"I don't see him much anymore." She knew she sounded bitter, though she would never apologize for it. "He comes maybe once a year. He says he's busy."

"What keeps him in Tadane?"

"It's been this way for over a decade. Most of the time, it's his parents. Queen Amry wants him to be involved in everything and I think she doesn't want him to leave again so she keeps him busy. Sometimes it's a girl, but he doesn't stay with them for long."

Rosalyn's body ceased all movement, except for a small and rigid nod of her head. She breathed in and exhaled, as if to clear her mind, then started walking towards the door. "I should let you eat and get ready for the day."

"Don't go," she called. She wished she could take back her last sentence, feeling her whole body reeling from seeing Rosalyn's reaction. "We don't have to talk about Azrael."

"It's not about him," Rosalyn assured. She put her hand on the door and pretended to be positive. "Your breakfast is getting cold. Besides, you have the ball tonight, and it should be quite the event."

Emmy all but let her walk out the door until something caught in what Rosalyn had said. She walked towards Rosalyn with a quizzical expression on her face. "Won't you be there?"

Rosalyn put forth a laugh that Emmy had heard many times, a laugh that covered truth. A defense mechanism that allowed Rosalyn to say what she was supposed to say, rather than her own thoughts. Rosalyn blinked a few times, let her gaze wander, then spoke. "I don't believe so, my father would prefer that I did not attend."

"That doesn't make any sense," Emmy remarked, her

tone blunter than she would have preferred.

Rosalyn waived away Emmy's comment and flashed one more smile, before pulling the door open. "I should let you get ready."

Emmy could read into Rosalyn's tone and attitude that Emmy would not see her again if she made it out the door. Rosalyn did not seem interested in staying, and part of Emmy thought that she should let her walk out of her life. They had only known each other for a few weeks, and they had both grown since. It was childish, but she could not help herself when she stomped her foot.

She reached out and grabbed Rosalyn's arm, "You trusted me once, and, now you can't stand to be in the same room with me. Is all of the Rosalyn that I knew gone?"

Though Emmy's grip on Rosalyn's arm was not forceful, Emmy was shocked by Rosalyn's reaction. Her face was one of surrender, and she cowered away. Emmy let her go, though Rosalyn's eyes scanned Emmy's movements like a hurt animal.

"My father wouldn't approve," she said, still trembling. Rosalyn rubbed her arms and looked outside the door for anyone coming or going.

Emmy lowered her voice, so as not to scare her. "You told Dorian that your father gave you a short leash with me. What did you mean by that?"

Rosalyn's head snapped back towards her, "You weren't supposed to hear that."

Emmy slowly reached up, this time putting a comforting hand rather than a confrontational one on her arm. Her breathing slowed, and her posture straightened.

"Your father hurt you when you were in Valandyl." Emmy knew the answer, but her question had trouble forming itself. "Has he...?"

Rosalyn scanned the hallway outside Emmy's room again, then shut the door with a forceful push. She pulled away from Emmy, walked over to her bed, and started pulling open the fixtures of what Emmy realized was an overcoat that Rosalyn was wearing. The decorative lacing and ribbon of it had meshed together to create the illusion that the coat, undershirt, and floor-length skirt were all one piece.

As Rosalyn peeled away the tailored jacket and lifted her undershirt enough to expose part of her rib cage, Emmy saw massive bruises all along her left side. She could not be sure, but she could tell the bruises were at least a couple days old. However old they were, the bruises still looked like they were causing widespread pain. The swollen purple marks that followed her ribs and extended up to her shoulders were outlined in yellow-tinted skin. Emmy walked up to get an even closer look, but Rosalyn coiled away.

"As you can imagine," Rosalyn prefaced. "I'm rather sensitive to the touch at the moment."

Emmy nodded.

Rosalyn started to say something, paced around, then tried again. "About a week ago, my father thought that I had this grand plan to reunite with you and Azrael or make a scene at the ball. And maybe I did. I was feeling confident, and so I challenged him. As you can see, he did not care for that too much. In the end, he made it clear that I should stay in my room for the night."

Rosalyn sat down on Emmy's bed and instinctively reached up to cover her bruises with her hand. She forced a smile, hoping to lighten the situation. “And I'm not one for large gatherings anyway.”

“I’m sorry,” Emmy whispered.

“I don’t need your pity,” Rosalyn snapped.

Emmy stared at her friend, crossing her arms in front of her. Rosalyn may not have needed her pity, yet she had never felt such a strong outpouring before. Emmy could not imagine living in fear of her father, or having to worry about what might set him off that would cause a beating. Rosalyn had put forward an image of herself for Lucan and the weight of sustaining that image was too much for her. Lucan would have known that, yet Emmy suspected that he did not care.

"You are my friend," Emmy pointed out. "And I care about you."

"You should choose your friends more wisely," she said as she put her overcoat back on.

Emmy felt a lump in her throat, and she tried to ignore it. She let her head sink, "Do you not want me as a friend anymore?"

Rosalyn looked up, registered Emmy's words and physical reactions, then resumed standing. She walked over to Emmy and lifted her head up. Emmy thought Rosalyn was taking on the mannerisms of her tutors until she saw Rosalyn's expression was calm.

"There is a big difference between me not wanting you as a friend and you not wanting me as a friend. The later is what I would prefer."

Emmy scoffed, "To absolve you of guilt?"

"No, to absolve you of guilt."

It took Emmy a moment to realize what Rosalyn meant. If Rosalyn became the heir that King Lucan wanted, she would need to be as ferocious and manipulative as her father. Lucan was known for his violence, which would mean that she would have to be violent towards Emmy and Azrael's people. Any friendship with Rosalyn would implicate her friends, and the people of Valandyl and Tadane would not approve of any relationship with her.

"I've thought of you often," Rosalyn confessed. "Our time together, spending hours with you and Azrael, confiding in you...Those memories are pure. They are valuable to me. But I seem to only remember them when I'm doing something that you would disapprove of. I remember you both when... A couple of years ago, I had a private tutor. She would follow me around and shout at me when my head wasn't straight enough or I wasn't speaking as clearly as I should. It was aggravating. Do you know why?"

Emmy shook her head.

"Every time she grabbed me and told me to keep my

shoulders straight or to focus on my studies, I imagined you were there. Always out of the corner of my eye, just out of sight. Out of reach. Or when my father includes me in his military briefings, all I see are the people I interacted with when I went to the street fair with Azrael. How he would be disappointed in me for what I've done.

"Your opinions have weight to me."

Rosalyn paused, shaking off her previous train of thought.

"I wish more than anything that I could go on a walk with you or even relax around you. I wish I could dance at the ball with Azrael, but my father will have eyes on me the whole night. And for what? A small amount of time with a princess destined to kill all that you love. Destined to drown out your opinions, lest I suffer every day for holding to them."

"I won't let that happen," Emmy promised. A smile grew on Rosalyn's face at Emmy's commitment, and Emmy returned the gesture.

"And I won't let you or Azrael near my father," Rosalyn countered. "So we are at an impasse."

Emmy's smile turned coy, "The last time I talked to Azrael, he hoped to see you tonight."

Except for the rustling of Rosalyn's skirts, the room grew silent. Emmy thought she saw a change on Rosalyn's face, though it was gone before she could be sure. With a clap of her hands, Rosalyn pulled away. A clear intention of retreat on her face, even though she had not physically left yet.

"I hope you enjoy your night, Princess Emmelina, and give my regards to Prince Azrael."

She left.

Emmy thought about chasing after her, but she stayed. As much as she did not want to admit it, Rosalyn was in no position to be vulnerable and Emmy would not be able to convince her to change after years apart and only hours of contact.

CHAPTER 23

Emmy stared at herself in the looking glass and twirled to see the layers of her dress. She felt foolish, but, considering what she was walking into, she allowed herself to be fanciful. The last time Lucan had allowed her people inside the walls was over fifty years ago, and her father was on high alert. No one trusted Lucan, yet, if anything, Emmy trusted his daughter.

Her bodyguard, Asa, peered into her room, "Princess Emmelina?"

She turned around, the layers of her purple dress following her spin. The long sleeves were too warm and the color was not her favorite but her father went on about the optics of wearing closer to the wardrobe of Helios.

"We should leave. The ball is supposed to start soon, and the King will want you at his side."

She flashed a courteous smile, "Of course."

After one last glance at the mirror, she walked out the door. The hallways still made her nervous, though the few days she had been in Helios had given her enough confidence to walk through the halls without showing her discomfort. She envied her father's calm mentality or at least envied the collected look that he wore every time she saw him.

Asa held out his arm, which she took, and they made the journey from her room to the great hall. Square side tables lined the hallways, ornamented with bowls of glass orbs and roses the color of currants. Everyone was dressed in beautiful robes or dresses, a clear sign that everyone in attendance came from some source of money. The silks and soft fabrics were enough to make anyone want to reach out and touch, were they not attached to an elf.

They were almost to the great hall when Emmy heard someone clear their throat. "Might I have a word with the Princess?"

Emmy smiled, knowing before she turned around who spoke.

"Why would you want one?" Asa quipped.

Rosalyn pressed her lips together, her eyes gleaming with comments she chose not to say. She flashed a smile, "My reasons are my own."

"Asa, it's alright."

As she let go of Asa's arm, Emmy noticed who she assumed was Rosalyn's bodyguard. His eyes were the most striking part of him, as they seemed to see every movement done by all those in the room. He scared her, though she guessed that was why Lucan had hired him.

Emmy turned back towards Asa, "Please, wait over there."

"Is that your bodyguard?" Emmy asked and nudged her head towards the man behind Rosalyn.

After turning around to see, Rosalyn nodded. "Kieran? Yes, my father asked him to stay close to me tonight."

It dawned on Emmy that Rosalyn was dressed as if she were coming to the ball, and she realized that Rosalyn had changed her mind. The dress in question was unusual compared to the garments Emmy had seen, though it was nothing short of stunning. Her arms were exposed, yet her shoulders and upper arms were covered by a sheer beaded capelet. The beads were in rows, connected by strands of silver thread that resembled wings. Her dress was covered in a silver brocade, which shimmered amidst the light of the torches on the wall.

"You're dressed. Does that mean that you are coming?" Emmy stammered. "Tonight? Now?"

Rosalyn saw her gawking and smiled, taking her staring as a compliment. "You inadvertently talked me into it."

Rosalyn looked around the room out of habit. The smile lasted until she caught eyes with Kieran, then it faded. She stepped to the side, blocking his view of her face. There was an audible deep breath before Rosalyn was able to get her words out.

"My father dresses me up all the time, but tonight, I dressed up for you and Azrael. My father won't let me speak to you anymore, I've tested his patience long enough. But I want how I look tonight to tell you what I can't. I miss you both, and I hope you two find all the happiness in the world."

Emmy could tell that Rosalyn's speech had been rehearsed, but that did not lessen the impact of what she had said. She looked nervous and rubbed her tattooed arm with her other hand. Rosalyn, after a quick glance at Kieran, gave a slight bow to Emmy.

"Enjoy your night," she added then turned away from her.

"Rosalyn, it doesn't have to be this way."

Emmy did not think that Rosalyn would stop, but she did with enough grace to convince anyone watching that she had a purpose for the double-take.

"You don't have to become your father, and we don't have to be enemies."

Rosalyn's mouth fell open as if no one had ever told her such a thing before. "What are you saying?"

"Don't you see?" Emmy exclaimed. "The three of us could stop the war if we only wait until we are crowned. Your father won't have control of you forever."

Rosalyn clenched her fist, "What you have is an impossible dream, while I have physical blood and bruises. The girl you knew is gone, so stop trying to revive a corpse."

"Is that how he thinks of you?" Emmy faltered. "That you are nothing more than a corpse."

"Walk through those doors and enjoy the party," Rosalyn urged. Her tone was restrained, not wanting to let her emotions be seen by anyone else. "Then do yourself a favor, and never think about me again."

"Why won't you fight this?"

"What would be the point?"

"We care about you," Emmy admitted.

"Because it's easy," snapped Rosalyn. "You will go back home to your father and your friends. You will love me because I'm far away, because you don't have to face me or any consequences. But you don't know what fighting every day would entail for me."

By this point, Rosalyn's voice showed her fervor yet also revealed a mourning that Emmy doubted anyone had addressed. Rosalyn grabbed Emmy's arm. "You've seen what he does to me, and he does not hesitate."

For all the building of emotion, it was gone in an instant. Rosalyn lifted her hands up, and Emmy saw that Asa had his sword slid under Rosalyn's neck. Asa spoke through gritted teeth, "Take your hand off her and back away."

As Rosalyn did as she was ordered, Kieran came forward. Rosalyn held her arm out, and her bodyguard paused. He had his hand on his sword, and his whole body was tense. She nodded towards Asa, showing that she was compliant with him. Emmy parroted her, "It's alright. Stand down, Asa."

Kieran put his hand on Rosalyn's shoulder, "It's time for you to join the King."

Asa removed his sword from under her neck, and Rosalyn cleared her throat. She rubbed her neck and then motioned for Kieran to step back. Turning towards Emmy, she looked around the room, then leaned in close.

"Trust me," Rosalyn whispered. "There is nothing for you here."

Emmy looked at Rosalyn, trying to comprehend the 'nothing' before her. Rosalyn's face, despite the sadness, glowed. The fire softened her hard jawline, and Emmy saw the light shine on her colored lips and clear skin. Rosalyn had admitted to caring for those her father would condemn, and had taken the brunt of her father's anger with admirable strength.

"You are beautiful," Emmy muttered as Rosalyn turned to leave.

A smile like one Emmy had not seen since Valandyl lit up her face.

Rosalyn nodded, then turned and took her bodyguard's arm. If Emmy had not known better, they looked like a couple. Their pace together had a natural flow, and Kieran looked at her with as much gentleness as a dark elf could muster. Emmy wondered if perhaps Rosalyn had moved on from her experiences in Valandyl after all.

CHAPTER 24

Azrael did not like big groups. It was not the idea of meeting someone new or the awkward conversation, but rather the overwhelming mix of emotions that accompanied the large group. Parties and meetings drained him, though he was thankful for it at the moment otherwise he would have been flooded with nervous energy. He pulled at the cuffs of his robe and proceeded into the Great Hall of the castle at Helios.

Every elf in the room was dressed in finery with airs and graces to match. He laughed at the fact that all the self-importance was lost within the vacant space of the towering room. Despite only a distant echo off the ceiling at least 200 feet above his head from those below, Azrael could feel more emotions than he could identify and wanted more than anything to leave. He breathed through the pressure in his head and tried to focus on the physical.

Tapestries had been hung on the walls depicting great battles, and large plush rugs were placed along the center of the room. Along one wall, Azrael saw small balconies, closed off by curtains but the light from the candles could be seen through the fabric. As he walked further into the room, Azrael noticed a familiar smiling face and proceeded to the owner.

Emmy looked radiant, taking in the sparkling decorations like she did every moment. His nervousness eased as her excitement filled him with each step closer.

He walked up behind her, leaned in near her ear, and whispered, "You look wonderful."

She turned around, and, after seeing that it was him, Emmy embraced him.

"Thank you," Emmy said after she let go. "You clean up well too."

Azrael pulled at his sleeves, releasing the fabric bunched up towards the middle of his arms. "Well, you know my mother would have my head were I to show up in any other way."

Emmy nodded, "That's true." The corners of her smile sagged, and her mood resigned. "How have you been?"

Azrael shifted his weight to his other leg and took a breath before answering. He had not been to Valandyl in over a year, and the last letter he had sent was months ago. He had no excuse. It was not that he forgot about her, but rather time seemed to get away from him.

He apologized with his eyes, "My parents have me running around meeting with everyone and their mother, it seems."

"No girl this time?"

"No, not yet," he chuckled. He ran his thumb across his jaw, then hesitated. Seeing Emmy after so long was a joy, but he had been ignoring the anxiety pooling in his stomach. "Speaking of a girl, have you seen her yet?"

She hesitated, "I have."

"And?"

"She's different," Emmy replied without elaborating. Her tone grew dark, biting at him. "And, like you, her father keeps her busy."

Azrael groaned, "I'm sorry."

Emmy nodded once, as a sort of silent acceptance of his apology. She turned at the sound of the great hall doors being opened wide and watched, as everyone in the room did, the entrance of the King of Helios and his entourage.

Azrael saw that while many were focused on Lucan, Emmy watched his daughter walk in with her head held high and her tattooed hand effortlessly holding the folds of her dress out of her way. With all the elves in the room, Azrael knew she was too far away for him to feel her emotions with any precision.

"I think she's hurt," Emmy said under her breath.

"Physically?"

Emmy chuckled, though Azrael did not know why. She did not take her attention off of Rosalyn, and Azrael felt as though Emmy was far away. "I know she's hurt physically, but it doesn't matter now. I don't know how to explain her, other then she is different from the girl we knew years ago."

Lucan sat down on his throne at the end of the hall, Rosalyn stood near him with the poise befitting a queen and was followed by three males that Azrael did not recognize. The first bore an unmistakable resemblance to the two royals that held the focus of the room. Rosalyn had mentioned her brother during her stay in Valandyl, and he could distinguish the familial glances between them. The second man had his hand on the hilt of his sword and watched the room with experienced eyes.

The last man stopped in front of his King, yet turned to face the hall and its inhabitants. He cleared his throat loud enough for most of the room to hear, then spread his arms in a gesture of welcome. "Elves of the Three Kingdoms. Thank you for your attendance. My name is Jalen, and I am the master of ceremonies for this evening. We have prepared a great party in your honor and, I think I speak for all of us when I say, that we look forward to a night of revelry. We hope that this day marks progress as we strive to work towards a time of peace. Enjoy your night."

The guests partook of the food displayed on a long table, and to the casual observer, the party began without any sign of trouble. However, Azrael saw it in the eyes of the guests what many others failed to see. The eyes of his parents stalking Lucan and the simultaneous glances at Lucan's staff that served them, hoping to catch any signs of poisoning or threat. Meanwhile, Lucan was focused on his meal, yet Azrael felt his alertness. Doranen, alert as was everyone, seemed to ignore the tension and make conversation with those around him.

Azrael felt eyes on him, and though he found his appetite minimal, he kept his hands busy by shuffling a plate of food between his hands.

"May I speak to you for a moment?" His mother asked once she had eaten the acceptable amount of food. She was never one for excess, and Queen Amrydalis was known for her control and discernment as far as the Elestren.

He excused himself from Emmy's side and allowed her to pull him out of the great hall and into the narthex. "Yes, mother?"

"Have you talked to her yet? Emmelina?"

Azrael groaned, knowing without clarification what his mother was referencing. It was a topic he had hated and had gone to great lengths to avoid his mother and the conversation altogether. She brought it up usually when the two were alone, though she had been finding more and more public places to discuss the topic at hand.

"I was just talking to her," Azrael responded with obvious annoyance. "But you have to refresh my memory as to what you wish me to discuss."

"Marrying Princess Emmelina," his mother urged.

"Mother, we've talked about this." Azrael could feel not only his irritation on the subject but his mother's irritation at his unwillingness to cooperate.

"And we will talk about it again," she said, this time with more force.

"You know the Elestren won't allow royals to marry unless we have consent from all three kingdoms. Those are the rules."

"And Lucan is jovial tonight." Azrael saw a smile appear on her face, though to the casual observer it looked more like a face of indifference. Her lips were thin, and a smile from her was only a slight raise of the corners of her mouth. Azrael's father told him that the only genuine smile that he had ever seen from her was when her son was born, everything else could not compare. "It would be a good time to ask."

He crossed his arms in front of him, "You've known Lucan longer then I have, but even I know he's planned something for tonight."

"Of course he has something planned," she said. "However, we will adjust. This matter needs to be settled."

"He is not going to agree to an alliance that would strengthen the two kingdoms that he is fighting against."

Azrael turned away, indicating that was all he would say on the matter, then turned to go back into the room. He felt his mother's impatience before he felt her hand pull him back towards her.

"Azrael, I want you to be happy, but I also want you to be the king that you were meant to be. It is your birthright, and you will be a wonderful king. Your father and I have felt a change in you these past few years. We want to help you, but nostalgia for something long gone is only heartbreak. And marrying Emmy could be a solution for all of us."

Azrael's eyebrows furrowed, "You and Father would have to die for me to be king. Have I not been informed of something?"

His mother took a step back and found looking him in the eye difficult. Amrydalis cleared her throat, then forced the words she had been holding onto out of her mouth. "Your father and I have been thinking about abdicating and taking up a post in the Elestren."

Azrael sputtered, "How long have you been thinking of this?"

"We have been considering this option for a while," she hesitated. "But we need to know that you are ready to take the responsibilities that would be given to you."

Azrael lost the feeling of his body, drowning in the possible outcomes of his parent's decisions. His parents were the oldest of the rulers, and often their age was used to prove their arrogance. Instead, he saw the exhaustion they hid from the world, but he always thought that they would work through it. Some of the immortal rulers had abdicated in past generations to make way for their children, so the idea was not unheard of. His parents were significant players in the Elestren that he wondered how he had not seen this coming.

He wanted to fight, to give them reasons to stay but stopped. Somewhere inside his mother there was peace. Her face calmed, knowing he grasped the reality of the situation. He was still young, but he had been training his entire life for the day that he would take over.

"I'll do what I can," he tossed to quiet his mother.

Azrael was pulled out of his thoughts, by Emmy's voice calling his name. She was flustered, and her face was grave. "You both need to come to the great hall now."

"Vipers!" boomed Lucan from inside. All three elves ran into the room and saw Lucan pacing and screaming in the center of the room. "How dare you wear your smiles. You take advantage of my generosity, but it is all lies."

Doranen approached Lucan and tried to calm him down. "King Lucan, what is this?"

"As if you don't know," Lucan scoffed. "Or perhaps it is just as pathetic that you really don't know."

Rosalyn forced her way through the crowd, dragging a struggling figure behind her. "You requested the leech, Father."

"Yes." Lucan grabbed the man by his collar and held him up in display. "One of you sent ahead a spy. As if I would attack when we agreed on peace."

"King Lucan," Doranen coddled. "I am sure we can work something out."

"Work something out? You want to make a deal to make me forget this treachery?" Lucan dropped the man without a thought to him feeling the blow. A smile appeared on Lucan's face, amused at Doranen's attempts.

Doranen backed up, "That's not what I meant."

"King Doranen, does this man belong to you?" Amrydalis interjected.

Doranen waved her away, "Of course not."

"And how do I know, Queen Amry, that he isn't yours?"

Lucan spoke to Amrydalis with such malice, yet he did not talk down to her. Azrael was struck by the sudden civility. For the first time, he grasped the type of relationship that his mother and King Lucan had. Doranen was the middleman, an irrelevancy that they both needed to deal with. They hated each other, but their respect for each other's strength seemed to be what bonded them together. "You have been silent up until now."

"I have never seen this man in my life," Amry replied.

Lucan smirked, "Then perhaps your government isn't as secure as you'd like it to be."

Amrydalis' nostrils flared, "That is unfair."

Lucan stared at her, as if he were trying to think of what to say, then turned away. "I don't care who he belongs to, the treachery is clear."

Doranen fussed with his sash, though his face showed no sign of uncertainty. "And what if he doesn't belong to either of us?"

"You'd like that, wouldn't you?" Lucan patronized. "It would be simple. Wash your hands of the situation, and have no responsibility."

Aldan, who had been skulking behind Lucan, pointed to the spy in question. "One of the Vestans just gave him a look. I saw it."

Lucan's eyes volleyed between his man, the spy, and the other rulers. He turned to Amrydalis then to Doranen, all attempts at saying something seemed insufficient. His frustration had been building and his anger was peaking. Everyone could see the tension rising, yet no one was courageous enough to stop the momentum that was driving him. He yelled, in an action similar to a toddler but an accompanying fear that spread through the spectators that no infant tantrum could dream of spreading.

Lucan grabbed the spy by his neck, and then snapped it like a twig.

"I cannot tolerate lies!"

Emmy grabbed Azrael's arm and buried her face in his shoulder. Azrael wrapped an arm around her but kept his eyes straight ahead. He was intent on watching what Lucan would do next, though he found his attention being pulled away by a singular feeling of guilt from someone in the room. Everyone was feeling anger and fear in a swirling mix that made them indistinguishable from each other, but only one person felt guilt.

"Forgive me, My King," said a meek voice behind Lucan. Rosalyn appeared at Lucan's side and put a hand on his arm to restrain him. "This is not the place."

Lucan relaxed his shoulders and took a glance around the room before relinquishing to his daughter. His frustration eased enough to allow everyone in the room to breathe, but his anger could still be felt. He stepped away from Rosalyn, with a movement that seemed natural, and made his way towards Doranen and Amrydalis.

"You want to work this out? Let's work this out." He looked straight ahead, then forced out a word he hated. "Privately."

The tension and empty space lingered long after the four rulers and their security detail left the room. Everyone went back to mingling, but only because it was better than silence and whispers. He found the false civility disgusting in how everyone could go back to each other, but then soon realized that the alternative was drawing swords. Before the smell of blood could permeate the room, the body was cleared as soon as the royals had left. Everyone tried to avoid looking at it, but each elf cast a look at the cleaning process at least once.

Emmy ran to one of her father's advisors, meanwhile, Azrael would see to her safety. Regardless of his mother's request of him, he would see that his friend was safe from anything that may come from the results of Lucan's talks.

"Asa," he called.

The elf came over, "Yes, Your Highness."

"Keep a sharp eye," he warned. "If this tension erupts

into anything more, I want her secured."

"Of course, Your Highness."

Azrael dismissed him when Emmy came back over.

She rubbed her neck as she returned to Azrael's side, "Davis refuses to speculate what the repercussions are of this."

He was about to answer Emmy when he felt a familiar guilt pass through him once again. A silver dress smeared his peripheral vision, and he was drawn towards her. Rosalyn's face was blank, a face he recognized as one all royals stowed away for when the people preferred an image rather than emotions.

Being the youngest of them, the change from the Rosalyn that he knew in Valandyl to now was the most drastic. There was a darkness, a seriousness, that had not been there before. He had often wondered how she would have changed, but seeing her with her father now made his stomach turn. And yet, so much of her seemed the same. His memories and thoughts overlayed with what was real and in front of him that he took a step forward as though to test the boundary of distance that had kept them apart for so long.

"Azrael, don't." Emmy pulled on his arm and wore the same mysterious expression she had on earlier.

"I just want to see her for myself," he said as he pulled away from her.

"She will get in trouble," Emmy warned. "And Lucan is just as violent towards her as he is towards us."

"He's out of the room now."

"And if someone says something?"

He smiled, then pulled away from Emmy and followed Rosalyn through the banquet hall towards the balconies. The silver of her dress and the shimmer of the light on the curtains made him pause. She passed through the sheer curtains like a ghost. The full moon only added to the ethereal image that she was no doubt unaware of, and one that he alone saw. She covered her face with her hands to hide the weight of the blank stare he had noticed earlier.

He pulled the curtain back and stepped onto the landing of the balcony. Between his footsteps on the marble or the audible sway of the curtains when he pushed them aside, he thought she would have reacted.

"Rosalyn," Azrael said softly.

"Prince Azrael?"

Her voice held a fear that made Azrael nervous. She backed up against the guardrail and searched what she could of the room behind him. He wondered, for the first time, what kind of trouble Emmy meant when she warned him not to interact with Rosalyn. Without warning, her mood changed.

"You shouldn't be here."

Her low voice dripped like honey.

Azrael held his hands up, "I just want to talk."

She looked back towards the hall and nodded to someone behind him. "My father would be cross if he knew I was talking to you. I can't. I'm sorry."

Rosalyn cleared her throat, pushed past him, and walked through the curtains. He ran after her, painfully aware of the number of people now able to listen in.

"Later, perhaps." he offered. "When there aren't as many eyes."

It looked as though she was going to refuse him, but she stood stammering instead. She closed her eyes, bent her head down, and regained her composure. Azrael felt her helplessness, her desire for safety.

"Alright," Rosalyn said, trying to keep her voice quiet. "Just outside the castle."

Azrael's head perked up, surprised that she had agreed to meet with him. If she could not see his excitement, his voice revealed it. "Where outside?"

She grabbed her arms, and shook with impatience, "I'll find you. Now, please, go."

Azrael did as she asked, and hustled back towards Emmy with a giddiness that he hoped was not apparent. He knew it was apparent to Emmy, whose eyes looked concerned but her mouth smiled. Azrael turned to watch Rosalyn, expecting her to remain where he had left her.

However, Rosalyn had made it to the other end of the room, only to be grabbed by her father. Her brother, much like a magnet, made his way to his family with surprising speed. Lucan let her go, and, for a moment, as he talked with his son, Azrael hoped that Rosalyn had escaped the eyes of the room. It was not until Lucan grabbed Rosalyn's left hand that her physical pain was sharp enough for Azrael to feel. His own hand tightened and shook. He had never felt someone's pain like this, and suspected magic was the source.

Before he could search for a further explanation, Rosalyn was pulled from the room by her brother, leaving Azrael to wonder if he would see the Princess of Helios later that night. He turned towards Emmy, who had also watched the scene play out, and she looked as though she were on the verge of sobbing.

"Emmy?"

She gathered up her emotions and crossed her arms. "I told you that she would get in trouble. Why did you have to go over there?"

His stomach sunk, weighed down by what he could not bring himself to say. "You know why."

"Whatever she said. Whatever you said. Please don't go see her again, because, believe me, that was Lucan being lenient."

CHAPTER 25

Azrael shivered, more out of nervousness than because the night was cold. He took a step to his right, wondering if the moonlight would help Rosalyn find him better but then took a step back believing that the darkness would keep him out of sight from elves that would tell Rosalyn's father of their meeting. Azrael took one more step, not sure of which goal he had in mind, only that he could not stay still.

He heard the crack of a twig behind him and nearly jumped when he saw Rosalyn. She had a dark cloak over her dress from earlier, the glass beads at the front caught the light of the full moon. Her body took the uneven forest ground with easy strides, and her fingers lingered on the trees she touched as she passed.

"I didn't think you'd come," he said when Rosalyn stopped in front of him.

"I almost didn't."

Azrael wanted to get to pleasantries, but the guilt he felt from her earlier nagged at him. "Did you have anything to do with the spy?"

"I can't talk about that." She wrapped her cloak around her, and let her eyes wander.

"We were friends once," he petitioned.

"And you had the good enough sense then not to ask about issues or situations that would make me a traitor to my own people. What was it you said back then? 'We are not our titles when we are together. We are just us.'"

"Fair enough," he consented. "What have you been up to? Since I saw you last."

Her stance strengthened, and Azrael realized that, even now when they were alone, she was crafting an image for him. No longer was she the girl who worried about being seen, but, instead, she had been replaced by someone who well understood the power dynamics in every interaction. An attribute of Lucan's that Azrael was disappointed she had acquired.

"I probably shouldn't talk about that either. The past can get so political."

Her words sounded so sweet in his ears that he almost missed the slap within them. Azrael wiped his mouth, and let his fist rest on his lips. He did not know what he had expected from seeing Rosalyn, but he had expected more than her controlling the conversation into sentiments that meant nothing.

"What did you talk about with Emmy? We could talk about the same thing."

"Go ask her," Rosalyn snapped.

Azrael's frustration grew, diminishing his sense of decorum. "I could, but I want to talk to you, not her."

"Well, here I am. Sorry if I disappoint you."

"I haven't seen you in years. I finally get an audience with you, but all you are doing it evading."

"And why do you think that is?" she hissed.

"You weren't like this before."

"I wasn't a lot of things before."

"I just wanted to talk to my friend. Someone that once meant a lot to me. If she's not in there anymore, then what's the point?"

She stopped, pressing her lips together. "I'm sorry. Ask me how I am, and I promise I'll answer."

Azrael looked at Lucan's daughter, realizing for the first time his distrust. His voice was weary, "How are you?"

"I'm fine." Rosalyn rubbed her arms to fight off the cold, then proceeded to elaborate. "I'm glad the ball is over. I don't like the show that events like that require. It was good to see you and Emmy again. How are you?"

"I'm better. Big events make my head ache."

"Too many people?"

He nodded.

"I saw your father hurt you." His skin tightened at the memory of her father's grip. "It was my fault and I'm sorry."

She waved away his apology as though it were nothing, but he saw her hide her left hand behind her back. "It's fine."

Azrael rolled his eyes and was glad for the darkness that hid his irritation. Again, it felt like Rosalyn was evading. Lucan's castle loomed over them like an intruder into their conversation. As his eyes grazed the walls, the impact of the castle and Lucan on Rosalyn hit him in the gut. She was holding back, but it was not because she did not care as he had thought.

"I didn't know that he had magic," he coaxed.

"My father's magic is reserved to controlling the corins on dark elves' arms." She scratched at her arm, then continued. "When he does, it feels like your arm is being sliced up and struck by lightning all at the same time."

"Again, I'm sorry," he repeated. Rosalyn squirmed, and Azrael searched for a new topic of conversation. "You look breathtaking tonight."

She beamed.

"Emmy told me that you no longer stay in Valandyl," she interjected. "What changed? You loved it there."

"Yes, I did. Do. I will always love Valandyl," he said, lifting his eyebrows in shock and confusion. "And it will always be my home."

Rosalyn shrugged her shoulders, as if to dismiss her own words, but stuttered like she had more to say. She sighed, knowing her hesitation was only hurting her. "I don't want to be presumptuous, but Emmy said it's been some time since you stayed."

"It is because of you," he admitted. His voice was flat. As his words came back to him and her jaw dropped, he knew he had to explain further.

"It is because of you, but it isn't your fault." He hesitated but managed to get the rest of the words out. "Does that make sense? I believe that life can be defined by moments."

"Moments?"

"I wanted so much back then, but so much time has passed now."

The air around them was thick, and Rosalyn pulled at the clasp of her cloak. Her expression was like something had died deep inside her. "Do you ever wish that we had never met?"

"I've wished for many things the past few years, but meeting you has never been something that I've regretted."

Rosalyn was cold, her physical body too, but the only thing he sensed was a deep ache. The guilt and fear he had sensed all stemmed from that ache that he could not place with any certainty. Even though numbness was not the right feeling, it all clustered into something akin to overwhelming numbness that worried him with its complexity.

"You're harder to read," he added.

"What does that mean?"

"It's like you're numb," Azrael observed. "Or you are trying to force certain feelings that you don't feel."

Rosalyn scrunched up part of her cloak and smiled without amusement.

"I said that you would ruin me, but I never imagined how much. You made me feel cherished and I have never felt that way since. I want that feeling here, but everything I do is wrong or undesirable. I force myself to act to their standards, but nothing comes close to what I felt with you years ago."

"Then don't." He reached his hand out, without knowing how the gesture would help or what he would do if she took it. "Don't conform to them."

Rosalyn laughed without humor, "You and Emmy make it sound so easy. Like I could fix my problems with a snap of my fingers, but you two don't know anything about my life here."

"Azrael," came an urgent voice in the direction of the castle.

Rosalyn tensed at the sound, and Azrael blocked Rosalyn's body with his own. The castle's shadow hid the intruder until Emmy's face became noticeable at the edge of the forest. She was out of breath, and her hair had fallen from the pins and ties put in place for the ball.

Azrael steadied her with both hands, "Emmy? What's wrong?"

"A guard saw you," she wheezed. "Your parents are coming."

"You should go," Rosalyn said from behind him. Azrael knew Rosalyn had stepped closer, by the sound of the leaves and soil being crushed under her feet.

Emmy nodded, took his wrist, and pulled him with her towards the castle. The repetitive nature of his situation locked him in place. Was he not in the same situation twenty years ago, with Emmy pulling him away from Rosalyn as their parents closed in?

"No," he argued.

"What?" Rosalyn and Emmy said at the same time.

Azrael turned his focus on Rosalyn, "The last time I saw you I was pulled away with barely a thought to what I was doing. I've never regretted meeting you, but I have regretted not putting up a fight for you."

She sputtered, but could not form words. When she did not give a rebuttal, he turned towards the sound of people coming.

He saw an outline of figures following the nearest door and knew that Lucan was among them. His anger was easy to pinpoint. As the light hit the faces of the crowd, he recognized Rosalyn's brother from earlier and a brutish man that had been shadowing the royal family the whole night.

He pulled his wrist away from Emmy, who still had a firm grip, leaned in close to Rosalyn, and whispered, "We can hide or run. This is your home, you have to know some way to get away from them."

"Rosalyn," Emmy urged. "If we go now, you won't get in as much trouble. Azrael, we have to let her go."

Their parents were still far off, but Rosalyn's fear was spiking. Her breathing was ragged, and the part of her cloak that she had been wringing was wilted and creased.

Azrael could not run or be led away by Emmy, it felt too much like cowardice. All the memories of Valandyl and everything he had done in Tadane since was culminating in what he did in this moment. If he went with Emmy, he would regret it just as he regretted not standing up for Rosalyn years earlier.

"I love you."

The moment seemed to stop.

"You what?" Rosalyn asked. Her eyes wide as saucers.

He took her hand, "What I felt all those years ago, nothing has compared..."

Emmy pulled Rosalyn around to face her, "I don't want you getting hurt again. You know that I want this for you, but being discovered will only give your father more reason to hurt you."

"I haven't been able to stop thinking about you," Azrael admitted. He knew she was stressed and indecisive, but fighting for her was all he could do. With her magic, they would be safe. "Since we parted, I've realized that you mean more to me than you know, more than I ever could have predicted."

Rosalyn looked back and forth between them, clearly unsure which side she should choose. Lucan was close enough to hear his anger and yelling.

"Rosalyn!" Lucan roared, only a quarter of a mile off.

Emmy pulled on Azrael's arm, "Azrael, they are coming. We have to go."

"No," he uttered, still focused on Rosalyn. "I'm not leaving her to face this alone. Rosalyn, please. There has to be a way to avoid them."

Rosalyn pulled away from them both, clutching her head and mumbling to herself. Her stress was building as her father got closer. Emmy tried to steady her, but Rosalyn would not let her touch her. Her fingers dug so deep into her skin, that Azrael thought he could feel them himself.

"Rosalyn, get away from them," Lucan yelled.

“He’s coming...” Rosalyn whimpered, as she cowered down to the ground. “I can’t. He said. He’s coming."

Emmy shifted, "They're coming. Azrael, we have to go."

Rosalyn screamed, and a buzz penetrated the air. Her corin hand was outstretched, the muscles in her arm and knuckles tensed as if she were lifting something. Lucan approached in an expected huff but was blocked by a magical barrier around them. He banged on it with all his strength, though the only effect it had was causing purple ripples at the site of impact.

Emmy gasped, “How is this possible?”

“What have I done?” Rosalyn lifted her head up and stared at her father beyond the force of her magic. “My father will be so furious.”

Azrael bent down. Emmy had warned him about the punishment that Rosalyn would receive from her father, and, though he did not regret fighting to stay, he was aware of the consequences as he stared at the royals standing outside the perimeter.

Rosalyn screamed again. The outline of her corin turned red, and Azrael knew without looking that Lucan was the one behind it. He gritted his teeth at the resurgence of the pain in his hand. “He’s hurting you, isn’t he?”

She let her legs go beneath her, and Azrael pulled her into his arms. She screamed again-- a sound that tore at his heart-- and she nodded into his chest. Rosalyn shifted her weight upwards and placed a kiss on his neck. She let her head rest against his cheek, and whispered in his ear, “I have to let them in.”

Her voice was strained, as the strength to keep her magic going amidst the pain from her father caught up with her. He ran his hands across her hair, and let her cry into his shoulders.

"You are strong enough to fight them," he tried.

"Azrael, look at her," interrupted Emmy. She bent down, and her face pleaded for his understanding. Her voice cracked, but she was determined to speak up. "What is your plan? That we stay in this bubble she has created for a hundred years. You have to let her go."

"I will," he yelled, more out of frustration that he would have to bend to the will of others again. He put his hand under Rosalyn's jaw and caressed her cheek. If Lucan had his way, which he would, Azrael would never have another opportunity to talk to her.

"You will always be strong enough, Rosalyn. I'll never forget that."

The magic dissipated, and Lucan went straight for his daughter. He grabbed her by the arm and pulled her into the castle with no thought towards Emmy or Azrael. In his mind, his daughter was the only one at fault and would see to the rest later. Azrael heard Emmy's whispers, but more as a series of dissonant notes instead of words. His hands felt the emptiness that Rosalyn left with as much force as if she had fought hard to stay there. As he had many years before, he felt the defeat of losing something that mattered to him.

CHAPTER 26

Doranen watched Princess Rosalyn be lead into the room with her hands tied behind her back and clear signs that she had received preliminary punishment. She had been changed into a shirt and pants, and he knew that she had been changed by someone else because the row of buttons was off by one. Her hair was a disheveled mess pulled back by a thin strip of leather. Red cheeks told him that she had been crying, and her hoarse groaning told her that the crying had only stopped recently.

Aldan and another elf of Lucan's pulled her forward with unnecessary force, slamming her down in the chair that was the focus of the panel before her. He sat at a long table with Queen Amrydalis on one side and Lucan on the other. Rosalyn's breathing was shallow, yet no one seemed to notice. Doranen looked down at her wrists, that had been rubbed raw or worse depending on the section, by the rope that bound them together.

"Please remove the ropes from her wrists," proposed Doranen. "They are unnecessary."

He heard a small clink, and his eyes were drawn to the source. Around her neck was a chain and pendant that seemed out of place with her current state.

The silver metal was unassuming, though the raw quartz bound together by rows of wire were sharp at the tips. His eyes widened, realizing what the necklace was and why Lucan had not torn it off of her. The kyri pulled at her neck, severing her body from the magic she possessed. Kyris were rare, and the reports he had read said the experience of wearing one was a slow progression from dull to excruciating.

"Why?" Lucan asked, with an edge to his voice.

"You have her properly restrained with that..." Doranen made a vague gesture towards Rosalyn's accessory. "That thing. She won't hurt anyone."

Lucan consented with a small flick of his wrist. "Untie her."

Queen Amrydalis cleared her throat and tapped on the table to draw attention to herself. Rosalyn looked up from her wrists and turned towards the Queen. "It is a bold move sending for all three of us, so I hope that you have not wasted our time."

"I have come to petition an alternative to the punishment that you three have agreed upon." Rosalyn's voice was strained, yet Doranen noted the strength of will she inherited from her father in her straight posture and her confidence in asking for such a request from three royals without breaking eye contact.

"There is no chance of lessening your sentence," Lucan growled. "I am being lenient as is."

Doranen let out an audible sigh to pull attention back to himself. "King Lucan is right, you cannot lessen your sentence. To be clear, your punishment is fifteen lashes to be dealt tomorrow morning. What do you wish to dispute?"

Amry pulled on Doranen's sleeve, "There is nothing she can dispute. This is a waste of time."

Doranen kept his focus on Rosalyn. Though he agreed with Amry, he was willing to hear what the Princess had to say. "Princess Rosalyn, you have little to help your case."

"I do not wish to lessen my sentence," Rosalyn clarified. "I wish to add to it."

Doranen had to push past the growing lump in his throat to get the words out of his mouth, "Why would you want that?"

Rosalyn looked down at her wrists, then wiped her eyes. "I know that in addition to my punishment of fifteen lashes,

Azrael has been assigned ten, and Emmy five. I sent for you three to petition to give them to me, all thirty lashes."

"Explain your reasoning," he demanded.

"You taught your daughter to be kind and compassionate. No doubt something she took to well considering both of her parents. While she should have been more discerning, should she really be punished for doing what you have told her to do all her life."

"Your son," Rosalyn looked away from him, towards Amrydalis, "Has a good heart. His feelings for me are misguided, and, with the right guidance, he will see that. His affair with me will soon become a dalliance of his past. And yet, those lashes will leave scars.

"What will happen when he begins looking for a wife, his future queen? Those scars would be a constant reminder to his future wife and his people of a mistake."

Lastly, she turned to her father, who was sitting with his arms folded in front of him. He flashed a sarcastic smile and rested his head on his hand. "And your argument for me?"

Rosalyn dropped her head, a clump of her hair falling from the strap and covering part of her face. Doranen caught her small gestures--a quick touch of the area below her nose, digging her fingernails into her palm, pressing her lips together-- and knew that, no matter what words came out of her mouth, they would be a lie.

"I wanted your attention."

Lucan scoffed, "A cheap excuse."

"In Valandyl," Rosalyn countered. "My feelings for the Prince were genuine but they have cooled."

While Lucan sat back in his chair, Doranen leaned forward.

"It wasn't some long-term plan," she added. "Seducing the prince was a matter of convenience."

Amry slammed her hand on the table, her eyes seething. Lucan chortled. His daughter paused until Lucan got control of himself, then returned her focus to him. Rosalyn's face changed to disgust, yet her tone grew sweeter, "I think I rather enjoyed it.

"When I arrived at the ball, I saw him and knew that you would be watching. If I hadn't come last night, you would have no reason to see me until the next battle was planned and even then there is no guarantee."

Her excitement had built as she talked, so she had to pause and catch her breath. Her voice shifted to a more formal tone, "The punishment would fit my actions and my childish behavior more appropriately."

Lucan, who was still wearing the remnants of a smile, cast a skeptical glare on his daughter. "The problem I have is that I can't be sure that you aren't doing this out of love for the Prince and Princess."

"The way I see it," Rosalyn opened. Her head cocked to the side, and her gaze was leveling. "You were going to punish me, why not do it more?"

It was then that Doranen saw the real request that was being proposed. Rosalyn was not asking the three rulers if she could take the punishment. She was asking her father to allow her to take the punishment for elves he hated; elves that she loved and could no longer hide her feelings towards. No matter what excuse Rosalyn gave, Amry would do anything to keep her son away from the dangers of Helios and he would do anything to protect his daughter. She was baiting her father, telling him what he wanted to hear but also challenging him to punish her the way she knew he wanted to. While he looked out for Emmy and Amry looked out for her son, no one was concerned about the small girl in front of him that had managed to figure out the heart of each of them.

"You have made your arguments, Princess Rosalyn," Doranen said as to end the power struggle happening in the eyes of Rosalyn and her father. "We shall deliberate."

"Thank you."

Rosalyn was led off as forcefully as she was brought in, only she did not resist. She had her request, and all she could do now was wait for her father's decision.

CHAPTER 27

It was as though Emmy were watching her body walk through the cells of Lucan's dungeon. Her father had told her what had happened, and her imagination had been picturing it all day. Rosalyn had been moved after the incident to one of the cells below the castle so her father would not have to deal with her any longer. Aldan had been the standing guard but was leading Emmy and her father to the cell as a personal favor. Her father had asked Lucan to see Rosalyn before they left.

She heard whimpering at the beginning of the hall, getting louder as she drew closer. Rosalyn's brother, Dorian, was in the room, consoling her and tending to her wounds. For all that had transpired, Emmy realized she still expected the dark elves to treat Rosalyn with some amount of respect. However, seeing her friend cast aside on the floor in the same shirt that she had worn during the incident removed all hope Emmy had.

Dorian's back was to them as they approached. All the Lassehelins moved with a hypnotic slowness about them, but Dorian's movements stood out. His hands worked with gentle precision, the speed at which he moved controlled and measured.

It was not the blood that shocked Emmy most, but the way Rosalyn flinched and the sounds she made that made her stomach turn. The marks on Rosalyn's back stretched as she breathed, and her movements were rigid so as not to aggravate her condition further. Rosalyn let out a scream and Emmy gasped at the rawness of it.

Dorian turned around at the sound. He stood, looking at Aldan as if a crime had been committed and Emmy was the culprit. "What are they doing here?" he asked.

"Dorian, you forget your place," Aldan scolded.

Doranen held out his hands, "It's alright. Thank you, Lord Aldan, that will be all for now."

Aldan's mouth dropped at both being dismissed and by a foreign king. He unsuccessfully tried to hide his disgust, giving a rigid bow before leaving. He got to the door, then added a curt "I shall be down the hall when you are finished."

Dorian watched Aldan like a puppy who had disappointed his master. His shoulders were stiff, and he rubbed his hands, reminiscent of his sister when she was nervous. "I'm sorry, I just don't want her to get in any more trouble."

"I understand," Doranen assured. Her father's relaxed voice eased Dorian enough to take the edge out of his posture. "Your father is aware of our visit and we will not stay long."

Doranen motioned for Emmy to stay where she was, as he went over to check on Rosalyn. Though the order was not directed towards him, Dorian stayed near Emmy and the doorway. The folds in his shirt and the red in his eyes implied he had not slept. His sleeves were rolled up, and dried blood could be spotted on parts of his shirt.

"You've been up all night," Emmy observed.

Dorian's head popped up, "I had to stay with her. I couldn't leave her alone, considering what she was facing."

Emmy knew there was no malice in his voice, but she felt the jab anyway. If she had known, she would have stayed with Rosalyn as well. She would have tried to talk her out of it. "I only found out after it happened."

"Is she lucid?" Doranen called. He had bent down and was examining her. "Is her body experiencing shock?"

"She comes and goes," Dorian answered. "I've found she doesn't tend to respond unless she needs to, but you should take her hand so she knows you are talking to her. She drowns everything else out."

Doranen did as was instructed, stroking her arm with his other hand.

"They gave her a choice," Dorian whispered. Emmy looked over and asked him to clarify. "They stopped at fifteen, and asked her if she wished to continue."

"And she did?"

Dorian's jaw hardened, "Let this fact dictate all future relations with my sister. She fights for those she loves and few people in this world are so lucky. But that luck does not often find its way back to her."

Rosalyn shook as she breathed through a wave of pain, which pulled Emmy's focus. Lucan gave his daughter every opportunity to change her mind, yet she chose to have her shirt ripped open and be whipped for those she loved. Emmy felt like weeping.

Her father motioned for Emmy to come to his side, which she did and bent down to Rosalyn's level if only to keep from crying. Doranen's demeanor changed from his usual calm to a tenderness that Emmy recognized for when she was hurt or in distress.

"I'm sorry," he whispered a couple of times. "You are such a brave girl."

Tears streamed down Rosalyn's face and fell on her sleeve as she laid on her side, her corin arm outstretched under her. The sleeve of Rosalyn's shirt covered most of it, but Emmy could see signs of inflammation around the marked lines of the tattoo.

"I know what you did," he said without changing his tone.

"Did?" Rosalyn croaked.

"I do teach my daughter kindness and compassion as you said, but I also want her to know the sacrifices that others make for her."

He offered Rosalyn's hand to Emmy and stood up when Emmy took it. As she carried on her father's work of her hands over Rosalyn's, Emmy felt the clamminess of Rosalyn's skin as she held her limp wrist. Minutes passed before Emmy found that she could speak past the lump in her throat and the overwhelming guilt.

"You did all this?" Emmy said. "I would have taken the punishment."

"No," Rosalyn barked as if she had not been whipped in the past several hours. Her body tensed, and she cried as she paid the consequences for her movement. "I couldn't bear it."

Emmy put a hand to her own mouth, "It even hurts you to breathe."

Rosalyn made a vague motion with her head that Emmy assumed was her attempt at a nod. The fabric of what remained of the back of Rosalyn's shirt clung to her skin and moved with her breathing.

"Rosalyn, can I do anything to repay you?"

"There is something." Rosalyn took a moment to catch her breath, before continuing. "I seduced Azrael to get my father's attention, and I manipulated both of you because I thought it was fun."

"That's not true," Emmy objected. "You don't mean that."

"I do mean it," she pleaded. Her voice caught, and Emmy knew the pain in her eyes was not from her back. "If you wish to do something for me, repay me, you must mean it too."

Emmy paused, "I don't understand."

"You and I know the truth, but I had to say those words to save you. And now, you must say them to save Azrael.

"There is no future for Azrael and I," she added bitterly. "Yet he has shown that he does not forget easily."

"He loves you," Emmy countered.

"And that must end. No more secret meetings or lingering thoughts. Make him hate me, then make him forget me."

Emmy realized what Lucan was afraid of, that Rosalyn would choose to be selfless no matter the punishment he threatened her with or the bruises he caused. His rules had bound her, his prejudices had silenced her, yet Rosalyn fought her father with all that remained. Seeing her broken body, Emmy grasped the weight of her fight and why she had refused to be lenient when she had talked with Emmy a few days ago. Lucan had no qualms about punishing her if it meant that he could be one step closer to squashing all fight within her.

"I can't do this," Emmy stammered. "I can't lie to him about something this important."

"And the alternative?" Rosalyn asked.

Emmy wiped her eyes and explained, "He would know what you've done, and how you love him."

"To what end?" Rosalyn's eyes were heavy. The adrenaline that had allowed her to survive the whipping had all but faded. Her words slurred together, and her head dipped down. "He can have no peace so long as his thoughts are on me."

A tap on her shoulder grounded Emmy, reminding her that she was not alone in the room with Rosalyn.

"It is time to go, my dear," said her father.

She glanced at Dorian, seeing with renewed eyes the marks of his sleepless night. Without Dorian, Rosalyn would have no one. She would lay on the cold floor of this cell with her back torn up, and everyone in the castle could not care less. Meanwhile, Emmy would be in Valandyl with elves on standby, waiting to help her should she wish it.

"No, more time please."

Her father shook his head, "Say goodbye, my dear." He tapped on her shoulder once more, then proceeded out of the room.

Without warning, Rosalyn's grip grew tighter. Her tone dropped, "You would both do well to remove all thoughts of Helios."

Emmy leaned in and weaved strands of Rosalyn's hair back behind her ear. Lying to Azrael would be difficult, but forgetting Rosalyn seemed like an impossible task. How could Emmy forget someone who had sacrificed their own body to have a conversation with her? Rosalyn put Emmy ahead of her own interests and had done all she could to protect her friend, yet Emmy was expected to leave Rosalyn to become her father.

"Then who will think of you?" Emmy asked.

"The sooner you both forget me, the sooner I can."

Emmelina felt the world around her crumble. She was not naive; she knew she would go back home and her life would seem to be unchanged. It was the world she had hoped for that was dying. Rosalyn was giving up, Lucan would not trust her to be around Vestans for many years, and Emmy had to lie to a dear friend.

"Emmy," Doranen called. "You must say goodbye now."

"Goodbye, my friend," she whimpered.

Her legs felt weak, yet they moved of their own accord. Rosalyn let go, and Emmy stood up. The walk out of the cell seemed endless.

Her arm was seized, which jerked her back to the present. Dorian, who looked so much like his sister that Emmy no longer wanted to see him, forced her to turn to him. His grip all strength, but without causing her pain. "She needs this. Everything you do for her is one more beating she gets. I'm begging you. Do as she says, and never think of her again."

Emmy pulled her arm away and exited the room.

CHAPTER 28

Lucan rifled through his stack of papers and groaned when he saw his son enter the dining hall. Dorian talked to no one as he shuffled through the crowd, intent on reaching his father and did so as fast as his legs would carry him. A week had gone by since the Vestan rulers had left Helios after the disaster involving his daughter. The last two days had been a nonstop plea from his son to speak with Rosalyn, a plea he had been ignoring. He would deal with his embarrassment for a daughter in his own time.

"Father," Dorian said. "She needs to speak with you."

"Did she ask you to ask me again?"

Dorian shook his head, "No, I'm asking. You'll want to hear what she has to say."

Lucan gathered the papers, setting them down with an audible slap as they hit the wood surface of the table. "Has she recovered?"

"Not quite," his son hesitated. "Her muscles are still weak."

Lucan sighed and rubbed his eyes, preparing for a headache. "Bring her in."

Though there was not a smile on his face, Dorian's excitement changed his body language. He leaped from the room without a care as to the stares he received on his way out.

"Clear the room," shouted Lucan. The guards near the doors did as their king instructed, motioning the occupants towards the exits, but without an apparent reason as to why. They knew better by now than to ask, both of their king and in their own private conversations.

Dorian pushed through the crowd of people leaving with his sister by his side. She was pretending that she could walk on her own, yet she would instinctively reach for Dorian's shoulder to steady herself anytime someone got close enough to bump her. Her skin was pale, and her lips seemed drained of all color. When the two siblings found their way into the room, Lucan motioned for Dorian to step away from his sister.

"So what is it that requires you to pester me day and night?" Lucan proposed.

Rosalyn stood on unsteady feet, yet her attempt at strength was admirable. Her posture was straight, yet she clung to her arms and shook. "I know that I have no right to request anything of you."

"No," he quipped. "You don't."

Rosalyn pleaded, "Will you hear me out?"

"What is it?"

Whether it was his harsh glare or by sheer weakness, she wobbled and Dorian caught her by the arm. She stumbled down to one knee, catching her breath. Lucan rolled his eyes, regretting his decision to see her. It was a waste of time.

"Please don't invite them here again," she whispered, then clarified. "The Vestans, don't invite them. If you do wish to meet to discuss peace, meet in Tadane or Valandyl. Don't take me with you."

Even bent down, his daughter still had the nerve to order him around.

"You have no right to ask for any of that. You are my successor, I need you there and you will do what I tell you."

"I'm not saying forever," she excused.

"Then what are you saying," Lucan barked.

Rosalyn shook. She let herself fall the rest of the way to the ground and grabbed her head with one hand while supporting herself with the other.

"I'm vulnerable to them, papa."

Lucan paused. He was expecting her to ask for understanding and was prepared to punish her accordingly. Except this was something new, his daughter was admitting fault.

Rosalyn continued, "There is truth to what I said. I did want your attention. I want you to love me like you used to."

Lucan squatted down to her level.

"I'm confused," Rosalyn admitted. "And I need you to help me."

Lucan sighed, caving to his daughter. He stood up and motioned for his son to come forward. "Bring her to the table. Sit her down."

Dorian did as he was commanded, putting an arm under Rosalyn's and lifting her up. She hobbled to the dining table, needing Dorian to guide her into the chair. Even though his son had most of Rosalyn's weight, Dorian did not struggle to move her.

Lucan tapped his forefinger on the papers he had put on the table earlier, "I've heard this from you before."

"It hurts," Rosalyn mumbled.

"That is the point behind whipping you."

"That's not what I was referring to."

Lucan banged his fist on the table, "Then what? Rosalyn, I don't have all day."

"I love them. When they come here or I'm with them, they make my thoughts jumbled. I think of Emmy and Azrael, and everything else disappears."

He groaned, "I know."

"It hurts," she said again.

"And you're asking me to what? To give my blessing? To allow you to love the children of those I despise?"

"Take it from me," Rosalyn begged with tears in her eyes. Lucan froze. "My love for them, it hurts. I can't keep living in two worlds, and I need you to help me. Cut my heart out. Whatever you need to do to make the pain stop, do it."

She looked exhausted as if her request drained her of all strength.

"Do you mean it, my daughter?" he asked, annoyed at the

hope in his voice.

"I told Princess Emmelina to forget what she thought she knew about me. However, I can't forget the part of me she knew without your help. She put all these ideas in my head of who I should be."

Lucan interrupted her, "I will rid this pestilence from you."

Rosalyn nodded, a wash of relief apparent. She wiped the hair out of her face and took the time to catch her breath. "Take it from me, then try to forgive me."

Lucan sat down in his chair, pulled it forward, and put his hand on his daughter's cheek. "You've done the right thing coming to me, my daughter."

"I'm sorry, papa," she murmured into his hand.

He had waited for the moment his daughter would come to him, and, as he held his daughter's teary-eyed face in his hand, he smiled at his newfound opportunity.

CHAPTER 29

Two Years Later

Rosalyn looked out from her hiding place and watched soldiers run towards the other end of the hallways. Attacks from Tadane and Valandyl had increased in the past two years, though they had never gotten as close as today. Catapults had sent boulders pounding into the side of the castle and into the surrounding capital city. She had hidden in an alcove during the first barrage and would search out her father before the second.

She stood up, still weary that another attack would come. The castle could take the bombardment, yet the sounds of windows shattering and pillars falling gave her pause. Stepping out, Rosalyn set out to find her father or her brother and get instructions.

"Help me."

Rosalyn turned towards a voice and saw a servant girl trapped among fallen stones. She rushed to the girl's side, "It's alright, you're safe. Are you hurt?"

"I think it's broken," the girl said, holding up her arm. The arm in question had already swollen up, making the joints of the fingers and wrist undefinable.

There was a cracking sound above Rosalyn and she looked up only to see it was too late to save herself from the falling stones of a weak arch above her. Pieces that varied in size from a blackberry to a book fell on her and the girl. The pieces of rock scratched her face but managed to avoid any serious injury to either of them.

"Your Highness," Rosalyn heard from behind her. She turned around once the cascade stopped. Kieran had his hand on her shoulder and was examining the scratches on her face. "Are you alright?"

He stared fixated at a scratch on Rosalyn's head, and, when Rosalyn reached up, she felt the sticky liquid of blood. "It's just a scratch, but this girl needs your help."

"Come with me," he said to the girl. Kieran and Rosalyn lifted her up, and Kieran took her weight on his shoulders as he escorted her down the hall.

"Wait," Rosalyn said, pulling on Kieran's shoulder. "Have you seen my brother or the King?"

"They are in the dining hall."

"Then that's where I need to go."

Kieran grabbed her by the wrist, "No, I won't have you running through the halls by yourself."

"She needs you more than I do. Go, now."

Before Kieran could argue with her, she slipped her hand free and ran in the opposite direction. The hallway grew crowded as she made her towards where her father and brother were. Soldiers and elves moved past her in a flurry of bodies and colors. She looked for a familiar face, her anxiety growing when she could find none that were useful.

"Dorian?" She yelled. "Dorian? Father?"

"Rosalyn, over here." She followed the sound of her brother's voice, and he pulled her out of the crowd. "Rosalyn, here. You need to get to the throne room."

Her eyebrows shot up, "Why? What is going on?"

"Not only is the castle under attack, but Vestan soldiers have gotten behind our defenses. The inner wall has been breached, and our people are being evacuated to safer parts of the city. Father has requested you go to the throne room, it's the safest place for you."

"What about you?"

"Go," Dorian ordered. "Don't worry about me. I'll be

fine."

Rosalyn squeezed through the crowd, quickening her pace as the number of soldiers increased in the halls. Vestans had never before made it past the border towns, but, despite the surprise, her father's army was prepared for such an event.

The castle shook again with a low rumble, and Rosalyn looked around for any loose material that should fall. She felt a sinking in her stomach as she thought of Dorian fighting. He had been trained by the best, yet her worry persisted. She wondered if the castle had been stormed or if scouts had gotten lucky.

Rosalyn put away her thoughts knowing they were useless speculations until she got to the throne room and someone could give her a status report. The clapping of her boots seemed dwarfed by the voices of those around her and the sounds of battle outside. As the lower hallway narrowed, as did the number of people until Rosalyn found herself alone.

She continued on until her body was pulled into an alcove. One hand grabbed her around her waist, while the other covered her mouth. She struggled, trying to scream and break free from her captors' arms.

"Don't fight," whispered the mouth just behind Rosalyn's ear.

Rosalyn reached out with her left hand and shoved the person back with physical and magical force.

"It's me," she heard as she turned around.

Her arms relaxed, and gasped at the last face she thought she would see. Tall in stature with dusty brown hair, the intruder smiled weakly at her.

"Emmy?" Rosalyn gulped. "What are you doing here?"

Rosalyn saw her friend's body shake, a fear that would have paralyzed an average elf. Her armor seemed out of place as if it were stolen or placed on her by elves who did not know her. She stood at the edge of the alcove, the wall hiding her from view.

Emmy's face went pale, "My father feared that I would

be at the front."

"And now that fear has been realized," Rosalyn observed.

Rosalyn's body tensed, her skin feeling like armor. She knew Emmy's situation without being told. Emmy had gotten separated from her group, and, should she be discovered, she could be held as a political hostage. Rosalyn, more than any other, could imagine how her father would treat her friend and what life would be like in her father's cells.

"Come with me," Rosalyn said, taking Emmy's hand and pulling her out of the alcove. Emmy stopped and put on her helmet to hide her face.

"Where are we going?"

The suspicion in her voice was apparent. Even though Rosalyn could not blame her, she could not fight the pinch inside her when she saw Emmy's apprehension.

"If my father finds you, I can't help you like I did last time."

She did not wait to see if that answer satisfied her. With every turn, Rosalyn feared that her father or his soldiers would be on the other side. The throne room was the easiest way to cut out the long hallways it would take to get Emmy to her army, Rosalyn thought, but she knew it was a risk. Dorian had sent Rosalyn to the throne room for one of two reasons, either because it was empty or because it was densely populated with her father and his soldiers. She would not have much time to check which was the case, but she knew she had little choice.

When they arrived at one of the entrances, Rosalyn pulled on the large bronze doorknob and grimaced when it screeched open. She peeked inside and was relieved to find it empty. She ushered Emmy in, shutting the door behind her. The room felt cold as if it had been uninhabited for centuries. Emmy's breathing resounded in the emptiness of the towering room and the spire that pulled the ceiling together.

"I never did thank you," Emmy interjected.

Rosalyn turned around as if startled that Emmy was still behind her. She did not let her face change. Whatever Emmy was thanking her for would not take away the nostalgia for the times when they were together, it would not save her from her father or her fate, and it could not take away the scars on her back.

"Don't thank me yet," she countered. "I still have to get you out of here." She guided Emmy to the opposite side of the room before she could add anything.

Rosalyn felt time stop.

Emmy's hand slipped from hers.

A clang of metal against stone rang out.

Emmy screamed so loud that Rosalyn clapped her hands over her ears.

She saw that her father had advanced from whatever corner of the room he had been skulking in and was fighting with Emmy, who had drawn her sword after the first blow. Lucan sidestepped with the ease of a cat but charged at her with all the force he would use on an opponent of his size. His swing crushed her, and she fell to the ground clutching her sword arm to her.

"The Princess of Valandyl," her father announced, as though there were people in the room that could hear his reveal. His smile was open-mouthed and his teeth flashed like a wolf before wounded prey. "I expected better from you, Rosalyn."

Rosalyn sidestepped in front of Emmy, then held her hands out to keep her father away. "She's not supposed to be here."

"Which is why she is such a prize."

She pulled her shoulders back, "I won't let you touch her."

Rosalyn gathered up her strength, held out her left hand, and seized her father with her magic. He resisted, which Rosalyn had expected, but the stall allowed Emmy a reprieve. Lucan's eyes burned black at the betrayal, fighting to get free.

His anger made Rosalyn shake, but she did her best to fight through it.

She grabbed Emmy's hand and yelled, "Run for the door."

Emmy had only begun to run when Rosalyn felt the familiar lacerating pain of her father's magic. Her ability to keep her own power steady depleted and her father reached out. He grabbed her marked arm, adding a new level of pain as though her skin was being torn off. Her concentration broke, unable to sustain her magic and experience her father's wrath simultaneously.

"Your Vestan is giving me too much grief," Lucan said through gritted teeth. His expression was one of exhaustion, not physical but exhaustion of the situation. He threw her across the room and chased after Emmy, his sword held high as if it were an extension of his own flesh.

Rosalyn's eyes went dark.

The room faded away, and she clawed at nothing to force herself back. When her vision returned, her head felt thick and heavy. She pulled herself up.

Another scream tore through the room, and she searched for the source.

Lucan pulled his sword back to him, and Emmy crumpled to the ground. The warm smell of blood reaching Rosalyn before seeing the stain on her shoulder. Rosalyn struggled to get up, wheezing and unable to walk straight, but moved by willpower alone.

"What have you done?"

She fell down at Emmy's side, reaching towards her wounds but instead hovering above her for fear of damaging the Princess further. The sword had sliced through skin and muscle without precision, creating a gash that would be impossible to heal. Emmy moaned and twitched from shock and nerve damage. Rosalyn took Emmy's hand and ran her other hand across her hair.

"Emmy, I'm sorry," Rosalyn repeated as she looked

around for help.

"Get away from her," Lucan ordered.

"Help her," she pleaded. "Summon a doctor."

Lucan pulled a cloth from his pocket and wiped the blood from his sword to show his indifference. He shook his head, sheathed his sword, then flung the cloth in Emmy's direction. "Back away from her now. I will not ask again."

Rosalyn lifted her head, shaking not out of fear or weakness but out of anger. She felt the blood rushing below her skin and, despite her injuries, she stood up without difficulty. Her left hand glowed with power, and her eyes filled with deadly fire.

"I won't let you touch her again," Rosalyn growled.

Her magic wrapped itself around her father and threw him into the very throne that gave him power. She pulled stone from the ceiling above them and sent it crumbling on top of the heap of flesh and wood.

Rosalyn took deep breaths, knowing her father would survive but realizing what she had just done. She turned around, her father's punishment was a problem she would deal with later. Everything that Rosalyn had done for Emmy in the past was dwarfed by her need and vulnerability in this moment.

Rosalyn bent down to Emmy's level, the helplessness of her situation threatening to overwhelm her. She picked Emmy up by her torso and cradled her like a child. She had tried to help her, to get her to safety, to get her away from her father. Thick blood seeped into her sleeve; though between Emmy and her father's damage to her arm, she could not tell whose blood she felt. Tears welled up in her eyes, and she made an unsuccessful attempt at keeping them at bay.

"I'm sorry," she said again. Rosalyn knew she could say more, yet all words but those escaped her.

"This is not your fault," Emmy managed.

"I have to make sure you're safe," Rosalyn whimpered. "I'll take you home."

Emmy nodded, then closed her eyes.

It was a fragile hope that willed Rosalyn to pick Emmy up and leave the room. Emmy was strong. If she could hold on, then Rosalyn could still save her. Emmy would never be allowed in battle again, and Rosalyn could rest knowing that Doranen would keep her safe from any further harm.

The castle and the forest passed by her in a blur. She knew she had started running, carrying Emmy's tall, limp body in her arms. The people, the walls, and even her physical limitations seemed to fade away, erased by adrenaline and determination. She felt like she was disappearing, as though the body that ran was separate from her mind. Valandyl seemed both far and close, her sense of time and distance contorting into a jumbled mess.

And then the world stopped.

Emmy was gone. She knew without having to check as if she felt Emmy's soul pass through her own on its way out. Rosalyn let her knees drop out beneath her, and placed Emmy on the ground in front of her. After a few moments of silence, Rosalyn released her grief. A scream that captured her anger and mourning resounded through the quiet forest. It was a shame that such a scream went unheard, as it was the most desperate cry for help that Rosalyn had ever uttered. She let her head fall into her hands, sobbed, and rocked herself back and forth.

Her sobs were reduced to tears and whispered apologies until her body pulled her up to continue her journey. Doranen deserved to have her back, Emmy deserved to be returned home, and Rosalyn could do this last thing for them both.

CHAPTER 30

Rosalyn arrived just before dawn. The sky was lilac above her and streaked with clementine orange at the horizon. She made her way towards the palace unencumbered due to the battle and her early arrival. The town felt still, awaiting word about the outcome of their attack on Helios. Under lighter circumstances, Rosalyn would have chuckled at the irony of their halt in information, only to have the Princess of the enemy kingdom in their midst. She walked to where she and her father had been greeted on her first visit to Valandyl and was met by a nightguard.

"State your business," the guard said. He looked half asleep. Most likely on his second shift of the night, Rosalyn thought to herself. Emmy's face was buried into Rosalyn's shoulder, but the guard noticed parts of Rosalyn's tattoo.

"Bring your king out, now," she ordered.

As the guard ran inside, Rosalyn felt a tug at her heart that pointed out how much she sounded like her father. Her harsh tone, the expectation that her order would be followed, and the fear she instilled were trademarks of his. She knew that she was becoming more like him every day she spent in Helios, with only her love for Emmy and Azrael to pull her back. However, they could no longer help her, and once she gave Emmy to her father, her connections outside of Helios would be gone.

Rosalyn paused, focusing on the girl in her arms. "You are home now," she coddled. "My father can't hurt you anymore."

As she waited for Doranen, the exertion of the last day

hit her with force. Emmy's body felt heavy in her arms, to the point that she crumpled under the weight. Her feet throbbed as she realized that she had walked from Helios to Valandyl. Pain and exhaustion hit her at once, only made worse by the thought of making the return trip.

With his sword drawn, the guard returned with Doranen and the Prince of Tadane close on his heels. "Put her down, and step away."

Rosalyn laid Emmy down on the marble floor with caution and backed away with her arms raised in surrender. Doranen rushed to the body, while Azrael searched Rosalyn for an explanation.

"I brought her back," she muttered.

"You brought her..." Doranen's voice trailed off as he saw his daughter's wound and grasped her condition. He shook her as if it would revive her. "Emmy? Emmelina!"

Doranen picked her up and held her, shaking her every so often, still hoping that it was a cruel trick. He wept into Emmy's hair. His anguish was despairing to watch, as he held the body of his only child.

Azrael cleared his throat, "What have you done?" He fought his grief, only to be taken over by rage.

Words sputtered out of Rosalyn's mouth, but none formed a complete thought. Between Doranen's sorrow and her own, coherent thoughts seemed beyond her. "I couldn't... My father... I tried... She's dead."

"I can see that." Azrael's anger was building at such an astronomical rate that she half expected him to get violent. "How could you?"

Rosalyn stopped, "You think I did this."

"I thought I knew you," Azrael said under his breath. "And now this."

Doranen let out a lamenting howl, pulling his daughter's body closer. His voice broke, "She was my world."

Tears burned in Rosalyn's eyes and fell down her cheeks. She had cried the whole journey here until she thought she had no tears left, yet seeing and hearing Doranen's heartbreak renewed her agony.

"You just keep on killing everything good, that's your way."

"Azrael," she urged. "I didn't do this."

"You took her, she's gone."

He looked towards Emmy's body, the first signs of grief passing over his face. Rosalyn knew without having to read his mind, that he saw memories of his friend and part of him tore open. It was the realization that the memories he had of her were all he would ever have, locked away in the past. His fist closed, and he tried to keep his face blank.

"Leave."

"Azrael, I didn't..."

"I said go!" he interrupted. Azrael cast a glance at Doranen and Emmy, then grabbed Rosalyn and pulled her away from them. "I'll not start a war, and you've done enough damage. Go, before I kill you myself."

He cast her away from them, though she felt the force of Valandyl behind him.

Her head pounded, her throat felt as though she had been strangled, and pain coursed through her to the point that she would have believed her blood had been replaced by venom or some kind of poison yet she ran. She ran because Azrael would be after her soon. She ran because no matter how hard she wished, Valandyl was not her kingdom and she had to return home. But above all, she ran to escape the blame they placed on her.

Though the capital of Helios was still far off, she collapsed when she reached the line of trees that marked the border between Valandyl and her father's kingdom. The guards that patrolled the border would find her and take her back to life at her father's side. He would punish her, her brother would pity and comfort her, but life would go on in Helios as if nothing had happened and no one had died. Yet, the tears that fell into her hair and the forest floor told her otherwise.

Azrael's voice and Doranen's screams rang in her head. They blamed her for Emmy's death. She had tried to defend herself, but she was guilty in their eyes the minute they realized Emmy's condition. They saw her as the dark elf destined to turn and betray their trust. Her love for them, the blood she had sacrificed; none of it mattered when confronted with an idea that was easier to accept than the truth.

The brush scratched at her raw skin, yet getting up felt impossible. She cried out for help but knew that there were no guards near the area. In her head, she prayed for someone to find her or death, whichever would come quicker. It was not long before she passed out from sheer exhaustion, her mind now quiet.

CHAPTER 31

Rosalyn was awake, she was sure of it. However, she laid in her bed dreaming away Emmy's death. Emmy's last words told Rosalyn that her death was not Rosalyn's fault. In her dream, she saw Emmy getting out of the room when she had told Emmy to run. Emmy would have made it to the south hallway, where no one would be and would have escaped out the kitchens. The forest would have been overwhelming, but all the patrol guards would have been called to defend the castle and she would have found her way to safety.

While her face burned, Rosalyn found the rest of her body shivered. She willed her arm to move but found her body unresponsive. The wrap around her left arm reminded her that magic was not an option. Every time she tried, it felt like lifting a heavy object with a broken bone, weak and near impossible. Before she could drag herself to get the blanket, she felt the same blanket brush up her leg, down the curve of her hip, and came to rest on her shoulder.

"I'm sorry about your friend," Dorian commented. When he received no response from his sister, he sat on the bed next to her. He urged her further, "Rosalyn? Did you hear me? I said I'm sorry about what happened."

She had heard him, but he only reminded her further of what she tried to push away. He reached out his hand, hesitant to how she would react. She chose not to do anything. If her brother dared to take her hand, she would not resist. However, if he let her be, then she would go back to her dreaming.

Dorian took it and stroked it with his own calloused hand.

Rosalyn had cried all she could in the past few days but felt all the build-up of emotion and pressure in her face as if she were crying again. "He killed her. She was in his way, so he got rid of her."

She paused, her tone changing to one of matter-of-factness. "If I defy him, he beats me down. If I befriend someone he disapproves of, they are eliminated. He always wins."

"It's a trait that I pride myself on," Lucan interrupted, appearing at the end of her room. Despite the shock experienced by his children, his body lounged against the wall. He looked unconcerned with his daughter's condition and carried a sarcastically calm disposition.

Rosalyn sat up, "You control everything about me."

She exhaled the best she could, as she looked back at all her father had done to make sure she was the heir he wanted. The stone walls of the room closed in around her, with her father growing more significant in her mind. He was the gauntlet, the funnel her life had been filtered through. Emmy had threatened that dynamic, so she had to be dealt with.

She only realized that she had started shaking when Dorian grabbed onto her shoulder to steady her, looking her over with a worried expression in his brown eyes. "Father, I think she needs to talk to someone."

Rosalyn did not want to talk to anyone, and, by the eye roll her father exhibited, he concurred with her that it would be a waste of time. This was a dispute between father and daughter, one that Rosalyn believed would go on forever. Dorian was fretting. While endearing, she did not need his pity or concern. She fought through her weakness, shoving her brother away from her with her magic.

Dorian looked betrayed, "I'm just trying to help."

Lucan pulled his son by his shirt, shoved him through the door, and slammed it in his son's face.

"Walk away," he boomed.

Though they could not see his face, Dorian's disappointment could be felt from inside. He walked away from the room and the situation with heavy steps.

Rosalyn pulled her legs close, "You killed the Princess of Valandyl because she was friends with me."

"She would have been a danger in the future," Lucan replied. "And she was causing too much trouble with you now."

"You've won." Rosalyn did not know what he had won, all she knew was that that was the phrase that kept repeating in her head. She felt powerless, meanwhile, her father looked as he did whenever he came home from a victory.

Lucan straightened his tunic, "I need you by my side."

"You've said that before," she droned.

"I have," Lucan said, nodding. "What I haven't said, is how hard I intend to fight to keep you there. I've only won when I don't have to worry about you running off when I let go of your hand after I've raised it in the air. I've won when you accept who you are meant to be, who I am training you to be."

He paused, his face softening. Lucan waltzed over to the bed, sat down, and held out his hand. "Let me see your arm."

She did not relinquish her arm right away, fearing her father would hurt her. When she did extend her arm, her father held it gently and unwrapped the bandage to inspect the damage he had done to it.

"Are you going to punish me?" she asked.

Her father did not look up, "I haven't decided yet."

She did not like his vagueness but knew that prodding for more information would be a fruitless endeavor. Rosalyn watched her father handle her mangled tattoo with unusual delicacy and found her fear subsiding. He would punish her if he wanted to, but whatever punishment he enacted would not compare to the pain she already felt. Her friend was dead, her father was disappointed in her, and she was hated. Nothing seemed to matter curled up amongst her bedsheets. "I came to you when loving them hurt more than I could bear. But this feels worse."

"I told you that they would betray you," her father commented. She had half expected him to sound prideful, yet his tone was as if he were repeating a fact. "Nothing good can come from them."

She matched her father's tone, "Emmy is dead, and Azrael hates me. I don't know what to fight for or what to believe in."

With prompt quickness, Lucan let go of her hand and stood up. "I won't punish you. You've learned your lesson." He wiped his finger across his mouth, then pointed to her as if he were scolding her. "As for your conundrum, you fight for your kingdom and you believe in your family."

Rosalyn did not feel like fighting, and she did not think herself capable of believing in her father. He had taken everything from her all her life. She hated how nothing was ever good enough, and hurting her was the only response he seemed to have to her presence in his life. When she did something that pleased him, he hurt her with his callousness and his demand for something better. Yet when she did something wrong in his eyes, her wrongdoing consumed him.

She wanted to hate him, but, seeing her father standing in front of her, he seemed to be the only object with any permanence. Rosalyn tried to force the world away but felt shackled to her father and her role. Her face flushed and her legs kicked in frustration. Beneath her irritation was the slow grasp that bending to her father's will was the only way she would feel a sense of home and her father's love. Her brother had managed to find a way to keep his kindness while obeying her father. The influence of Vestans felt far away, yet her father loomed over her.

It was not easy, but Rosalyn pulled herself out of bed. Her hands were limp at her sides, her shoulders straight, and she leveled her chin with the floor. Removing all defiance and rebellion in her voice, she asked, "What do you want from me?"

"I want you to keep asking that question." Her father cupped her face in his large hands. "To be mindful of my answers. I am your father and I am your King. You will do what I say from now on."

He patted one of her cheeks, then walked towards the door. Lucan paused before leaving, "Now, be a dutiful daughter and say, 'Yes, father.'"

Despite her reluctance, she uttered the words with surprising ease.

"Yes, father."

CHAPTER 32

Five Years Later

Lucan ambled his way to the library, where his daughter was reported to be spending her time. While he knew every inch of his castle, he had not walked the path to his library in decades, perhaps centuries. He did not read often, and, when he did, he had the book sent for. However, Rosalyn had taken to hiding herself away there and he wanted to catch her off guard.

It had been years since her trip to Valandyl, years without so much as a minor refusal from her. He had trained her as he had Dorian, and, despite the years of catch up, she had surpassed him in most areas. The training also set the groundwork for the image he was crafting for her both in and outside of the kingdom. No matter the test or conditioning, his daughter excelled in all areas. He wanted to be proud.

Instead, her success made him anxious.

Rosalyn had never gone this long without incident. As he went through his day, he found his suspicions nagging at him and kept him from focusing on his work. As he approached, he studied her for echoes of rebellion. The books she had piled on the table in front of her were histories, though her face was blank and she saw past the pages.

"All these dusty, old books and you can't find one you like?"

She did not lift her head but cast a glance up at him before returning to her book. With an aggravated sigh, she closed it and tossed the book in the direction of the stack. "It appears not."

Lucan surveyed the room for anyone, only finding the caretaker of the library on the far end of the room. His hand migrated to Rosalyn's shoulder, "What troubles you?"

"I'm fine," she replied.

She pushed her chair back, gathered her books and walked away from him. The building seemed to elongate itself to accommodate her desire to be left alone. He followed her regardless, running his fingers across the spines of the books on the shelves. The dust he had mentioned in passing when he entered the room caught on the pads of his fingers. As he wiped it away, he regretted not just sending for his daughter to a place of his choosing.

She stopped, "Is there something you need from me?"

Lucan raised an eyebrow at her tone, feeling his frustration peaking. He had asked for her to be mindful of his demands, and she had obeyed all that he had put to her. However, he was uneasy, expecting defiance over every decision. That was her way. Yet, his daughter remained passive. He suspected a grudge or worse a plot against him.

"I need honesty."

Rosalyn tapped on a book in her hand, "Honesty, father?"

"Ever since your unplanned trip across the border, I have noticed a change in you."

Her straight face only served to aggravate him further. His daughter's voice turned obliging, "Tell me what you disapprove of and I will change such behavior."

He gestured in her direction, "You see, it is this calm facade that confuses me. Your obedience is often short-lived. I'm worried that your current behavior is masking something sinister."

"There is no facade so your confusion is unwarranted."

She put her books away without haste and then walked up to him. Her arms were at her sides, her tone was nonthreatening, yet her eyes challenged him. "Is there anything else that you need from me?"

Lucan smirked. He put his arm around his daughter's shoulder, walked her to the nearest wall, and then cast one more glance at the caretaker of the library. It was the smallest defiance in her eyes. He dug his nails into his palm to fight the urge to tear those eyes out. Rosalyn searched him for an explanation and tried to pull away from him but he held her by the collarbone.

"Father?"

He grabbed his daughter by the neck and shoved her against the bookcase. The books around her fell to the floor, causing the caretaker to fret over the damage done by Rosalyn's body and the journey downward.

Lucan flexed his marked hand.

The man howled, which made Lucan laugh. A weak old immortal with nothing but books to watch over.

"Your Majesty, please."

"The books will survive. I will have to decide your fate, Woolf, if you don't keep to your own business."

Lucan glared at him to back away, which he did with a groan.

Meanwhile, Rosalyn grabbed at him and made frantic attempts to grab at the shelf around her when his grip was unrelenting. When she looked around for help, he pulled her face back towards him by her jaw.

"I would prefer that you dispel of any plots against me and you be outright with your intentions." When she struggled to breathe, he threw her across the room. "You are a Lassehelin. You will tell me of your true motives."

She rubbed her neck and her breathing came out in gasps, "I have none."

"I mean it," Lucan said through gritted teeth. "Fight me fairly, or don't fight at all."

"I will not fight."

Lucan eyed her left hand, "Why?"

"What would be the point?" she yelled. Rosalyn straightened her clothes, then her posture. "I have no plots. You successfully separated me from the Vestan Prince, and you killed Doranen's daughter. They were my attempts at fighting you, and I lost. I am not calm, what you see is resignation. You want your heir, then you have her. I'll do whatever you want me to do."

Lucan smiled and walked over to his daughter. She took a step back, her neck straightening. Beads of sweat grew on her forehead, yet she did her best to hold her composure. "You have no idea how pleased I am to hear that."

Rosalyn clenched her jaw, "I will ask again, is there anything else that you need from me?"

"No," he answered. Lucan patted his daughter's shoulder, a bright smile infecting his face. "You have given me all that I could have hoped."

She put on her cloak and bowed to her king, "I'll be in my room."

Lucan wanted to say that his daughter's answers had calmed him, but, as she walked away, his body was still tense. Her anger was useful. The fact that she was obedient pointed to her value in future endeavors. Her magic would be a boon when he deemed it appropriate. And her recent loyalty made him want to hope. However, he replayed his interrogation in his head and knew there was something that would keep him coming back.

CHAPTER 33

Rosalyn exited the library, trying to hold in her emotions. Her hands trembled. The feel of her father's muscular arm still caused her pain, and the sound of her coughing resounded in the hallways. Everyone heard her cough, she was sure of that, but no one dared to look at her. Her head stayed low, only watching the people she passed from the occasional upward glance and the spaces between her hair.

She felt the familiar change in the air that told her Kieran had started tailing her. The soft sound of fabric apart from her own clapped against itself, and the chink of his sword hitting his chainmaille. She did not say anything and neither did he, walking in agreed silence. When they arrived at Rosalyn's room, they entered and Kieran closed the door behind them.

"Do I detect the signs of your father's affection?" Kieran asked.

Rosalyn turned around, her brow furrowed. Her hands began to shake, and she buried them in the folds of her cloak. Kieran ambled his way over, pausing in front of her. He reached up, unhooked her cloak, and peeled it away just enough to reveal the red on her neck from where her father grabbed her.

"May I ask what happened?"

Rosalyn took a step back, slipping her cloak off and placing it on her chair. The physical contact did not bother her. What bothered her was that he knew her well enough to know to look for marks on her. She missed the years when she could hide the damage her father did. However, a part of her was relieved that someone had noticed.

"I'd rather you didn't," she mumbled. "The King was just in a foul mood. It was bad luck that I ran into him."

Kieran scratched his head and shrugged, "I think your luck will change."

"Possibly," she said without conviction.

Rosalyn made her way over to the wood desk and took out one of the books that rested against the wall. Her eyes flicked towards Kieran, seeing his reluctance to leave. The position of his feet, strong yet eased, and his visible hesitation to make conversation were endearing in a way.

He took a step towards her, "Do you have any plans to-night?"

"I imagine that I will just stay in. You?"

"I'm on duty."

Rosalyn nodded, expecting Kieran to carry on with the conversation but he had shut his mouth. He took another step forward, bridging the gap between them. The heat from his breath made her look up, only to realize how little space he had left. Had she been facing him, the edges of their boots would have been touching. She felt her heart rate increase, and her instincts telling her to be wary. The door was behind Kieran, making it so that she would have to climb over her desk or push Kieran out of the way to reach it.

"You're skittish today," he chuckled.

"My nerves are shot."

"I could help with that."

"How?"

"Not every touch from a man has to be a hard one," Kieran whispered. He reached out and caressed her arm with the back of his fingers. "Some can be gentle."

Rosalyn forced herself to breathe, "Please don't."

"Why?" he asked, without stopping.

"I don't like to be touched." The edge in her voice and strong glare should have made him panic, but he smirked in-stead.

"I could change that," he offered.

She pushed herself away from him, not any closer to the door but far enough to get away from his hand. "You're making me uncomfortable."

Kieran scratched his head again, drawing Rosalyn's attention to the pulsing vein in his forehead. He followed her deeper into the room. "So, your father mistreats you and the minute someone tries to offer you a gentle hand, you refuse it?"

"Yes," she argued, backing up as he got closer. "And the reasons for it are my own."

Kieran's body flexed and his skin turned red, except the white of his knuckles. Everything in Rosalyn told her to run, that his anger would erupt and it would be no different from her father's displays of anger. If she could squeeze into the space between her guard and the bed, she could break free of him.

She lunged forward, only half looking where she was going. Her father had already hurt her today, she could not take another outburst directed at her. The door seemed in reach, her hope peaking and her internal voice repeating "just get to the door."

All breath escaped her, and Rosalyn felt pain radiate from the back of her head outwards. It was only after the impact of the blow subsided did she process what had happened. Kieran had caught her around the waist and had slammed her against the opposite wall. He used his body to pin her in place and grabbed both her arms.

"I tried to be kind," he began before she could scream. "I would have been good to you, but you wouldn't have it."

Her throat was like stone, and her voice came out in a feeble whisper. "Let me go."

"Here is my new proposal. No magic. And you tell Dorian about this, and I'll have my men kill him."

Rosalyn's eyes widened. Kieran had been around her long enough to know that Dorian was the only person left to threaten, and she melted in his hand. However, she knew her brother was well guarded and had ample skill to protect himself.

As if hearing her thoughts, Kieran added, "And believe me, it will look like an accident. They've been shadowing him for months."

"I'll tell my father then," she threatened.

He shrugged. "It's your word against mine. Who do you think he'll believe? His disappointment for a daughter, who fell in love with Vestans and used them to garner his attention? Or me? A soldier of exemplary record, who has proven his kindness with his daughter on many occasions?"

Rosalyn was well acquainted with the feeling of helplessness, her father made her feel it every time he scolded her. This time, her body felt paralyzed. She knew that she could use her magic to force him off her, but her mind focused on Dorian. None of his friends or fellow soldiers were new, which pointed to the genius of Kieran's threat. His men were undetectable, and therefore everyone could be a threat.

She let her arms relax and Kieran let them go, resting his hands on the wall behind her. Her eyes moistened and her mouth scrunched up. Tears would not fall from her eyes, she determined. She would not let the man see the damage he was causing. He would feel vindicated like he had conquered her, and she would not give him that.

"What do you want from me?" Rosalyn submitted.

"Freedom." He paused and inspected her body with fresh eyes. "Freedom to explore."

With an odd softness about him, he kissed her full in the mouth. His body arched over hers as he pulled her close to him. She did not want him, but her lips moved with his of their own accord. Kieran was experienced, and she hated herself for noticing such a thing. She ripped her mouth away from his before she could feel anything else.

"I don't want this," she whispered.

He ran his hands over her hair, "In time you will."

"And what if I don't?"
"In time you will," he repeated with an edge to his voice.

CHAPTER 34

Rosalyn felt Kieran's hands lift her dress up above her knees and squirmed deeper into the alcove. All he had done was kiss and touch her for the past week, but it was more than enough to bring her to tears when she was alone. She did not want him anywhere near her and felt like a hypocrite when his unwanted advances made her feel something akin to pleasure. It was a reaction to stimulation, she told herself, though the logic brought her little comfort.

His body pressed her against the wall, and he went for another attack on her mouth. One hand stayed under her skirts, while the other grabbed a clump of her hair to steady himself. She tried not kissing him back, which only made him kiss her cheek and down her neck. His hand slithered out from under her dress and traced the edge of her neckline. She prayed that someone, anyone, would walk by and stop them. If they were interrupted, she could try to find her brother or an excuse to get away. It was a stalling tactic, but at least he would be stopped long enough for her to recover.

She heard footsteps from the hallway and felt washed with relief. As they got closer, she tried to catch a glimpse but Kieran pulled her face back towards him.

"Make a sound," he whispered, "And your brother will pay for it."

Kieran did not turn around but did his best to hide his actions. He pulled at Rosalyn's sleeve until it covered the corin on her hand, then pressed it against the wall to keep her pinned. His other hand slipped around her neck and blocked her face from view with his own.

Her body tensed.

Her skin felt weak from trying to hold in her panic.

A scream would have brought the stranger over, but she buried it deep inside her.

"Get off her!" A voice yelled like a crack of thunder.

Kieran's weight lifted off her, and he was thrown behind her rescuer. The familiar short brown hair of her brother was the first thing she saw, before grasping that someone had stopped Kieran from touching her. Kieran fell into the hands of soldiers ready for him, and Dorian followed them.

Her father came into view barking out orders. "Take this pathetic wretch away! Tie his hands back."

Though she was not the target of his rage, Rosalyn shrunk down into the corner and put her arms above her head. Kieran grunted as he struggled to get back at her. Between Kieran and her father, she lost the ability to distinguish who was yelling. She heard the soldiers scuffle off, Kieran's protests dying in the enormousness of the hallway.

Then, it was quiet.

Soft steps advanced towards her.

She peeked between her arms and saw a man that looked like her father, yet he wore a gentle expression. He extended a hand down to her.

"Rosalyn, come with me," Lucan instructed without force.

For a second, she did not believe that he was there or that she was. The walls were cold against her back. She wanted to scream, as she had wanted to do for the last week. Her father's voice was different and he was trying to help her, but she wanted him to leave her there on the floor.

Lucan's hand flexed, reminding Rosalyn that his hand was still there for her. She took it and was whisked out of the alcove. Her father walked towards the narrow hallway that led to his bedroom, wrapping his arm around her and moving her away from anyone who walked past.

Though she had not been in her father's room in years, it

looked unchanged. Lucan sat her down on the plush grey comforter, grabbed a nearby blanket from the large wooden chair at his desk, and wrapped it around Rosalyn's shoulders.

"How did you find us?" Rosalyn asked.

Lucan pulled the chair over and sat down opposite his daughter. "Dorian stumbled on to you both a few days ago, but we had to have proof."

"He confronted me about it," she mumbled.

Lucan nodded, "And he didn't believe you when you said nothing was wrong."

Rosalyn pulled the blanket tighter around her shoulders, as all the emotions she had been suppressing bubbled to the surface. She wanted to break something, cry, and scream all at once. Instead, her body shook and she crumpled the blanket into a tight ball. She pressed the ball tighter, growing frustrated when it reached its limit. When it would not budge, she ripped the blanket off of her and cast it aside, burying her face in her hands.

Her father sighed, then peeled her hands away. His voice was soft, "Why didn't you come to me?"

"He threatened Dorian," she answered.

Lucan stood up and walked to the open door. Fresh air crept into the muggy room and pricked at Rosalyn's skin. Aldan was waiting like a loyal hound outside, attentive to Lucan's demands.

"The prince may be in danger, go see to his safety."

"Yes," Aldan bowed, "Your Majesty."

Aldan rushed off and Lucan turned back towards his daughter, deciding to keep the door open. She had not moved an inch, except to watch his movements. Her father returned to his seat and wiped his face. He would not say it, but his stress could be heard as he sighed. Regardless of his concern for her and his son, he would not want to deal with this situation much longer.

She turned her face away from him, "He said you wouldn't believe me."

Her father's head popped up, "That's ridiculous."

Rosalyn flinched, expecting her father to get angry. Maybe she should have confided in him when Kieran's advances started, but she had believed bringing this to her father would have been yet another strike against her. Even if he believed her, she thought he would find it tedious, telling her to either deal with it or enjoy Kieran's attention.

"I thought he was right."

She could not have predicted the concern he had shown when he found her, nor could she have foreseen the shock on his face now.

"You thought that I wouldn't believe that you were being assaulted?" he said in disbelief.

"A long time ago, I was with a Vestan and you didn't believe that I could be happy with him. Why would you believe that I was miserable with a dark elf? Kieran was from a good family, and was without incident until now."

Lucan hesitated, searching for words.

"He is locked away," Dorian announced, entering the room. "And he won't bother you again."

Rosalyn shut her eyes, breathing a sigh of relief. "Thank you."

Lucan lifted her chin up, "If this ever happens again, you tell me and I will stop it immediately. You are my daughter."

Rosalyn nodded, then bowed her head under the stares from the two men. She fingered the neckline of her dress that felt as if it was loose enough to fall off of her and tight enough to strangle her at the same time. Her father's room was stifling, and she wanted to retreat back to her own. Her face flushed.

"You're shaking," Dorian observed. Her brother took another glance over her body before reaching a hand out to steady her. "Rosalyn, how far did he go with you?"

The question weakened the last bit of resolve she had, and she managed to get her words out but only through broken sobs. "Tonight would have been the first time that we..."

Dorian's hand felt like a crushing weight on her shoulder, and she slithered away from him and her father. She did not want her brother's hand or anyone touching her. Her breathing came out in shallow gasps. Sleep called to her, and she wanted nothing more than to curl up amongst her blankets.

"I just want to go to bed," she groaned.

Lucan stood, "Dorian, take her to her room and see that she is settled."

He turned towards his daughter and ushered her to the door.

"I will find you a new guard," he urged. "I will personally see that he is vetted thoroughly."

"Thank you," she mumbled, but it was lost as she left the room.

It did not take long for Dorian to pick up on her disdain for physical contact. Her skin recoiled from his first attempt, and she threw his hand off her before she realized what she was doing. She wanted to wrap her arms around herself but her body seemed to fade away as she neared her room, and, she wondered were she to surrender to the weightlessness, if she would float away until she forgot herself entirely.

The warmth of her breath on her hand brought her back down, her knuckles covering her mouth. She did not remember lifting it or much of the trip from her father's room to her own, but she heard the click of her door as the bolt was unlocked.

"How did you know?"

Dorian's head jerked up, startled at the sudden, yet monotone voice.

"That you were lying?" he clarified.

She managed to nod.

He hesitated, as though his answer was sure to hurt her. From the way he stood to the restlessness of his hands, her brother pitied her. She hated it, even though she knew it was his version of an apology.

"There are two types of lies. The ones you tell other people, and the ones you tell yourself. He was hurting you, and no matter how much you wanted to, you couldn't lie to yourself with enough conviction to make it go away."

She nodded again, then walked over to the trunk near her wardrobe. Opening the lid, she pulled out her nightgown and hoped Dorian would leave soon. He had done all he could to comfort her, but the only thing that would help her now was for her to be alone.

"Shall I stay tonight?" he asked. "I can have a cot brought in, I don't mind."

"No, that's not necessary."

His tone grew quiet but more endearing. "I would like to."

"He would check on me when he thought that I was asleep. I could always feel him standing over my bed, and stroking my hair. I would prefer to sleep alone for the first time in awhile."

"Alright," he conceded with a sigh. "Will you come see me in the morning?"

Rosalyn plopped the nightgown on the bed, then ushered her brother out of the room. "Of course," she added to take away the rudeness of her pushing him out.

He let her push him until the door, where he stopped and let his hands rest on the frame. His voice was dripping with regret, "Be honest with me. How long had this been going on for?"

Rosalyn shrugged without knowing why, "A week."

* * *

In bed, Rosalyn felt as though the world could swallow her up and she would not notice. Her breath had steadied at least. The blanket below her had spots from her crying, and she scratched at them. She had thought that being alone would make her feel better about what had happened. Yet, she found the loneliness only opened herself up to flashbacks. The week came at her intermittently, and she banged her fists against her temples.

Something moved across the room, which made her prop herself up.

The room was empty. She could have sworn she saw something, searching every item in her scope of vision. It felt as though someone else was in the room. She knew the person that she wished was there, but laid back down on the bed because that person would never appear. It was an echo she felt, and a ghost she longed for.

A thought began repeating in her head until it forced its way up her throat. "I wish you were here."

CHAPTER 35

The fire made it too warm in the library, but Rosalyn believed the protection she gained from long sleeves made up for the minor discomfort. She had come to the library for the past few weeks, trying to put the situation with Kieran behind her. Her father even had a chair made for her with extra cushions and armrests. He had not said anything. She came into the library one day, the caretaker had offered it to her, and she knew the origin at first sight.

Enough time had passed that she could be around people without them mentioning what happened or pestering her with questions about her mental state. If she heard one more pitying tone directed at her, she would scream. How they had found out about the whole incident she had not idea. She only let herself think of Emmy and Azrael when she was in her room. Outside, she belonged to her father and her tutors. The constant flashbacks to Kieran's actions and her friends made her avoid her room except to sleep.

The door at the end of the room creaked open and she smiled when her brother entered. His face tan from dirt and sun exposure. A natural smile grew on his face when he saw her, and he ran to her with the haste of a man newly rested and hugged her tight. After an extra squeeze, he let out a relieved sigh.

"How was your trip?" she asked.

"Uneventful and long," Dorian stressed. "I always hope that just once I won't have to deal with so much politics when I go to the Elestren, but what should I expect from a place meant for the politicians of the world."

"I'm just glad that I don't have to make the trip."

Dorian nodded, knowing her aversion to the Elestren.

A great idea, in theory, the Elestren was where representatives of every kingdom met to discuss problems and resolve conflicts. Her father hated dealing with the politicians in the Three Kingdoms, having to deal with the conflicts of an area that was not his own was his idea of torture. However, what sealed his hatred of the Elestren and sparked Rosalyn's was her mother had retreated to the Elestren after her flight from Helios. Lucan handed the task off to his son, who was willing to take the journey if it spared everyone from a chance reunion with Rosalyn's mother.

Dorian made a vague gesture towards the door, "Have you eaten yet? I'm starving."

"You go," she said. "I'm not hungry."

Her brother raised an eyebrow, a clear skepticism on his face. "Have you eaten today?"

"No," Rosalyn murmured.

"Then I will have to drag you to the dining room," he said with a smirk.

Rosalyn relaxed, "Fine."

She knew her brother meant well, and he would be hungry after his journey home. With a quick gesture, she ushered him towards the door but he stopped her. He clicked his tongue, and he reassured her with a playful smile.

"Did you think I had forgotten?"

Strapped to his shoulder was a tanned leather satchel, which he ruffled through and pulled out a book. It had been a tradition since his first trip to the Elestren to bring back a spell book for her. Few elves in the Three Kingdoms had enough magical power to have a use for spell books, so most libraries only had a few, if any. Dorian had surprised her on his first trip, and she had tried every spell within a week.

He wrapped his free arm around her and they walked out of the room, admiring the present. The spine and front cover were embossed with gold, and Rosalyn scanned through the stiff pages with wide eyes. Her mind was already thinking of how to perform the spells she saw.

"So I've decided something," Dorian began. His head raised and he strutted through the hallways with all the swagger of a man keeping a secret.

"And what is it you've decided?"

Though his body language did not change, his tone grew more serious. It was a tone he had been using with her all her life, but more so since the incident weeks ago. Inside the deep tone of voice, he showed his love for her.

"I would see you smile again."

His comment did just that, though she knew it was not the kind he was looking for. She put her hands behind her back, then asked, "And how would you do that?"

Dorian hesitated, "I have yet to decide."

She chuckled, "Your specificity in this matter gives me confidence."

They arrived at the dining hall and Rosalyn reached up to open the door. Her hand was intercepted by her brother, and she thought about pulling away but stopped when a different smile appeared on his face. He held her wrist without force, which made her calm down. "I promise you that I'll do what I can."

Dorian let go of her, and they both entered and made their way towards the large wooden table that was big enough to accommodate an entire feast but seemed barren and unnecessary for daily use. Elves would migrate to the table at all hours and servants stood attentive to those that sat down. One elf standing against the wall lifted himself off and approached them.

"Would either of Your Highnesses like anything specific?" he asked.

"Whatever the cook has prepared is fine with us," she assured. The man nodded, then she looked over to see her brother pulling out the chair at the head of the table. Dorian motioned for her to take it but she stayed where she was. The chair was reserved for her father and him alone.

"Oh, come on," Dorian urged. "He was deep into a meeting last time I checked. Besides, it will be your chair soon enough."

Rosalyn tiptoed over, still unsure, and sat down with all the care as if the chair was made of glass. Though her father was healthy, it was only a matter of time before she would rule. She did her best to ignore the future that awaited her. She looked around at the dozen or so people in the room and knew that eventually they would all look to her. Rosalyn shook her head and let the smell of food pull her out of her own thoughts.

She had not realized the deep-set chill in her body until she smelled the warm bread and sweet tomato stew from the plates of food that the servants brought to the table. Dorian attacked the bread first as if he had not eaten in days. When he paused to breathe, he looked around expecting to see that time had sped up around him.

He cast a sidelong glance at her, “Perhaps I’ll look for a husband for you.”

The dull thud of Rosalyn’s spoon falling on the tabletop was drowned out by Rosalyn’s laughter. “Good luck with that endeavor.”

“Have you given up?” he asked, with no threat or judgment.

She shrugged the question away, “Why would I need someone when I have you?”

“I missed you too.”

A tone in the room changed, and Dorian shifted in his chair.

“Is something wrong?”

“I’m fine,” Dorian replied, sounding tired. “I’m just glad to be back. You know I do my best work here.”

“Father isn’t there to scare you.”

“And you aren’t there to motivate me.”

Dorian’s focus turned back to his food and she let him

eat. No matter how mundane, these were the moments when she had missed her brother the most. When he was away, she realized how isolated she had become when she went about her day without him there. She reached over and took her brother's hand, which made him pause.

"It'll always be you and I," Dorian said in a low voice. "Together."

"Always?"

The desperation and fear in her voice surprised her, but she did not change her voice to make it go away. As though to match her tone, Dorian squeezed her hand tighter.

"I'll be right here at your side, always."

She smirked, "Well, in that case, maybe I should look for someone for you."

Dorian let out a laugh from deep in his throat. "How about we agree not to look for anyone for each other?"

"Fine by me."

"My children are enjoying themselves," Lucan said, appearing behind Dorian's chair. "What a rare sight."

Rosalyn froze, remembering where she was sitting and glared at her brother for encouraging her.

Dorian ignored the glare and smiled at his father. "It does happen on occasion."

"True." Lucan motioned for a plate of food and made his way around the table. "Though they are few and far between."

Rosalyn squirmed.

"No, you are already settled," Lucan said as he pulled out the chair next to her. "Besides, I think I can sit at your right hand for one meal."

The same elf who had interacted with them earlier brought another plate out but attended to his King with a slew of pleasantries. Rosalyn knew that her father hated the formality but enjoyed that the motivation for such flattery was that the man feared his king. The servant left with a low bow but was soon replaced by Aldan. The old man whispered in the King's ear, and Lucan groaned at the interruption.

"Father, you just sat down." Dorian watched Aldan leave, then returned his attention back to his father. "Surely whatever the business is can wait."

Lucan scoffed. "When you are the king, it seems as if all business can't wait. However, this business is not mine."

"Then what news has Aldan brought?" Rosalyn asked.

"Your new bodyguard has been selected."

Rosalyn's posture straightened, "And he's here?"

"Yes," Lucan said between bites and pointed towards Dorian with his fork. "And he has been vetted by everyone except your brother, who requested the privilege."

"Then that is my queue to leave," Dorian interjected. He dropped his spoon and got up. "Don't worry, the man has yet to impress me."

Dorian followed Aldan's path, leaving behind an awkward silence. Rosalyn and her father had avoided each other ever since the incident, refusing to discuss what happened further. She stirred her soup, but then resigned herself to the back of her chair.

"Have you met him?" Rosalyn asked when the silence became unbearable.

"I have, and I think he will do nicely."

She intertwined her fingers, "Whatever you think is best."

"Rosalyn..." Lucan tried to be caring, yet his voice came out as a low growl. "Though I punish you harshly, I do care for you and your happiness."

Rosalyn pushed her plate away with enough force to send the stew sloshing over the rim of the bowl. She shrunk back in her chair and looked away from the table to ignore the mess she had made.

"Of course," she tossed in her father's direction. "Is there anything else? This food is no longer appealing to me."

Her father let out a resigned sigh and gestured towards the door, "You are free to go."

She left without another word and ignored the tug inside her chest. An apology tried to force its way up her throat, but she fought it away. All she wanted was to get to her bedroom and shut the door, shut the world away.

CHAPTER 36

Rosalyn sat down in her chair, pulled her legs up onto the seat, and stared out her window at the grey clouds passing by. The door was closed, yet she knew that it was only a matter of time before someone would come in. She pretended that someone else was in the room with her, though even in her mind, she would not say her name. Rosalyn did not say anything, lest the echo of her voice would remind her that she was in fact alone.

The sound of footsteps in the hallway startled her, and she hoped that they would keep walking. When the pair of elves stopped at her door, she groaned. She had had at least some time to herself. There was a knock on her door, and her projected companion vanished from the room.

"Rosalyn?" her brother called from the other side. He knocked one more time, then opened the door.

Her voice felt small, "Yes?"

Dorian motioned for the elf behind him to stay back, then he entered the room. "Your new guardian is outside. Would you like to meet him?"

She stood up, "First, I want to hear what you think of him."

"He's kinder than your last one," he answered. "I think you will like him."

"Like him? Have you found a husband for me already?"

"Not like that," he assured.

Rosalyn hesitated, "But you trust him?"

Dorian walked over to her and put his hand on her shoulder. "I do, but if he does do anything, you know to tell father or I right away."

"I will," she replied without conviction.

"I'll bring him in." Dorian turned back towards the door, gestured for the man to enter, then escorted him further into the room. "Rosalyn, may I introduce Lord Codi Antien."

Lord Antien looked like every other dark elf, or so she told herself, though she felt an odd desire to look away. His face matched that of the men in her life, angular and set in a rigid position. His dark hair and eyes were the same hickory color as her own hair. It was as if someone had taken all the tropes of dark elves to create the abnormally common man standing in front of her.

Rosalyn nodded as if to answer a question Lord Antien had not asked. "A pleasure to meet you, Lord Antien."

"The pleasure is all mine, Princess Rosalyn," he said with a pleasant smile. The smile was the only original thing about him and shattered the mundane nature of the rest of him. "And you may call me Codi if that isn't too informal."

Inspired by his, she flashed a courteous smile. "Codi, then. Are you settling in well?"

"Of course, your father's attendants have been helpful and kind."

Rosalyn thought to herself that she never would have picked those words to describe her father's men, but she shrugged off the thought.

"That is good to hear," she added.

Codi cast a look towards Dorian, then looked at her like a puppy to his master. "Is there anything that you would like of me?"

"No, I don't..." she said shaking her head but stopped. Like his smile, there was a glimmer of something that made him seem unreal. As she stared at him, she could feel what could only be magic that forced her away. She should have noticed the magic earlier, and, now that she was aware of it, she focused that much harder on trying to see the face beneath.

The weight of Dorian's hand on her shoulder startled

her, and she realized that she had been staring for some time, without any sense as to how long, at a man she had only met minutes earlier. Dorian's eyes were laced with confusion, and she shook herself out of her skepticism.

"Are you alright?" Dorian asked when she did not say anything.

"Yes, I'm fine." She waved his hand and concern away. "May I have a moment to talk security with Codi?"

"Certainly." The hesitation in his voice was clear, but not enough to stop him from leaving the two alone. "I'm going to unpack from my trip."

Rosalyn watched her brother leave, waiting until she was sure that he was down the hall and there were no more prying ears. The muscles in her arm flexed, and she focused her magic and energy on shoving the man against the wall. He protested and grabbed at the air in front of him as if that could save him.

"What are you doing here?" she barked.

Codi's voice came out in harsh gasps, suggesting that he was being strangled though she knew that she had no pressure on his neck. "Your Highness, I don't know what you mean."

Her voice lowered to a growl, "I know who you are."

"You must have me confused with someone else," he sputtered.

She examined him once more, as he was pinned and unable to move. It took all her concentration, but she could see every detail in his face. That face had haunted her dreams, and it was one she thought she would never see again. She was not confused and plopped him down in front of the mirror to prove it.

"This spell works on Dark Elves, yes?" She asked, without expecting an answer. "That is your mistake."

Rosalyn spread her feet to a shoulder-width apart and searched her body for the magic required.

The man stood up wearily, "I don't understand."

"You will," she responded. She reached out, her palms

open, and found the glamour that surrounded him. The words that came out of her mouth were from no language that she knew of, only that when she read it in books part of her knew how to say them.

The magic that had latched onto Codi's body was powerful. Her hands were half closed as if she were clawing at something. She tore his glamour off in thin strips to reveal long blonde hair and a soft face that contrasted with every other face in Helios. Standing before her was Prince Azrael of Tadane.

"How did you know?" he asked after she released the glamour back into place.

"You forget. Dorian's mother is a dark elf, mine is not. You better pray that I'm the only one with mixed blood that sees you."

She pulled on his arm to get him up and then shoved him towards the door. "Whatever you are doing here, you end it and you return to your own kingdom."

With a flick of her left hand, she opened up the door and gave a short but final shove on Azrael's back. He left in confusion, and she slammed the door behind him.

Her mind filled with questions. What was he doing here? Where did he get the magic for a spell like his glamour? And how could he risk his life like this by infiltrating Helios alone? She did not expect to get answers to any of them, and none of them screamed in her head as the one taking over. After all she had been through and all she had done to forget her past, why did he have to show up just when she was forgetting about him?

CHAPTER 37

Azrael grabbed the library door as it was opened from the inside, smiling at those exiting but tapping on the door's frame when they did not move quick enough for him. The interview process had him questioning the spell's capability to hide him, but he had relaxed by the end of it. Now, the elf that was the reason for his infiltration could see him. He had thought of retreat, and he was not ready to dismiss that option. There was still a chance with the right persuasion that Rosalyn would keep quiet.

The sound of his steps was dulled by the stone floor as he walked through the shelves of books. Though she did not look up, he knew Rosalyn was aware of his presence. She sat in her library chair almost every day and knew the footsteps of everyone who came in. She adjusted her position in the chair, closed her book, but kept her eyes down.

"May I speak with you?" he asked.

"About what?"

Azrael shifted his weight from one foot to the other, "You know what."

"I haven't the faintest idea," she lied. Her head rose to reveal a facetious smile. "Perhaps you could shed *light* on the subject."

Azrael had hoped to remain calm, but she was toying with him. Even the glove on her left hand seemed more like a taunt than a precaution, and he was not about to believe that she could turn against her father after so many years away from Vestan influence. He looked around for any elves that were left, finding the caretaker to be the only other soul besides Rosalyn.

He walked over to the man and forced charm. “I’ve been informed of a threat against Princess Rosalyn’s life, and it would be easier to brief her here. Do you mind giving us the room?”

The old man in drab grey robes scratched at his head. Azrael’s muscles weakened because of the man’s hesitancy. “That is most irregular,” the caretaker added and cast a glance toward Rosalyn.

“It’s alright, my lord,” Rosalyn acknowledged. “Please make sure we are not disturbed.”

Once the room was vacated, Rosalyn rested the book against one leg of her chair and stood up.

“Did I say something that hit a nerve?” The smile had not faded from her face, only teasing him further. "I thought I was being rather amusing."

The muscles in Azrael’s jaw clenched. Except for a slight tremor in his hands, he gave off no exterior signs of the seething anger inside him. Comments like hers could get him killed, though it did not come as a surprise since his first meeting with her had shown all her concern for him was gone. With a forced swagger, he walked over until his face was inches away from her and chuckled.

Azrael grabbed her by the neck and shoved her against the nearest wall. Once the shock wore off, Rosalyn reached up and pulled at his grip.

“You’ve gotten violent since I saw you last.” Her words were hardly distinguishable, but it was all she could muster until he let go of her.

“Believe me, I could show you just how violent I’ve become.”

Rosalyn exhaled, and he guessed it was the closest thing to a laugh that she could get out. “Oh, I wish you would.”

His eyes narrowed.

Azrael shoved Rosalyn against the wall again and pinned her in place. She cried out when her head hit the stone, and she breathed through the pain. Once it subsided enough for her thoughts to clear, her breathing turned into full laughter. It was a laugh that masked something darker, but it unnerved him all the same.

"What is so funny?" he snapped.

"You actually think this will get me to talk or spill some big secret of Helios?" Her body relaxed, but her face turned dark. "Do you think this is the first time that I've been threatened? Or even the first time recently?"

He released his grip on her, "I don't need information."

"No, you want me to keep your identity a secret."

"You tell anyone and I will..."

"Threatening me will get you nowhere."

She stepped to her side and then walked deeper into the room, away from him.

"I won't tell anyone who you are if you tell me why you are here." She stopped, cocked her head, then flashed that same spiteful smile from earlier. "No, even better, I'll guess. It's because of me."

Azrael was uninterested in games, and this game risked his life. The only viable route he could see was to pull out, remove himself and take the losses for what they were. After all, he should have realized that the glamour spell would not work on Rosalyn. She had mentioned her parentage before, and he should have considered it a factor.

"My plan isn't for you to know," he announced. He saw the wheels of thought turning in her expression, and knew that she had not heard his declaration.

"No, it is because of me. If it was for information, they would have sent any other spy. The only thing that you have in common with Helios is me."

Azrael's palms began to sweat. He could feel her curiosity and confidence grow as she pieced his plan together. If he ran now, he could escape before Rosalyn and Lucan had time to lock down the castle. Longer if he could knock her out and lie to the librarian outside. He made for the door but felt

Rosalyn's magic stop him before he reached the middle of the room.

At first, he had thought Rosalyn's magic was an incredible gift. Now that she was using it against him, he found her "gift" irritating. He fought her hold on him, but it left him squirming in mid-air.

"It is because of me," she repeated. "Admit it."

She pulled him around and forced him against the same wall he had pinned her to a moment prior. As her face came into view, he saw that the smile had gone and was replaced by one of contemplation. The tone and volume of her voice dropped.

"Tadane or Valandyl could get information from far more relevant sources than me. Any of your spies could have told you that I'm not close with my father."

"We don't have spies."

The fire in her eyes flared up, reminding him that she could be fierce when she chose to. "Lying doesn't suit you, Lord Antien."

She said his name with obvious disdain as if it were a poison in her mouth.

"No," she began again. "You aren't here for information. Torture won't work on me and your clear disdain for me makes seduction not an option."

There was a pause then another realization, "Doranen sent you, didn't he?"

Azrael did his best to keep his face blank, though it was hard when she made such an accurate leap. "How could you possibly know that?"

"Because I know why you are here."

She let him go, letting him land on his feet as opposed to in her room when she dropped him on the floor. Her body resigned, and she rested her weight on the table edge near her. Her face drained of emotion, "You intend to kill me."

Though he was afraid of being discovered, the anger towards her and the anger that drove him to Helios made him tighten his fists. “I intend to kill Emmy's murderer.”

“Your hatred of me runs that deep?” she asked after she processed his words. She looked hurt, though he saw no reason that she should be. Rosalyn had brought this on herself, and he would not grant her his sympathies.

His mind flashed back to the last time Rosalyn was in Valandyl, a memory he relived often. He had visited Emmy a month prior and had no idea that that would be the last time he would see her. Emmy was beginning to forgive him for spending so much time away. Doranen’s screams seemed to be sewn to the inside of his ears, filling his mind whenever he thought of Emmy’s death.

Azrael reached out and grabbed her, “She was my friend.”

“Then do it.”

Rosalyn did not resist his outburst, nor did her tone carry any sense of defiance. He felt the familiar pang of guilt, though he soon realized that the guilt was not his but belonged to the woman in his arms.

He raised an eyebrow, "I've never met such a willing subject."

"Kill me," she demanded. She broke away from him, yet she did not run. "For I am not innocent. I have taken lives, and I have behaved in ways natural to Helios."

Azrael knew that meant something. He knew that he should care about the rest of her actions. Yet, it was Emmy's death that drove him. "Admit it. Admit to Emmy's death. Or is that the one thing you feel shame over? The one action you hide away."

"I will not admit to it because I didn't do it." She looked straight into his eyes, her chin raised and her diction overemphasized. "Would you care to know her last words? The last words your dear friend ever said."

He grabbed her by the neck, his own tempestuousness taking over. "I would though you have no right to utter them."

“She said, ‘Rosalyn, this was not your fault.’” Her voice

was strained, but clear.

Azrael wanted her to be lying, it would be easier if she was lying. He felt her guilt, the lack of confidence needed to sustain a lie. Her gaze did not waver, and she had stopped resisting.

"She said none of this was my fault," she said again when he let go of her throat. "I will not admit to her death, because to do so would mean that her last words were false."

He felt her magic again, this time on his hand. She forced him to grab the dagger at his waist and raised it so that the tip was on her neck. She let him go, but he kept his hand where she had placed it.

"Why?" he asked.

"The man I love hates me so much that he would kill me. I live in a prison of my father's making. And I walk by the man that took our friend from us every day and can do nothing about it. So kill me."

Desire with confidence was a dare. Guilt with confidence was a lie. However, he felt desire and guilt from her and that gave him pause. He had been convinced that Rosalyn had killed Emmelina, and part of him was not yet ready to give up that belief. She could have been a good liar, and she could have been telling the truth. There was enough doubt to get him to lower his weapon.

"No," he said and took a step back.

Rosalyn released the breath she had been holding and relaxed her posture. "Can't do it?"

"I don't know what to think," he admitted.

"Then I will make it clear," she snapped. "Do what you came to do or leave. While I will keep your secret, you will be in terrible danger should anyone else find out who you are."

She turned and left the room, much to his dismay and to the surprise of the caretaker outside.

CHAPTER 38

Rosalyn fingered the thin straps of her dress with her gloved hand, hoping that it was not Azrael walking towards her door. Dorian had a quicker pace, and he walked with a heavier gait than Azrael. She hoped that it was Dorian, taking his time and trying to walk with a lighter foot. However, she knew she was wrong long before Azrael gave a short knock then entered.

He did not say anything at first but paced in the space between her bed and the wall. The layers of clothes he wore to fight the winter chill contrasted so starkly with her own that she tried to cover herself to make up for it. She pulled her legs up on the chair, covered her legs with her skirt, and wrapped her arms around herself. Her bare arms and shoulders were rigid from the cold.

As he walked the room, she remembered the strides he made when they danced together. The muscles in her hands felt the echoes of her memory. She thought she would forget the softness of his hands on her skin or what it was like for someone to look at her in adoration. Azrael was a stranger to her now, yet, with the help of her father, she had tried to convince herself that she did not need what Azrael and Emmy gave her. They gave her back a part of her soul every time they were together and she had been living for too long without it.

"Have you thought any more about your mission?" she asked.

"I have."

"And what conclusion have you come to?"

"I just had a conversation with your father."

She chose not to hide her disapproval, "Why would you do that?"

Azrael stopped and took a deep, focusing breath. "After he talked to me about various security measures, I pretended that I was interested in Emmy's death. I had to act like I was happy that my friend was killed."

He wiped his forehead and scratched at his arms before pacing again. She knew his frustration better than most. It never got easier to lie to her father, but she knew that the first time had the most significant impact.

"It's not easy, is it?" she said without defiance or attitude.

Azrael threw his hands up in the air, "And then he just admitted to me that you weren't capable of doing it."

Her father would say that, she thought to herself. She rested her head on her fist, "Did he go on to say that it has only been recently that I've been making an improvement?"

"Yes," he agreed warily. "Were you listening?"

She shook her head. "No, I just know my father."

Azrael sighed, sat down across from her on the bed, and looked at her for the first time. "You tried to tell me in Valandyl. You said that you didn't kill her, and I didn't listen."

The weight of Azrael's gaze and words made her uncomfortable. She intertwined her fingers, looking away from him. "You and Doranen needed someone to blame. I can understand that."

"It was easier to blame you than accept that she was dead," he admitted. When she did not look at him, he shifted forward.

"Rosalyn," he said to get her to look at him. "I'm sorry that I didn't listen and that I blamed you. And, most of all, I'm sorry that I thought you were capable of killing Emmy."

All air seemed to escape from her lungs. She blinked away the tears that formed in the back of her eyes, forcing herself to breathe. Lucan had lied to the Three Kingdoms, making her the villain of Valandyl. She had given up on anyone believing that she had done all she could for Emmy, and never expected Azrael to apologize. Yet, here he was in her bedroom doing just that.

"Thank you," she responded. Her voice cracked, which made her wince. She took a breath to make sure her voice would not give her away. "It's all in the past now. Apologies won't bring her back."

"You've grown hard," Azrael remarked.

"It's what dark elves do."

"So you're becoming one of them?"

Rosalyn dropped her arms, grabbing the armrests of her chair. "Becoming? I've always been one of them."

Azrael stifled a laugh but shook his head. "No, you haven't."

Her strong facade faltered. Her father had trained her to be the type of dark elf that he wanted, though she had never believed she had it in her to please him. All her hard work for over a century to become what an entire kingdom wanted her to be and Azrael could tell she was failing. Despite what she was, she was no dark elf and she wondered if she ever would be.

"I've figured them out," she began. "At first, you see them and everything they do is wrong. And like an interrogation, they strip everything from you until all you are left with is your loyalty."

"And they are wearing you down?"

She thought he was judging her, only to look up and see his eyes were not condemning her but were concerned for her.

Her mouth opened to answer, but she refrained from giving that information up. She wanted to admit that, to scream down the halls that below her strength was someone who was breaking. Azrael had always managed to uncover her vulnerabilities when they were together, but this time was different. She had been under her father for long enough. Whether Azrael stayed or left, she would have to make a choice to either succumb to her feelings for Azrael or forget herself for her father.

“Are you going to kill me?”

“No,” he vowed.

“Then you should go,” she ordered. The mountain air blew the unlatched window open, and, rather than shut it, she got up to get a blanket. "The longer you stay, the more at risk you are. The consequences are unthinkable if you are discovered."

Rosalyn hoped that by turning away from him, he would take her advice and go.

"Wait, stop."

She turned around, only to find that he had moved closer to her instead of the door. He moved forward with cautious steps, unlike Kieran who had charged at her.

"Turn around."

Her brows furrowed, "Why?"

Azrael put his hands behind his back, "I won't hurt you."

His voice was soft, yet it broke her faster than any of the words yelled at her by her father. She did as she was told. The awkwardness of the situation was not lost on her, and she glanced back to see what had caught his eye.

“When did you get these?” he asked, staring at her back.

Rosalyn jerked away from him when she realized that the dress she was wearing exposed her scars. She made Emmy promise not to say anything only for her to reveal her own secret. Her frustration manifested in her quick foot stomp, before turning her attention back to Azrael.

“They happened a long time ago,” she excused.

Even though she had turned her back to the wall, Azrael stared at her as if he could still see them. He stammered, trying to figure out where they were from and why she hid them. When he found the words to speak, they were not in complete thoughts.

“Emmy said that you were punished,” he managed.

Rosalyn backed up against the wall, the cold surface startling against her skin. “Emmy told you? I begged her not to."

"What did you not want me to know?" Azrael took a step forward, then thought better of it. The volume of his voice was elevated, and she shrunk back. "That you were punished? My mother told me that before Emmy ever mentioned it."

She mumbled, "I didn't want you to know."

"Know what?"

"I didn't want you to know because if you knew what I did, then I thought you would never forget me. That you wouldn't move on.

"After decades apart, you made it clear that you still thought about us, despite the vehement opinions expressed by our parents. And maybe that's selfish to think that you would think about me that much, but I believed it at the time."

Azrael pulled his shoulders back, his attitude one of surrender. When his lips did not move, she thought over what she had said. Perhaps she had read into Azrael's intentions and been mistaken. She did not want to admit that she was wrong, because it would mean that the marks on her back meant nothing and that everything she felt for the elf in front of her was based on her own foolishness. His voice, sudden and desperate, silenced her.

"I've thought of you every day since I met you."

"You're just saying that."

"I've missed you," Azrael returned. "After I left Helios, I still thought of you because it didn't make sense how I felt about you and what I was being told. I hated myself for believing that you could have done all that my parents said, and what I thought I witnessed when you brought Emmy back.

"Tell me what I don't know," he pleaded with a final breath.

"You and Emmy were supposed to be punished that day too," Rosalyn admitted. "I took care of it."

Azrael's eyes widened, "What does that mean?"

"Fifteen, ten, and five," she enunciated. "Those were the punishments that we all were supposed to receive. I met with your mother, Emmy's father, and mine to arrange to take the ten lashes from you and the five from Emmy so that you two wouldn't have to suffer."

Azrael looked up as if recalling the memory of his last trip to Helios. The more he thought about the past the longer his face became. He stared at her like the wounds on her back were fresh or that he was watching it happen.

"Thirty?" he asked more to himself than to her. "You were whipped thirty times?"

She pushed past him and made her way to the window. If she could get him to leave, she could keep her heart intact and she would have no repercussions from her father. He would never have to know that a Vestan had slipped through the ranks.

Rosalyn waved away any further comment, "As I said, you are at risk as long as you are here. You should go."

"Is that what you want?"

"Don't make this about me," she argued and turned around. "This has never been about me. Go back to your home where you are loved and never spare me another thought."

"And you?" he asked, putting the focus on her again. "What will happen to you?"

"I said this isn't about me." She hoped that her voice did not sound as annoying as it did in her head.

Azrael crossed the room, stopping just short of her. His jaw was rigid but his eyes and voice were soft. "And what if I wanted to make it about you?"

"Why?" she asked in earnest.

"Because I love you."

Every muscle in her body froze. She had wanted to hear Azrael say that for as long as she could remember. However, all she could do in the moment was doubt him. Her fantasy was just that, something she made up to fight away what she felt.

"You were willing to kill me," she pointed out.

"And I was wrong," he urged. "I know that."

Her tone grew dry, "And you can be that changeable?"

"I thought you had killed Emmy, but my feelings for you never went away. They were just ignored."

She leaned in for emphasis, "Then ignore them further."

Azrael seemed unfazed. "I'll go or I'll stay, the choice is up to you. But know this, I will love you no matter what you decide. Tell me what you want me to do and I'll do it for you."

"I want you to..."

Her voice started off strong but faded into a whisper, then silence.

The right thing for both of them was for him to leave. He would be safe, and that was all she wanted. Or at least that is what she told herself. She knew what she wanted from him as if the words were itching to come out. He had said all she had ever wanted to hear.

"I want you to," she started again. She shut her eyes, exhaled, and cleared her throat for one last attempt.

"I want you to kiss me."

The words were out of her mouth before she could stop them, though she felt relieved once they were out.

Azrael took a slow step towards Rosalyn, bridging the gap between them. He reached up, slow enough so as not to scare her, and rested his hand on her cheek. She felt a slight pull in his fingertips, but, other than that, he made no more attempt to force her. She leaned in, and he kissed her as if his life depended on it.

The voice of reason in her head told her to hold back, but she had been waiting for too long for the feeling of his lips on hers to listen to reason. She wrapped her arms around his neck. He gave her freedom, a freedom to be herself that she had only ever had in Valandyl. It made her vulnerable, and, were she to follow her feelings, would give her the courage to fight her father's control of her.

When they released, she took a clearing breath. The thoughts and feelings ebbed away, and she paused to think over what had happened.

"This is wrong," she whispered past the lump forming in her throat. The glow was wearing off, and, like her time with Emmy before the ball, the reality of her situation hit her soberly. She pulled away from him with only the force needed to remove herself from his grasp.

"We won't get caught," he tried.

She scoffed, "I always get caught."

Azrael started to say something that would make it right, but she turned away. She could not deny that being with Azrael was what she wanted. However, the more she thought about it, the easier it was to recall the pain in her corin and the impact of the blows her father would deal out.

The hairs on her arm stood up as she felt a gentle caress glide down her arm. Before her body could think or freeze, she pulled away from him and used her left hand to shove Kieran back. She would not let him touch her again.

It was only when she stopped and saw Azrael's hands up that she remembered that Kieran had been imprisoned. She resigned, letting her hands fall to her sides and breathing through her embarrassment. Tears fell from her eyes before she could hold them back.

"I'm sorry," she rasped.

Azrael approached her again, his hands still raised. She nodded, indicating she would not lash out and that he could put his hands down. Written on his face, the look of pity that she had wanted to avoid.

"They're wearing you down, aren't they?"

The answer seemed to scream in her head, but years with her father had blocked it from breaching the surface. She half wondered if the thoughts she fought were even her's anymore. A couple of tears escaped and burned as they scraped the side of her cheek.

All she could muster was another small nod in Azrael's direction.

One more step forward, and he was back to his original

place. "You mentioned the mask you wear for them the last time I was here. It's getting harder to wear, isn't it?"

"I can't do it anymore," she admitted, her hands waving around. "Be who they want me to be. Hate you and Emmy. When I'm with you or I help you, it hurts. When I'm away from you, it hurts. But when I do what they say, it hurts even worse."

Rosalyn stopped moving but knew that she had said enough that she could not stop her train of thought. She did not want to keep suppressing how she felt or giving in to the fear of her father. Even if Azrael rejected her, she had waited long enough to say what she was about to say.

"If this is love and happiness," she began, with a quick motion towards the both of them. "Then let me drown in it. Let me fall because of it. Love me, if you can stand it, because I love you, Azrael. I love you and that is the only thing that I have been sure of here in Helios. I know we haven't known each other every day of our lives but..."

He reached out and pulled her into a kiss, making the end of her thought irrelevant. Any doubts or thoughts of her father, she fought off and surrendered herself to the moment. One hand held her close, while the other smoothed over her hair.

Azrael gasped for breath, "Ever since you left Valandyl, I've been searching for you. Trying to find you in other people, and I've come up empty. I don't want anyone else."

His hands caused her skin to tighten, an ache to be touched growing faster than she knew what to do with it. She wanted him everywhere at once. He pulled her closer to him, and she wrapped herself tighter around him.

Azrael took a breath, releasing her.

"Why did you stop?" she asked.

He hesitated, taking her in.

She stared at the curve of his bottom lip, wishing he would go at her again. In his eyes, there was a worry detached from any words that he could find. "I won't hold back from you. Ever again."

Relief swept through him, “Neither will I.”

She smiled, flicked her wrist, and pulled him closer. “Thank heavens for that.”

CHAPTER 39

Rosalyn refused to move. She feared that any disturbance of the bed would highlight the other occupant or, rather, she feared the lack of another occupant. Azrael's arm laid limp across her side, his fingers brushing against the curve of her hip. It was only when she felt the bed shake from underneath her as Azrael got out of bed that she opened her eyes and breathed through her fear.

Azrael's breathing was husky and deep, as he urged himself out of bed and searched for clothes. She smiled and turned over to watch him. His body pointed towards a soldier with trained muscles, but the politician in him had the muscles hidden under an average physique. At first, she felt embarrassed for looking at him, but brushed her feelings away and continued to stare. For however brief a time, he belonged to her and she would make the most of it.

"Where are you going?" She asked when he walked toward the door.

"I was going to get us some breakfast while you were asleep, but I don't think that is going to work anymore."

She could hear the smile in his voice and stretched out under the blankets to release the warmth that his smile brought. The linen was cool against her bare skin. Her face changed to match his, "And now it seems I've ruined your plan."

He cocked his head and looked at her with soft eyes. She felt seen as if he saw through her flesh and saw the aura beneath. More so, his face brightened every time she let him in. He swaggered over to the bed, crawled in, and pulled her towards him. The fabric on her left hand lagged as he moved her, and she clamored with her other hand to pull it back into place.

Azrael did not hesitate this time.

“I love you,” he said. He pressed his lips against hers, and the fullness of his lips combined with her own. When the kiss broke, the after effects came down in a haze.

“I love you,” he repeated.

He had said it many times, but, even now, the statement stopped her heart. The words filled her ears and lingered in the space between.

Azrael pulled his face away and leaned his weight on his elbow. “What is it?”

She leaned back onto her pillow, biting her lip. "You just have to realize that everything you say... Well, I don't get comments like that often and it takes me by surprise every time you say them."

"Then I will shower you with them."

He leaned towards her and kissed her shoulder. His hands trailed over the thin sheet covering her skin, reminding her how vulnerable she was under the blanket. She exhaled audibly and laughed when she saw the responsive grin on Azrael's face.

She was about to kiss him again when she heard her brother's footsteps in the hallway outside her room. There was a visible pause in her body, as she listened to Dorian's footsteps close in. Azrael stopped as well but stared at her instead of the door.

Dorian knocked, "Rosalyn? Are you awake?"

"My brother," she mumbled. With a flick of the sheet, she shuffled out of the bed and Azrael did the same. Her robe was nearest Azrael, so she pointed to the article. "Hand me that."

"I could try to explain why I am here," he began.

"Rosalyn," Dorian called and knocked again. "Can I come in?"

"Just a minute," Rosalyn yelled. She grabbed her nightgown from Azrael and pulled her glove off. As she tied the wrap around her torso, she lowered her voice and explained. "No, trust me. He won't listen to a word from you. Let me."

Every step closer to the door made her more anxious. "Stay here, just for a minute."

No sooner had she opened the door, did she slam it behind her and come nose to nose with her brother. He gave her a once over, his knuckles resting against his mouth.

"Are you alright?" He queried.

Rosalyn slipped in a breathy laugh. "I'm fine. Why?"

"Because you walked out here in a robe when you are usually dressed by now and you shut the door rather quickly."

Dorian gave her one final glance then switched his focus to her door. "What don't you want me to see?"

"No."

Rosalyn winced as soon as the sound of her voice stopped. It did not matter what was in her room, her protest had exposed that there was something she did not want her brother to see. It was all he would need for his curiosity and protective instincts to kick in, and he would not stop until he knew.

"Do you have someone in there?" He looked at the door as if he could see through it. "You do. Who?"

Rosalyn chewed on her lip, "Codi."

Her face grew hot as she realized the immediate implication that she slept with her new guard after only a week of knowing him. Meanwhile, Dorian fumed. He banged his fist against the wall, and his chest expanded as all his anger seemed to build up there.

"I swear, I'll kill this one. I'll guard you myself from now on."

Rosalyn rushed in front of the door and held her arms out to keep her brother back. His eyes begged for an explanation.

"Stop," she urged with a bite in her voice that her brother knew all too well. "I want him there. It was consensual."

"Consensual? You're sure? He's not blackmailing you or anything."

Rosalyn cleared her throat and crossed her arms, feeling vulnerable. "I promise that I want him in there."

"You are attracted to him?" Dorian asked, his temper cooling.

"Yes, I am." She rubbed her arms and tried to make a joke to ease away her anxiety with an accompanying shrug. "You said that I would like him."

Dorian chuckled, "I didn't imagine this much so soon. Did he stay the night?"

She looked around, trying to hide her blush. A small part of her was ashamed at how much joy was in her brother's voice. The years of walking the halls and her kingdom alone came to her like a cluster around her that she tried to push away. As she fussed with the neckline of her robe, she remembered that Azrael was in her room and his touch would keep the memories at bay.

"I would really like to get back to him."

"Oh," Dorian smirked. "I'm sure you would."

Rosalyn smacked her brother in the arm, but the smile on her face was hard to ignore. "Go."

Dorian turned to leave but reached out for her chin before making the full turn. His grip on her was slight. "I'm glad he makes you happy."

Rosalyn watched her brother leave, feeling warmed by his sentiment. With a quick breath, she backed into her room. Azrael was now fully dressed and was slowly exploring the space. She bent down to grab the glove she had thrown on the floor in her rush to get out the door, and secured it back to its protective place.

"I'm sorry about that," she whispered.

"Blackmail?" Despite the confusion, Azrael's voice tossed out the word in a casual tone. "He'd kill me?"

"My last bodyguard was less than ideal," she explained.

Azrael got up and made his way across the room. "I heard a little about that during the interview process."

"Of course you did," she said and flashed an awkward smile. "Well, you aren't like that."

Azrael saw her shift and laughed off what had happened with Kieran. He shrugged his shoulders, cocked his head, and pulled her close to him. "That is a goal of mine. Did he hurt you?"

She nodded, "Not like my father hurts me though."

"What can I do? I want to make everything better. I know I can't heal everything, but..."

Rosalyn cozied up until there was no space between them. His arms wrapped around her, and she felt the heat from his body through her robe. She let the fingers of her right hand wander around in the open space of his shirt.

"Spend the day with me?" Her voice was small, but she was close enough to him that her volume did not matter.

He began to sway as if they were dancing, "Doing what?"

"Anything. Everything. Nothing. I don't care, so long as I spend it with you."

The sound that came out of Azrael's mouth was the middle ground between a chuckle and a scoff. Before she could guess his mood, he smiled then placed a kiss on her forehead. "You are easy to please. We could take a walk, though I don't have any candles this time."

"I think I'll manage."

"Shall we get something to eat first?" he asked.

"Sure, I should probably make an appearance outside my room anyway. My father gets nervous when I don't."

Rosalyn let her fingers linger on him before removing herself from his arms to get dressed. While the warmth from his skin still beamed beneath her own, she was thankful for the feeling of clothing covering her skin. The purple dress she had chosen was a favorite and came with a feeling of familiarity compared to the dresses her father preferred she wear. She also found the companion glove to the lone glove she had taken to wearing and slipped that on to avoid suspicion.

Once she was dressed, she turned around and saw Azrael open the door for her. "After you," he smirked.

She made an unsuccessful attempt to hide the smile on her face as she walked through her bedroom door. Azrael followed behind her, not touching her with his fingers but walking close enough to make up for the feeling. Rosalyn expected to see the stares from the elves she passed, though she was surprised when they ignored her as they always did.

Azrael leaned towards her, "What are you smiling at?"

"It's odd keeping a secret like this. I should feel guilty, but I don't."

"What do you feel?"

She lowered her voice but kept her head straight. "I would think you already knew the answer to that."

"Because of me?" he asked with a childish grin.

Rosalyn gave him a slight shove, not enough to move him any considerable length but with enough force to stop his incessant beaming. However, it only made his joy grow. "You're fishing for compliments."

"So it is because of me."

By the time they reached the dining hall, she found herself laughing at the persistent grin on Azrael's face. It was an expression that dared the dark elves around him to discover his identity. He was unafraid of his surroundings, though he did not pretend to own them either.

The room looked as it always did, yet Rosalyn's pace slowed. Something she could not identify pulled at her, like a subtle shift in the air that made her nervous. She looked around. The guards and attendants were at their places near the doors. Elves meandered through the room, going about their lives and duties. Even Azrael's presence that made her nervous about the potential discovery was not enough to explain her hyperfocus.

A servant approached her, "Shall I fetch some food for you, Your Highness?"

"Yes," she whispered.

As she searched, she felt a presence in the room circle her. Her eyes unfocused and she tried to isolate her feelings. It stayed out of view, but, by the time she isolated it, the elf had already grabbed her. She felt the sliver of steel under her chin, and another curved blade just above her Corin. The man had her pinned, a careful wrapping of his arms that eliminated any means of escape. She heard Azrael's blade leave his side before she saw it pointed in her direction. The tension in the room erupted as the civilians ran, and the guards weaved through the crowd to get to her.

"Stand down or she dies," the assassin growled.

Azrael's hands were poised upward, ready to strike at the first opportunity. "By the look of it, you're going to kill her either way."

"You guard a murderer."

"And if you kill me, what does that make you?" Rosalyn said through gritted teeth.

The assassin jerked her back and pushed the blade deeper into the soft flesh of her neck. "Quiet, you don't deserve to speak."

Azrael cleared his throat, pulling the focus back on him. "You are surrounded and have no chance. Surrender, now."

"I would rather die."

It was then that Rosalyn saw the stark difference between Azrael and her father's men. They were ready to attack as soon as was warranted, without that nagging question as to why they were doing what they were doing. They believed in Lucan's orders and the mentality he had instilled in them. Meanwhile, Azrael was trying to reason with the man. The assassin could have been a kinsman of his, and Azrael bothered to take the time to find out. He inched forward, still hoping that the elf would surrender.

The difference was also his weakness. Azrael was hesitating. He did not want to kill one of his own, and, if her father saw his hesitation, he would be punished or dismissed. There was no place in her father's kingdom for such weakness, and there was a possibility that it would expose him.

Her tattoo tightened as she took control of the elf that threatened her. She did not just force his hands away, she forced his whole body to obey her. Moving him away was not enough, but what she had to do did not frighten her. She lifted him by his head, and, with a nasty snap, ripped the head around before the elf could register the end of his life.

All the men in the room, including her father, rushed over to her and her victim. She had not seen him come in, but, when she felt his hand on her, she worried about how much he had seen. He asked her if she was alright, which she nodded and shrugged his hand off.

"Lord Antien," Lucan summoned. "Take her back to her room, and make sure she is secured. I'll not give any straggler Vestans another chance at my daughter."

Azrael did as he was ordered, grabbing her by the arm and pulling her away. Neither said a word until they were inside her room, though Rosalyn's mind was far from quiet. When he did let her go, she felt the blood return to her arm as Azrael forced the door shut.

"You didn't have to kill him."

Rosalyn forced herself to take deep breaths. "You hesitated. Either I kill him, or my father kills you for having a weak stomach."

Azrael shook his head, "No, I could have gotten him to surrender."

"Did you know that that was going to happen?" She yelled.

The volume startled him, but it was the power in her voice that made it seem like the world stopped.

"What?" Azrael asked. "Of course not."

"Did you know?" She wrapped her arms around herself in a futile attempt to stop shaking. "Did you know that there was another Vestan? That he would try and kill me?"

"No." His tone dropping down to a gentle whisper.

Azrael reached out to her, but she smacked his hand away. If he touched her, she knew that she would be taken in by whatever he said. The elf who attacked her could have been part of Azrael's plan all along.

"Why should I believe you? You came here to kill me. And now, you have been sharing my bed for one day and then he takes me in the dining hall."

Azrael scoffed, "But I wasn't involved."

"But I don't know that," she declared with as much power as her earlier question.

A silence descended and it was then that she realized the real weight of Azrael's presence in Helios. To her, it did not matter whether her father found out about him or that he was here for her. The consequences of Azrael's stay in Helios was dependent on her opening up to him. His mission was to reach her vulnerabilities and use them to get what he was after. He had denied trying to seduce her, yet he had succeeded.

"This could all be a trick, and I can't be sure."

Azrael's mouth hung open, but closed when he shifted his weight. He began pleading, "Whatever you want me to do to show you I wasn't involved, I will. How can I prove that I am loyal to you?"

"You can't," she muttered.

He struggled for words, but one glare from her silenced him. No matter what he said, she had no way of verifying any of it. The past few days had been some of the happiest of her life, only for them to be under scrutiny.

"Do you want me to go?"

She was not sure if he meant leave the room or the kingdom, but she wondered if he should.

"You were looking around my room earlier, and maybe it was curiosity or you were looking for something. The point is I don't know anything about your being here except what you tell me. I've spent years trying to forget about Valandyl and all that my association with Vestans has cost me. I could be put to death if someone found you and I was willing to take that risk because I will always come back to you. And right now, I hate myself for that."

Azrael nodded.

He sighed, searching for anything persuasive but came up empty.

"I hate that I keep losing you," he admitted before exiting.

As she heard his footsteps travel away from her, something in her throat caught. Her heart sank and, she knew that however counterintuitive it was, Azrael leaving was not what she wanted. This would be the moment down the line that she would look back on and curse herself for causing her own broken heart.

"Wait."

She was not sure if Azrael heard her, and wondered if it would be better if he had not. His footsteps paused and he entered her room with timid steps. His eyes were unmistakably hopeful.

She took a deep breath, "If you love me, then stay and love me. If this is all a trick, then stay and pretend that you love me."

Azrael's face was a mix of concern and horror, "Are you giving me permission to hurt you?"

"No," she snapped then regretted it. She straightened her dress and began again. "I feel as if the proper response to all this would be to let you go and save myself from the hurt, but I don't want that. I don't want to be alone anymore, and I certainly don't want to be away from you. What I want is to experience your love, whether real or pretend, as long as I can."

"Why would you do that to yourself? If I were to betray you, that would only prolong your agony."

She did not want his pity, or anyone else's. She was strong. It was the one part of her that her father never contested, because, even when she disobeyed him, she fought him with all she had. It was the one attribute that she inherited from him that she clung to, knowing that giving up would tear her down faster than any punishment. Azrael's pity was like a stab in the weak part of her armor, the hole in her barricades. It reminded her that her strength could be taken from her, that she could lose that too.

"For someone like me, pain is common but happiness is rare. And don't you dare think any less of me for it. If I get to choose, I'd rather take fake happiness for now, than real pain."

Azrael's shoulders fell, and his voice lost all sense of strength. "I love you, Rosalyn Lassehelin. I swear it."

She wanted to believe him. His words made her heart leap inside her, and she had dreamed of those words for countless years. She had had her heart broken by her father and by Azrael being forced from her life. However, she could not imagine the pain were he to break it knowing just how much it meant to her. The walls around her seemed to move in closer, as though the world outside her door dwarfed her feelings in this room. A breeze blew in from outside but grew stale by the time it reached her. She forced herself to take small breaths and grabbed on to Azrael's shoulder to steady herself.

"Show me," she requested. "Show me every day, even when you return to Tadane. By acknowledging that right here and now, your feelings for me are genuine. Years from now, you may regret being with me, but never say that your love for me was anything else than what it was."

Azrael bridged the gap between them and wrapped his arms around her.

"Show me," she whispered into his ear.

As his hands traced the curve of her body and his lips set to work on her neck, she surrendered. Azrael would leave and her father would punish her, but this moment belonged to her.

CHAPTER 40

Lucan watched his daughter laugh and realized that he could not remember the last time he saw her laugh in earnest. He hated to interrupt such a rare sight, but the issue he wanted to address could not wait.

"Rosalyn, can I see you a minute?"

"Yes, father," she called, after motioning to her guard to stay where he was.

Rosalyn walked over to him, and he pulled her further out of earshot of those in the hallway. He eyed Lord Antien for a moment until the guard turned his back towards them.

"Dorian mentioned your new romance, though it has come at an odd time."

"Do you disapprove?" she asked plainly.

"No, quite the opposite. I am happy that you have found someone that brings such a rose to your cheeks."

She fought the smile that tried to make itself known on her face. "Then where is your displeasure?"

He cleared his throat, "I know Dorian already asked you but I need to be thorough. Has he in any way threatened you?"

"It is genuine, I swear."

He searched her face and body language for any hint that she was lying. Yet, she did not blink, her jaw remained in its natural tightness, and her body did not fidget. Had she moved on from the Vestan prince? He was not foolish enough to hope that the relationship would be her last, but he was glad that she was branching out to spend time with someone other than her immediate family.

His posture relaxed, "Is the relationship serious?"

Rosalyn blushed, "I don't know, it's too early to say. He may not even be permanent."

"What do you mean?" Lucan diverted his attention to the elf in question as if he could see the answer just by looking at him.

Rosalyn chewed on the inside of her cheek, choosing her words with care. "He is a skilled guardian, but it does not suit him."

"Shall I find a replacement?" he asked, more out of concern for his daughter than the vacant position.

"Not yet." She followed his eyes and smiled at Lord Antien's slow pacing back and forth. "He may stay. I'd rather see how his time here goes."

Not only had he seen his daughter laugh and blush, but it was then that he saw longing. Regardless of if the relationship would last, it was the desire and the belief that someone could make her happy that was foreign to her usual demeanor. For once, he was not annoyed when she wanted to parted from him.

"Well, be off with you."

She scampered away, with a smile written across the length of her face.

A tinge of pain from somewhere he had long since forgotten about made him pause. He watched Lord Antien gaze at his daughter and he remembered a time when he made a woman feel as Rosalyn felt. There was a time when a woman had a hold on him, but he had done everything to break loose since she left.

Rosalyn would learn, he thought. The relationship was young and probably would not amount to anything. She would learn that it was best to lock her heart up so that no one could hurt her. She would be a better queen for it.

CHAPTER 41

Rosalyn thought the glow would fade over time. She thought that she would grow tired of the uneasy happiness she felt with Azrael, even though he might betray her. Yet, she walked from the library back to her room where he was waiting for her, and her heart was full. He had wanted to accompany her, and, probably should have, but she wanted the quick trip to examine her thoughts. Her skin felt alive when he touched her, and his sweet words had awakened a part of her brain that she thought was long gone.

She knew that her whole demeanor had changed. The not-so-concealed stares of those elves that she passed in the hallway, as well as her father taking an interest in her love life indicated something had changed about her. It only made the feelings inside her bubble over, and she found herself stifling laughter as she walked down the halls.

The sound of voices from inside her father's study drew her off her path, and towards the door. It was only open enough for Rosalyn to see a sliver of the room inside, but enough to hear her father and Aldan talking.

"Our reports indicate a spy," Aldan admitted.

Her father scoffed, "Why is this news? We know they have spies here and we have used them to our advantage for years."

Aldan groaned, "This one is different, your majesty."

"Why?"

"Because we know nothing about him except that he exists."

"How is that possible?"

Aldan hesitated, "Our informants have only received limited information."

"Then how can it be verified?"

"It comes from reputable sources," Aldan assured. "A spy has invaded our inner ranks."

Rosalyn pulled away from the door, resting her weight on the nearest wall. Someone in Valandyl had talked, and, even if they did not know it was Azrael, they would know soon enough. Aldan would press his informants, who would press their Vestans, only for Azrael to be discovered and Doranen's treachery known.

"Search for the breach, but be discreet," she heard her father say before she tiptoed away. When she was far enough down the hall, she broke into a sprint to her room.

Rosalyn pushed the door open, and it smacked against the adjoining wall. Azrael spun around, startled by the loud crack of the door as well as her panting and excitement.

"What is it, my love?" he asked as he got up from the chair in the corner. He had removed one of the books from the desk opposite him and had been perusing it until her sudden arrival. She could not form the words right away. It was only after he came over to her side and rubbed her arms that she found the will to speak.

"It would seem that our borrowed time is up," she lamented. "How fast can you be ready?"

Azrael's eyes were wide, but he kept his composure. "I'm ready now."

Of course, Rosalyn thought, he would not have much with him. Outside of Helios, he was a prince. Here, he was a spy. Anything that could identify him was left behind and nothing of value would be packed in case he needed to make a clean exit should his cover be blown or his mission accomplished.

She ripped the blanket off her bed, haphazardly folded it in her arms, and ushered Azrael out the door. "I'll tell the watchmen we are going on a walk."

Every eye felt like a spotlight on her motives, which made the journey from her bedroom to the end of the city a torturous ordeal. She forced her shoulders back, despite the pain in her chest that felt as though it would split her ribs apart. The echoes of his touch all over her body came in full force, and she scratched at herself to make it stop.

CHAPTER 42

Rosalyn brushed away some branches that obscured their path and held them away to let Azrael pass. In the distance, a cliff face seemed to grow taller as they approached. They were half a day's ride from the border, but it was nearing sundown. If her father did not know she was missing yet, he would realize soon enough and send out scouts to look for her. Dorian could have lied, but he had no reason to cover for her.

Azrael paused, "Isn't this?"

The rest of his sentence was lost as he gaped at the impending natural structure. He did not have to finish it, because she knew why he hesitated.

"Is this the same set of caves that you found me in years back?" She kept walking, not waiting for him to catch up. "Yes, they are. The area is still rarely occupied. We'll camp here for the night."

Rosalyn led, though they both knew the route without help. The air was thin, and the rocks dampened the sound of their feet. When they reached the bottom of the stairs and entered the sizable makeshift room, Rosalyn dropped the blanket on a dry patch of rocks near the wall.

"We can stay here tonight," she repeated with a forced formality. "Then part ways in the morning."

Azrael looked around the room with an unidentifiable expression.

She avoided his gaze, not wanting to acknowledge that she would have to let him go. If she looked at him, she thought she would lose what composure she had. She straightened the blanket, checked outside the door, and took a few deep breaths.

"What if we didn't have to?" came a small voice from the other side of the room.

Rosalyn whipped around. "Azrael, they know. They may not know it's you but they know that someone has gotten through. You can't stay here."

"Come with me," he petitioned. He came over to her and took hold of her hands.

"To Tadane?"

"You could keep wearing a glove and we could..."

"I can't, and you know I can't."

She thought he would keep on talking, trying to convince her further, but he took a step back. It was as if for a moment, he believed that he could hide her. He walked past her and slid down the wall in defeat.

"I keep feeling like I need to apologize for what I am," she admitted.

Azrael let out a sigh, "Don't."

"I wish I wasn't a dark elf. I've wished a thousand times that I could change."

"Come here," he said without force or command. She did as he requested, and sat down close enough to feel his arm brush against her's. "I wouldn't change you. You are fire and passion and strength, all things that you wouldn't be if you were different. It hurts to love you, but not because of anything you or I could fix."

"I just wish it was easier. Your parents know my face, and Doranen wants my head. I wish that I could hide, even if I had to wear a glove, but it's impossible."

"Wishful thinking, I guess," he said in a voice that was both wistful and one of mourning.

Rosalyn leaned her head on Azrael's shoulder, "What if I had said yes?"

He placed a kiss on the top of her head. "What do you mean, my love?"

"I want to live in the realm of wishful thinking a little

longer." She slipped her exposed hand into his and snuggled close. "Where would we go?"

"The elven kingdoms are out," he ruled. "But the druid lands are beautiful."

"I'd rather avoid those."

"Why? You would blend in easier than I could since you are half druid."

"Exactly. I'd rather not run into family."

"I haven't been to the human lands," Azrael brought up with renewed speculation. "Though we would certainly stick out."

Azrael stopped, smiled, and chuckled at his own thought. "No, I know where we could go."

"Where?" She asked with a definite smile heard in her voice.

"There is a village on the edge of Valandyl and the humans. It's remote, and no one would know us. It's near a lake, but with snow covered mountains in the distance."

"And we could live there?"

"I'd build you a house myself," he answered with confidence.

Rosalyn lifted her head up, "And do you know anything about building houses?"

"Not a thing."

"Sounds perfect."

The happiness drained from his face, as he fell back into reality. His eyes lingered on her, and he reached up to a small strand of her hair. Stroking it absently, he fantasized about the life he wanted again. "It would be."

Azrael cleared his throat, and let go of her hair. "What is your father going to do to you when you get back?"

"You don't want to know."

"I do," he urged.

"I'm telling you that you don't."

Azrael stood up.

"If you're going to bear it, the least I can do is know what you will endure because of me."

Rosalyn stood up to match him but leaned against the wall. She would be lying if she said she had not already thought about what punishment her father would deal out to her when she got back. This was yet another topic that had been vying for her attention, and one she had been trying to keep at the back of her head.

"I don't know. Honestly, I haven't done anything like this before. This is treason. If my father doesn't kill me, he'll make it something that will make me wish he had."

He sighed, not satisfied with the answer. "I wish I could save you from it."

She wished he could too. Rosalyn pulled at the glove on her left hand, then intertwined her fingers. "Will you promise me something?"

"Anything, my love," he whispered.

"Years from now," she started. "When you are King and I'm Queen. I don't want to become my father, but, if he doesn't kill me when I return, he will do anything and everything to make me hard like him."

Azrael stopped her, "You aren't like that."

"Now, I'm not. But after many years with him, I could be. I could be in so much pain that hurting others could be the only thing that helps. He could turn me. It's as likely for me to become what he wants as it is for you to wake up and realize that I'm dangerous."

"So not likely," Azrael quipped.

"Promise me. Promise that you will keep trying to find me; this part of me that wants the Elven War to end and the killing to stop. Remind me of Emmy and these feelings right now and..."

Azrael shook his head, "I don't believe that you have it in you to be like him."

"You saw me kill that Vestan," Rosalyn fumed. "And it was easy."

One tear escaped and ran down her cheek. Azrael saw

her begin to shake, and he went over to her. He wiped her cheek with his thumb but left his hand on her throat.

"Please," she pleaded. Her lungs felt heavy, and her body seemed distant. "Promise me."

"I promise."

Rosalyn bit her lip, forcing away all thoughts on the future. "Show me you love me. One last time."

CHAPTER 43

"Azrael, wake up." Rosalyn shook him, then rolled over and sat up. "We have to go."

They folded up the blanket, straightened their clothes, and emerged from their hiding spot in business-like silence. No eye contact was made, or else the emotions that lurked behind their skin would unleash in full force. Rosalyn led the way, while Azrael lagged behind.

"That hill marks the border," she announced. "And Tadane isn't much further."

She could see past the forest and at the edge of the horizon were the silhouettes of the spires of one of Tadane's fortress cities. Dascaul, the most heavily fortified because it was so close to Helios, remained one of the only cities her father had yet to attack successfully.

A sharp sound she could not identify pulled her attention away.

He put his hand on her arm, "Do you hear something?"

"I don't know," she whispered. Rosalyn scanned every tree and shadow in case something would suddenly make itself visible. She turned back to Azrael and pulled his arm around in the other direction. "You need to go, now."

Despite her statement, Azrael looked as if going near that area would kill him. She pushed him further away, but he resisted her.

"If my father's men are close, you have to run."

He pulled her to him and kissed her full in the mouth. When the kiss was finished, Azrael rested his forehead on hers.

"I keep coming back to what I've said before. Two days

or two hundred years."

Rosalyn forced herself to speak past the lump in her throat, "I wish we could have had two hundred years together."

She pushed herself away from him, ignoring the tears that were falling from her eyes. Her hands lingered in the air, as though she would pull him back. "Please, go. I won't stop worrying about you until you're across the border."

He glanced at his home in the distance but stayed where he was.

"Rosalyn, you aren't your father."

She gasped for breath, but none seemed to fill her lungs. "You don't know that. I could be."

"You aren't. No matter what they tell you. You are stronger than that."

"It doesn't feel like it."

Her heart, her rib cage, her skin. It all would break open, she was sure of it. Leave, her mind screamed. Azrael had to leave now before she collapsed. Before her father's men caught up with them. Before Doranen found her.

Before.

Before.

Before.

He reached out and held her together. The world on pause.

"What happens now?" she asked.

"Emmy used to talk about this idea that the three of us could change the course of history. Doranen's daughter, I can't speak to."

"His daughter?"

"His wife had another one," he explained. "He has kept it as quiet as he can for her protection."

"After Emmy, I don't blame him."

"She is young, but you and I… I know what I'm saying won't be easy, but if you and I can be better than our parents, I believe that Emmy's idea isn't impossible."

She wanted to rip away.

Away from this elf so unlike her.

Away from his optimism.

But, without any force, his hands kept her in place.

"I'm not giving up on you."

She sputtered, "What if I...?"

"Never."

It was time. Something in her gut told her so. If he did not go now, her father would come or, perhaps, she would go with him. He had to be safe.

"Please, go." Her voice was smaller than she had ever heard it. "I can't lose you."

She guided his hands away from her.

He surrendered, feeling the end too.

It was a slow and painful walk back to Helios. Every step seemed forced, and the walk itself seemed to be never-ending. She counted the trees to give herself something to focus on other than the pain. By the time she reached the outer bailey of the castle, she had lost count at least three times that she could remember.

Dorian was talking to the watchman on duty but stopped mid-conversation when he saw her meander up the path.

"Rosalyn?" he called. "What are you doing out of the castle?"

"I was out on a walk."

"Princess Rosalyn," said the watchman behind Dorian. "You never checked back in yesterday."

"I got in late last night."

It was a flimsy excuse, but a plausible one. She had snuck past the guards before, trying to spite her father.

Dorian wrapped an arm around her, "Well, let's be glad you're safe and that it was just an oversight by our guards."

He ushered her up the broad staircase to the main portal entrance, past the befuddled guard in question. While Dorian would often keep her close, she soon discovered that he was forcing her forward. He pushed her into an alcove, waited until the hallway was vacant, then turned and lowered his voice. "I know when you are lying. You were out of the castle when the security breach happened."

"You don't know that," she objected.

Dorian cast her a disapproving look, "I came to check on you last night."

Rosalyn swore in her mind. "What did you tell father?"

"I didn't tell him anything. It isn't the first time that you have stayed out all night on one of your walks and the watchman said that Codi went with you."

Rosalyn nodded, "That's what happened."

She looked down at her now bare arms, thankful she had tossed the glove along the way.

He took a step towards her, forcing her into the corner. "Then answer one simple question. Where is Codi?"

"I mentioned to father that he might not stick around. We had a fight, and he left."

"That's it? He just left, and had you give his resignation?"

She had no answer to that.

Dorian's breath caught, and his eyes went wide. He breathed through the shock and turned away from her.

"You know that I have to take you to him," he managed.

Rosalyn was not angry. Just because she had lied, did not mean that Dorian had to. She preferred he did not. The consequences were hers alone to bear.

"I don't expect you to lie to him," she said evenly.

Meanwhile, Dorian was shaking and distraught, wishing that he had not pushed her for information. He took her arm and led her towards her father's dungeon. She would be locked up, he would report to the throne room, and talk to their father. Lucan would be furious, but unable to show his anger. His daughter and heir was a traitor.

By the time her father came in to scream at her the first

time, she had already shut her brain off.

Before.

Away.

The words swam in her mind.

She wanted to go back to before.

Away from here.

Instead, she was weighted. Left holding out her hands, unsure if she were pushing away or reaching out.

At least, Azrael was safe and she would never give him up.

CHAPTER 44

Rosalyn looked straight ahead, hearing the footsteps of her father's men coming from down the hall. She had memorized the sound of their steps at this point, visualizing their feet hitting the ground hard in their stride. Her body was positioned opposite the door to her cell with her legs folded in front of her and her eyes locked in a vacant stare in the direction of the side wall. She knew they were coming for her.

Her abdomen hurt from the last time they had followed their orders. All they did was yell and scream at her until they figured out that that did not work. They beat her, though nothing she could not handle. Dorian had to have worked something out with them, or they would not have been so lenient. The bruises were nothing compared to the pain of the kyri pulling down on her neck. However, she refused to let her face show anything that could give away what she knew. The slightest clue could tip off her father.

The men stopped outside her cell door, one unlocked it while the other entered. He was muscular and angry like all her father's men. She turned her face away, not out of fear but to dismiss their power. They would not break her.

He came over and pulled her to her feet, only to pull her out of the room so hard that she lost her footing. The one who had unlocked the door laughed, but she did not fight them. They were following orders. Her shackles jingled and clanked as they rubbed against the floor and themselves.

At the end of the hall was a room about the size of her bedroom with a grisly stone table, often used during interrogations. She eyed it with apprehension knowing soon they would fix her to it. Her father, who was pacing the room, made a vague gesture towards the table.

They did as they were instructed, pulling her arms and legs taut by weaving a chain bolted to the table through the chains connecting her shackles. Even though they were anything but gentle and the way they threw her around made her head ache, she did not resist.

"Everyone out," her father growled once they had finished. He paced the length of the room a few times before he spoke again. "I have been racking my brain trying to figure out what I did to deserve a daughter like you."

"And what conclusion have you come to," she quipped.

Lucan cocked his head to the side. The death glare was enough to make her afraid for her life. His voice snapped like a whip. "Don't act like you've done nothing wrong."

The intense pain in her corin seemed like it would come from a punch or a stab, as opposed to a quick flick of his wrist. While the pain started in her hand, it extended upwards as fast as the sensation started. She tried to breathe through it but the pain tugged at her lungs, so her breathing came out in wheezes.

Lucan let his hand fall, and her breathing released back into a normal rhythm. "You have committed treason. I need the name of the spy."

"I can't give you that."

He flicked his wrist again, this time shouting over her screams. "You refuse to acknowledge that you have betrayed your family and your people."

Again, he let her go. Rosalyn only shook her head in reply. Her father's own breathing seemed to fall into sync with her's, only his was because his anger had reached its apex.

Lucan stopped pacing, came to the edge of the table, and banged his hands on the surface near her hip. "I should put you to death for what you have done."

Rosalyn shifted in her chains but dared to look her father full in the face. "Then do it."

Her father's body stopped moving.

"If I'm such a disappointment, then get rid of me and claim Dorian as your heir as you should have done in the first place."

For a brief moment, her father's gaze did not challenge her. He looked at her and wondered if he had been wrong. She had magic unseen in the Three Kingdoms, the strong lineage, and had inherited his fire.

But was it enough?

Lucan motioned with his hand again, and, like a maestro, Rosalyn's torment started at his cue.

"You have put elves in danger," Lucan said through gritted teeth. "I need to know who and what is vulnerable. Give me his name."

Rosalyn tried to focus on anything but the pain. The feeling of the cold stone beneath her, likely something that many other victims of the table had tried. When that did not work, she tried to imagine the pain away. She tried to picture her bed, her blankets, and Azrael sprawled out amongst them. When it started to take her away, Lucan pulled her out of the illusion by shaking her back to reality.

"We didn't discuss any secrets," she admitted.

Lucan fumed, "Stop protecting him!"

"I didn't tell him anything."

Lucan scoffed, his voice changing octaves. "You really think that he wouldn't have killed you if you gave him the chance."

If she thought admitting that she had in fact given Azrael the chance would change his mind, Rosalyn would have mentioned it. Her father would only chastise her further for her actions. That she knew the spy had malicious intent would only add to her guilt.

"I'm not giving you a name, and I didn't leak any information to him." She flashed a crooked smile, finding her last pocket of strength. "Now, if you did during any of your security briefings that you had him attend, then that is on your hide, not mine."

With one last flick, the pain came again. However, Lucan did not stay to watch. He walked away and swung the door open, half tearing it off the hinges. The guards wore the shock on their faces with unabashed clarity. When Lucan saw this, he convinced himself that they were staring at his daughter and only furthered his own shame. He flew out of the room and down the hall screaming, "Get her away from me!"

Rosalyn felt rather than saw them release her. She waited for the pain to subside before opening her eyes. Even the thought of opening them seemed too taxing on her body. They lifted her off the table only for her bulk to fall in their arms. When she did not respond, an unspoken but unanimous decision was made to drag her back to her cell. Her ankles and toes dragged against the stone, but she was not strong enough to walk to correct the problem.

When they returned to her cell, the guards plopped her down then promptly left. Whether she was passed out or dying, they had completed their instructions. Rosalyn could have sworn she heard a slight pause before they left. She felt the stone under her fingers and cursed her father in her mind. However, no matter how vehement her cursing was out loud or in her head, she could not convince herself that Lucan was wrong. She had committed treason, and, though she regretted nothing, she deserved to be the subject of Lucan's rage. He had a kingdom and a prejudice to protect, any weakness in either would be seen as a weakness of his own self.

The pain subsided enough for her to pull herself off the floor, noticing her brother leaning against the wall in the corner. Either he was not aware of her rousing consciousness or he was lost in his own thoughts, but his face was turned away from her. He looked as though he had not slept yet, though his posture was stiff like his father. When he did bring his face towards her, he took out a tiny bundle of fabric from his satchel and threw it over to her.

"I brought this for you."

Her body seemed heavy, but she managed to propel it forward with her right hand towards the parcel. She unwrapped it and found a pilfered loaf of sourdough bread. Though she could feel his disappointment in her and her betrayal, his eyes were still soft as he watched her open the napkin.

"Thank you," she whispered, as she rewrapped it and placed it next to her for later. "Dorian, I'm sorry."

Dorian nodded, then sunk down to her level. "I want to ask you something."

"I'm not giving a name."

"I know that," he sighed. "That isn't the question I want to ask. The question I'm going to ask I don't think you are going to answer.

"I've been thinking about this whole situation. You loved and trusted him, two things that don't come easy for you. He had to be someone special to get you to be so vulnerable."

Dorian gave her a pointed glare, but his words stopped.

"I didn't hear a question," she remarked.

"The spy was Prince Azrael, wasn't it?"

Rosalyn bit her lip, slowly releasing it as an excuse to let out the breath she had been holding. She did not look up at her brother, yet she knew him well enough to know he had his answer. He could not prove it and he would not bring his speculation to their father. It would only make him angrier that someone as high profile as the Prince of Tadane could slip through their ranks without anyone knowing.

He nodded, though his face was anything but positive. "It was good to see you happy, even if it was only for a few weeks."

She gave a nod of her own, then watched him get up to leave. With a quick wipe of his pants and tunic, he crossed the room with all the haste of a snail. She did not expect him to pause and looked up at him when she heard his feet stop.

"I can't protect you anymore," he admitted while tapping on the wall.

"I know. You've done what you can, and I appreciate it all."

Dorian pounded his fist against the hard stone. "Rosalyn, I'm begging you. Tell him. If you do, father will stop hurting you. Please, do it for me. I can't take this..."

He waited for a response, but she would not give him one. Dorian sighed, "What good is this love you feel if he's warming his feet by a fire and you are being tortured within an inch of your life. Maybe killed?"

Rosalyn shut her eyes, trying to drown his words out. Her love meant more than that. It had to, she told herself.

"Enjoy your love," he taunted with grim finality. "I want nothing to do with it."

She watched her one ally walk away and pulled her legs in. Her love was gone, her ally had jumped ship, and her father would in all likelihood kill her before she would break. She wiped the tears from her cheeks with shaky hands and felt the fear she had fought off find its way to the surface.

CHAPTER 45

Lucan scanned the battlefield and breathed in the familiar scents of sweat and adrenaline. His feet were spread apart, his hands resting on the opening of his cloak on his chest, and his face was a surprising reflection of his pleasant mood. Today, he hoped to get a name from his daughter or provoke a confession from the kingdom at fault, either would satisfy him. He turned around at the sound of Aldan clearing his throat and saw his daughter being dragged to him.

"It's good to see you this morning, Rosalyn."

His daughter was barely conscious, with an outline of red on her eyelids and a cold sweat on her brow. He lifted her off the ground and forced her up.

"I don't understand," she moaned.

"You won't give me a name," he said flatly. "If you had, I would have simply asked the rulers of his kingdom for his head and be done with it. But now, I will attack at random."

Rosalyn's eyes widened and pleaded with him in a pathetic attempt to save the lives of Vestans or herself. "Why are you doing this?"

"They tricked me," he growled. "And you're defending them. If I attack the kingdom that the spy is from, then I get my revenge. And if the kingdom is wrong, then his kingdom knows just what I'm capable of."

Lucan adjusted his hold on her and forced her to look at the soldiers starting the attack. She tried to pull her face away, but he only tightened his grip on her chin. He would strap her to a chair and make her watch if he thought it would demonstrate his point.

"They will know what I'm capable of, but do you know who will be responsible? Every life lost on both sides will be because of you. All because you wouldn't give me a name."

Rosalyn struggled in his arms, "Please don't do this."

Lucan let her drop to the forest floor, and he turned back to watch the battle. "The attacks and punishments will stop when I get a name. You care about the lives of Vestans? How many must die before you give up the life of one?"

He ignored her sobs and petitions. They would not change his mind, and her pain would not make him reconsider having her interrogated. He looked to Aldan, hoping that her next interrogator had arrived.

"Take her away," he dismissed.

Aldan motioned for the guards to come forward, "Soren's here."

"Good," Lucan commented. "Hand her over."

Aldan nodded, then turned to leave him.

"Tell him," he started, but then reconsidered his words. "Tell him just don't kill her. She needs to be whole to be queen."

Aldan nodded, "Yes, your majesty."

Rosalyn was pulled away amidst her groaning and weak resistance. She would tell Soren or die in the process, both of which he was prepared to deal with. He would get retribution from his enemies and his daughter would know how serious her betrayal was to him and her people.

CHAPTER 46

Azrael stepped over a fallen tree trunk, his ears sensitive to any foreign sounds coming from Lucan's scouts. The battle had raged for a few hours, but Lucan's drive pointed to the battle lasting for days. His elves had made an initial raid, then pulled out only to barrage the city with catapults of stone blocks. Azrael had just gotten back into Tadane when the reports came in that Lucan's army was on the move. He and Marcus rushed towards Valandyl to help.

"And you had no idea that Lucan was planning something like this?" Marcus asked.

"Don't you think I would have said something if I had," he quipped. "No, this can't have been planned. He has more soldiers than he needs to attack these towns, and the towns themselves are of no political significance."

"So he's attacking Valandyl because he's angry?"

"Is that really so far-fetched?"

"No." Marcus kept walking, his hesitancy heard over his heavy breathing from trudging through the thick forest. "What was he like? I mean you dealt with him on a daily basis."

Azrael had hoped that he could avoid any poignant questions about his trip across the border, but he knew they would be asked eventually. He sighed, "He honestly believes that his cause is justified and that he's doing the right thing."

Marcus shrugged, "Don't we all."

Azrael nodded, though he hated to agree that Lucan thought of himself as a hero. He continued walking, then stopped when he heard a sound he could not identify. When he heard it again, he recognized the sound as a scream.

"Did you hear that?" he asked and stopped moving.

Marcus kept going, excusing the sound. "Must have been a bird or an animal."

The scream rang out again, not far from them. "Sadly, I don't think it was. It came from over this way."

He pointed up the ridge, motioning for his friend to join him. The scream could be a trap, which made him pull his sword from its sheath. There was something in the pitch or tone of the scream that struck a chord with him, but he could not place its origin. Marcus' face showed his disapproval, but he followed with his sword drawn and raised to attack.

Azrael saw the outline of an elf tied to a tree at the bottom of the draw, and then another elf circling the prisoner. He motioned toward the clearing they occupied, but Marcus held him back. If they moved in too quickly, it could draw attention or send the elf running to Lucan.

As Azrael moved closer, he saw the dominant elf in more detail. Poignant, forward reaching features only made the sinister glare on his face that much more frightening. He held a thin, glass instrument, like a giant needle, with a demented smile on his face as he fingered the weapon with great care. Azrael shut his eyes, knowing the weapon all too well. He pulled at his collar and scratched at the skin underneath.

The elf circled the area in front of his victim, waiting for his desired response.

"You will tell me, eventually," said the elf.

When he did not get what he wanted, he shoved the needle through the poor thing. Azrael was surprised that the weapon did not make a sound as it went in nor did the elf scream. The only noise that reached him was the scraping of the rope as the elf struggled against her bonds.

"Would you like to know why I brought you out here?"

The man's voice was melodic, almost drunk in the way his words were delivered with unusual lifts and inflections.

The other silent.

"We could have spent our time together back in Helios,

but you have allies there. Your screams would have been noticed."

Another stab, only this time the woman screamed.

"You will tell me the name I'm looking for," he sang over her.

Marcus drew his sword.

"Like always?" his friend whispered.

Azrael nodded.

"Give me a couple beats, then we go."

"Take it slow," Azrael cautioned. "Wide berth, no room for error. You take the back, I'll come up the front."

He shut his eyes and listened to Marcus leaving. The elf below laughed, his feet shifting and crunching on the forest floor. His victim whimpering and groaning as the wounds sunk in.

One beat.

Two beats.

Azrael opened his eyes and began.

His pace was careful. The wrong quick step down into the draw and the whole plan would be ruined. He knew without seeing that Marcus was equal to him as they cornered the two at the bottom. His sword raised and guided his eye line.

After the initial shock, the elf poised the glass weapon in one hand and drew a back sword with the other. Marcus, his sword matching Azrael's height, sidestepped to angle the man in between him and Azrael.

"Light elves?" the man observed. "You two are far from home. The battle is that way."

Marcus tapped the man's blade, taunting him. "We are quite well-oriented, thank you."

The man turned around, trying to find an out but Marcus and Azrael matched his frantic steps.

"Oh, I see. You heard her scream and wanted to be heroes."

"Something like that," Azrael quipped.

"I know you have no reason to but believe me when I tell

you that she deserves none of your concern."

"What do you think, Marcus?" Azrael asked. "Should we believe him?"

"I'm a bit restless and could use the exercise. Let's not."

The dark elf swung first, slicing with his sword then thrusting the shard. Azrael blocked both attacks and lunged forward with unexpected speed that made his opponent stumble back onto Marcus. His friend, at the ready, grabbed the man under his arms. With Marcus' sword across his chest and the man's arms flailing, Azrael ran him through the middle with one clean blow. The elf slipped from Marcus' grip with a painful gurgle.

"All you've done is saved a corpse," said the elf while he spat out the blood that was filling his mouth.

"Lucky for you," Azrael reasoned. "She's still alive."

The elf coughed up more blood, and his head wobbled. "She won't be for long," he managed before slipping away.

He looked pitiful, his own blood down his chin and all down his shirt. Azrael wanted to dismiss him but the glass weapon caught the sunlight, diverting his attention. He wanted to look away from it, but an onset of hatred and disgust for it kept him fixated. All the pain that weapons like that had caused but, for all his disdain, he was afraid of it. He lowered his sword, frozen in place.

"Azrael? Why did you stop?"

He shook himself out of it.

It was just a weapon.

He picked it up and broke it over his knee.

Marcus scanned the area with the trained eyes of a scout. "Dark Elves have to be close. We need to leave or we'll be caught."

Azrael turned around and walked over to the poor woman still tied to the trunk. Her long hair covered her face, her arms pulled tight, and her belly looked like a bloody pincushion. He wiped her hair away from her face to check her heartbeat and pallor but lost his own coloring when he saw her face.

"He's right," he observed in a low voice. "She won't last long."

He rushed to the other side of the tree and hacked with his sword at the knot. When the knot was hanging by a strand, he moved to the other side and caught the woman as she fell.

"What are you doing?" Marcus asked.

"I'm not leaving her like this."

Azrael laid her against his chest and examined her wounds in better detail. Her head fell against his shoulder, exposing her face to Marcus. Azrael heard him sputter, but he chose not to look up to see his facial expression.

"You're not leaving her?" Marcus' tone dripped with heavy disapproval. "Azrael, you know who this is, right?"

"Of course I know, and that's why I want to save her." Azrael pulled her closer to him and put his ear close to her mouth. "Now, keep quiet. I need to listen."

Rosalyn Lassehelin looked like death, and, if Azrael had to guess, she was not far from it. Her hair was plastered to her forehead from the sweat and stress of being interrogated, and her breathing was composed of desperate, wet gasps. Superficial cuts meant to inflict pain riddled the exposed parts of her arms, while deep bruises infected large sections of her body.

Meanwhile, the damage from the shard stood out among the rest. Her upper abdomen, near the joints and her stomach had punctures from the weapon. Her interrogator had been careful to focus his attention away from her major organs, except for the freshest that seemed to move inward.

He swore under his breath.

"Azrael, what is your plan? Take her back to Valandyl? Heal her and send her back with no problems or concerns from Doranen?"

"I don't care," boomed Azrael. He flinched, knowing that his temper would get them killed if he was not careful. He gave Marcus the eye contact he deserved and lowered his voice. "I don't have a plan. The shard over there had an enchantment on it that was keeping her alive, but I broke it and I don't even know why I did that. I just know that she is not dying on me."

Rosalyn's breathing grew worse, so he laid her flat on the forest floor to expand her airways. He took her hand, and, looking heavenward, hoped that the enchantment would keep her stable enough until he could get her to a doctor.

"I have you," he cooed. "Rosalyn, you're safe now."

Her eyes fluttered when he said her name. The leap in his own stomach startled him, but he gripped her hand tighter.

"I'm here," he whispered.

"I need you safe."

Though her voice was steady, it was said through chapped and damaged lips. A bruise one week old, Azrael guessed, began at the corner of her mouth and extended down her cheek.

"I am safe," he assured. "Now, so are you."

She looked around for an explanation, and, when she did not find one right away, she grew frantic. Anything that touched her skin agitated her, while every movement to free herself from what irritated her pulled at her wounds. She groaned in frustration, then fell limp in resignation.

"My father wants your head, but I won't give it to them. He keeps asking for your name."

Marcus tapped Azrael on the shoulder, "She knew who you were?"

"The magic didn't work on her," he answered Marcus, before turning back to Rosalyn. "You don't have to worry about that any longer."

Rosalyn formed a fist and hit the ground with a barely audible thud. "But they keep hurting me. My father keeps asking... I think I'm going to tell him soon."

Tears welled up in her eyes, and they fell straight back into her hairline. Whatever her father had done to her, the physical toll was brutal and had aged her considerably in the last week.

"Everything hurts, and I can feel your name in my

throat. My father wants me to talk."

"We can't stay here," Marcus interjected. "It's too close, and we don't know who this man told that they were out here."

Azrael shrugged off his friend's hand. Here Rosalyn was dying, and Marcus was concerned about being spotted. He did not care if they were found. If this was what Rosalyn had to endure for him, he would confess to Lucan himself what he had done so that Rosalyn's torment would end.

Marcus pulled him around, and up to his feet. Before Azrael could raise his voice, his friend began in a low one. "I don't understand this, any of it. But I can see that, for whatever reason, you care for her. I know that you always have. If you are going to take her, then do it now. We've been out here too long."

He sighed. Azrael wanted to be mad, even to rebel against Marcus' insensitivity, but he looked around at the clearing they found themselves in and knew he was right.

"We should get going," he said with a nod.

Azrael bent down once more, putting one arm under Rosalyn's legs and the other under her shoulders. She did not look like she would weigh all that much, being at least a foot shorter than him. He lifted her up but stopped when she cried out.

"She isn't going to make it very far," Marcus observed. His tone filled with worry.

Rosalyn shut her eyes and pushed him away. "I'm not going to talk. I won't."

"We'll have to take her to Valandyl," Azrael tossed over his shoulder. "She won't last long enough to make it anywhere else."

When her panic subsided, she reached for his arm again. Her eyes pleaded with him, though he did not understand why.

"I'm sorry," she moaned.

"You have nothing to be sorry for."

She reached up and wiped away the new streams of tears. “People are dying because I won't give him a name. It's all my fault.”

“We'll make everything right.”

“I wish I had run away with you,” she whispered more to herself than to him.

Rosalyn tried to reach further for his hand, but her arm could not extend far enough. When her hand hit the ground, she began to feel the impact of her injuries rather than the immediate pain. Her eyelids were heavy, her lower extremities were cold, and her mind felt like it would burst with all the activity of trying to keep her body functioning under the stress and damage.

Marcus peered over at her, scanning her body with a calculating gaze. “She'll never make it if we don't go now. She's lost a lot of blood. Absalom is her only hope.”

He did not want to pick her up. Lying on the ground, he could see why her interrogator had called her a corpse. She looked like one wrong move and she would break. And yet, it struck him that she still looked like herself. Had she always been this small and fragile? With a quick intake of breath, he submitted himself to the urgency and anxiety of the situation. The best course of action for her now was to be taken to Valandyl. He picked her up with unsettling ease and held her tighter when he thought about the moment when Doranen would see her.

CHAPTER 47

Azrael adjusted Rosalyn's body to a better position and whispered in her ear that they were almost there. He had been telling her that for the last hour, more to make himself feel better than a belief that she could hear him. She had passed out soon after he had picked her up, though her breathing had steadied as a result. To keep anyone from identifying her, Marcus wrapped his cloak over her body. He knew it would only do so much if the wrong person were to recognize her resemblance to the Scourge of Helios.

They walked through the towns without any trouble, though he had not expected anyone to stop them. It was Doranen he was worried about. Doranen was the one who sent him to Helios for Rosalyn's head in the first place. Now, he was bringing her to Doranen for help while a battle was going on. Azrael hoped that the King would allow her inside if only to get her out of sight.

When he saw Doranen coming to greet them, Azrael shifted her weight to a more stable position then walked up with as much strength as he could muster. Doranen's face was stressed, clear lines written deep into the sides of his eyes but he greeted them with a smile.

"I am happy to see the both of you have returned," he stressed. Azrael tried to keep walking on the off chance that he could slip her past and get her to Absalom. Doranen held out a hand, his face scrunched up in confusion. "Azrael, I need to speak with you about..."

Doranen's face went pale.

"Guards," he called, ushering behind him. "Take her."

The men moved forward, but Azrael only held onto her tighter.

"She's hurt," he pleaded. "She needs Absalom."

"What she needs is a cell. Now, put her down."

He had never heard the King of Valandyl's voice so severe in all his years in Valandyl. Doranen's face had grown increasingly hard, and his command was as sharp as talons.

"Put me down," he heard softly in his ear. He knew the voice came from the bundle in his arms, yet even her voice disagreed with him. Though every muscle in him ached to do so, he put Rosalyn on the ground in front of him and stepped back. Her limp body released from his with ease, falling from his bulk to the stone floor of the atrium. Doranen's guards picked her up by the arms and dragged her inside. Azrael took a step to chase after her, but the King stopped him.

"Whatever you think you are doing with her, put it out of your mind. I will make sure she never sees daylight again."

"She could die," he protested, but Doranen shook his head.

"Then I will be obliging and help her along."

Doranen turned and followed his new prisoner down to the cells.

Azrael watched him disappear.

The only thing he could feel was Rosalyn's blood on his clothes. He pulled at the damp fabric, then threw his hands down. He wanted more than anything to pull out his sword, and fight until Rosalyn was free. Why could no one see that she was hurt? Even Marcus was willing to ignore that she was tied to a tree and injured all because of who and what she was. Doranen wanted revenge for Emmy's death, and, left to his own devices, he would kill Rosalyn in the process.

He ran.

Azrael knew that Rosalyn was dying, and he was not going to abandon her now. The tapestries and the walls passed by in a blur, and he could feel his chest tightening as he broke out into a sprint. Absalom's infirmary was on the other end of the castle, any delay could spell death for her.

The door swung open with such force that it smacked the adjoining wall. Absalom jumped at the noise but watched Azrael enter with the steadiness of a doctor used to emergencies.

"Absalom? I need your help."

"With what?"

Azrael's breathing came out in gasps. "Rosalyn is dying, and you are the only one I know with the skills to help her."

"Rosalyn?" Absalom questioned. There was a momentary look of confusion on his face but changed to one of recognition as quickly as the other had come on. "You mean Rosalyn Lassehelin?"

He felt Absalom's confusion and his own impatience mix together, yet he pushed them away. Absalom would want more information, a long story that would take time to tell. Everyone, it seemed, wanted the story of his time in Helios. When he had arrived in Tadane, he sent a letter to Doranen explaining that Rosalyn was innocent of Emmy's death though he had apparently chosen to ignore it. He meant to send more of a briefing, but Lucan's attacks deterred him back towards Helios.

"There isn't time for a debrief," he stressed, hoping that Absalom would understand. "She's in the cells now and the King won't listen to reason."

Absalom groaned, "Why does she need me?"

"She's been stabbed by a shard multiple times, and Doranen is so blind with rage that he doesn't care."

Absalom rushed over to the station on the side of the room, threw bandages and jars in his bag, and made his way back towards the door. Azrael moved out of his way, but Absalom lifted a finger to him.

"You will explain this to me later," Absalom assured, then disappeared down the hallway. He followed at a pace somewhere between jogging and running.

Once they rushed down the stairs, they could hear Doranen's shouts from down the hall. "I trusted you with her. Oh, how I was wrong!"

When Azrael grew close enough to see inside the cell, the two guards had Rosalyn held against the wall while another one stood next to Doranen. He and Doranen paused, and, when all they got in return from her was dazed silence, the third man threw a punch in Rosalyn's stomach.

Her body recoiled against the blow, but her head fell forward and her breathing stopped. Not knowing how to handle a subject who could not physically resist, the two men holding her let her drop to the floor.

Absalom pushed his way through them, "Your Majesty, step aside."

He bent down, laid her flat on her back, then set out to check her injuries. He lifted her shirt and glanced at the punctures to her stomach.

"Absalom," Azrael hesitated. "She... She's not breathing."

Absalom glanced around at the rest of the cell. He noticed the cot in the corner, then motioned towards it with his head. "Azrael, help me get her up."

Azrael helped her up, hoping that Absalom could fix the lack of emotions he felt from Rosalyn's body. He would save her, Azrael told himself. Her lips were blue, but he would save her. Azrael half wondered if Absalom had even noticed it, with his focus on her abdomen.

Lifting up his long fingers, Absalom placed his hand on the area just below her neck and mumbled under his breath. The words seemed to spring her back to life. She gasped a couple times before her breathing steadied, being sustained by Absalom's hand pressing magic into her lungs to keep them going.

"No," Doranen protested. "Rosalyn killed my daughter. She doesn't deserve your help."

Absalom motioned for his bag, then cast a final glance at his King. "With all due respect, I'll decide who I treat and who deserves my services. She may be Lucan's daughter, but I'm keeping her alive."

CHAPTER 48

Azrael ran his hand over Rosalyn's hair, enjoying the fact that she was breathing. She had not woken up yet, but her abdomen was wrapped in bandages and Absalom had assured him that he was doing his best. The doctor had attended to the punctures before the enchantment wore off, and, aside from a trip to get more bandages, he stayed in the cell with his patient so that he could monitor her progress.

Rosalyn's skin felt thin, her natural pallor had paled due to the blood loss, but Absalom seemed unconcerned which he trusted meant that her coloring would return in time. The only blessing that gave Azrael any real comfort was that she was breathing on her own. He did not know if it was the contrast of the white sheet and pillow or if her body had caught up with her lack of movement in the last few hours, but her bruises seemed more prominent. What cuts she had sustained seemed to fade amongst the red and purple splotches that were even more common on her body than he had initially thought.

A small moan startled him, pulling his attention forward. He shuffled, lifting himself up and rubbing the tiredness from his eyes. Her head wobbled from side to side, a motion that made him giddy. He ran a hand through his own hair and allowed himself to hope for the first time that she would make a full recovery.

Rosalyn moaned again. This time, she managed to open her eyes.

Azrael breathed a sigh of relief, "You're awake."

"I thought I was dreaming earlier," she said through

cracked lips. "I didn't think that you were really saving me."

He encased her hand in his and stroked her hair. "I was just glad that I found you. How do you feel?"

"I feel like I'm wavering." Her voice was clear, though it looked as though it took considerable effort to speak. She searched the room for something, then returned her eyes back to him.

"What does that mean?"

"Like I'm here with you, yet my body hurts. Like I'm still there."

Her corin hand had been tucked under her blanket to keep any prying eyes from seeing it, though she used it to search the damage done to her. When her fingers met the stiff cloth wrapped tightly around her stomach, she grew agitated. She tried to move, to where he did not know, but Azrael put his free hand on her shoulder.

"Absalom is helping you," he assured. "But it takes time."

Rosalyn turned her head towards Absalom, "Thank you."

"You're welcome, Princess," Absalom said with a bow of his head.

While they were civil, the interaction was laced with the tension that they both tried to hide. Both of them knew that Absalom was treating two people, the Princess with all the political connotations and the real elf that bled and felt pain. He was treating the Princess as a favor, but treating Rosalyn out of compassion.

Absalom turned away, and Rosalyn tried to lift herself up again. She fought against Azrael's hand, only for her head to fall back against the pillow. Her hair pooling behind her neck and above her shoulders.

"I just want the pain to stop," she sobbed.

"It will..." His voice sounded empty, and he wished he could do more. Azrael straightened her blankets and adjusted her pillow. "I'm sorry for how Doranen's guards treated you."

Her face went blank. “It's natural. Doranen needs someone to blame.”

“You almost died.”

Rosalyn winced, “I wish that I had.”

His heart skipped a beat, while his lungs emptied of air.

“Tell me you don't mean that,” he pleaded.

Rosalyn closed her eyes, her voice steady as if repeating a mantra. “Better I die at the hands of King Doranen, then be sent back to my father.”

He looked beyond her, realizing, without magic, what she was feeling. It was defeat. She was giving up on the possibility that anything good could come from this.

“I wish we could avoid both outcomes,” he advocated in a shaky voice.

“Promise me you won't fight Doranen,” she continued. “If he decides to kill me. I don't want to go back to Helios.”

He scratched at his ears, wishing that he could cover them completely. His throat and mouth felt dry, while he was trying to wipe the moisture from his eyes. “I hope it never comes to that.”

“Promise me,” she insisted.

Azrael stroked her hand, feeling like someone had punched him in the gut. Laying in the cot was the small, broken body of the woman he loved pleading him to allow her to be broken further. What was he supposed to say? Yes? Doranen would understand once he had some room to breathe, or at least Azrael hoped so. However, he could not be sure, and he had no idea what he thought Doranen would do if she did heal.

“I can't not fight for your life,” he lamented.

“Please let me go, while I'm still myself. Don't make me go back. Don't let him hurt me anymore.”

Absalom turned around at this point, his arms crossed in front of his chest. His face held no answers for Azrael, even though both men wished it had.

“Promise me,” Rosalyn insisted again.

Azrael did not want to say it. He told himself that he

would not say it. If he could move away from her to illustrate his point further, he would have done so.

"I promise."

The words had forced themselves out from somewhere beneath the pain that filled his chest. Promising her was not what he wanted, but he knew it was the only way that Rosalyn could see to get out from under her father.

The soft skin of her hand brushed against his as she struggled to hold his hand with a stronger grip. She stared at his hand in wonder, then she saw past her surroundings. Her voice struggled to stay above a whisper. "I wish I could have spent my life with you."

Azrael forced the words past the lump in his throat, "I still hold the hope that we can still be together."

"I have dreamed of that everytime I close my eyes. But it's just that, a dream."

Absalom took a step towards the cot, hearing her sharp intake of breath and worrying that she tore something. He came over, undoing her blankets enough to uncover her hand and abdomen, then checked both. "You shouldn't move. Just lie still."

Though he had seen them when Absalom was bandaging her up earlier, Azrael had not grown accustomed to the severity of her injuries. Her corin arm was the worst looking of them all, with her tattoo close to disappearing from her wrist because the bruising was so dark. The only thing that Azrael could guess was that Lucan or his men had used a rod or beam against it. When she had been kidnapped as a girl, Azrael realized that her corin arm could heal faster since her abductors had seen fit to show their disapproval at her claiming by hurting her corin arm. Her father had done the same but this was to make Rosalyn suffer, seeing the corin as the way to carry out his will best. He began to wonder if she had already healed from some of her father's punishment and what he was seeing was the second or third round.

Absalom lifted up Rosalyn's arm and felt for her pulse

with a delicate touch.

"What did they do to you?" Azrael asked.

"I was chained to a table," she began. "They interrogated me for days, mostly just my father's men beating me when I didn't give them the answers they wanted. It wasn't anything I couldn't handle, though I have a feeling my brother had something to do with that. Then my father came in and started asking me the same questions. Who you were? What information did I give you? He used his magic...

"He's never used it on me for that long before. He said the attacks were my fault. That they would stop when he got a name. And then he handed me to Soren."

She pushed away the blanket and pulled at her bandages. "The name."

"The name," she repeated, this time imitating Soren's melodic voice. "You give me a name or I'll end your life now."

Despite her weakness, she pushed away the strips of cloth with surprising determination. Her breathing quickened, the vein in her neck bulging under her skin. Azrael cooed and shushed her until she calmed down.

"They can't hurt you now."

Rosalyn's wide eyes flashed around the room. "They're still looking for you. They won't stop, and they'll keep asking me."

Azrael rubbed her arm, but Absalom motioned for him to stop. Absalom's head cocked to the side, suspicious of something she had said. It was as though he was horrified or insulted, neither which Azrael could understand.

"Asking you for what?" Absalom uttered. "What will they keep asking you?"

"The name," Rosalyn said again.

Absalom urged her further, "Which name?"

Rosalyn's breathing seemed to stop altogether, "... his name."

"Tell me his name."

The darkness in his tone started to concern Azrael, fearing what Absalom's goal was through this line of questioning. He motioned for the doctor's attention, "Absalom, what are doing?"

Absalom whipped his hand out and motioned him to be quiet. His gaze did not waver from the elf in the bed. "What is his name?"

"I won't tell you," she whimpered. "I can't."

"Why?" Absalom's voice cracked like a whip, reverberating off the walls. "Lives are at stake, and he's right here. Tell me the name."

Azrael reached over and tugged on Absalom's shoulder. He shook it off as if Absalom was disgusted by the touch.

"Give me the name."

"Azrael!" Rosalyn screamed. She repeated it until she was out of breath. Until she had said enough times to make up for all the times her father had asked.

Absalom put his hand down, his body and demeanor softening. "It's alright. It's over. No more yelling."

"What was all that for?" Azrael objected. He pulled Rosalyn up into his arms and did his best to soothe her. She clawed at him, trying to pull herself as close as she could get to him.

Absalom reached under her chin and felt for her pulse. She resisted, yet Absalom waited with patience and understanding until Rosalyn was calm enough for him to check her pulse after the incident. His eyes were gentle. While he disapproved of his actions, Azrael felt Absalom's guilt show through his checking.

"You hadn't said his name yet," Absalom remarked as he stood up. "Had you?"

Azrael felt her shake her head deeper into his chest.

"You were even scared to think it, lest even your thoughts put him in danger. You don't have to worry about that anymore."

Absalom nodded, more to himself than to Rosalyn. "I'll let you rest now."

Though his method was questionable, Azrael realized what Absalom had given Rosalyn. Her father had nearly killed her in pursuit of the name of the spy, while Absalom had brought her out of the mindset in a controlled environment. He had not hurt her, or even threatened to hurt her. It was a purge to get the name out of her system without the threat of violence towards her or Azrael.

CHAPTER 49

It was two days later that Azrael found himself being pulled away from Rosalyn by Absalom.

"I must get more supplies," Absalom excused then tugged on Azrael's arm. "May I have a word with you?"

"I'm not going far," he promised Rosalyn before leaving her.

Azrael followed Absalom outside the cell, where he was waiting with his arms crossed against his chest. Absalom tried to look him in the eye but changed focus to Rosalyn through the barred doors. "She is not healing as fast as I would like."

"Are you saying that she's dying?"

"I'm saying," Absalom stressed. "That her lungs have healed, but the other damage, mainly the punctures, is not healing quick enough. She's stable for now, but she could take a turn at any moment. I just want to prepare you for every eventuality."

The air seemed to escape from Azrael's lungs. She did not look frail or that she could take a turn, whatever that meant. Rosalyn appeared to be healing, as evidenced by her clear breathing and the bruises lightening. Her mood seemed to be growing more alert as well, asking about the battle and what steps were being done to push her father back. The idea that in a random yet brief moment, Rosalyn could go from healing to dying scared him more than he thought possible. He wanted to do more, but, until Doranen saw reason, Rosalyn was a prisoner confined to the cot in a damp cell for a murder she did not commit.

The tapping of feet echoed in the corridor down the

hall, and they turned to see Doranen. He stopped at the bottom of the stairs, then ushered with his finger for Absalom to come to him. In all his years staying in Valandyl, Azrael had never seen Absalom hesitate around Doranen. He did not know the origin of their friendship, but Doranen sought Absalom's advice as often as his team of advisors. Watching them now, Azrael saw that they were straining for the first time.

Azrael made his way back into the cell and sat down on the chair that Absalom had brought in for him yesterday. His eyes stayed on Doranen, hoping to hear bits of the conversation. He heard echoes, but nothing to make out any specifics of their conversation.

"What's Tadane like?"

He glanced down at Rosalyn, then inched his way towards the end of the cell. The voices at the end of the hall rose above a whisper, but he still could not make out anything.

"I'll take you some time," he commented over his shoulder. "And you can see for yourself."

Rosalyn reached out for his hand and nudged his arm. "Please?"

He turned his face back to her, realizing that this conversation was more important. If Absalom was right, he may not get many more opportunities to talk with her. He thought about telling her Absalom's prognosis. Would telling her be cruel or kind?

"Tadane is beautiful," he answered. It was an answer to stall his decision, and he would readily admit that to himself. "Towering spiers and light shining through every hall."

She closed her eyes, smiling at what she saw with her mind's eye. "It sounds wonderful."

"It is when my mother isn't there."

Rosalyn gave his hand a small squeeze, likely as much force as she could muster.

"You said that you would never give up on me," she mumbled.

"I meant it. I still mean it."

Tears burned the back of his eyes, and he cleared his throat to force them away.

"Rosalyn, I don't know what's going to happen but..."

He could not say the words that Absalom had told him. Rosalyn was perceptive, and he guessed that she already knew the likelihood of her chances. He had hoped that Doranen's temper would cool with time, but what little he could hear from the hallway told him that Doranen's anger was steady. This may be the last moment he would have.

"I just want you to know, before everything gets complicated, that no one in my life means more to me than you. I would fight for you forever. We don't have forever, but I would."

The corner of Rosalyn's mouth lifted into a slight smirk, "I love you too."

Amongst everything, his lips curved as well.

"I don't want to disappoint you," she said once her smile faded. "You said that I was strong enough, but I told you that I could feel your name about to come out. I was going to break. Someday, I will.

"But this time... for once, I didn't feel alone. For so long, all I felt was alone."

Suddenly, Doranen's voice shot through from the end of the hall. "I need to know the truth!"

Rosalyn grimaced, opened her eyes, and looked towards the cell door for an explanation. Her voice a low murmur, "What are they talking about?"

He shrugged.

Rosalyn's eyes grew darker, and he felt the room change. The objects around him tensed, and the air pricked at him. The wall of swords and armor hung on a board of begs not far from the entrance of the cell shook, and the bottles and supplies that Absalom had left in the room lept from their spots. He looked down at Rosalyn's corin hand to see it palm extended outward and the muscles flexed.

"I want to know," she commanded. Her voice had a dangerous tone he had not yet heard. Everything in the room, including the cell door, rattled in its place. The sound of all the objects hitting the walls and bars was ominous as if foreshadowing what would happen were Rosalyn to let them crash. Doranen and Absalom ran inside, looking for the source of the disturbance. When they came into Rosalyn's eye line, she barked out, "You two are talking about me, I know you are."

Azrael flashed a look of apology towards them, before returning his attention back towards the girl. "Rosalyn, you need to calm down."

"Our discussion is nothing to concern yourself with," Absalom added.

"You were talking about me," she growled.

Doranen, who had yet to say anything, took a step towards Rosalyn. "You want to know?"

"Your Majesty, please." Absalom held out a hand and shook his head. "She is too weak for it."

"She wants to know," said Doranen, matching Rosalyn's tone. Absalom recoiled away from his King, giving Doranen even more access to Rosalyn. "I need to know if you killed my daughter."

The objects stopped, some falling to the ground but others resolving themselves back onto their pegs or places.

Azrael stood up, ignoring the complicated feelings that he felt from Doranen. "She's told you that she hasn't. I've told you what Lucan said."

"I need to know for sure. If even part of the rumors of her are true, it tells me that I can't trust a word that comes out of her mouth. And I won't trust a word out of Lucan's either."

"What are you going to do?" Azrael asked, scared of the answer. Doranen was fuming and glared at his intended victim.

Absalom cleared his throat, "Doranen wants me to look through her memories."

"Her memories?" Azrael stuttered.

It took Azrael a few minutes to piece together what Absalom was saying. Few creatures in Arthanya were capable of executing the spell Absalom was proposing, and even fewer were willing to cast it. The mind was the most private and revered place of a creature, to breach that privacy was reserved for only the most drastic of situations. "You want him to read her mind? You can't do that. It's wrong, and you know it."

"Killing my daughter was wrong," Doranen growled.

"So you would use one wrong to justify another?"

Doranen's voice cracked like a whip, "I would use it to get the truth."

"Absalom," Azrael turned. "You can't think this is right when the King has reputable sources that he refuses to believe."

Absalom bowed his head. "He is my King. However, I have told him that she is too weak. Accessing her memories in her current state would most likely kill her."

"I need to know," Doranen urged as if to incite another argument.

Azrael stepped in front of Rosalyn, blocking Doranen's view of her. "You are risking her life."

"Any day now, Lucan is going to realize that we have her and he will fight to get her back. Every day she is here and I don't have answers, means another life at risk. But I will risk the lives of my men if I can find out what happened to my daughter and get justice for her death."

"Do it."

They were the last words that Azrael had wanted to hear, and, though they were said in a weak voice, it attracted the attention of all three men in the room.

"Do it," Rosalyn repeated when she assumed no one heard her.

Azrael winced. He turned to her, and let his every move show his submission. The weight of his arms made them drop to his sides, his stomach sunk, and his knees buckled under him. "It's wrong."

"Everyone will know the truth." Rosalyn stopped and breathed through a wave of pain. When it did not subside in a moment, she took his hand and spoke through gritted teeth. "I'm in so much pain, Azrael. This will make it stop. I can still feel the glass inside me. The burning. I want the pain to stop. You promised me."

Azrael's voice caught, "But like this?"

She only nodded.

Though he had never seen the spell done, Azrael felt Absalom and Rosalyn's despair. He knew without knowing the spell that it would be painful, and they knew that she would die. Both felt like a knife in his heart, all because Doranen could not believe him. Yet he knew that it was not just his lack of belief. He saw Emmy's body lying cold and in front of him. The memory seemed as real as Rosalyn, with Doranen's grief fueling it. He stood up and walked towards the opposite wall so that Rosalyn and the others could not see his face.

Absalom stepped past him, his long sleeves following him in his stride. He bent down to her level. "If you are to agree, you have to understand this. Memory is fluid. One memory is connected to another and connected to another after that. I can't just see Emmy's death."

"You have to see everything?" she clarified.

"Yes."

"Do it," Rosalyn said a final time.

Absalom nodded to her, then turned to Doranen. "I will prepare for the spell."

CHAPTER 50

Rosalyn watched Absalom's movements with precision. Whether it was the way his hands curved around bottles of herbs or the way his mouth moved to form the enhancements needed, it all captured her attention. She had not read about the particular spell, though Azrael's reaction told her more than enough.

"Will it hurt?" She asked, her voice sounding surprisingly even to her ears.

"Unfortunately," Absalom remarked, focusing on his craft. He stopped, looking as if he were going to apologize. "Don't fight me when it starts. It will be uncomfortable, reliving past memories in rapid succession, but you need to let it pass or it will only be more painful for you."

More painful, she thought to herself. How could it be more painful? It would likely kill her, yet it had the opportunity to be more painful.

"Are you ready?"

She looked into the eyes of her killer then her lover, both holding a fear in their eyes that she did not possess. Her body felt numb, but she was not afraid. Soon the pain would be over for her.

Rosalyn nodded.

CHAPTER 51

Absalom wiped his brow.

Rosalyn's memories were arduous to sort through. She had lived a lonely life, locked in a cycle of rebellion and submission to her father. He hated that he had to see her suffering like he was intruding into her bedroom when she cried.

As soon as he had released his hand from her head, she had started seizing. It had lasted for five minutes before the fit finally broke, and somehow she had come out the other side still breathing. It did not take long for Doranen to come barging in to ask what he had discovered. Absalom, however, refused him, citing that regulating Rosalyn's health was a priority. When Doranen pushed him to answer him, he told him that Rosalyn did not kill Emmy before bodily shoving him away from the dying girl.

The next day, he found that Rosalyn had been moved to one of Doranen's guest rooms in the castle and the door was guarded. Though he could see a visible change in her health, she had yet to show any signs that her mind had made it through the spell. He did his best to heal her, however, if not for Azrael's sake, but to make up for his intrusion.

"How is she?" Doranen asked, sneaking into the room.

Absalom rubbed the sleep from his eyes. "She has been interrogated for the last couple weeks, and then we proceed with a spell like that. Her mind is... fractured, is the only word that comes to mind. I'm surprised she's still breathing."

"And Azrael?" Doranen inquired.

"I made him go get some rest." Absalom straightened his robes and adjusted his place in his chair. He knew that he deserved some rest as well, but he wanted to give Azrael time to sleep while making sure that Rosalyn was not left alone. "He had been up for over two days, and couldn't keep his eyes open any longer. I told him I would send for him if something changed."

What he was not going to say was that it was more like he had to pull Azrael from the room. Azrael had looked worn through, and, in his tired delirium, threatened Absalom were he to remove him. He realized the severity of his threat, then apologized. He allowed Absalom to pull him away, only on the continued and repeated promise that he would send for him were Rosalyn's condition to change.

"She didn't kill your daughter," Absalom remarked without warning. "I know that's why you came down here."

Doranen faked a sense of shock, then dismissed his own emotion and looked at her with skepticism in his eyes. "She has incredible magic, perhaps she..."

"Your Majesty, you can't keep blaming her. You have been given more than enough proof."

Doranen relented, "What happened?"

"Your daughter found herself in the castle." She should not have even been there, and Absalom suppressed his own anger at Princess Emmelina's superiors for losing track of her. "Rosalyn tried to save the Princess. They ran into Lucan, and he killed Emmy because she was getting too close to his daughter."

Defeat crossed Doranen's face, knowing that the spell was the final test and Rosalyn had passed. Absalom could not tell if it was the guilt of blaming the wrong person for so long or that his daughter's murderer was still out there that hit harder, but he knew each would hit him in time.

"Then that is an end to it all," Doranen managed. "No more doubt."

Absalom turned away from his king and watched as he had done for the last hour. He watched for Rosalyn's eyes to flutter, a bobble of her head or a twitch of her fingers to show that there was life still inside. He wanted to hope, to believe that she would wake up and do what he hoped she would do.

"What is it?" Doranen asked, seeing his contemplative gaze.

Absalom pointed to her, though it took a moment to find the right words to express his sentiments. "This girl is leading a revolution. If I could predict her future, by what I've seen of her past, she will change everything."

"How?"

"Well, to start, she cares about the fate of all Three Kingdoms, not just her own. And she admires you, much to Lucan chagrin, and thinks you are a King worth serving."

Doranen let his head fall, "I don't feel like it now."

Absalom waved his King's comments away, "She is in love with Azrael, a light elf."

"And you're sure of that?"

"I am." The time he had spent seeing Azrael and Rosalyn interact had convinced him of their love, not to mention all that he had seen in Rosalyn's mind. "Lucan is afraid. He wants the world to stay the same, and he's afraid because he knows that she has the power to change it."

He could not remember the last time he had seen a couple with such drive and fight. Tadane had an uneasy alliance with Valandyl, but Helios had always remained separate since before Lucan's great-grandfather. The Elven War had its roots in Lucan's hate, but Absalom dared to hope that the hate and prejudice could be defeated by such a love as what existed between Azrael and Rosalyn.

A shadow passed over his face, "If she wakes up."

"Do you think she will?" Doranen asked with genuine concern.

"I don't know," he mumbled.

He shifted again in the hardwood chair. His back ached and his eyes drooped. It had been a long few days.

Doranen turned to him and put a hand on his shoulder before leaving. "You should get some sleep too, my friend."

"What will you do?" Absalom asked before Doranen reached the door. "If she wakes up, will you give her back?"

"Perhaps I'll see if I can change a little myself."

CHAPTER 52

Rosalyn was only half listening.

She had woken up, to as much surprise to herself as it was to Absalom. Nothing in her body felt as though it functioned as it should. It took her a day for her mind to sort through the resurgences of memories she thought were long dead, and four days for her legs and arms to remember how to work. Even now, she felt that everything she did was with new muscles.

As soon as she was conscious in the room she did not recognize, Azrael burst in and coddled her. Today, he felt compelled to make her laugh and forget. He started out reading, only to switch to telling his own stories. Most of them were about adventures that he and Marcus had experienced, with the occasional story about his family sprinkled in.

"My father seems harsh," he cautioned. "But we both could not help but laugh. My mother was furious at us."

"Seems like a common occurrence."

"Clearly, I take after my father."

Her smile faded. "I take after mine more than I'd like."

"I'm sure there are some good qualities associated with your mother," he tried.

Rosalyn crossed her arms, "Yes, leaving my homeland, betraying the people I love. All admirable qualities."

The wound from her sharp tongue was evident on his face. She sighed and leaned her head against the headboard of the bed. "I don't want to fight. My relationship with my parents will always be... Complicated."

He took her hand and stroked the back of it. The gold

flecks in his eyes caught the light and she fixated on them.

"I know I can't, but I wish I could fix everything for you. Make all the pain you feel vanish."

His words made her heart leap, dripping with a tenderness that only he could give her. Azrael may not have been able to make the pain go away, but he was able to make the pain bearable. She pulled his hand up to her lips and placed a small kiss on his fingers.

She stopped.

He did too.

"I..."

Her breath shook, as she let his hand go.

"Time has always ruled over the two of us. Had more of a say about what we can and cannot be than we have. We talk about two hundred years, or that we would fight forever. I can't think like that. It's hard for me to think that the future can change or that there is anything to hope for, because, for me, there is everyone else's opinions, their eyes, and everyone else's words. Not mine. But..."

Her voice dropped so low that she half wondered if any sound came out at all.

"No matter what happens or who I become, I love you. It scares me, how much I love you. How strong you make me. And how vulnerable too."

She eased herself forward.

He reached up and guided her to him.

They were a breath away when there was a knock at the door, followed by Absalom shuffling his way in and they broke apart.

Who it was that entered did not matter. Always another pair of eyes on them.

"And how are we feeling today?" Absalom asked, rummaging through the satchel that seemed as much a part of him as any other body part.

Rosalyn clenched her fists. She wanted this doctor to go away, this time to never end, the pain to go away, to go back to the moment before. The bed she was in was so big. The warmth from outside poured in and suffocated her. She did not want the moment to end. She wanted to go back to the coolness of her bedroom at home, with Azrael lying there, and the glow that filled her to bursting. His touch on her skin and his fingers in her hair and around her.

She took a breath.

Rosalyn reached out her hand and he took it once again. She knew that even without his magic, that he could feel her anger and disappointment.

And she could feel his.

Without giving the doctor any notice, Azrael kissed her knuckles. Then, turned around, his face he wore for the world now on. “Oh, just another day.”

The words themselves meant nothing, but Absalom nodded and continued on to her.

“Good enough to stand up,” she managed. “I think.”

Absalom came over and did his usual checking of her heart, her breathing, and her general appearance. “Do you mind if we test your strength?”

Rosalyn allowed him to help her out of bed, where Azrael took her by the other side. She managed to stand up with some ease, but, after a few steps, her strength began to fail. Her brain clouded and her feet stumbled forward clumsily. By her fifth step, she could not push herself any further and fell forward.

Hands grabbed at her and wrenched her up. Her arm was forced above her head, while the rest of her ricocheted from the fall. Although her eyes told her she was in Valandyl, she recoiled away from the men in the room. Her mind thought of her father, of all the times he grabbed at her. The skin on her arms remembered his touch and the pain.

She thought she had escaped.

She thought her father was in Helios.

Azrael was there.

He was there and had grabbed her arm.

Her body began to shake and she pushed away the hands trying to touch her. “Get away from me.”

“Rosalyn,” she heard in a calm voice. “You are safe.”

She reached out with her corin, pulling the body nearest her over to the opposite wall. “Just leave me alone.”

“Rosalyn,” she heard again, this time in a different voice. “Let him go.”

She fought her body’s weakness, focusing on the strength needed to keep the body against the wall. “Why?”

“Because you love him. Let him go.”

Rosalyn exhaled, allowing herself to see Absalom in front of her. He was wary of what he should do next, but still, she held her shaky stance.

Absalom took a cautious step towards her, “You’re frightened, and I see that. I’ll listen to you, but you need to put him down.”

She did as she was asked, released her grip, then fell to her knees.

Absalom came over and bent down to her level. “You are safe here.”

“But he grabbed me,” she whispered.

Absalom’s eyes narrowed in confusion, “What are you afraid of?”

“My father would beat me all the time.”

“And you think that he’s going to hurt you?”

“No, I think he would be justified if he ever did.”

“What?” Azrael interjected.

“My father would beat me within an inch of my life,” she explained again, unable to make eye contact with Azrael. “And my people hate me. As far as I’m concerned, they have good reason. He deserves better than me.”

Azrael came closer, “What brought this on?”

She let the tears that burned the back of her eyes fall down her cheeks. The air around her was hot and sticky. The room dwarfed her, making her wish she could go back to the room in Helios she knew.

"You've risked so much because of me."

Azrael extended an arm to her, but she shook her head. He urged her further, coaxing her to him. She did not want to take it, and everything in her made her recoil. And yet, she looked into the eyes of the man who knew her.

"I love you," he added.

She took his hand, and he pulled her into his arms. His love was terrifying. It was the possibility that she could be loved that kept her hoping and fighting, but it made way for the possibility that she could be wrong. What if she did take after her mother and it was a matter of time before she would see why her mother left, and do the same. What if Azrael did?

"For how long?" she mumbled against his shirt. "How long will you love me until you finally realize that being with me is a mistake. That I'm dangerous."

Azrael lifted her head up just enough for him to whisper in her ear, "Loving you is not a mistake, and you will never convince me otherwise."

Though his voice was still quiet, it carried his conviction. If she had had any doubt of his feelings, it was removed when she felt him around her. She could not tell if her knees weakened because of Azrael or because her strength had finally given out, but he caught her. "You should be in bed. You aren't strong enough to be up for this long."

"What do you see that's worth all this?" she petitioned. "That my father can't see? My people? Your people can't see?"

"I see what they do to you."

CHAPTER 53

Azrael smiled to assure Rosalyn that she was fine and to assure himself that he would only be gone a few minutes. She had only been awake for a few days, getting out of bed this soon was a mistake.

Though the air was an improvement on the previous room, it had its own problems. The cell in Doranen's dungeon was drafty, the wind blowing through corridors made a terrible gasping sound as it made its way through.

Meanwhile, this room was much warmer and he could tell that the speed at which Rosalyn was healing was faster. Here, she had a bed and the warmth made her skin feel soft but durable. However, as he walked out the door with Absalom, he felt the fresh air flood the room as soon as the door opened. He took a hearty breath at the entrance of the room, before exiting.

"What was that? A side effect of the spell?" he asked Absalom in reference to her previous outburst.

"The way you grabbed her set off an emotional reaction."

"How do you know?"

Absalom looked exhausted, and he gave off all the visible signs that he would rest as soon as Azrael was done with him. His voice strained, "One of the unfortu nate consequences of proving she was innocent of killing Princess Emmelina is that I've seen every traumatic event she has ever experienced. Not the type of information that I enjoy knowing."

"I understand," Azrael replied, though he did not. What Doranen had asked of him was detrimental to not only Rosalyn but to Absalom as well. He would live with the memories of another life coexisting with his own. The pain and joy of both lives swirling and combining that contributed to the seriousness of the spell. Only the most powerful and adjusted magic practitioners in the realm were permitted to cast the spell, let alone the few among those willing to cast it. A few had been rumored to have lost their sanity over the aftermath.

"You love her," Absalom observed without warning. "But knowing all that her father did to her, it will take a long time for her to believe that you love her, and that is if she ever fully accepts it."

"What do I do?" Azrael asked, then clarified. "To convince her..."

"That's simple." Absalom flashed a weak smile, the lines near his mouth creaking under the unexpected expression. He put a hand on Azrael's shoulder and patted it in approval. "Tell her how you feel, every day."

"Absalom?" Both men turned to see Doranen peeking his head around the corner and into the hallway they occupied. When they noticed him, it was too late for him to turn around so he stepped out into full view. "Is something wrong?"

"No, not at all." Absalom waved his hand to further emphasize his point, bowed to his King, then excused himself. "I'll leave her to you. Let me know if she needs anything."

He nodded, "Thank you."

Azrael let him go and motioned for Doranen to come towards him.

Doranen intertwined his fingers and shifted nervously. "I seem to have interrupted something. Perhaps, I should come back later. I don't want to overtax Rosalyn."

"We can check, but I believe it would be alright if you came in."

Azrael ushered him into the room, leaving the door open a sliver to keep the fresh air circulating. Rosalyn was sitting up and watched them come in with an eager smile. "Rosalyn, King Doranen would like to speak to you."

"Only if you are feeling up to it," Doranen cautioned.

"Please." As her smile grew wider, she motioned them forward with her hand. "Come in. I'm feeling much better."

"I'm glad to hear that," Doranen expressed.

Between him and Absalom, a chair had been placed on the side of the bed opposite the door. Azrael walked to it and sat down, allowing the King to come to the side closest to the entrance of the room.

Rosalyn turned her attention to Doranen, "I was amazed by your generosity when I woke up here. You didn't have to move me."

Doranen's face sunk, "Yes, I did."

"You could get in trouble if the wrong person were to find out that I was here. The sacrifices that you have made for me..."

Doranen's previous nervousness melted away into a much darker shadow passing over his face. He shuffled around, and could not keep eye contact for longer than a few seconds. "You talk of my sacrifice, but I don't think you realize your own. What you have done for me, my daughter, and Azrael is worthy of praise."

He paused, "And yet, we live in a world that is not yet ready to hear it..."

Doranen ruffled through his overcoat and pulled out a small stack of parchment wrapped in a leather cover with a tie to keep it taut. He extended his hand and placed the parcel on the bed, letting it go as if it were made of hot coals.

"What I have here is my attempt at thanking you." He shrugged, though it was the shrug of someone trying to ignore his own nervousness. A sweat developed above his lip and his hands had a slight tremble to them. "It isn't much in comparison, but I hope that it will help you. You and Azrael."

Rosalyn picked up the parcel and opened it up with care. Her fingers moved over the parchment with particular grace, guiding her eye over the parchment's surface. As she did so, her face grew long with shock. Her voice struggled to remain steady, "Is this real?"

"Yes," Doranen answered.

Azrael stood up to get a better view of this item that shocked Rosalyn and left Doranen quiet. The parchment was a series of documents that described the life of a woman named Lina Meleigh. She was a distant cousin on Doranen's side of the family, was born a year after Azrael was, and had been traveling for most of her life between the Three Kingdoms and the human lands. However, Azrael was acquainted well enough with Doranen's family to know that no such person existed.

He looked to Doranen for an explanation, "This is an entire person, an entire identity."

Doranen nodded to Azrael but explained himself to Rosalyn. "One that will allow you to go anywhere you please, aside from Helios of course. I've made all the arrangements, and Azrael's parents already know."

"This..." Rosalyn stammered. Though her eyes teared up, her face was full of joy. "This isn't much? This is everything I have ever wanted. Thank you. From the depths of my soul, thank you."

"You're welcome," Doranen said with a smile that conveyed his relief. "It's what Emmy would have wanted."

"My mother agreed to this?"

Doranen crossed his arms and took a step back. "No, she did not. Contrary to how your mother perceives the world, I do have sovereignty over my own kingdom."

"She won't be happy about this."

"You let me worry about that."

"Thank you."

"Your welcome," Doranen said, as he turned to leave.

By the time that the mechanism on the door slid home, the shock on Rosalyn's face had not worn off. She kept reading over the papers as if expecting them to evaporate in her hands. The rest of her body remained still to avoid shattering the moment.

Azrael looked up from Rosalyn's new life with giddy anticipation, "Let me take you to Tadane."

Rosalyn's eyes traveled between him and the parchment in her lap. "You just told Doranen that your mother won't be happy."

"We don't have to see her much," Azrael chuckled. He shifted to the end of his seat, holding her hand just a bit tighter. "When we arrive, we'll have to. But, after a couple days, she'll be busy and Tadane will be ours. We could have a life there."

Rosalyn pushed the paper to the end of the bed, then forced herself to the edge closest to him. "We'd be running away after all."

"Is that a yes?"

"Yes."

CHAPTER 54

Lina Meleigh felt Azrael's grip on her tighten as soon as they reached the border of Tadane. For all his disdain for his parents, she saw his excitement and smile through his body as he saw the tall spires in the sky and his own people on the streets.

Part of her thought that she would hate everything about Tadane like she could not get away from the prejudice that she had fought all her life. However, Tadane felt like Helios reflected in a mirror. Tadane was as grand and built up as Helios because Queen Amrydalis was as obsessed with image as her father. The sun showed through every hallway she passed, giving each building a glow that was unmistakable. Just as Azrael seemed to have an aura that radiated from him, so it seemed that the city matched him.

When they reached the castle, her eyes were as wide as they could be and her own doubt of herself was high. There was no question that she stood out amongst the typical fair-haired Tadanian dressed in silver and white robes. She had attempted to blend in, wearing a pale blue dress that Doranen had given to her, but not only did she stick out in the color but it was too long for her. When they dismounted from the cart, she almost tripped even with Azrael helping her down.

The sight before her was more intimidating than any entrance at Helios. While her father hated fanfare, it seemed that Queen Amrydalis lived for it. First, and purposely, stood the hardened generals of Tadane at attention. If there was anything that she took from her childhood, it was the ability to spot a soldier and a politician. Lined up after were some of the queen's train, looking almost too enthusiastic about their Prince's return home. As Azrael greeted everyone by name and with light chatter, some of them seemed not to notice her stumbling next to him while others eyed her with confusion and suspicion. Lastly, Marcus stood trying to hide his excitement under his usual composure and doing a decent job, she thought.

Marcus, dressed in finery, stepped out of line to greet them. His pace faltered when he saw her, but he recovered himself. His smile was genuine when he turned his attention back to Azrael. "It's good to see you again, my friend."

Azrael wrapped his arms around Marcus' narrow shoulders and patted his back, "You as well."

When they released, Marcus turned to Lina and tried to be cordial. "And you brought..."

"Lina Meleigh," Azrael finished.

"Of course, right," he returned. "Lady Lina, it is good to see you as well."

Lina bowed her head, then intertwined her fingers. "I hope you will forgive the intrusion."

"It's no intrusion," Azrael countered. "You are my guest."

"He's right," Marcus agreed. His tone grew more cheerful as the conversation went on. "You have every right to be here. Come. The King and Queen have planned a meal for you, as they surmised that you would be hungry after your journey."

Azrael nodded, "They have surmised correctly. Do you mind, my dear?"

"Not at all," she answered. "We left so early that we didn't have time to grab anything."

Marcus ushered them forward, falling back so that his pace was even with Azrael's. They began talking as old friends were apt to do, while Lina studied her new surroundings.

Everywhere she looked, there were intricate carvings in the stone and wood that weaved its way like a marker directing guests. History overflowed from the carved moldings and icons that highlighted how much older the elves of Tadane were compared with the other two elven kingdoms. The soldiers that dispersed behind them were as formidable as the Queen and country they served. For all of Tadane's strength, an ingrained order was just as vivid and stable as it's history. The white marble columns that lined the tall corridor were not just symmetrical but marked by the same ornamental pearl urns after every fourth column and one pale wooden lattice in the middle marking the pathway onward. Out past all these markers was an indoor garden that appeared to be for display only. The grass and plants were without any visible marks that anyone had touched them in some time.

Measured. Tailored. Sharp.

Rosalyn squeezed Azrael's hand tighter, hoping for some sort of protection from it all. "You did tell them that I was coming, right?"

"Of course, I did," Azrael assured. She hoped that her nervousness was not as noticeable as she thought, but cursed under her breath when Azrael stopped walking. "Marcus, do you mind giving us a minute?"

"Sure," Marcus paused, looked around, then the brightness of an idea illuminated his face. "I'll tell your parents that you both have arrived."

Marcus dawdled off, disappearing into the ballroom at the end of the hallway.

Lina let go of Azrael and crossed her arms in front of her. "I'm fine," she stressed.

"It's alright to be nervous."

Lina took a step back, "Is it? One wrong move and I could ruin everything."

"That isn't going to happen."

"Besides, the world may see me different now, but people like Marcus and your parents still know the truth."

"I see what they don't," he countered with a smile. "Remember?"

A smile tugged at the corner of her mouth, "You're just

trying to make me feel better."

"That I am," Azrael admitted with the charm he would need to be a good king.

"So you don't mean it?" she asked.

To her, it seemed insincere. She did not need charm. She did not need comforting. Part of her did not know what she needed, aside from assurance that she would not be discovered. However, her doubt was so strong that she wondered if she would even believe it were he to give it to her. She scratched at her arm and looked away from the man in front of her.

"Of course, I mean it." Azrael sighed. He scanned her, thought for a moment, then gave a gentle tug at her arms to uncross them. Once free, he pulled her in close and rubbed the tension from her arms. "Lina, this isn't going to be easy, but we have a chance to start over. To make our own way. I will be here with whatever you need, but you shouldn't worry. Doranen has given us something no one in our position has ever had."

"I wasn't aware there were others in our position," she replied.

"I'm sure there are, but, if not, then all the more reason to make our own path."

His charm still oozed from the broad smile he wore, but it was beginning to work. His body seemed to glow in a way that made her jealous of his warmth and confidence.

"You seem happy," she said to mask her own insecurity.

"I'm hopeful," he replied, then placed a kiss on her forehead. "Come on, let's get some food in you then we can rest."

Azrael interlaced his fingers in her right hand and nudged her forward towards the double doors. Two attendants nodded at their Prince, then opened the door as was their job.

The first thing Lina noticed was the smell of food that released once the doors swung open. Crisp greens, warm spiced almonds and walnuts, plus the familiar scent of chicken with rosemary filled the room and looked even more delicious than it smelled on the large table in the middle of the room.

The second thing she became aware of was the presence of Azrael's parents. She had not seen Azrael's mother, Queen Amrydalis, since before her whipping, and she had never spoken with Azrael's father, Aurelius. The moment she made eye contact with the pair, she felt small. Everyone seemed to be taller than her, and, as Emmy had, the King and Queen of Tadane towered over her.

At the end of the room and already seated, Amrydalis and Aurelias were like statues. Their mouths curved into forced smiles, and their bodies thin like trees. Rosalyn observed as Amrydalis leaned over and whispered comments to her husband that the two were inseparable. Divorcing her personal opinions on the Queen, she could see that Amrydalis and Aurelias were of the same nature.

A nature that their son did not share. Perhaps, she wondered, Azrael had somehow drained them of their sincerity and light when he was born.

"Oh, my son," Amry cried. Despite her fervor, there was still a reserved quality about her. It was as if she was always being watched for weakness, that any emotion could reveal something useful to her enemies. "It's been so long."

Azrael broke away from her and gave a short bow with his head. "It's good to be back, mother."

Though he had to let go of her hand to receive his mother, Lina felt her doubt slip in as his fingers slipped away. She saw Amry's glares in her direction, and Aurelius stared at her as if she had horns growing from her head. What would they disapprove of most, she began to think. Every object and person that surrounded her seemed so beautiful yet untouchable that she wanted to retreat.

"Where did Marcus go?" Azrael asked, looking around. "Did he not just come in here?"

Amry pointed to the other door out of the room. "I dismissed him. We wanted to talk without being censored."

"He's like a brother to me."

"My son, you will have plenty of time to catch up with your friend, but you will do it later."

Amry turned towards her, "So, this is Ros..."

No, do not say her old name. Anything but her old name.

Amry stopped herself before she could say anything incriminating, but the first syllable of Lina's name was enough to make her palms sweat. She bowed, then recited her new identity as she had in her mind the entire journey to Tadane. "Lina Meleigh."

"Of course," Aurelius said, ignoring the slip up by his wife. She noticed the same smile and cheekbones in Aurelius as was in his son, which gave her a familial sense of calm. "It is good to meet the woman our son has written to us about."

"Yes," Amry agreed dryly. "We are glad to meet the woman who has stolen our boy's gaze... and time."

Azrael cast a disapproving glare, "Mother..."

She waved away his comment with one hand and ushered them towards the table with the other. "Come, rest your legs. We had the cook make your favorites."

Lina breathed a sigh of relief, hoping that she could let Azrael reacquaint himself with his family rather than the focus be on her. She made her way to the table with her head down, focusing on keeping her skirts out of her way and attracting as little attention as possible.

"Lady Meleigh," Amry called. "You can't sit next to the Prince, it would be improper."

Lina stopped, unmoving for a few seconds as she processed what she had just heard. She searched the table, wondering what seat was proper enough for her to sit in, and half believed that she would be sent away. Azrael would have never allowed something like that, but the idea crossed her mind.

"Sit here, near me," Amry offered. She patted the armrest of the seat on her left side. "I'd relish the opportunity to get to know you."

Lina hoped that she did not look as scared as she felt, and wished more than anything that Azrael would say something. When he did not, she proceeded to the other end of the table. Queen Amrydalis wanted to get to know her? Her hands shook at what that could entail, but she managed to sit down without tripping or knocking anything over.

"So, Lina," Aurelius began. His voice much deeper than Azrael's, a smooth bass that somehow managed to sound refined. "My son tells me you like to read. I hope you will pop into the library we have in here. Has Azrael told you about it?"

She flashed a courteous smile, hoping the attention would soon shift away from her. "He's mentioned so many things in Tadane. He speaks of this place with such fondness."

"Oh, Aurelias, yes," Amry agreed, though her tone implied she did not. "Azrael, you really should take her over there. We have a particularly great history section. Though I'm sure you are well acquainted with most of the events."

Azrael dropped his fork, it falling onto the plate with a noticeable clink. "Mother, please."

"You said she reads," Amry excused. Her eyebrows shot up as if she was not expecting anyone to notice her inference, though she was not apologetic. "I just assumed she would have read books on every subject. That's all."

"I will be sure to visit it," Lina mumbled.

Amry continued with a bite in her voice, "There are many places you might enjoy. The library, the armory, the throne room."

"Mother."

Without warning, Amry stood up and waved her hands in Lina's direction. "I'm not on board with this plan."

Aurelius reached up, trying to grab onto one of her arms and calm her down. "Amry, not now. They just arrived."

Her movements stopped, but her attention turned in a drastic motion towards the elf in the room she despised. "She should know. I won't have her here under false pretenses."

However small she felt when she had walked into the room, she wished that she was smaller than that. She bent her head down and stared at her hands in her lap, wishing that she was back in her room in Valandyl. It was not even a room that belonged to her, a guest room that still seemed more welcoming than here.

"I'm sorry," she whispered.

"You're sorry?" Amry parroted. "If this falls through, we could have rioting all across our kingdom and don't think Doranen will be excused. He'll have it worse."

"It was his idea," Azrael cited.

Amry dismissed her son's comment and turned back to Lina. "A foolish idea. I can't make you leave, but I won't sit passively while you sow dissent in my kingdom."

Lina flinched, but she was surprised that it was not out of fear. She was afraid. However, that last sentence of Amry's seemed to catch on something in her head. Lucan had beat her many times, but there was a common phrase he would often yell at her while he hit her. Often he would tell her of the dissent that she was bringing to Helios every time she mentioned Emmy or Azrael, every time she stood up for herself. All the feelings she felt with her father moved within her now, and, while Rosalyn had been powerless against him, Lina did not have to be powerless against Amry.

She stood up, almost knocking her chair over behind her. "I wouldn't do that."

"Azrael, she needs training," Amry began. Her eyes, however, watched Lina's every movement. "Like etiquette. Not to mention that she knows nothing about our history, our culture. That's if people will look past the fact that she has darker hair and eyes than everyone here. And her gloves? Who will believe that she's not hiding something beneath them?"

Her voice was like a lightning strike in an otherwise clear sky, "I've already had etiquette training."

Amry pursed her lips. "Assuming that I trust your father's judgment when it comes to etiquette, you still don't know us. You haven't read Vestia by Archellias, The Towering Spires, or even Tadane: A History by Phineas."

Before Amry could say anything more, Azrael banged his fist against the table. His anger seemed to make his skin steam, and, for the first time, Lina noticed that Aurelius's eyes had been on his son. Azrael flew out of his chair, came over to her side, and pulled on her arm. "I'll not stand here while you insult the woman I love. Come with me, my dear."

She did not let him move her but stood with her feet planted. "I've read them."

"What?" Amry mouthed.

Azrael seemed startled as well, "You have?"

Lina gave a quick nod to Azrael, then turned to his mother. Her voice surprisingly calm. "You can make all the judgments you want about me, but I do know you. I can't change my face or my attire, but I have been trained by the best to walk in a crowd like I belong, and, unlike what you would expect of someone like me, I have read just about all there is when it comes to culture in the Three Kingdoms. Pardon me for saying so, Your Majesty, but it seems that it is you who doesn't know me."

"Forgive me if I want to make sure," Amry retorted.

"Check all you like, but tomorrow." Lina relaxed her arm that Azrael was still holding, letting him pull her away. "I'm tired from traveling."

Azrael pulled her closer and wrapped his arm around her. "I'll show you to my room."

"Your room?" Amry sputtered. "Together? No, we'll make up a guest room for her."

"No," Azrael decreed. "We'll be in my room."

Lina walked out and wondered why she did not feel better. She had fought against Azrael's mother and her every attempt to discredit her. Yet, she felt further away from herself than ever. Azrael held her close as they walked, whispering apologies in her ear.

As she followed the man she loved through his home,

all the politics that she had wanted to avoid thinking about came at her. No wonder Amry had built up the army she had and that the border had walls that had kept her father out for as long as they had. The castle was open, exposed ceilings and gaping corridors as far as she could see. If her father could only break through the fortifications, the kingdom would be overrun with dark elves and Amry defeated in hours.

"You said that she wouldn't be happy about me," Lina reiterated once they were alone in his room.

"I did, but I'm still mortified. That was..."

Azrael closed the door and hovered near it while he searched for words. He grew quiet, channeled all his frustration into a small bang on the wood with the flat of his hand, then turned around to face her. "Words can't explain how sorry I am."

She shook her head and hands, trying to release all the tension in her. "It isn't you."

"In a few days, she'll calm down."

"Calm?" she scoffed.

Azrael's head wobbled, weighing out his experience and his optimism. His thoughts settled and he relented. "Her attention will shift to something else. Something new always takes precedence. You'll see."

"You're sure?"

"No, but I hope."

As he came over and took her in his arms, her frustration eased. She was not optimistic, but she was in Tadane which had seemed just as unlikely as Amry's mood changing only a few days before. He smiled, and the last of her nerves fell away. She was here with him and that was all that mattered.

"I sent ahead for something before we left Valandyl."

He turned her around so they both faced the same direction, weaving one of his arms around her stomach and the other pointing to a work table. On top, in a white porcelain vase were a bouquet of honeysuckle, lavender, and roses. Once she saw them, their brightness made her wonder how she had missed them. The deep color of the petals and the light fragrance that reached her as far away as she was made her want to reach out and touch them.

"Are those for me?" she asked, even though she knew they were.

His free hand trailed up the skin of her shoulder, before landing on her neck and in her hair. "In some ways, my upbringing wasn't so different from yours. When you agreed to come here and having you standing in my bedroom, it redeems some of my childhood that I'd rather not remember."

Azrael winced, and she realized that, while she had shaken her feelings away, Azrael had not. He was the comforter, the one to always look after her, but it was in these rare moments that she saw him falter. The pain that he did not allow to the surface until it forced its way out, and pointed to some deeper trauma.

"She'll calm down," she assured.

He nodded into her, and she could hear a forced smile in his breathing as he pushed the trauma back down where she could not get to it.

"She'll calm down," he repeated.

CHAPTER 55

Lina walked to Azrael's room knowing that he would not be in there. For all their hope at Amrydalis's mood lightening, Azrael had been sent on a trip to Valandyl while she was left to periodic "training" from Amry on how to blend into Tadanian society. She came back from a session with the queen to a letter explaining the whole circumstance and a sincere apology, and with no one but Amry for company.

Company she had no interest in seeking out.

She opened the door, closing it behind her as if it would keep Amry away.

After pulling off her necklace, she stopped.

Lina felt a hand cover her mouth, and her body being pulled against the bulk of another. She struggled and pushed, but the arm around her was like a rock holding her in place. The arm pulled her around and relaxed his grip.

"Shhh. It's me."

She turned to see her brother and, while her body relaxed, her mind began to race.

"What are you doing here?" she whispered.

Dorian stayed silent, looking ashamed and anywhere but her eyes.

"It's good to see you too, Rosalyn."

Lina stopped cold, recognizing the voice that came from deeper in the room. The voice was one she thought she would never hear again, especially in Tadane. He stood in the shadows, glancing over the aspects of the room with clear disapproval before walking into full view. Her father cracked a gloating smile, "Or is it Lina now?"

In an instant, all the strength she had built up and the confidence that her new identity gave her vanished. Her body shook and cowered under her father's gaze. Flashbacks of her father pulling her away from Valandyl surfaced in her mind. She took a step back, reaching for anything to grab onto if her father tried to pull her back to Helios.

"What are you doing here?" she said again.

"Can't a father check in on his daughter?"

"No."

Lucan chuckled humorlessly, "You filthy traitor."

It was not the word traitor that caught in her mind. She was a traitor. It was the word filthy that unraveled her. Despite the residual pain from her injuries and Amry's temper, her new life was the happiest she had ever been. Tadane and Valandyl allowed her to walk around without fear of abuse or failing her father's expectations. However, her current feelings did not matter to him. She had mingled with Vestans and, in his mind, she was filthy and tainted.

"Leave Tadane, now."

She cringed, hoping that her voice sounded less pitiful out loud than in her head.

"Or what?" he laughed. "You have far more on the line then I do, if I'm caught."

"Please, just leave me alone. I have a chance..."

Lucan's sarcasm drained from his face. The anger she feared returned, commanding the room. "I don't care about your chance. You belong in Helios, with your people. With me."

"You don't want me," she exclaimed and gestured towards her brother. "You want him. Claim Dorian."

Dorian tugged on her arm, "It isn't that simple."

"It could be," Lucan mused. Both his children whipped around at his words, and he regretted saying anything. He sighed, shifting his weight to the other foot. "We are going to do this, now? Fine. Dorian, you were the obvious choice. You were the one that everyone wanted. But you, my daughter.

You were the one that no one expected.

"I flatly refuse to be predictable," he added with an air of superiority.

Lina struggled to say the words that were forming in her head, "So you chose me for shock value?"

"I chose you because you are stronger than Dorian, more powerful than Dorian." Lucan turned away, wiping his face and running a hand through his hair. "Traits that I, unfortunately, have to credit your mother for."

Rosalyn saw Dorian wince out of the corner of her eye.

"Dorian would be a good king," he explained further. "But you would be a great queen if I can just push you hard enough."

"I don't want this."

"And you think your brother does?" He bellowed.

Lina turned around and searched her brother for an explanation. "You don't?"

"I was relieved when he claimed you."

For all the years that she had relied on her brother, he had never admitted that he did not want the crown. He had been her rock through all of the torture her father had put her through, yet he had always done everything her father had asked. She had assumed that he obeyed him to secure his position in case she failed.

Lucan banged on a nearby dresser, "You don't think that we've discussed this before."

He stopped then looked up, forgetting that his children were even in the room. "I do everything for my people and then I get cursed with two children that don't want to succeed me."

"And you don't think that says something about you?" She sneered.

Lucan's eyes narrowed, the same fire in his eyes that made her knees weak appeared. He lunged at her, grabbed her by the chin, and slammed her against the nearest wall.

"Contrary to what you may think," he said through gritted teeth. "I didn't come here to ruin your little dress up game. I need something from you. You are the only one powerful enough to make me a weapon to help me with this war."

She clawed at his hands, though she knew from past experience how unyielding they were. "Why would I help you?"

Lucan let go of her, straightening his robes as if he were a proper gentleman. His voice mimicked a more formal tone as well. "Because I'll out you if you refuse."

Once she regained her breath, she felt a deep panic set in. She had been Lina for only a couple weeks and her life with Azrael was already in jeopardy. Her father knew that, as well as the fact that making him a weapon would put her loyalties into question.

"Why are you trying to ruin me?" she asked while wiping her eyes. She felt like crying, but she would not give her father the satisfaction of seeing her break.

"I don't mind if you have your fantasy that you can make it here," he lied. "Eventually, your Vestans will betray you and you'll come running back to me. In the meantime, you can be useful."

"I'll tell Azrael," she tried. "We'll figure out a way around you."

Lucan's jovial attitude returned, and he flashed a mocking smile. "Azrael isn't even here. You don't think I would have risked coming here if I didn't do any research ahead of time. Your lover is in Valandyl."

She swore under her breath, realizing that she was trapped in a corner. As always, her father had thought of everything to get her to do his will and she was powerless. She searched the room and her mind as if something would give her an out but nothing inspired her.

"You do this for me before your Vestan gets back," Lucan prompted in a voice meant to be charming. "And I'll leave you to make your own mistakes."

She could go back.

The thought entered like a poison, slow but with

powerful effect. If she went back with them, she would not have to ruin what Doranen had given her or betray Azrael. It would be a clean departure, one that left Azrael and Doranen without any blame.

Or she could run.

She snickered at that possibility. Her father was able to sneak into enemy territory, and into the bedroom of the Prince without being seen. Lucan would find her no matter where she went.

Lina retreated to the edge of the room, away from her family. "... Get out. I'll make your weapon."

The smile Lucan wore eased into the rest of his face. His victory was clear, yet his joy made her stomach turn. He ushered to Dorian, towards the balcony where they had apparently entered from and began his exit. Dorian crawled over the railing first, still unable to look her in the eye.

Lucan pulled his leg over but paused before committing fully to his dissent.

"I'll see you soon," he tossed over his shoulder.

She heard horses below and the quick stampede of hooves as they rode off.

Though it was mid-afternoon, Lina felt the room darken. Her legs lost the strength to carry her, and she resigned herself to the floor. In one brief meeting, she felt that her resolve was shot and sense of freedom shattered. The room seemed to swallow her up. She wished more than anything that she could run to Azrael for help and punched the marble floor when she knew that that was impossible.

While her father's presence reminded her of everything she lacked, what he had driven home was that, for all her attempts, she was still very much alone.

CHAPTER 56

Azrael stood at the top of the hill overlooking the castle that he called home and knew Lina was in trouble. Every step closer told him that dark magic was at work and he had a sinking feeling that Lina was at the center of it all. The air was ripe with magic. He signaled for his horse to move forward, and arrived at the castle within the hour.

When he arrived, he was greeted by Marcus and his parents fretting and commenting to each other outside his bedroom.

"Marcus, what is going on?"

"We aren't quite sure, she won't let us in."

His mother came over, arms waving and a tremor in her voice. "Azrael, please, make it stop. She's been at this for hours."

He looked at the guards that followed his mother around and gestured towards the door with his head. With a sigh, he ordered them to break the door down. The immediate smell of ash and incense filled his nose as smoke escaped from the room. He peered inside, only to find Lina in a circle marked on the floor with a white powder. The roses he had given her were lying in front of her with an eerie change in color.

"Leave me," Lina choked.

He entered the room, hoping that Marcus and his parents had the good sense to wait outside. As he made his way over, he noticed that the flowers were not the only thing in the room that had changed in appearance.

Lina was sitting on her knees, though her back was arched in an uncomfortable and unnatural position. Her hair was plastered to her forehead with sweat, and the vein in her neck and forehead were distended. However, her hands were the most frightening of her physical changes. They straightened and curled with no order other than what seemed to cause her the most pain. All her muscles in her hands were flexed, and her corin glowed.

"Lina," he hesitated.

"Don't touch." Her voice gurgled through her strained vocal chords.

He bent down to her level. "I won't touch you, but you have to stop this."

"Don't touch them," she spat. "Don't touch them."

"Alright," he surrendered. "I won't touch them. Stop this, now."

Her head fell, yet her body remained still.

"Away," she whispered.

His eyes narrowed, and he reached out to urge her to finish. The instant his hand touched her, she reacted as if his hand was red hot. She screamed, writhed away from him, and her body arched further.

"Away," she commanded.

Azrael backed up, feeling more distant from the woman in front of him then all the times they were separated by kingdoms. With a wave of her hands, the spell broke, the roses scattered across the room, and something in the air released. Lina fell, convulsing.

She grabbed at the sky, the ground, and him for help. He could still feel the magic working in her like a second heartbeat that pounded in her chest. As her shaking began to slow, she gasped for air. He pulled her close to him.

"Is she alright?" Marcus asked from the doorway.

"She needs a physician."

Marcus left, presumably to get a doctor.

As he surveyed the room, nothing made sense. Cold air blew in from the balcony and pricked at his dirty skin. The cold made him numb, while the girl lying limp in his arms pulled him away from all he knew. He carried her to his bed and covered her with the comforter.

Small footsteps marked his mother entering the room. She came up behind him, putting a hand on his shoulder.

“Azrael,” she began with a mix of disappointment and fear in her voice. "What has she done?"

"I'll sort it out," he hoped. "I promise.”

CHAPTER 57

Lina pulled at her blanket with futile effort. Every muscle in her body felt torn, and her head throbbed. She knew the spell was powerful, though she had not expected all that had transpired. Her memory was returning slowly, but she knew that Azrael was back.

She opened her eyes, hoping to find him somewhere in the room. Instead, covering a rose she had enchanted and placing it in a bag on his shoulder was her brother.

She wanted to move and even tried to speak. Both, with an aching physical reminder, were beyond her.

Dorian saw her notice him and came over to her. He placed a quick kiss on the top of her head, then made his way to his preferred exit.

"I'm sorry, Lina."

Her vision was blurred, so it looked as though he leaped off the balcony. Honestly, she would not have been surprised if he had. Lucan had put Dorian through his own training, often grueling work in swordsmanship, counterintelligence, and special operations.

Guilt ate away at her, realizing that she was a traitor to all three kingdoms. She had defied her father and protected Azrael's identity after his infiltration. Her father, now, made her betray the loyalties she had had since her first trip to Valandyl. She wanted to believe that he had made her do it, yet she had had a choice. Obeying her father avoided returning to Helios, but she feared that Azrael would send her back anyway.

Tears fell seamlessly from her eyes before her body shut

down. Whatever happened, she had chosen the action she thought was best to keep her with Azrael. She took a deep breath, hoping that he would see that, and find a way to forgive her.

CHAPTER 58

Lina paced across the length of the room, waiting for Azrael to enter as he had managed to only come in when she was asleep or nearly out of it. He had left partially full cups of water, still warm chairs, and, the latest, a note stating his intention to talk through what happened. She had spent the better part of the day shuffling around the room and waiting to explain her actions.

When he knocked on the door, she nearly jumped from her skin.

"Come in," she stuttered.

As soon as she saw his face, her heart broke. She would cut off her left arm if it meant she could stay with him. His face looked tired. What she had done had undoubtedly caused a reaction with his parents and she imagined he had been with them while he was away from her. She searched her mind for anything she could do to absolve the situation.

"I wish that I could think of something better to say other than I'm sorry."

Azrael looked startled when she spoke, but said nothing. He closed the door to give them some privacy, then walked over to her with an evident trepidation in his step.

"Please say something."

"What were you thinking?" he began, his frustration apparent. "You were worried about making a mistake, but I had no idea that you would make one like this."

"I know," she cried. "And I'm sorry."

Azrael raised his hands and paced. "I had my parents screaming at me all night. The guards didn't know what to make of the scene."

Her voice was a mere whisper, "I'm sorry."

"Is that all you can say?"

Lina shrunk back.

Azrael stopped and relaxed his body. Even in his frustration, he was sensitive to her feelings. He bridged the gap between them, reached out to steady her with gentle hands, and looked at her with soft eyes. "What happened?"

"My father snuck into the room," she explained. "He threatened to expose me if I didn't make him a weapon."

"Why didn't you tell me?"

"He said I had to do it before you got back. He knew you were gone. I didn't want to, but I didn't see another option."

She paused, reaching up to his collar. "I know that I made the wrong decision, but I was so afraid of losing you that I wasn't about to let my father ruin this like he had everything else."

Azrael sighed, "What did you make?"

"It's an enchanted object. A rose that hurts people similar to what a corin does to you, but on a grander scale."

"I guess we can find a way to work around that," he guessed.

Azrael stood contemplating his next move. His voice sounded hopeful, forgiving even, or at least that is what she told herself. Instead of saying anything, Lina watched him mosey over to the bed, sit down, and think more. She came over but did not feel comfortable sitting next to him.

"I made ones for Valandyl," she admitted.

He looked up at her, "You did?"

"My father doesn't know. I enchanted roses for Valandyl that will counteract the one I made for my father because I know that that is where he will strike. Valandyl is weak, far weaker than Tadane. My father believes that toppling Valandyl is the key to winning the war."

Azrael stood up, walking past her towards the door. "We need to write to Valandyl to let them know what is in store for them. The more that we can tell Doranen the better. Multiple roses will help when I present all this to my mother."

"Your mother?"

"Yes, I've had her screaming at me since I got back. She's furious."

"Azrael?"

He turned around, only to see her small frame shaking.

"Can you ever forgive me?"

Lina did not know how her emotions were interpreted on her face, though she could read enough on his face to get an idea. She blinked away the tears that were on the edge of her eyelids and scratched at the top of her arms. He ushered her over to him, wrapped his arms around her, and kissed her forehead.

"Of course I can," he whispered into her hair. "Let us craft a letter to Doranen and then we can spend some time outside. I think we could both use some fresh air to clear our minds."

She cracked a smile, "I'd like that."

Once the letter was crafted, Lina followed Azrael outside and into one of the many courtyards that Tadane's palace featured. The effects of her actions remained to be seen, but the mood began to lighten. Azrael smiled at her as they searched for a spot, and would place chaste kisses on her cheeks. If anyone had asked her what it was that drew her to Azrael, it was the way he made her feel like she was worth loving despite everything. He did not see her as a dark elf or even the Princess of Helios but as herself.

Azrael picked a spot with trees for shade and privacy and waited until she was seated at a stone bench before removing the sword from his sheath to practice. He explained that the Elestren had gotten reports that there was unrest among the humans nearest the border of Tadane and Valandyl. While Queen Amrydalis was not worried, Aurelius had expressed some concern. Azrael was told that he would be required to participate in battle were there to be one.

Meanwhile, she opened a book she had picked up at the library that Aurelius had raved about but could not concentrate. Her mind wondered about humans and roses, knowing that she could not hide from them all forever.

"Take that."

Lina jumped, more startled at the sound of Azrael's voice than the tap of the flat of his blade against her leg. "You know you're just lucky that I'm not armed."

"Luck? Is that how you would describe it?"

"Remember," she cautioned. "I do have magic."

"I'm so frightened. Really, I think I'm shaking."

Lina chuckled, then stood up with a dramatic flourish. She may not be Rosalyn anymore, but Lina would be just as powerful. With feet planted parallel to her shoulders, she lifted up her gloved hand.

"You would be smart to fear me," she taunted.

Feeling his weight not with her hands but from somewhere deep in her muscles, she lifted him back against a tree behind him and pinned him there. She took a few steps over to him, studying her work.

"Is that it?" he teased.

Before she could think of a next move, she winced from a sudden pain that began in her head. The pain was unlike anything she had felt before, putting pressure on her skull. It hurt to move, to think, and even just her acknowledging that the pain existed seemed to aggravate it. It grew so fast that she fell to the ground, unable to keep her legs steady under the weight of it.

"Lina," she heard amongst her own groans. "Are you alright?"

She felt her body reach out and a flood of magic release, but without seeing any of it. Everything seemed further away than seemed real, and the pain turned into a pounding. She clawed at the ground for any kind of relief.

As quickly as the feeling had come on, the pain vanished.

Her eyes cleared, the muscles in her arms relaxed, and only the prickle of her corin told her that anything had happened. She blinked until her vision was back to normal, only to see Azrael convulsing on the ground next to her. Moving her body felt foreign but she managed to crawl her way to him and held him down to stop the shaking.

"Somebody help me," she screamed. "The Prince needs help."

She turned her attention back to Azrael, pulling him into her arms.

"You are going to be fine," she whispered. "Please. Hold on, my love."

CHAPTER 59

Lina sat with her hands in her lap, studying the lines of exhaustion and weakness in Azrael's face. She reached up, as she had done several times, to take his hand but thought better of it. He was only in his bed with a doctor looming over him because of her. She had spent every moment since they were found in the garden at his side, attempting to figure out what had happened. The pain had come on without warning, but there had to be a reason for it.

The doctor was confident that Azrael's condition was responding well to the medicine he had given him, but refused to comment on whether he would survive. Azrael's breathing was small, and his pulse thready. His doctor eyed her suspiciously, and she could not blame him.

With a massive bang, Amry stormed through the doors of Azrael's room and ran to the side of the bed. She fussed over his blankets, felt his head, and straightened his hair. Aurelius came up behind her, with Marcus in tow, and began asking the doctor questions. Amry's gaze turned to Lina, taking notice of the small creature on the other side of the bed.

"You are a poison," Amry screamed. "He believed you to be different. But you aren't, are you?"

Lina knew she was merely reacting to her son's injuries, but the tone in her voice was sinister. Amry charged forward, moving to the other side of the bed with alarming speed. She pulled Lina out of her chair and pushed her to the center of the room.

"You monster," she growled. "You are a darkness, a curse."

Lina held her hands up in surrender, "I swear, I didn't know that this would happen."

"You didn't know?"

Amry ran at her, all rage and fury. She grabbed her hair and arm, then pushed her towards the ground so hard that she did not realize that Amry had torn some hair until her vision cleared enough to see the queen flicking it away.

"Staying down like a dog?" Amry taunted.

She pulled Lina up only to throw her back down with even more force.

"Please, Queen Amry," she begged between sobs. "I'm sorry."

Amry pulled her up again, this time bringing her within inches of her face. "I don't want your apologies or your begging. What did my son ever do to you? Of all the men in the world you could have tormented, you chose him."

Marcus crept to Amry's side. His voice was low but respectful. "My Queen, the stress isn't good for him..."

Lina looked over her shoulder and saw Azrael's breathing had become short gasps during the exchange. She wanted to blame Amry's shouting, but the Queen's words ate away at her. How could she put any blame on Amry when every word she said was correct. No reason or explanation would take back what had happened or heal the man in front of her.

"You are right about it all," she sobbed.

Amry grabbed her arm and pulled her further away from Azrael. This time she lowered her voice when she spoke. "And you think admitting that will save him? As though you could admit what you are, and that would heal him or make you better. You still did this, and you will never become better than what you are."

Lina's mouth fell open.

Amry dismissed her with a wave and turned back to her son. "Get out."

"No," she pleaded. "I haven't touched him. I won't. I just want to know if he's healing, if he's alright."

Amry tapped on Marcus' shoulder to get his attention, "Get her out of here."

She pleaded with Marcus, yet his loyalties carried him over to her and pulled her away. No amount of pleading or pushing weakened his resolve, even though she was clinging to him by the time they were out of the room. He whispered an apology in her ear, then shut the doors with a resolute thud.

CHAPTER 60

Lina wiped her face, even though she had not cried in hours. It had been three days since Amry kicked her out of Azrael's room, yet she had not heard any news about his condition. The only comfort she had was that she had not seen anyone wearing black nor had Amry come for a second run at her. She had been waiting in an alcove near Azrael's room, hoping that she could gain information from the reactions of the faces of those who left.

When she saw Marcus leave, she called after him. He did not stop, though she knew he had heard her.

"Marcus, please."

"I shouldn't be talking to you," he said, shrinking away from her. "I'm sorry."

She followed him a few more steps, then crumpled against the wall nearest her and fell to the ground. Marcus was her only possible ally and he had left her too. The tears began again, and she pulled her legs underneath her.

"I don't think you are as bad as Queen Amrydalis says you are."

Lina looked up and saw Marcus with an outstretched arm. She took it, nodding in a small gesture of gratitude. His tone and body language were gentle, but his eyes revealed something she could not place. It was not disdain she saw, though she knew it was not affection either.

"What do you think of me?" she asked. "Tell me honestly."

"I think that Azrael loves you," he began, eyeing her with caution. "But I don't think he should... He is my oldest and dearest friend. And as happy as you make him, I don't think that he should be with you."

Lina pulled away from him, wrapping her arms around herself. She had thought the same thoughts as Marcus, though this was the first time she had heard them from someone she trusted. Marcus looked apologetic.

She ushered him back to her alcove, sat down, but looked down at her gloved hand instead of looking at him. The glove hid her mark but she knew it was there. That twist of ink and magic represented everything she hated in the world. While the corin was visible to everyone else, only she knew of the scar just above her elbow.

"Do you think if I were able to cut it off that it would make a difference?"

Marcus' voice was heavy, "No."

"I wrote to Doranen and explained what happened. I'll leave for Valandyl in the morning."

"I hate to say it, but I think that would be wise."

Marcus stood, nodding to signify the end of the conversation. He took a glance back at Azrael's room. He nodded once more, then turned to leave.

"Please let me see him," she begged.

"I don't know if that's..."

She pulled on his shoulder, "I just want to say goodbye before I leave."

Marcus sighed, "Queen Amry and King Aurelius will be back in an hour. I don't want them walking in on you, so, if you are quick, you can come now."

"That's all I ask for," she agreed. "Thank you."

He ushered her into the room, making sure that Queen Amry did not turn into their hallway. Once he was sure she would not, he entered the room and walked over to one side of the bed and she took her place on the other. She wished that she could have a moment with Azrael alone, yet she knew the value of any time with Azrael considering Marcus' opinion of her and his loyalties to Amry.

Azrael's color had returned to his face and sleep had given him new strength. The room itself smelt of stale air and bandages. It was too clean, she thought. Something about the room seemed too perfect until she realized that what was off about the room was her own place within it. She could almost hear Azrael telling her that she belonged. In this case, staring at the result of her being in Tadane, he would have been wrong. She scoffed, then wondered if he could hear her. If she said goodbye, would he even know?

"How is he?" she asked. "Any improvement?"

"He woke up earlier, but he was only able to stay awake for a couple hours."

She went to grab his hand as she had contemplated a few days prior, but, after hearing Marcus' sharp intake of breath, she pulled away at the last second. Instead, she straightened a fold in Azrael's blanket, then pulled the sheet up to his shoulders.

"He asked for you," Marcus added. "Queen Amry did not say much, only that he needed to focus on healing."

It seemed like a thousand questions surged through her mind at once. Was he angry with her? Did he want to see her only to yell at her? There was the slim chance that he would understand that it was a mistake because that was his nature. She shook her head free of her thoughts and shifted her focus back to Marcus.

"Queen Amry is right."

Marcus tapped the edge of the bed, then walked to the end of the room. He did not trust her to be alone with him and, she realized, neither did she. Despite his distrust, he was kind enough to give her some privacy. With her newfound space, she leaned in close to him.

"It's me," she began. "I don't know if you can hear me, but I wanted to at least try to explain myself to you. I've replayed what happened in my head, and the only thing that makes sense is that my control over my own magic was crippled when I made the roses and I..."

Lina swallowed past the lump in her throat and looked down at the blanket that she had straightened. It was soft, with little pills of fabric that caught on her fingertips when she touched it. She scratched at one bit as she formed words.

"You shouldn't have to live with my constant apologies. You shouldn't have to live with any of this. I'm not leaving because of your mother, even though she was right. And I'm not leaving because I don't fit in here, even though I know I don't. I'm leaving because I hurt you. Because I no longer trust myself to be around you. You deserve to be with someone who loves you. And I do. When I'm not around you, I feel like I can't breathe. I love you more every day. But what I've done is prove that I cannot hide who I am nor can I trust myself with your safety."

With a final kiss on his forehead, she whispered, "I am so sorry, my love."

CHAPTER 61

Lina left the room, unable and unwilling to hold back her tears. The future was uncertain and she had no trust in herself or magic. She trudged forward towards the room she had found after the incident, grabbed what few possessions she had, and headed towards the stables. Doranen expected her tomorrow morning, but she had to get out now. Staying in Tadane was like a constant voice in her head telling her how opposite she was from everyone around her.

"Lina," she heard call out behind her. "I think you are doing the right thing."

When she did not stop, Marcus continued to chase after her. He had seen her cry and struggle before, but the fact that she was leaving made her want to hide from him. What could he do about anything she felt, and she had a sinking feeling that he would not want to help her even if he could. She was the unfortunate lover of his best friend who made countless mistakes at the cost of Azrael's health and reputation.

And yet, for all her logic and reasons, her mind ached to turn back.

"Then why doesn't it feel like the right thing."

"Because you love him," he cited and grabbed her arm. She tore her arm away but stayed in place. He looked at her as if she were a child, his voice as stern as Aldan's. "But you must stop that for his own good."

"And what about my own good?" she retorted. The weight of her tone struck her, and she muttered an apology. "What happens now?"

"You leave before you hurt him again."

Lina stomped her foot, "But I didn't mean to, you have to believe me."

"You may not have meant to, but you almost killed him. His physician doesn't think he will ever be able to use magic again."

"I could change," she whimpered. "Build my control back up."

"No," he barked. "You can't."

Lina stopped.

There was a flash of guilt in his eyes, one that she clung to. The moment he realized that it showed, he wiped his face and pulled his shoulders back. He clenched his jaw and crossed his arms.

"You and I are not friends," he explained. "The only reason that I don't hate you is because of his feelings for you and the fact that I trust his judgment. But you have hurt my friend time and again."

"So... You want me to leave. Not only should I leave, but you want me to leave."

"Yes."

She exhaled a shaky breath, while her arms clung to her.

"Ride to Valandyl, Helios, or anywhere you deem fit. Just keep your distance from Azrael or I believe you will kill him."

Without so much as a word, Lina left Marcus standing in the hallway and made for the destination she was headed before he stopped her. Her chest felt like it would break apart at the least provocation and her fingers shook. By morning, she would be away from Tadane and all she had hoped she would find with Azrael. More so than in her entire life in Helios, she believed in the moment that a life with Azrael was impossible. If she could not be with him, at least she would keep him safe.

CHAPTER 62

Though his voice was hoarse and his body felt like water, Azrael urged himself out of bed, through the halls, and into the stables. His muscles screamed at the exertion, but still, he moved forward. The pain, the wheezing, the real possibility that his body would give out, none of it mattered. He had to get there in time to stop her. She could not leave, not when they were finally together.

"Lina," he screamed.

The woman in question turned around, and, with shock clear on her face, she came over. His legs stumbled on the uneven cobblestones. Lina's shock turned to concern, and she guided him to a small wooden stool near the stable wall.

"You shouldn't be out of bed."

"I don't care," he wheezed. "Marcus told me that you were leaving. Lina, you don't have to go. We can figure this out."

"No, we can't."

The hand on his shoulder fell away, and the look on her face was one he knew well. The regret and guilt were easy to recognize, but it was the conviction that hurt him. He would do all he could to convince her to stay, but he knew that her mind was made up.

"I love you," he muttered.

She fussed with her glove and stood up, "I love you too, and that's why I need to keep you safe. Safe from my father, from my people, and, especially, from me."

"You aren't going to hurt me."

Lina scoffed, her eyes darting towards him.

"Open your eyes! I already hurt you, and now you can barely stand. I am not sticking around to watch you die because of another mistake of mine."

He pulled himself out of the chair using the wall as support, despite Lina's fussing. If he had to run after her, he would collapse not too far from his start but he would run anyway. He took a step towards her, slowly wrapping an arm around her. She eyed his movements with caution. The instant his skin touched her own, she relented and was pulled in more easily. He lifted up her chin and pressed his lips on hers.

Lina kissed him back but pulled her lips away after only a moment. She searched his face for answers and pulled herself out of his arms when she did not find them. Though she looked the same, Lina had changed.

"I don't want to go."

"Then stay," he petitioned in a small voice.

"We've been fighting for so long for something that shouldn't be."

Azrael stopped dead. No, he thought to himself again and again. Lina had not only made up her mind, but she had also given up.

"I have to think that whatever happened, happened because we are trying to force a relationship that should not work. As if there wasn't a long list of reasons why we shouldn't be together already, this is why I can't stay. This is why I need to get away from you and you can't chase after me."

He looked down, "I don't believe any of that."

"Then you are a fool," she spat, turning towards her ready horse. She adjusted the buckle on the saddle, lifted the reins over the horse's head, yet turned back to him.

"I've lost you so many times..." he hesitated.

"You aren't losing me." Her gaze softened. He took hold of her wrist to stop her from getting on the horse. She continued, "You will always have me, and will be the only man to ever truly have me. You just can't be with me."

Lina caressed his face, got up on the horse, and rode

away as if he were a villain. Azrael watched her go until she disappeared from sight then fell back onto the stool. He did not feel the pain from the accident nor the sweat that had broken out from his exertion. Laying his head in his hands, he wept until Marcus came looking for him.

CHAPTER 63

Doranen rounded the corner of the hallway leading to the main hall when he stopped without warning. He had not gotten much information from her letter, but standing in front of him was Lina Meleigh. She was leaning away from him against the balcony on wobbly legs, her hair clumping around her shoulders, and her eyes half closed. If he did not know better, he would think she had ridden through both desert and storm to arrive in such a state.

"Lina," he called. "When did you arrive?"

She turned around, as if expecting him to find her at that exact moment, and faked cheerfulness. "I got into town only a half hour ago, and was going to look for you."

He locked eyes with her, and she shrunk away from him.

"Don't lie to me," he cautioned with only the amount of force in his voice that he would use on a child.

"I got in yesterday..."

"What?" Aside from himself, Lina had no friends in Valandyl. His mind searched her for an explanation as to what she could have been doing all this time, before physically asking her. "Why didn't you find me?"

Pulling at her hair to straighten it and make herself look more presentable, she looked like a distressed child. Her height led one to believe she was young regardless, but her cheeks were red from salty tears and she wrapped her cloak around herself like a blanket.

"I didn't want you to have to deal with this," she stuttered then stopped to clarify. "To deal with me."

Doranen sighed, "What happened?"

"I don't know." Her shoulders were tense, and it was as if her hands held her arms to keep her body from falling apart. "I told you in the letter that I don't know. The only thing that I can think of is that in making the roses, I weakened my own strength to keep my magic in check."

The letters that Doranen had received over the past week were distressing, yet he had never considered the letter writers in all that time. Enchanted artifacts were rare, and the idea that Lina was powerful enough to create such artifacts was made all the more unique since most elves lacked the ability to perform magic at all. Many years ago, he had discussed the possibility with Lucan just after her powers were discovered and he had not believed it was possible. The first letter from Azrael reported that not only had she made one artifact but four roses in total.

Hearing from her that she had experienced side effects of such creations did not shock him in the slightest.

"And Azrael paid the consequences..." she said after a few moments.

The second letter was written, with evident distress on Lina's part, begging for sanctuary for "just a night if you can find it in your heart to spare one."

"What will you do?" he asked.

"I don't know that either." Lina fell back against the wall he found her on, her shoulders and hands relaxing. "I think I'm going to go to the human lands. Try to clear my head, but stay out of sight."

"The human lands?" Doranen protested. "I don't like that idea. When would you leave?"

She reached down to a large kit bag, threw it over her shoulder, and turned away from him. "I should probably go now. You shouldn't have to deal with my mistakes like this."

Doranen rushed in front of her, blocking her path. He was about to tell her not to go when he noticed her face up close. The dark circles under her eyes that were hardly distinguishable from the agitation on her cheeks caught his attention.

"When did you sleep last?" he asked, lifting her chin up so her face was in the light.

"... Tadane."

"You are not going anywhere until you have had some sleep." He took her by the elbow and led her in the opposite direction to a couple of spare rooms he knew his staff had ready for emergencies. "There is a bedroom this way where you will not be disturbed."

"I'm fine," she claimed while tugging at his grip. "I swear, I don't..."

He stopped, causing her voice to trail off. "Lina, though you may think that I don't know much about you, but I know enough to know that you love Azrael and would never want to do him harm. Whatever happened, however unfortunate, had to be out of your control.

"But, I know two things for certain. The first is that you are working as hard as you can to prevent another incident from happening. The second, your magic will be harder to control when you are exhausted."

Lina managed to nod.

He guided her through the maze of the palace to the empty guest room, opened the door for her, and beckoned her inside. It was a smaller room, though he doubted that she would protest. Her skin was weak and translucent, while her strength to fight him was gone. She dumped her bag on the bed, then turned back to face him.

"Thank you."

"Your welcome," he smiled. His voice low and gentle. "Take a few days to get your head on straight before running off. I'll have my servants bring you anything you should need."

"I don't want to inconvenience you," she insisted.

Doranen put his hands on both her shoulders and waited until she looked him in the eye before he spoke. "Lina, you are not an inconvenience, and I'll tell you the exact same thing tomorrow after you have gotten some rest."

CHAPTER 64

Lina peeked her head into Doranen's study. She did not know what time it was, only that she had slept for a long time and that the sun was in the same position when she went to sleep as it was now. Her body felt renewed with energy, her skin less blistered, and she could keep her eyes open.

"It's good to see you up," Doranen called from the other side of the large banquet table that spanned most of the room. She smiled and navigated her way around the elves that congregated in groups of three or four until she reached Doranen. "It looks like sleep has done you some good."

"I feel a little better." She eyed the rest of the inhabitants in the room with suspicion. Ever since the lunch with Azrael's parents after they arrived in Tadane, she had been wary of large groups of people. All she felt were the never-ending pairs of eyes that seemed to stare right through her secret and make her feel vulnerable to their scorn. She turned her attention back to Doranen when she finished the scan of the room. "Thank you again."

Doranen flashed a calm smile, then returned to the papers in front of him. "I was going to finish reading through these military reports then spend some time with my daughter. Would..."

"Daughter?" she asked.

Doranen took a deep breath, returning the papers in his hands back on the table's surface. "Yes?"

"I remember hearing about her, but I can't seem to remember her name."

"Larien," he answered. The glow in his face was instantaneous.

"That's it." She looked for any prying eyes, then lowered her voice so that only Doranen could hear. "Not much news of her made it to Helios."

"That was my goal."

Lina bit her lip, taking a step back. Of course, Doranen would want to protect Larien from her father after what happened to Emmy. The wrong bit of information or the smallest breach in security would give Lucan the opportunity he needed. Unlike his enemy, family was everything to Doranen.

"I'm sorry..."

Doranen's face popped up, and he waved away her guilt. "Don't be. I was just going to ask you if you wanted to accompany me."

"With Larien?" she sputtered. "No, I probably shouldn't, not in my condition."

Doranen tilted his head, "I'm not worried."

The warmth of his comment spread throughout her body until it beamed through her cheeks.

She stopped.

Her corin tingled as if she were casting a spell even though she knew she was not. The air felt ripe with excitement and anxiety, and she looked around for the cause. The energy she felt built up until she thought something would burst.

The room shook.

She searched for any reaction apart from her own.

"Lina?"

"Did you feel that?" she asked under her breath.

Once more, it shook. This time, Doranen was lurched forward.

"That doesn't make any sense," he whispered.

A third time it shook, only, this time, the shaking did not stop. The other elves in the room looked around for an explanation, grabbed onto furniture for support, and gasped at the realization that a quake was occurring. A metal spoon clanged like a bell as it hit the floor, followed by a louder shattering of a plate near the end of the table after falling to its doom.

"Everyone out of the castle," Doranen yelled. "It's not safe."

A few elves did as they were told and evacuated, while the sound of a glass breaking startled the rest into compliance. A servant in the corner was so scared that he dropped the tray in his hands while running out the door.

"Everyone out," Doranen repeated. He grabbed Lina's arm and they both raced to the other end of the room. The door quivered under the force exerted on it and slammed behind them.

Lina felt her body at the mercy of Doranen's grasp on her sleeve, while her mind filled with questions. A quake? The land was uneasy, but a quake this large was unheard of in the Elven Kingdoms.

"... Wait..."

Doranen stopped, only Lina and his guard remaining in the hallway.

"Wait, where is Larien?" he asked.

"I'm sure her maid got her out," the guard replied.

"No," Doranen protested. "I need to know she's safe."

Lina pulled him around, "Your Majesty, you need to get out."

"I'm not leaving her," he pleaded. "I'm not going out without her."

Lina paused, the shaking subsiding.

"I'll get her," she announced.

"I'm her father, it's my job to keep her safe."

“You are the King. I have to do this.” She turned to Doranen's guard, pushing Doranen closer to him. "Make sure he's safe."

Before either of them could protest, she ran deeper into the palace. Doranen shouted out directions, as his man pulled him further away.

The damage only grew worse as she wound her way through the halls and rooms. A fallen tapestry lying crumpled on the floor in the hallway. In one room, a painting had fallen onto a dresser, breaking the frame, and it rested inverted against a drawer with one corner folded against itself.

As the hallway narrowed, she saw cracks in the walls and ceiling. They split from the foundation, dropping small pieces as the weight built up.

A woman who had not yet gotten out ran past her. Lina tried to get her attention, but she kept running.

An aftershock rolled through, causing Lina to fall against the wall. The woman screamed, and a terrible bang followed.

Lina turned only to see a section of the ceiling give way, releasing pieces of rock the size of a chair and smaller onto the poor woman. She shut her eyes tight and covered her mouth to keep from reacting.

"I'm sorry," Lina whispered, then continued on towards Larien's room.

More stone continued to drop. Lina followed the cracks with her eyes, silently praying she would make it through and find Larien safe.

Another scream rang out, this one smaller and higher pitched.

Lina reached for the knob, only for the door to catch on the rubble behind it.

"Larien," she shouted. "Larien, can you hear me?"

Pounding on the door with her shoulder and all her weight, Lina forced the door open enough to get herself through. A bookcase, its contents, and more ceiling were scattered across the entrance sending Lina into a panic.

"Larien?" she called again.

A squeak sounded from under the bed, and a girl of only five or six crawled out from under it with a blanket clutched to her side.

Lina sighed in relief. "Larien, I know you're scared, but I

need you to come with me."

"I'm afraid," the young princess insisted.

"I know, my dear." Lina held out her hand and meandered forward. "Please, I know you can be brave. Come over to me, and I'll take you to your father."

The trickle of cracks sounded their anthem again, and Lina searched for the culprit. The section from the corner that had toppled the bookshelf, let loose more debris and made Lina wary that the entire wall would come down. She bent down and urged Larien once more.

With a hearty scream, Larien ran over and grabbed onto Lina's neck. Her grip surprisingly strong for such a small child. Lina pulled her up and hurried out of the room before any more cracks could form.

The incessant cracks, however, rippled their way through the castle, reaching their pinnacle in the atrium near the main hall. Strong columns struggled under the shifted weight and groaned as they let go.

"Larien, go." She put Larien down and nudged her forward. "Just down those stairs."

Larien clung to her leg, "I don't want to."

"You father is down there. Go!"

As soon as Larien started running, Lina lifted up her left arm and reached out to hold the cracks in place. She had fought so hard the last few days to ignore her magic, but the ceiling would give way without it. The chunks of rock edged closer as the pillars outside her magic weakened.

"What do you need me to do?"

Lina turned around to see Doranen's guard running up to her.

The pillars released, letting loose a shower of stone. She reached out for all the pieces, yet the hundreds of pounds of rocks knocked her to the floor. She caught them, yet she felt pinned. She could not release them or the pieces would crush both of them, but she could not hold the weight for much longer. Running was not physically possible because she was not able to pull herself from underneath them.

"Check that Larien is safe," she uttered with great difficulty.

"She is," he assured her. "King Doranen sent me in to help you once he had her. What can I do?"

"I don't know."

The man grabbed under her arms, "I can pull you from under them. Can you hold them until I do?"

"I can try..."

"Get ready to run," he cautioned.

Lina chuckled humorlessly, "Try to keep up with me."

The man did as he promised, pulling her out as the chunks of stone crashed behind them. The muscles in her arms relaxed, and, once outside, she caught her breath.

CHAPTER 65

Lina's face hardened, as Doranen made his way into the infirmary and towards her. She sat up and lifted her legs over the side of the cot.

"The damage?"

"Mostly structural." Doranen let out a heavy sigh and crossed his arms. "It'll be expensive, but easy to fix. I wish I could say that there were no casualties but..."

He did not have to finish.

"Absalom told me that you had no external injuries," he announced as if she were not aware already. The smile he wore was one that occupied his entire face and glowed from his cheeks.

"My muscles are sore," she clarified. "But, other than that, I'm fine."

"I'm glad to hear it."

"Is Larien alright?" she asked.

"A few scrapes, but she's strong." Doranen sat down on the empty bed in front of her and gave her a once over. He went to speak, but, after looking around for anyone who might be listening, he lowered his voice.

"What you said before? When we were evacuating, you said that you had to save Larien. Why?"

She paused, knowing why but not wanting to admit it.

"I thought that I should save at least one of your children."

"You tried to save Emmy."

She nodded, "I know."

"Then why do you feel responsible?"

"I didn't kill her. It wasn't my fault that she's gone, and I tried to save her. I have never fought my father that hard, but, in the end, I wasn't enough. When I saw your fear, I just reacted. I can only imagine how much Larien means to you, and I thought that if I could save her then maybe... I don't know."

"Then maybe you could find redemption..." Doranen filled in.

"Yes, something like that."

Lina paused. A flood of memories that she had been resisting came to a forefront in her mind as she looked at the King in front of her and thought about the little girl she had just saved. "I miss her. I haven't seen Emmelina in so long, but I still miss her."

A shadow passed over Doranen's face, and she felt the familiar pang of guilt. "I'm sorry, I shouldn't have brought her up."

"No, it's fine," he excused. "I'm glad that you miss her. Makes me feel less alone. People don't talk about her anymore. Like if they talk about her, that I'm not strong enough to hear it. I miss her every day."

In an instant, Lina became aware of a hollowness within the man in front of her. She saw all the conversations he wished he could have and all the potential moments that vanished when Emmelina's life ended. Doranen was not as concerned about image as Lina's father, but he knew that if his grief went on too long that public concern would turn to collective doubt.

"But," he began, wiping the hurt from his face and donning a practiced cheerfulness. "That isn't why I came to see you."

"Is something wrong?"

"Quite the opposite. I came to offer you a job."

Lina leaned forward, "A job?"

"What you did for Larien was impeccably brave. She is getting older, and you are one of the few people that understand why I want more security on her. I want you to be her guardian, protecting her from any threat that could arise."

Her jaw dropped.

"But you know what I've done," she whispered. "How do you know I won't do what I did to Azrael to Larien?"

"I trust you. Besides, I will never find someone more committed to keeping her safe than what I have found in you."

His eyes and tone gave off the idea that this reason would explain everything, as if she could accept such an answer. How could he trust her when she no longer trusted herself?

"I don't think..."

Doranen stood, buttoning his robe, and brushed off some imaginary dirt on the fabric of it to keep from looking her in the eye. "You don't have to give me an answer right away. In fact, I insist that you sleep on it."

"Your Majesty," she sputtered.

"A whole night's sleep. Perhaps a few."

Without giving her any more of his time, he promptly turned and made for the door. No matter how hard he ran, he would have to accept an answer sooner or later.

"Well, he made sure to give you no time to answer," said a voice on the other side of the bed that Doranen had been sitting on only a moment prior.

"Because he knows what I'll say," she answered. She looked over and saw the guard that had pulled her out from under the rocks laying down with a blanket over his legs and bandages wrapped around his shoulder. "Were you listening?"

"Not actively," he grinned. "But I am right here. It was inevitable that I would hear some parts of your conversation."

She nodded, more to acknowledge his opinion than out of agreement with it. "What happened to you?"

"I was pulling people out of the rubble and some of it caved in. But the bandages make it look worse than it is."

"How long have you been working for Doranen?"

"Not long," he told her with boyish charm and a lopsided smile. "The only reason I was guarding him yesterday was that his actual guard was sick. I'm just the backup."

"What a day to show your strength."

"You're telling me." He removed his blanket, and, with a few small groans, took Doranen's place on the bed next to her. "You refer to the King informally. Have you known him a long time?"

She eyed him suspiciously, "Yes."

"And you knew Princess Emmelina? You mentioned her before you retrieved Princess Larien."

"We were friends," she answered just as simply.

"I don't mean to pry or anything. I just know that her loss was hard on the King."

Lina leaned her head back and tried to force the memories away. Emmy's laugh seemed to ring in her ears like an incessant bird, yet, when she tried to hold onto a specific memory, it would vanish. She took a deep breath and focused on the man in front of her.

"Can I ask you something?"

The man nodded.

"If someone you loved and trusted offered you a job that you believed you weren't qualified for, would you take it?"

"I'd have my doubts, sure," he offered up while chewing on his answer. "I think I would trust the person as I always have. Well, in my interpretation of your hypothetical question, I've trusted this person for a long time."

She smiled at his comic clarity, then folded her hands in front of her. "Thank you for saving me."

"Of course. I'm just glad that you weren't hurt." He thrust out a hand, "My name is Rowan."

She took it gingerly, "Lina."

"I think you should do it," he announced as he let go.

"And what about all the things that I don't know?"

"You'll learn." His words seemed obvious, yet Lina looked at him as if he had given her an opinion she had yet to think of. "So will you do it?"

Lina went to answer but found all words beyond her.

The End

Made in the USA
Middletown, DE
26 September 2023